monsoonbooks

DEATH IN THE KINGDOM

In his fifty something years, New Zealand-based Andrew Grant has lived and worked in a variety of roles around the world, including being a professional hunter, merchant seaman and bodyguard. A small arms expert, competitive pistol shooter and keen photographer, he is a frequent visitor to Asia, regarding Thailand as his second home.

DEATH IN THE KINGDOM

ANDREW GRANT

monsoonbooks

First published in 2007
by Monsoon Books

No.1 The Lodge, Burrough Court, Burrough on the Hill,
Melton Mowbray LE14 2QS, UK

www.monsoonbooks.co.uk

ISBN (ebook): 9789814358217
ISBN (paperback): 9789810584924

This book is dedicated to Clara

Prologue

When you jam a .357 Desert Eagle, a gun the size of a small cannon, into the side of someone's face and it goes off, one of two things are likely to happen. One, you have a very messy body on your hands, or two, you have just created a very ugly enemy who will do everything in his power to kill you. The latter is exactly what happened.

The problem was now, six years on, I was about to meet the man to whom I had given the extreme facial.

To say I wasn't looking forward to the meeting would be a total understatement. The thing was, it was bad enough being faced with a disfigured, hate-filled gorilla, but this time he wouldn't be alone. Thailand's top gang boss, Tuk Tuk Song, would be there as well.

My run-in with the gorilla, Choy Lee, and the very reason things had got out of hand way back in 1999, was that shortly before I rearranged Choy's features, I shot dead Arune Song, Tuk Tuk's son.

Tuk Tuk was one of the reasons I was back in Phuket, putting my life on hold. Now Tuk Tuk and Choy were on their way to fetch me. I was shitting myself, as any sane man would!

1

It had been a hell of a long flight and business-class comfort or not, I'd spent the entire time awake thinking about what was to come and trying to figure out how I was going to stay alive. Now Geezer was trying to confound me with some Zen bullshit.

'Life is a street, not a bloody footpath, Dan,' Geezer said from behind his beer, cutting across my morbid train of thought.

I struggled to focus my tired eyes on my friend's face. It was a difficult task for me at that moment in time, given the amount of alcohol I had consumed in the last five or so hours since I had landed in Phuket. Prior to that there had been a seriously short overnighter in Singapore, following the gut-buster from Heathrow. As for the booze, if I had to die I wanted to be inebriated enough not to feel the pain because, sure as hell, if Choy Lee got his hands on me it was going to hurt big time.

My confusion or simple lack of comprehension at Geezer's words came from that shattering combination of fatigue, alcohol and sheer, gut-churning fear. Of course, there was always the fact that Geezer was out of focus to the world and me, whether I was drunk or stone-cold sober. 'Since when did you start this damn Zen thing?' I asked him.

Geezer didn't even smile at that. In the twenty years I had known him he had never once smiled, not to my knowledge anyway. In fact, I doubted Raymond 'Geezer' Terrant actually knew how to smile. Where he came from, displaying a set of teeth generally invited someone to knock them right down your throat, then kick your arse until they fell out on the floor.

'Zen be buggered,' Geezer replied as he reached for another can of Singha from the ice bucket that resided at his feet. 'Life's a fucking highway and if you don't get up to speed and learn the damn road rules, you bloody well die. Simple fact!'

'So what the hell happened to the footpath?' I wanted to know, my brain spinning like a damned dervish on speed. Geezer lowered his beer and reached for the cigarettes that sat on the rattan coffee table by his chair.

'What footpath?' he replied through a cloud of blue cigarette haze, nodding at the ongoing chaos that was happening on the street below us. 'You see a footpath down there?' He was right. There wasn't a footpath in sight, not from where we were sitting anyway. The only thing close to being a footpath that I could see had traffic lines painted on it in big wide white stripes. The wisdom of Geezer's words, Zen or not, was plain enough for even a blind man to see. In this place it was either drive the crazy streets or walk on the broken concrete and weeds alongside—there was no alternative.

We were sitting on the patio of Geezer's place at the northern end of Patong Beach. The house, a small two-bedroom Thai-style bungalow, was all tiles and plaster. It was cool and airy, most of the time anyway, and it had a view, a hell of a view.

Geezer had had his place built in 1986 with some of the proceeds of his retirement stash, when he quit the military. That was back in the days before foreigners could buy property in Thailand. The Thai Government had owed him some serious compensation for deeds done in his distant past up on the Burmese border, and appropriate arrangements had been made.

Now from the wide, white-tiled patio, Geezer lived the life of the perpetual voyeur with Patong at his feet. He sat, watched and smelt the world unfold below him as the entire known universe channelled itself into the two and a half very narrow lanes of Phra Baramee Road. The road was the main artery that allowed Geezer's universe to drag its tired arse over the steep-sided ridge that separated Patong Beach from the rest of the world.

'What a view,' I thought aloud. As for the perpetual smell of diesel fumes and the racket from the traffic, that part I wasn't so taken with.

'Isn't it just,' Geezer agreed. I think he almost smiled then. He'd picked the site of his home for that very reason. To the left the jungle and plantations covered the ridge that encircled three sides of Patong. The town lay in front and below us. To the right was the bay with its yellow sand. The waters of the Andaman would change colour with the mood of the weather and today the mood was grey. Tomorrow the waters could be green or a wonderful shade of blue. On the flip side, the ocean might just suck itself out to the horizon and come charging back, just as it had done on Boxing Day 2004.

Geezer had been sitting out on his patio having his first smoke of the new day when the tsunami came calling. He watched helplessly as the waterfront took the hit. Now the damage to the waterfront structures of the town had been repaired. However the damage caused to some of the people I'd seen in my few hours back here showed itself in their eyes. It was still as raw and as painful as in the immediate aftermath of the disaster.

Geezer prodded his beer can towards the black, midsized Mercedes that had pulled up on the street below. 'He's here!' The car was black in every sense of the word, with windows of mirrored glass. It sat low and heavy. I didn't need to be a genius to figure it was armour-plated.

The Merc was on the wrong side of the road, an obstruction to the oncoming traffic. No one seemed perturbed and the traffic just flowed on around it. It always amazed me how, being mainly Buddhists, the majority of Thais were pretty tolerant as a people. Road rage didn't seem to be as common an affliction here as it was in the rest of the civilised world.

As I stood to go and meet my fate, my mobile phone vibrated.

'Great timing,' I snapped as I fished the beast out of my jacket pocket. It could only be one person: Bernard. Or, to give him his full title, Sir Bernard Randolph Sinclair, MBE, my boss. Bernard was a twitchy old bastard. I'd told him that I would check in once I was on the ground. He obviously couldn't wait.

The mobile I carried was one of our special hybrid models and definitely wasn't for commercial sale. It wasn't a flip top and was fractionally larger than those cute fashionable ones. Apart from that it looked pretty standard and worked much the same as any other but sans all the bling. There was no voice mail function or address book. If the wrong person picked it up they wouldn't realise what they had. There was no ring tone, just vibrator mode. Silence was golden in my world at times. A couple of the features the phone did have, however, were a built-in scrambler and a big, power-off switch which was easy to reach on the side for those times when you didn't want to take a call. Moments like this. However I had no choice. I pressed the scrambler button.

'Swann!'

'You are precisely where at this moment in time?' The prissy tone of the old prick had the ability to raise my hackles, even though he was half the world away.

'Patong Beach and about to meet Tuk Tuk to get our little venture under way,' I replied.

'I require a daily progress report, Daniel.'

'I've only been here a matter of hours,' I replied, sounding like a sullen schoolboy even to my own ears.

'Once a day, Daniel. Once a day! I need to know where you are at all times.'

'Yes, Bernard,' I said. 'My ride is waiting. Goodbye.' I killed the connection and flicked off the power switch. I left the phone on Geezer's patio table. Where I was going I doubted I would need it. I quickly finished my beer, dropping the can into the empty carton that served Geezer as a receptacle for all things dead and finished with. I only hoped that by the end of the day I didn't find myself in the same position.

'Luck,' said Geezer almost to himself.

'Luck will have absolutely nothing to do with it,' I replied as I picked up my super-slim, super-sexy Toshiba laptop. I wasn't taking the laptop with me as some sort of yuppie fashion statement. It contained something that I knew might, just might, keep me alive.

I gave my old friend a sloppy salute and started down the steep steps towards the street below. It was a long way down to the asphalt but I wasn't in a hurry. As I emerged onto the roadside, the Merc suddenly swung across the traffic flow, causing momentary chaos. Vehicles braked heavily and took evasive action in every direction before the black beast alighted virtually on my feet. It barely rocked on its heavy-duty springs. I stood and stared at my reflection in the glass. Jeez, I looked shocking. My face sported three days worth of growth and my hair needed washing. I had the pallor of someone who had just escaped from a damp, sunless London winter, which was absolutely true.

The car's rear nearside door popped open. I didn't bother trying to blink into the Merc's dark interior. I stooped my six-foot-two frame and slid in. The door closed automatically and we were away, heading upstream with the traffic flow. A very big and definitely non-spec engine pushed our several tons of metal effortlessly along with a deep rumble. I glanced ahead. It always surprised me how the occupants of a car with mirrored windows could see so much of the world outside. We were heading uphill, following the sweeping curves in the road. The tail of a Jeep full of tourists hovered in front of the gun-sight emblem on the bonnet.

The man sitting in the front passenger seat turned and put himself between the view and me. Choy Lee was known by his friends and enemies alike as 'The Cabbage'. This was mainly due to the fact that the shape of his head resembled the Chinese vegetable *bok choy*. He stared back at me, not blinking. Once, his round basketball of a head housed a broad grin. Now, Choy had no grin. I'd heard he didn't speak much either. He didn't speak now, he just grunted. It could have been a greeting but I doubted it.

When I had shot him, the 180-grain hollow point bullet went up through the right side of his jaw. It punched its way out just below his nose, taking most of his upper lip, teeth and lower right jaw with it. The plastic surgeons had done their best, but some things just can't be fixed. It was no secret that Choy definitely wanted me dead, slowly and very painfully dead for what I had done to him, and despite the dark mirrored lenses in his sunglasses, I could feel the heat of his gaze burning holes in me.

'It has been a long time, Daniel,' a very familiar voice said. I turned to my right. Tuk Tuk Song was seated beside me. He extended a short thick hand. His grip was just as strong as his voice, despite the fact he was almost eighty years old. 'A long time, Daniel,' he repeated, 'and if I remember rightly, we left a little unfinished business hanging in the wind.'

'Yes, Tuk Tuk,' I nodded in agreement. 'Unfinished from your end only,' I added softly. This was the moment when I lived or died. Tuk Tuk's next words were the most important I would ever hear in this lifetime. Tuk Tuk's smile was little more than a faint grimace, a fractional movement of his lips. I saw a flash of yellow teeth and gold, a lot of gold. His eyes weren't hidden by dark glasses. They stared at me unblinking, jet black and as cold and hard as nuggets of coal. He regarded me for a long time, maybe a minute, maybe just a second, I wasn't sure because I was caught in a place between life and death—a place where time was made and not measured in neat, convenient units for mere mortals to toy with.

So, you ask, why the hell was I sitting in a car with a man who might have me killed at any moment and a sadistic ape who wanted me dead so badly I could almost smell it? And what the fuck did I do to get on Tuk Tuk Song's wrong side? I guess a little history might be in order here.

Tuk Tuk Song, a Chinese Thai, had made his name back in the late 1960s in Bangkok. Those were the days of the Vietnam era and R&R excesses. The days when literally hundreds of thousands of young men from the US military machine escaped Nam for a few short days to enjoy the delights of the ladies in the Land of Smiles.

Already a well-established gang lord, Tuk Tuk could see that there were plentiful suppliers of young ladies and countless bars on offer to the dollar-rich Americans. However, what he soon defined was that visitors to his city needed transportation, and plenty of it. In a matter of months Tuk Tuk Song moved into all things on wheels in a big way, hence his nickname. At that time the Thai Mafia was not the force that it is now, and Tuk Tuk formed the biggest criminal organisation in the land. So from about the time the world was starting to learn about Thailand outside of the nauseating film *The King and I*, just about everything you rode with wheels on it in Bangkok and most of the resort towns meant you were riding with Tuk Tuk Song.

The story of Daniel Swann and Tuk Tuk Song began in the early 1990s in Bangkok. I was doing unmentionable things for Betty Windsor's mob. Then, as now, the Queen's shilling was in my pocket. I am still a soldier in the dirty war, the war that takes place in the shadows, hidden from the world at large. It is a war that is seen by the public only in those occasional strobe flashes of violence and mayhem that make the headlines when some of the protagonists are caught exposed just for a moment, before they plunge back into the shadowlands.

In the 1990s I was attached to the British Embassy with the words FOREIGN AFFAIRS AND ASIAN TRADE CONSULTANT on my business card. I didn't know shit about any trade, other than dope or arms, and I didn't spend much time in Bangkok either. I was mainly up north in what was known to the world as the Golden Triangle. The Thai, Cambodian, Laotian and Burmese borders didn't really exist for me, or for the people I worked for. Bangkok, however, was a home base between trade missions.

It was during one of my decompression spells in the City of Smiles that I had the fortune, good or otherwise, to meet Tuk Tuk Song. It happened quite by accident, as these things sometimes do in the real world. I saved his life back then but that's a story for another day. Right now I needed to persuade Tuk Tuk not to kill his old friend, the man who had killed his son.

2

We approached the crest of the ridge that cuts Patong off from the rest of Phuket. The driver slowed without any signal from Tuk Tuk or Choy. In some sort of deference to the sheer volume of traffic on the road, Tuk Tuk's driver pulled us over to the left verge just opposite a shrine on the crest. It was a noisy place to be due to the local drivers who would toot at the shrine on their way past. The toot was a sort of thank you to the powers that be, or maybe they were just asking the buddha to ensure they had brakes for the trip down.

The driver moved us back to the centre line as the following traffic eased off. There was a break in the oncoming flow pushing up from Phuket Town and without prompting, the man at the wheel hit the gas pedal hard. We roared across the highway and nudged our way onto a small road I'd never noticed before, despite a dozen trips over the hill.

The hairs on the back of my neck were working overtime. Shit, I didn't have a weapon on me, apart from the stiletto taped to the inside of my left calf. The knife wasn't much, but it was all I had. That and a plan of sorts to convince Tuk Tuk not to kill me. I figured I could do it but it would be a close thing.

We drove a couple of hundred yards along a narrow dirt track. Rubber trees crowded in on us, shutting out the grey storm-laden skies. No one was talking. Choy was sitting sideways in his seat, watching me. Tuk Tuk was also watching me, contemplatively, slightly puzzled, obviously wondering why in the hell I had come back. Especially given how hurried my departure from Thailand had been.

We entered a clearing, a small, coarsely-grassed flat area the size of a tennis court on the eastern side of the hill just below the crest of the ridge. The trees dropped away below the edge of the plateau, forming what would have been a spectacular view under any normal circumstances.

There was one totally incongruous touch about where we were, and it bordered on the surreal. An open-sided green pergola sat in the centre of the clearing. Under the canopy was a small, white, plastic picnic table. A pair of matching chairs faced each other on either side of the table. The table setting included a bottle of Glenfiddich and two glasses, which were resting open end down on a white napkin. Even if Tuk Tuk was going to kill me, it appeared we would share a glass of whisky first.

The Merc stopped and Choy got out. He moved very smoothly for a big man. The butt of a cannon showed under his left arm. Was it the same Desert Eagle I had shot him with more than half a decade ago?

Choy opened my door and stepped back just far enough to ensure he had time and room to accommodate any aggressive moves I might make. 'Open,' he mumbled, confirming that, with half of the roof of his mouth gone, he no longer spoke with the smooth eloquence he had once enjoyed. I didn't feel guilty.

I climbed out of the car, slipped off my jacket and pirouetted for him, lifting my T-shirt as I did so. There was no room for a gun. I pulled up the trouser cuffs of my Levis so he could see that the tops of my boots didn't contain any hardware and I wasn't wearing an ankle holster. I didn't pull my left cuff up high enough to let him see the flat knife taped to the inside of my calf. Choy motioned for the laptop. I reached back into the car to retrieve the Toshiba and handed it to him. Choy opened it, grunted and handed it back to me. Computers didn't seem to figure largely in his lifestyle. He motioned towards the table and chairs, and I moved in that direction while Choy went to assist Tuk Tuk from the car. The driver sat motionless behind the wheel.

Tuk Tuk moved slowly with the aid of an ebony walking stick with a gold and ivory grip. Knowing the old devil, I was prepared to bet that the stick housed the blade of a sword or even a gun. He had never missed a trick in his long life.

I laid the laptop on the table and removed a packet of Marlboros from my jacket as I waited for Tuk Tuk and Choy. I lit up using the BIC disposable I'd picked up in a 7-Eleven on my way to Geezers. I left the cigarette pack and the lighter beside the computer. I'd given up smoking three years before but Tuk Tuk wasn't to know. However, I knew that of all the cigarettes on the planet, Tuk Tuk Song hated Marlboros. It had been something of a joke between us. I fought to keep myself from coughing and made a show of enjoying my fag and the view.

Tuk Tuk chose a seat and lowered himself into it. Choy moved to stand to one side of the table. When I sat he would be on my right which meant if I went for him, my striking hand would have to be my left. He knew full well that I was right-handed.

'Sit, Daniel,' Tuk Tuk said softly as he removed a cigarette from the flat gold case Choy extended to him, 'and tell me why you are here and why I shouldn't kill you.'

As I sat I picked up my fifteen-baht lighter and flicked it into life, leaning across the table to offer Tuk Tuk a light. He accepted, leaving Choy standing with a diamond-encrusted gold Ronson worth a couple of thousand pounds sitting uselessly in his huge hand. The big man straightened and dropped the Ronson into a side pocket in his jacket, his ruined face expressionless. He continued to stand like a miniature man-mountain with his arms folded, waiting.

'Firstly,' I said, my eyes meeting those of the man who had once almost been a friend, 'Arune attempted to kill me because I found out he was planning a coup against you. He was going to have your car wired to two kilos of Semtex.' My voice was flat and hard. I'd never had a chance to tell Tuk Tuk *why* it had happened. He knew *how*! Now I needed him to believe me. 'Old friend,' I said softly, 'Arune wanted you dead. He wanted to take over. He tried to kill me and I had no choice but to kill him. Then you sent Choy after me before we had had a chance to talk. The rest you know.'

There was a near silence. I could hear birds, the hum of distant traffic and the wind in the trees, but that was as close to silence as it would get. Tuk Tuk Song blinked once, then twice and then a third time. He leaned back in his seat. His eyes had lost that hard coal-black edge. Suddenly, he looked like an old man, a frail old man. He knew the words I had spoken were the truth. We had that much trust still between us.

Despite his dark glasses I knew Choy's eyes were on Tuk Tuk, and there was a look of concern on his face that even the damage I had inflicted could not hide. He had been Tuk Tuk's right-hand man for most of his own sixty years. Tuk Tuk was his father in all but birthright. There was no doubt that he still wanted me dead, but there was something else there. He and I had also almost been friends in the days gone by.

'Why didn't you tell me?' Tuk Tuk asked in a whisper.

'I didn't have time,' I replied. 'I was involved with the Cambodians on a matter for my people. It was purely by accident that I found out about Arune's plans.'

I paused for a moment to draw smoke into my lungs. What the hell! I prefered to die of lung cancer than Choy's bullet in my brain, and the nicotine hit was making my head buzz.

'Arune bought the Semtex from Savang over in Savannakhet. It was part of a tagged shipment we were monitoring. We'd tracked it in from Europe. We busted Savang and found that a big chunk of the pie was missing. With a little persuasion, he told me Arune had bought it. We handed Savang over to his people. That was one hell of a big mistake. He made some sort of deal and was free in ten minutes and on the phone to Arune.' Tuk Tuk was leaning forward slightly in his chair. I had his total attention it seemed. 'Arune and his goons were waiting for me when I went back over the border,' I continued. 'Incidentally, I'd assumed that Arune had bought the plastic for you.'

I accepted the tumbler of whisky that Choy handed to me. Tuk Tuk's hand shook as he raised his glass to his lips. I could see in his eyes that he knew I was speaking the truth. 'Go on please, Daniel,' he said as I took a sip of my drink. It tasted better than any other I'd ever remembered.

'Arune took me to a warehouse on the bank of a river up at Lopburi. Somewhere along the line he had had the bright idea of implicating my people and me in your death to take suspicion off him. He was showing off, Tuk Tuk, showing how bright he was.' Tuk Tuk nodded. He'd known his son that well at least. 'He told me everything. They were going to wait until you went to Sakura's for the weekend and plant the explosive under the seat of your Lincoln when Choy brought it back to the city.'

Sakura was Tuk Tuk's Japanese mistress. At weekends Tuk Tuk used to stay in the palace he had built for her down the Gulf at Phetchaburi. Usually Choy would drive him down there in the Lincoln and leave him while he returned to Bangkok. He would then go down on the Sunday or Monday, pick up Tuk Tuk and return with him to the city.

Arune had apartments in the city but he lived at Tuk Tuk's magnificent Bang Khen mansion most of the time, and had plenty of opportunities to do the deed. Choy personally favoured big black Jeep Cherokees as his choice of vehicle. So when Choy was away visiting one of his many girlfriends, Arune's plan was to plant the explosive and a remote detonator in the massive Lincoln. 'Arune planned to have some of his guys go down to Phetchaburi, wait for you and Choy to leave Sakura's place and bingo, all over.' I illustrated the latter by flicking the remains of my cigarette away. 'Meanwhile he planned to be very much in public view, going about the city creating the perfect alibi.'

'Two kilos?' whispered Tuk Tuk in sheer disbelief. 'You said two kilos of plastic, Daniel?'

'Yes,' I replied. 'Ten kilos and all of it under your seat.'

'Oh,' Choy spluttered. All three of us knew what that amount of Semtex could do to any automobile, but ten kilos inside an armoured vehicle was totally over the top. Firstly, it would vapourise everything inside the car then, because the blast was being contained beyond critical mass by the armour, it would turn the car into a second bomb, a huge bomb that would devastate anything and everything within a hundred yards in all directions. Talk about overkill! Half or even a quarter of a kilo would have done the job fine.

'Did he hate me so much?' Tuk Tuk whispered almost to himself. And then his voice hardened. 'The stupid, stupid boy!' He swallowed the remaining whisky and held out his glass for more. Choy moved to do his bidding. 'Go on, Daniel.'

'His plan was to kill me, then make sure enough of me was left close enough to the blast area to get an identification. He was even contemplating shooting me and putting me in the trunk of the limo.' I shook my head. Arune wasn't the sharpest tool in the workshop. I would have been vaporised just like Tuk Tuk and Choy. There would have been nothing left to identify. Of all of Tuk Tuk's eleven sons and eight daughters, Arune had been the oldest, the heir, and that had been a problem. Unfortunately he had also been very stupid and very violent. A most dangerous combination!

'Arune got careless,' I said. 'I got free and took a gun off one of his guys. We had a shoot-out and I killed Arune and one of his men but the other got away. I guess he called you with some fairy story and when I arrived back in the city, you had Choy waiting. You know the rest.'

'Stupid greedy boy,' Tuk Tuk said shaking his head. 'I'm sorry, Daniel. The fault was mine for breeding such an imbecile.'

'He did what he did, Tuk Tuk. It happens,' I replied, accepting more whisky. 'A father cannot be responsible for the actions of his son. Not in the real world,' I added, thinking of my stepfather and the way we had parted. It hadn't been quite as drastic as in Arune and Tuk Tuk's case, but the end result had pretty much been the same.

'Enough of that past, Daniel. I apologise anyway. Let us toast to our renewed friendship and the future.' Tuk Tuk held his glass out. I pushed mine to his and they touched.

'Indeed, old friend,' I replied, reaching for another cigarette. I was well on the way to becoming a human chimney. I lit up and stood. 'Before we talk business I must alleviate the pressure in my bladder,' I said. Tuk Tuk chuckled and Choy just watched as I walked away to the edge of the plateau. There I unzipped and did exactly as I had indicated I would.

The tiny radio microphone in the cigarette pack I'd left on the table was on, and the signal was loud and clear in the equally tiny earpiece built into the ear stem of my Ray Bans. They were speaking Cantonese. My Thai was excellent, as was my Lao. As they both knew this they spoke the language of their birth. Neither of them knew that I had been born in Hong Kong and Cantonese was virtually my first language, compliments of our nanny. Mandarin came in a close second thanks to the cook. It was always wise to keep some secrets in my business.

'He is telling the truth,' Choy mumbled.

'I know he is,' Tuk Tuk sighed. 'Arune was an idiot, but he was my son. Only a father has the right to kill his own son.'

'You will kill Daniel?'

'Not yet, Choy. It will pain me to kill him, but eventually I must. Not now, later! First let us hear what business he has for us.'

'Can I kill him for you then?' Choy was asking. Damn him, he was so eager to have me dead.

'Maybe when the time comes, but not until I say so,' replied Tuk Tuk as I zipped up and turned to go back to the table. Immediately they both switched to Thai, talking about nothing to create a smoke screen. I sat down and smiled at Tuk Tuk.

'Okay. It goes like this,' I said. 'Yamashita's gold!' Those two words dropped into the near silence like a depth charge.

'Just a legend,' said Tuk Tuk at last, looking faintly disappointed. Choy's expression didn't change, but he was looking intently at his master, as if willing him to give the word.

'Wrong,' I said. 'The truth has been presented as legend by those who have the most to gain, namely the former allied block who defeated Japan and recovered much of the gold. That includes, of course, my people, the Americans and the Russians. I have read the most secret files on Yamashita's mission.' I paused purely for effect because the next bit was the one that was going to set the hook I had so carefully laid out for Tuk Tuk Song.

'General Tomoyuki Yamashita gathered an estimated four billion dollars worth of gold, precious stones and artworks from China and Southeast Asia.' I paused to let the figure sink in. Even as fabulously wealthy as he was, this was something else for Tuk Tuk. 'Those were the dollar values of the day. Imagine what it would be worth today!' Tuk Tuk's eyes widened and even Choy gave a grunt. Inscrutable Orientals my arse. When it came to wealth they were all too scrutable, just like the rest of us. 'Yamashita raped half of Asia of everything of value, and when the war was being lost and his retreat cut off, he hid his loot all over the place. The location of most of his bootie is still unknown.'

'You know where it is?' Tuk Tuk said, his eyes once more bright and hard.

'Some of it,' I replied. 'About a hundred tons of gold, give or take,' I added and watched Tuk Tuk's eyes as he did the maths. I'd checked my figures before leaving home and gold had been sitting at over six hundred US dollars an ounce for months. Figuring that as the minimum, the little pile of bullion in the Andaman was worth two or three billion dollars, depending on whether you were into US billions or the other sort. Whichever, it was a lot of dosh.

'Where?' he whispered at last.

'Close to here,' I replied. From where we were seated, it was about 150 miles as the crow flies. 'There is more than gold.' I reached for the laptop. Choy tensed, his gun hand hovering close to the butt of his hand cannon. I gave him what passed for a reassuring smile as I gently opened the Toshiba. I didn't want Choy to do something I was going to regret.

The first of the two pictures I had loaded appeared on screen. I turned the computer around so that Tuk Tuk could see the black and white image. He focused intently for a second or two before he raised his head and stared back at me from across the table, a puzzled expression on his face. 'What do you see?' I asked.

'A small buddha,' he replied, shrugging dismissively, 'probably gold and covered with gem stones.'

'Not just a small buddha,' I said, preparing to drop the choicest morsel of bait into the shark pool. 'That is a photograph of the Ruby Buddha of Pha To.'

'Pha To!' Tuk Tuk exclaimed. Suddenly he was interested, very interested. His eyes went back to the screen and he hunched closer to examine the image of one of the greatest of all Thai legends.

The Ruby Buddha of Pha To had been crafted in the sixteenth century. It was one of the truly unique artworks of Thailand, or of any other nation for that matter. Standing a metre high, the gold seated buddha was encrusted with more than 3,000 rubies that formed a robe covering part of its chest, shoulders and back. None of the rubies was reputed to be less than a carat in weight, most of them three and four carats. In addition to the rubies, there were more than two hundred large diamonds and dozens of other precious stones creating designs against the ruby background. All in all, the buddha was worth possibly a couple of hundred million dollars just for the gems and gold. However, as a work of art, it was priceless.

'But when the Japanese came it was hidden, and the monks who hid it committed suicide rather than tell the invaders where it was,' I said as Tuk Tuk searched his considerable memory bank. 'Afterwards, people searched for decades but it has never been found—until now.'

I reached across the table and tapped the enter key to bring up a second image, this one in colour, mostly tints of green. I couldn't see the screen from where I was sitting. I didn't need to. I just leaned back in my seat and watched Tuk Tuk's face. His brow furrowed as he squinted at the laptop. I knew it was a difficult image to decipher. The photographer had been hampered by bad light. After all, he had been a hundred or so feet under the surface of the Andaman Sea in the rusting hulk of an old freighter. Gradually Tuk Tuk made sense of what he was seeing and the frown became a question in the making.

'The Japanese found the buddha,' I said. 'They moved it to the coast along with their other loot. They loaded it onto one of the freighters that Yamashita had working the Burmese coast to collect whatever his raiding parties found. Shortly afterwards, the freighter was sunk by marauding American fighter-bombers. A year or so ago, a scuba diver found the ship. He wasn't looking for it at the time. Inside, he took that photograph.' I paused for a moment to let this sink in.

'So, old friend, the Ruby Buddha is still in one piece. The man who returns it to Thailand will become an instant hero. He will have the gratitude of the nation forever.'

A look of understanding began to form on Tuk Tuk's face. He knew exactly what I was getting at. He didn't need gold, despite the lure of a hundred tons of it. He had more wealth than he could use in a dozen lifetimes, and despite everything else, his life was coming to an end. However, like most mere mortals, he craved immortality, and here was his chance to become truly immortal in the eyes of the Thai people. Tuk Tuk wasn't a Buddhist, but to return the famed statue and become a national hero, that would be his legacy. It was infinitely preferable to the alternative of being remembered as a cold-blooded thug, complete with a five-star rating in the great book of infamy. I could see by the expression on his face that the hook was well and truly set.

'Why has this diver not claimed the buddha?' Tuk Tuk wanted to know.

'Because he was one of ours,' I replied. 'He was looking for something else when he found the ship and this.'

'Why did your people not recover it?'

'Because it is in Burmese waters and, as you know, our relationship with Myanmar is not as it once was.' I was understating the case there. Britain's relationship with the military regime was at an all-time low. 'A large-scale salvage operation would attract too much attention, including that of the Burmese authorities. I also doubt that if they found the buddha themselves they would even acknowledge its existence. We decided another approach might be in order.'

What I didn't tell Tuk Tuk was that Bernard, in his infinite wisdom, had decided that the buddha and the gold were the bait I needed to persuade Tuk Tuk to, in the first instance, not kill me, and in the second, set up the nautical aspects of our mission. I had tried to argue the old sod out of involving Tuk Tuk at all. I could have used a common smuggler or fisherman and paid him a few thousand baht to take me to retrieve the object of the exercise. That object was, in fact, a lead-covered box, the contents of which I had no idea. We could so easily have recovered the box and left the buddha and the gold for another day. Bernard, however, had other ideas.

'Understand me, Daniel,' he'd explained in that damn schoolmasterly tone of his. 'The buddha and the gold do not matter to us. All that matters is the box. Use the buddha, use the gold as bait and payment for the boat and crew. The box is the be-all and end-all. Everything else is unimportant.' Those had been his exact words. 'Also, we may need Tuk Tuk's services later. This will clean the slate and ensure he is on our side.'

Knowing the convoluted logic that the old bastard was capable of, I had eventually conceded, not that I had had any choice at the end of the day. He was the fucking boss after all. Bernard had come up with the strategy to lock Tuk Tuk into the game, now I had to deliver the sell in my own words.

'And you came to me, why?' Tuk Tuk brought me back to the present and it was time for me to perform. I shrugged and gave him a half smile. 'I knew you well and you knew me well. We were friends before Arune's death.' I switched to English because some words did not translate well. 'Of all the people in Thailand who have the resources to help, and who, perhaps, deserve a chance at redemption, the choice was you.'

'Redemption.' Tuk Tuk repeated the word slowly in English, rolling it around his lips. 'An unusual choice of words,' he said at last reverting back to Thai.

'Apt, I think. History will bear your name proudly.' Tuk Tuk chuckled at that and nodded as he reached for his whisky.

'Yes, Daniel. Very good! Very clever! You knew how to get through to me. That is something few have ever managed to do. Well done!' We touched glasses again. Tuk Tuk chuckled on for a moment then asked the question he had to ask. 'If not the gold and the buddha, what is it your people want, Daniel? We know it isn't to help me redeem my soul.'

'There is a small box that I must find,' I replied. 'I have no idea what it contains. My orders are to find it and get it to my people.'

'A most valuable box,' Tuk Tuk said thoughtfully, 'if a hundred tons of gold and the most valuable buddha in the world are in the balance.'

'The buddha and the gold for you, the box for me,' I reiterated.

'Of course, Daniel,' Tuk Tuk replied raising his glass to mine, a broad smile on his face. 'Redemption for me. The box for you.'

Choy wasn't smiling. He knew that it could be a long time, if ever, before Tuk Tuk called down the hit on me. Dead son or not, the prospect of achieving immortality appealed immensely more to Tuk Tuk Song than any crude revenge on me. The goal posts had been shifted and Choy, waiting on the penalty spot, was staring at the back of the net from the wrong side.

3

There are several sensations that defy description. One of them is being dragged up from the depths of the deepest sleep by a skilled set of lips and a tongue as they give you an expert blowjob. That was what happened to me the afternoon of the day following my meeting with Tuk Tuk Song. I'd been dropped back at Geezer's place and I had crashed out in his guest room.

I awoke as I came. Jesus, what an experience! For a second I didn't know where I was, and I didn't care. Then I stared down my naked body to the equally naked woman who was kneeling beside me. She was a young Thai, waif-like, with golden skin and a mass of long, gleaming ebony hair that touched the sheet below her. I fell back against the pillow and let her continue doing what she was doing.

A minute or two later she crawled up my body and propped on her elbows so she could smile down at me. 'I'm Nan,' she said. 'Mr Geezer said to come in and wake you the special way. You like?'

'Hi, Nan,' I said blinking up at her. 'What's not to like? That was very amazing.'

'Good,' she said. 'Now you want to fuck?'

'I don't think after that I am going to be capable,' I replied honestly. She just smiled and vanished back down to where she had been. Within a minute she was astride me and yes, I wanted to fuck. When she proposed a repeat performance fifteen minutes later, I begged off. At forty-two I have to conserve some resources. We did, however, have a delightful shower together.

Later, I said farewell Nan with the promise that we would do it all again very soon. The whole thing had been a treat from Geezer. 'Out of the housekeeping budget,' he said when I tried to settle up.

Over coffee on the patio he expressed his amazement that Tuk Tuk hadn't killed me. I told him just enough for him to know that it was extremely unlikely that Tuk Tuk would whack me in the foreseeable future. I also told him that Choy, perhaps, didn't have quite the same motivation. 'You going to see Tuk Tuk again today?' Geezer asked.

I glanced at my Seiko. It was already 15:30. Nan's ministrations aside, I had slept for about fifteen hours straight. I shook my head. 'He's flown back to Bangkok. We're meeting at Sakura's place in Phetchaburi the day after tomorrow.' I didn't tell Geezer that Tuk Tuk was already working on what was to come. I had outlined the basics of my plan to him, sitting up there in the pergola on the hill as afternoon had started to turn to night. I didn't elaborate for Geezer's benefit.

The timetable I'd given Tuk Tuk meant that I would hire a car and drive up the Gulf the next day. Phase two of the operation would come into effect at the palace of the beautiful Sakura. My last memory of Tuk Tuk's mistress was of a breathtakingly stunning, graceful, humorous woman of indeterminable age. If pushed to describe her I would liken her to an oriental Audrey Hepburn. To say I was looking forward to seeing her again would be an understatement.

I took Geezer to dinner. Yin, his long-term live-in woman, declined the invitation, citing urgent household duties. 'She's shy in public,' was all Geezer said as we walked down to the road to pick up the cab he had called. He didn't drive any longer, and maintained that motorcycles 'were for fools'.

Safely on board a late model Toyota with an icy air-con, Geezer directed the cab to a small restaurant high on the hill that separated Patong from Karon. The meal was, as expected, absolutely sensational.

Of all the cuisine on the planet, the broad palette of the Thai kitchen was my favourite and I pigged out. As we ate, Geezer and I put away copious quantities of beer along with a couple of bottles of good wine. When I paid the bill it only amounted to the equivalent of about fifty quid, and most of that went on wine. In a restaurant back home I regularly blew that much on a very ordinary meal sans wine.

'No wonder you love this place,' I said to Geezer as we made our farewells to the restaurant owner and started down the hill on foot. We'd both agreed that some exercise was more than a little necessary. The alcohol had loosened us both up in the brain as well as the joints. Geezer was almost gregarious. As we made our way down the steep street he actually put a hand on my shoulder, either in friendship or to steady himself.

'No other bloody place in the world I want to be,' he replied. 'You know, I went back last year for my brother's funeral. I'll never go again. Mean fucking streets, meaner people.'

Never in the years we had known each other had he ever called England 'home'. For him, Thailand was home. England, specifically the backstreets of Birmingham, just happened to be the place where he had been born. It had never been his home. At seventeen, eager to escape, he had become a soldier and left.

We stopped on the bridge at the southern end of Patong Beach, where the river crept into the sea. There were a couple of dozen long-tail boats and the bigger shrimp boats moored upstream, but not as many as there'd been the last time I'd been there. Most of the trees that had lined the banks were gone and on the true left of the stream there was a row of new concrete cabins, replacing the fishermen's shacks that used to be there. 'The tsunami blew right in here,' Geezer said. 'Took out just about everything. Put boats up into the jungle. I lost some good friends,' he added. A few of the local fishermen were sitting eating, drinking beer and smoking under one of the few remaining big trees on the riverbank. Their conversation and laughter drifted down to us over the noise of the traffic from the town. 'I go out with them every so often,' Geezer volunteered. 'Hard cases, most of them. Good blokes. Always have a laugh.'

Looking at the boats riding the current above us, I couldn't help thinking of what was to come. There would be a shitload of 'mucking about in boats'. There would be pirates to dodge, and the Myamanian or Myamese or whatever navy. Shit, like all of the old school I still called it Burma. Some habits die hard, if at all.

Fact was that, apart from the pirates, Thai boats fished the southern Burmese waters with impunity. The pirates, however, were a grim reality and they had a million hiding places in the archipelago and on the mainland itself. In the south, Burma was not exactly a populous place. Roads and anything other than villages were few and far between, so travel was mainly by boat. Sea gypsies could be found there and the nomadic Moken were constantly on the move through the archipelago with its thousands of islands. However, few permanent settlements existed. Many of the islands were home to tigers, elephants and all sorts of poisonous and dangerous beasts. It was a place that man had left alone, for the most part. How long it would remain that way, only time, tourism and the Burmese military rulers would tell.

The plan I'd cooked up with Tuk Tuk had been simple. He would arrange for a fishing boat, a biggish prawn boat probably, and a team of divers. He would also enlist a bunch of his goons and a second boat to act as a deterrent to the pirates. I hadn't told him where we were going in any detail. I'd just said Burmese waters. We'd join the boats at Ranong, the nearest Thai port to the Burmese border.

Then, while Tuk Tuk went after his buddha and his near sainthood, I was going to be looking for my metal box, and not on or in the wreck of the freighter. I had another destination, albeit adjacent to the sunken cargo vessel. I knew the exact where and what, right down to the precise physical dimensions of the damned thing. In fact the box would fit precisely into the tailored cavity in the bottom of my leather holdall which, with its wire-mesh reinforcement and wire-cored handles, had been made specifically to carry it. Weighing twenty-three pounds the sealed, lead-sheathed box measured twelve inches along each of its sides and was four inches deep. I wasn't privy to its contents, and I sure as hell didn't want to be. It was clear that knowledge could prove to be a fatal distraction.

Bernard's parting words at my final in-car briefing, delivered as the department Rover pulled up outside the terminal at Heathrow, had given me a distinctly uneasy feeling. 'Collect the box, Daniel. Get to the embassy. Kill anyone who tries to stop you. Under no circumstances is it to fall into anyone else's hands. Progress report to me daily without fail.' That had been it. No goodbye or good luck! The car door had thudded shut and I was on my own, standing on the pavement looking like a slightly dazed mullet.

'What's in the fucking box?'

'What box?' Geezer wanted to know. I hadn't realised that I had spoken the question aloud. Alcohol could do that sometimes.

'Just a box,' I replied. 'A box no one has opened since the end of the war.'

'Oh, one of those boxes,' said Geezer as he lit another cigarette from the one he was finishing. 'You watch your skinny arse, boy. Those sorts of boxes are nothing but grief.' He dropped the remains of the first smoke down into the tide and we started to promenade our way the length of Patong Beach. As we walked and talked, his words automatically replayed themselves over and over in the back of my consciousness. He was damned right. What could be so important about a sealed box left over from the tail end of the war? A hundred tons of gold and the Ruby Buddha were, in my book at least, a hell of a lot more important than whatever was in the box. Or were they?

There was a series of questions I had been asking myself over and over since Bernard had briefed me. What the hell was an unidentified and un-flagged British submarine doing rendezvousing with a Japanese freighter off the coast of Burma during the last year of the Pacific War. Had it been mere bad luck that a flight of three carrier-based Grumman Hellcat fighter-bombers, carrying out nuisance raids on Japanese shipping in the Andaman, had just happened by?

Maybe it had been fate or damned good flying that had dropped a lone 1,000-pound bomb right on the torpedo room of the sub. The resulting massive explosion had sent both vessels down to the bottom in seconds. It may have been pure fate, too, when the Hellcats had been caught in a monsoon gale as they had attempted to return to their carrier. All three aircraft and their pilots had been lost.

Point was, at the end of the day, given the combination of high explosives, sharks and monsoon seas, no one from either vessel—or, as it turned out, from any of the aircraft—had survived to tell the tale. A short broken radio signal from one of the aircraft gave news of the sinking but the atmospheric conditions caused by the approaching storm had cut communication before the carrier operators had been able to get the co-ordinates. Exactly where the two vessels were lying had remained a big fat mystery for decades. Not that anyone, except perhaps Whitehall's secret squirrels, had actually been looking. After all, my guess was that no one but a few top-secret British Government departments and presumably the Japanese hierarchy had known about the operation, whatever that had been.

However one aspect of this whole thing bothered me. How the hell did anyone know what happened out there in the Andaman if no one had survived to tell the tale? Undoubtedly Bernard had been selective with the truth when he had briefed me. But then his kind always were secretive. Truth to guys like him was always relevant or irrelevant, depending on the position he and his puppet masters wanted to maintain.

According to Bernard, the discovery of the wrecks had come about when a sonar reading from an oil-exploration vessel licensed by the Burmese Government had identified the remains of two vessels lying close together in the area known as the Loughborough Passage. The captain of the survey ship was former 'old school' British Navy. He sat on the information until his return to the UK on leave in 2003, when he visited a former shipmate who was still on the Navy payroll in an intelligence capacity. The information obviously caused a few ructions in the basements of Whitehall.

It had taken some time to arrange a charter scuba-diving expedition into the area using some of The Firm's divers posing as enthusiastic amateurs. The tsunami and the second Iraqi war caused the project to be temporarily shelved. It seemed that a couple more years weren't going to make any difference. In late 2005 the covert expedition went ahead and divers identified both of the vessels. One was HMS *Victor*, the other, an old former Dutch freighter, *Ziderzall*, captured by the Japanese in Singapore and thinly disguised by being renamed *San Tao*, a supposedly Philippine-registered cargo tramp. The vessels lay within a hundred feet of each other on the bottom of the Andaman, fifty miles off the coast of Myanmar. The time window the divers had available and the presence of Burmese naval vessels in the area, plus uncertain weather, had made them pull out before they had achieved any of the additional objectives they may have had on their agenda.

Now, all things being equal, I, within a week or two, was going to be somewhere out on the bloody Andaman with a bunch of Tuk Tuk's cut-throats. I was a trained scuba diver, but I hated boats at the best of times, and stinking fishing boats and rough water were not my idea of fun. However, that was the only alternative as I saw it.

As for Bernard, well, he would get his daily call while I was on the dry, but I wouldn't be telling him my plans in any detail. I didn't trust long-distance communication, coded email or satellite mobile phones, scrambled or not. I'd also learned that the closer to your chest you played your hand, the less chance you had of a screw up.

4

I enjoyed the drive up the Gulf. It was a trip of 500 miles or so from Phuket to Bangkok, a big hit in one stint but perfect with an overnighter. Despite the popular misconception and generalisations many in the West make regarding Asian drivers, Thai's are not that bad. It's just the sheer numbers that give the illusion of chaos—that and the constant sound of vehicle horns. The horns aren't saying, 'Piss off, Noddy', or worse, as we do in the West. Here they are instead saying, 'I'm here, look out for me.' Driving in Thailand is a matter of self-defence and anticipation; it can be fun if you have the right attitude.

I cruised on up the highway in the rented Nissan. I stopped at Chumphon for a street-stall lunch and then carried on with a full belly, lips tingling from spices.

I didn't head straight on up into Phetchaburi. There was no point if Tuk Tuk wasn't there yet. I wasn't about to presume and crash Sakura's palace. Instead, I stopped in Cha-Am mid-afternoon. I anticipated a few hours to enjoy the sun and sea, followed by a relaxing evening. The summer tourist season was still building, and I had no trouble picking up a room at the Golden Sands. In the bar I picked up Suzie from Boston overnighting with her coach party. She found my accent 'kinda cute'. I found her body definitely cute.

In the morning Suzie left my room before her tour checked out of the hotel. I showered and went down to one of the restaurants where I just managed to keep down a breakfast of essential grease and black coffee. Someone should ban Jack Daniels—it's just too damn easy to drink.

I powered up my mobile phone. I'd ignored my instructions and not called Bernard the previous day. He was not amused. After copping the usual load of crap, I cut in as he began to reiterate. I was feeling shitty-livered. 'Bernard, I've heard it all before,' I snapped. 'Just let me get on with my job.'

'It's my job to know where you are in case things go wrong. And I am your superior,' he replied primly.

'I'm going to Phetchaburi to see Tuk Tuk. I will touch base tomorrow. Over and fucking out!' I flicked the power off and pocketed the phone. I didn't want him calling back. Bernard was as queer as a two-bob watch. Maybe that was why he was such an old woman. A fucking vicious old woman! I always talked to him like that when the booze had got to my liver. His S&M side seemed to enjoy it. I risked a cigarette as I took a constitutional along the beach. The sun was up and smiling and it was getting warm. Today would be an ideal day to spend doing a lot of nothing. Unfortunately I had a date. I checked out and at a few minutes past nine I started for Phetchaburi Town, a forty-minute drive up the coast. Tuk Tuk and I were meeting at ten.

The palace Tuk Tuk had built for Sakura wasn't hard to find. It was a magnificent structure set on the hill up near the palace at Phra Nakhon Khiri, just off the highway. The old palace was now a museum and, in many ways, so was Sakura's place, albeit a modern one. Physically they were both imposing structures by any definition.

Tuk Tuk's creation had a high outer wall and behind that was a moat ten yards wide, and behind that again, a high inner wall. The moat, at first glance, looked like a water feature, with floating lilies, many species of carp and even turtles. The peaceful calm was an illusion. With its sloping bottom and smooth walls, it was a mantrap. Anyone trying to wade through it would drown unless he could swim really well. Once in the water even a good swimmer would eventually run out of energy, that was if he didn't encounter one of the extremely poisonous water snakes in residence. Not a good place to take a dip.

The remote-controlled gate of the outer wall gave access to a narrow car bridge that led to a second gate in the inner wall. This wall had a gatehouse built into it and was always manned by a guard armed with a sub-machine-gun. Did I also mention that there were CCTV cameras everywhere? There was another entrance and exit to the palace: a hidden tunnel that ran from the underground garages back into the small mountain the palace was built into. The tunnel emerged in a warehouse in a street half a mile away, and was big enough to take Tuk Tuk's largest armoured tank. Armed thugs and booby traps guarded the disguised tunnel entrance. Not even the Thai Army could get through that one.

Both gates slid open simultaneously as I approached. I was well and truly expected, it seemed. I drove on into the huge gardened courtyard I remembered so well. There was a heavily armoured Lincoln Pullman parked in the white pebbled parking area. The ageless Lincoln was a real heavyweight beast, akin to a Centurion tank. It was very probably the same limousine Arune had intended vaporising. I parked beside the behemoth and got out. Choy was waiting, standing motionless in front of the Lincoln like one of the many priceless marble and bronze statues that decorated the whole area. The Cabbage really was the only ugly thing there, with the possible exception of the big black limousine and me, but compared to Choy I was Pierce Brosnan.

The Cabbage was motioning me to follow him inside. He started away and I fell into his wake as he led me away along a white marble pathway spanned by fountains and pools of hundred-year-old carp. It was a truly beautiful place, no doubt due to Sakura's influence. Her class and serenity juxtaposed Tuk Tuk's violent power. Yin and Yang, the crippled philosopher in my brain muttered. That was the thing: the hard and the soft, the beautiful and the ugly. Without one you could never truly know the other. That was Tuk Tuk and Sakura.

Choy and I passed through tall, black glass doors into the cool of the main building. The massive foyer was almost as large as the courtyard. As with the gardens, the theme was white, with marble the colour of the purest snow dominating. Serene white was Sakura's colour, just as blood red was Tuk Tuk's.

They were both waiting, standing side by side at the balustrade on the mezzanine level above. I started up the wide staircase while Choy remained at the foot of the stairs, as watchful and as spiteful as a junkyard dog.

Sakura glided forward, smiling, and I felt my heart immediately do a back flip. If anything, she was more beautiful than the last time I had seen her all those years ago. She was dressed in a pair of simple white trousers and an equally simple white top. There were small gold earrings peeking out from under the gleaming cap of jet-black hair. Her eyes were enormous, separated by a tiny elegant nose. Her lips curved upwards in a genuine welcoming smile. Those lips, they were just about perfect, touched as they were with a slight shade of rose that glowed against her alabaster skin. She was stunning. There was no other word for it.

'Daniel,' she said in the clear, singsong voice I had heard in my dreams numerous times since my very first meeting with her. 'It is so wonderful to see you again.' She extended her hand and I took it gingerly. It looked so fragile, so cool and smooth. But she squeezed with a sudden pressure that belied the illusion she was delicate and weak. Then she came closer and stood on tiptoes to kiss me on the cheek. 'So very, very good to see you again.'

'And you,' I replied, 'the most beautiful woman in a land of beautiful women.' I looked into her eyes and could have fallen in as she laughed away the compliment, but I could see she enjoyed it. It would have been so damned easy to fall in love with this amazing creature, or the ideal she represented. I looked beyond her to see Tuk Tuk standing smiling at me. It wasn't the gloating smirk of a man showing off his trophy, but rather a genuine smile. Sometimes that man could be so fucking confusing. Sakura swung to my side and took my arm, drawing me forward with her. 'I will make tea and then I will leave you men alone to discuss what you will.'

The tea ceremony was a traditional Japanese one. It was held in a small lounge of polished wood and glass panels set back off the mezzanine. Thank god we didn't have to sit on the floor. I hated that. Instead we sat at a modified table with a pit for our feet and thick cushions for our behinds. It was comfortable in every way.

Despite the fact she wasn't dressed as a *geisha*, Sakura's ceremony was every bit as elaborate as those I had partaken of on my visits to the Land of the Rising Sun. It was a pleasant and quite beautiful interlude. Very civilised and civilising. The tea helped get rid of the remnants of my hangover. Almost too soon, the ceremony was over and our smiling hostess departed, leaving Tuk Tuk and I alone. Choy appeared.

'We have the boats, Daniel. Two of them: a prawn scow, and the other a highly modified deep-sea trawler,' Tuk Tuk said as he removed a cigarette from the gold case that Choy passed to him. He pushed the case towards me. I smiled, declining, and took the pack of cursed Marlboros from my shirt pocket. The radio transmitter wasn't in this particular pack. Choy held a flame under Tuk Tuk's cigarette tip, and then mine.

'Crew?' I asked.

'We have three divers coming up from the south. The boat handlers are all sailors used to the Andaman. The guards will all be my men. They will be well armed and they will use the trawler. It is a smuggler's boat, very fast, but it looks just like any other boat of its kind.' Tuk Tuk smiled the self-satisfied smile of the cat that would soon get the cream. 'So, Daniel, in five days the boats and the crews will be ready and waiting for you at the dock at Ranong. It just remains for you to pass over the details of their destination so they can plan fuel and supplies.'

'Lord Loughborough Island,' I replied. Tuk Tuk glanced at Choy who left the room, no doubt to fetch a map. Tuk Tuk and I sat in more or less companionable silence while we awaited his return. I had a hand-held GPS in my kit. It was programmed to get us within half a mile of what we were looking for. The exact co-ordinates of the vessels were committed to memory. Survival was high on my personal agenda and I was not going to be giving away more than I needed to at this point in time. I was wondering if Choy was coming with us. Tuk Tuk had already indicated that he himself would not be sailing on the Andaman.

Choy rejoined us carrying a large framed map of southern Thailand and the Andaman coast. We cleared space for it on the table. Tuk Tuk squinted at the map, perhaps too vain to put on the glasses that I could see in the breast pocket of his jacket. I leaned over and indicated the island. 'Only fifty or so miles out from Ranong,' I said. 'I estimate we might need three days in the area.'

'It will take more than that to recover all the gold,' Choy mumbled.

'If you want all the gold in addition to the buddha, it is yours,' I replied, directing my words at Tuk Tuk. 'I want three days and then I'm gone,' I added. 'If you want to spend a year getting the rest of the gold that is your affair.'

'I still find the deal we have struck quite fascinating,' Tuk Tuk said, leaning back against his cushions. 'A hundred tons of gold bullion and the most valuable buddha ever created and your people want just a simple metal box.' He paused. 'That is a very valuable box, Daniel, or for someone, a very dangerous one.'

Tuk Tuk was echoing the very words Geezer had uttered only a matter of hours before. I had to agree. It was a very fucking dangerous box. I worked hard to keep my voice steady when I replied, 'This is one deal I think it would be very wise to keep, my old friend.' Tuk Tuk's black eyes sparkled dangerously for a moment, then he slowly smiled and nodded. Sending warnings Tuk Tuk's way was fraught with danger at any time. For all that, killing me, a mere operative, was one thing but even Tuk Tuk Song knew that to cross our mob on a major issue was the equivalent of putting your head in a tiger's mouth. Many years before, a contemporary of his with business in the far north had tried to cross us and our CIA partners of the day over an arms shipment. His helicopter and a ground-to-air missile collided somewhere near Phou Bia up in Laos. That lesson had not been lost on Tuk Tuk Song, or the others who worked the shady side of life in the region.

'Yes, Daniel. This mysterious box is for your people,' he agreed at length.

'Choy will accompany you to Ranong and introduce you to those on the boats. He will not be going to sea. Like me, he has no stomach for it.' Tuk Tuk chuckled and Choy looked almost embarrassed.

While Choy wouldn't be watching over my shoulder on Tuk Tuk's behalf, I guessed he would have other eyes boring holes in the base of my skull. Despite the fact I was almost back on the dance card of the most dangerous man in the Kingdom, I didn't trust Choy. If Choy killed me without Tuk Tuk's approval, he would beg forgiveness of his old master and Tuk Tuk would surely grant it. That being the case I had to be very fucking careful around The Cabbage, ready for anything he might try. The one thing I was sure of was that he wouldn't attempt a hit on me until Tuk Tuk had his buddha. To do otherwise would be to guarantee his own very painful demise. Tuk Tuk might forgive Choy just about anything, but not for screwing up his chance at a Thai sainthood.

5

I had five days to kill so I headed the Nissan north towards Bangkok. I was on the verge of a nostalgic episode, wondering what had changed in the almost seven years since I had been there. The traffic had got worse, that much was obvious from the moment I got to Samut Sakhon on Highway 35. From there into the city it was controlled chaos.

Hell, the pollution quota, that was something else. The city streets were filled with the grey haze of too many cars. I had the windows up and the air-con churning its little heart out, but still the smell of the city seeped into the car.

First call was to the British Embassy. The embassy compound was huge. It was virtually a walled park with the embassy proper, residence and offices, lawns, ponds and beautiful gardens inside. A third of the compound had been sold off in 2006, but the remaining eight acres or so of prime inner-city real estate still had Bangkok's developers slavering at their collective mouth waiting for the rest to go on the block.

Embassy business was done off Wireless Road. Here there were a series of entrances, all guarded and each with specific functions. The road itself was a wide, pleasant tree-lined avenue. There were no street parks, stalls or street peddlers, just embassies, offices and Nai Lert Park, one of Bangkok's true gems.

It took me five minutes to find somewhere to park in a side street down by the canal. I had the necessary ID to drive inside the embassy compound but I wasn't ready to stand on any soapbox and announce my presence back in town. Maybe I never would be. Tuk Tuk wasn't the only enemy I had made in Thailand and some of them still resided in the embassy of old.

I walked back down Wireless Road to the embassy and presented myself at the public gate under the eagle eyes of the guards. The insignia on their uniforms told me we had elements of the Royal Marines on duty. That was absolutely fine by me.

Nothing had changed in the main foyer in the years since I'd last been there. There were still familiar faces around. One of them, Roddy Thomas, had been a junior attaché when I had been there in my other life. Unfortunately he intercepted me just as I walked in and was orientating myself. He was all over me like a pissed matron on a hen night. 'Daniel the Swann.' Roddy was shaking my hand as if he were trying to jack up a car. 'What are you doing back here?' Roddy had never been the brightest of the bright. As he asked the question, his face slowly clouded over as he remembered the rumours of the circumstances relating to my sudden departure from the City of Smiles and Thailand.

The rumours—only half-truths—about my departure had been created and circulated by the masters of misinformation and I knew I hadn't come out of it in a good light. Word, as I heard it later, was that I had been fraternising with the wife of a wealthy and influential Thai businessman and had barely escaped with my manhood intact. The things we put up with in the line of duty, huh? 'It's okay, Roddy,' I replied, giving him a man-to-boy smile and half a wink. 'All friends again.' I then immediately changed the subject by asking what he was up to. I realised that this might have been a big mistake, but I didn't want to talk about myself, not to him.

Roddy, it appeared, had gravitated up the diplomatic food chain a little to become an under-attaché or big satchel or similar. He would never be anything more than that and he probably knew it himself. He would serve out his time, collect his pension and retire back to the UK to 'something on something'. There was a Thai wife and three kids now. That was going to make life awkward in freezing, wet, grimy, expensive something on something. Thais, cold and wet do not really go together in my experience. It would be a miserable existence for the delicate flower of the East who had had the misfortune to marry this crushing bore.

After five minutes of Roddy's excruciating company, I moved my agenda abruptly forward. 'Who is in charge of security these days, Roddy?' I asked. I knew damn well who was in charge. That had all been part of my briefing. However by asking the question, I managed to stop Roddy mid-sentence. He looked at me slightly surprised at what could have been considered a rude interruption. 'Security, Roddy old lad, and I mean security with a capital S,' I repeated in a conspiratorial tone that caused Roddy to drop his voice and lean closer. Not a pleasant sensation for me.

'Donald's your man. Donald Wisehart,' Roddy said, looking around with an earnest expression on his face. 'All hush, hush stuff,' he confided in me in a stage whisper. He probably had no real idea what Wisehart actually did. Roddy was very, very low in the need-to-know department.

'And where might I find this Mr Wisehart?' I asked.

Roddy pointed towards the basement stairs. 'In his den. Trevaine's old office. You remember it?'

'Oh yes,' I replied. Neville Trevaine had been a controller for our group. He'd been transferred out to Lahore a few weeks after I'd flown the coop. I don't think the two things were related, but the poor bugger was killed on the Afghan border a few weeks before the allied invasion.

'Drink later?' suggested Roddy hopefully.

'We'll see how this goes,' I replied, heading for the stairs. The last thing I wanted to do was end up in a dance bar with Roddy at my shoulder.

Donald Wisehart was about thirty-five, but his face was in the process of changing from young and idealistic to cynical. Middle age was on its way early, as often happened to those in this business. It was a fact I had observed casually over a bourbon too many back in London. There happened to have been a bar mirror staring me in the face at the time.

'Don Wisehart,' he said, shaking hands with a grip that stopped about one psi short of being a bone cruncher.

'Dan Swann,' I replied, thinking that we'd make a great double act: the Dan and Don show, or Don and Dan or just Don Don the Security Man and Dan the Whistling Dog. Whatever, Don Don stuck. He would forever be embedded in my memory bank as Don Don the Security Man. Stupid stuff like that helped me remember names, faces and deeds.

Wisehart hadn't done much to the décor he had inherited. There was a woman at a desk just inside the door who looked like a secretary. He introduced her as Janice. He asked Janice for coffee for two. She left. The office was your basic pre-war Whitehall two-person issue. A couple of space-age communications units and a pair of PCs were the only concession to fifty years of some sort of progress. It appeared to me to be exactly as it had been when Trevaine had been in charge, even down to the circa-1965 picture of Betty on the wall. There was a large NO SMOKING sign beside the portrait. Damn! Political correctness and all that crap!

Janice returned with the coffee. She was a tidy-looking brunette with a big chest and slightly heavy thighs. She was maybe a couple of years Don Don's junior. I noticed the engagement ring on her finger and caught a glimpse of something pass between them. She would attract a fair bit of attention on the street or in the pub back home, but here in the City of Smiles, as far as the feminine stakes were concerned at least, she wouldn't raise an eyebrow. European women, even relatively trim ones, all complained of feeling like 'fat cows' around the petite Thai girls. It was a fact of life.

My instincts told me that Janice and Don were keeping house. I wondered if there was a Mrs Don or a Mr Janice in the mix. That would complicate things here just as it would anywhere else in the world. Neither wore a wedding ring on the telltale finger, however someone had to have put the sparkler on Janice's finger. My money was on Don Don. Either way, the coffee was drinkable.

I left the embassy two hours later, having successfully dodged Roddy on the way out. Wisehart had filled in a few blanks as to the where, what, how and why of Bangkok 2007. American paranoia had been hiked to levels previously unheard of. The Yanks didn't have a hell of a lot of friends anymore, especially in the Middle East. On the broader scene even old friends had been relegated to another file. Perhaps old Osama had achieved more than he'd intended with 911. Or had he known the US psyche better than the experts had anticipated he did?

The apartment Wisehart had given me the key for wasn't a safe house as such. It was a unit used for visitors in what was basically an annex for the lesser lights of the embassy staff, along with the employees of various British trade and government agencies and the like who had bought into it. Don Don told me they had a pool, a club bar that looked like a set from *Coronation Street* and a restaurant that did passable English food. I didn't yet have a good enough handle on the guy to know whether or not he was taking the piss about the food.

I anticipated that the nightly pool and bull sessions in the boozer would be like the usual bloody Whitehall piss-ups. The sort of club gatherings where everyone was intent on getting one up on each other and attempting to swing a leg over the latest young wife or single guy or girl in town. In principle I wasn't against it, but with bloody bureaucrats and diplomatic types and their hangers-on I just found it so fucking boring and predictable, no matter where in the world it occured.

This little oasis of British heaven was only 300 yards away from the embassy, up around the corner on Soi Chitlom, right behind the Central Department Store, or CDS as everyone in Bangkok refered to it. I found the annex first try. There was a gate man on the vehicle entrance. He was asleep in his cubbyhole.

There were two basement car parks dedicated to Flat Eleven. One contained a Honda step-through. I pulled into the vacant space at about the same time as two bright young Thai girls emerged from the lift twenty feet away. I cast an appreciative eye on the pair as they came towards me. The girls both showed a lot of skin wearing tiny tank tops and tight jeans. They were giggling and talking in Thai.

I got out of the Nissan and collected my bag from the trunk. I couldn't help but tune in to the girls' animated conversation. That they were working girls, to use old-speak, came as no surprise. They were discussing the couple who had hired them for a foursome. 'She was like a cow, so fat,' one girl was saying. 'I was scared she was going to squash me.'

'And he was so skinny and so white. He never got hard, it was like a soft noodle.' One of the girls caught sight of me and nudged the other with her elbow. The smiles broadened, the eyes widened and the hips, ensconced in their stretch denim, began to sway with every stride. It was some sort of carnal poetry in motion; a Thai mating dance without the headgear and six-inch fingernails.

'I think this one would get very hard for you.' The girl who said this looked at me with the big-eyed innocent smile of a pretty twelve year old. All she needed was the school uniform. It was a wonderful piece of acting. 'So sorry we are in your car park,' she said in English.

'No problem,' I replied in English. 'I only have one car,' I added in Thai.

Both girls looked startled, but only for a second. Then the laughter started. Fingers were pointed accusingly at me and heads nodded, sending waves of dark hair shimmering.

I had always appreciated the fact that most of the Thai women I had met had a very robust and quite crude sense of humour. Being caught out by assuming I was a visiting Englishman not able to speak their language was, to them, a good joke in itself. Knowing I had understood the remarks they had made was another. I joined them in sharing the joke.

'Maybe you do want me to see if you can be hard,' the second girl said, giving me the full works in the eyes and teeth department as she pushed her hair back off her face. The same movement projected a pair of pert nipples my way through the thin fabric of her top.

I smiled back and gave her a mock pout. 'Not tonight,' I replied in Thai. 'I have a date with a cow.' That set them laughing again. It was my cue to head for the lift and navigate my way to the fourth level.

The flat was off a corridor with seven doors. One had an exit sign above it, the others bore fake brass numbers running from seven to twelve. I keyed the lock and went into number eleven.

The place was basically designed to a conventional motel format. There were two bedrooms, each with double beds. One had a view and a balcony, the other stared at a blank wall across a narrow alley. The living room-cum-lounge had a dining nook off it connected to a small kitchen. A door off the kitchen ran into a bathroom with a shower, bath, toilet, washing machine and dryer. A second door gave access to the larger bedroom.

Having done the complete circuit, I took the bedroom with the view. From the tiny balcony with its two plastic chairs and side table, I could look down at the deserted pool with its fringe of potted palms and plastic sun loungers. It was obviously too early for the horde of expats to be out and about. Either that or they had chosen not to swim under the grey–blue haze that filtered the sun down to the sparkling blue waters of this little ersatz nirvana.

I didn't hang about admiring the view. My hunger was growing hot in the pit of my gut and I didn't do starvation well, not unless absolutely necessary. I stowed my few clothes and went to check out the kitchen in detail. There was a microwave, gas hob and a small oven. The fridge was empty. Don Don had warned me of that. The food court in CDS would take care of my inner man.

Before I left the apartment I put my passport collection, emergency funds and my Walther P99 in the under-floor safe in the bathroom. Don Don had given me one of the only two keys that existed for it. He assured me the other was in the embassy main safe. I had to trust him. I kept the knife. It was sheathed on the inside of my left boot. The key to the safe went into the pocket in the lining of the right. Okay, so I was a Brit who liked cowboy boots. Not the fancy Rudy-of-Hollywood type, but plain black and solid ones. Apart from being useful for hiding weaponry, keys and cash, they were comfortable. They were also very handy when things got a bit untidy. The square toes had steel under them and the heels were solid. Footwear like that had saved my life in the past, so why spoil a good thing?

I went out on my supply run and shared the apartment lift with a couple riding down. She was a big richly dyed redhead. He was a balding stick insect. They both had the look of being long-time residents. They didn't speak—not to each other and not to me. I resisted the temptation to mention cows or noodles. They got off at the first level.

I was showered, shaved and the washing machine was on. I'd devoured two sandwiches and was on my third Singha. It was time to call Sami. Sami Somsak was an old friend and associate. We had worked and played together over many years. The last time I had seen him was when he had visited London maybe eighteen months before. Once upon a time we had been joined at the hip as we did all sorts of tricky stuff out in the bush. Since his semi-retirement from Black Ops, where he worked as a freelancer for our side, Sami had been doing things with illicit substances. The Golden Triangle was still very golden for him. I didn't begrudge him the wealth he'd accumulated from drugs. Personally I hated drugs, but The Firm, the CIA and damned near everyone else I knew had used them for profit over the years. Sami was just getting his share, and if the sick fucks around the world wanted to stew their brains, hell, that was their perogative.

Sami wasn't home. He had departed the City of Smiles for the City of Angels. We talked for ten minutes. He would be back in Bangkok in a week or so. I'd go do what I had to and we'd catch up. I flicked on my laptop and checked for messages. Nothing of any significance, not even any SPAM! The souped-up agency-supplied Toshiba was equipped with all the filters known to man. I shut down the magic box and sat debating whether to go out on the town or visit the pub-cum-club downstairs and maybe risk an 'English' meal in the restaurant. In all my years in Asia, the only time I had ever caught a dreaded stomach bug was in a European-style hotel with European food. I'd never been sick on so-called street, bush or peasant food.

First I had to call Bernard. I fired up the mobile and called home. If the Right Honourable Sir Bernard Sinclair was overjoyed to hear my dulcet tones he didn't let on. I informed him where I was and of the timetable as I saw it. I didn't go into detail. I just told him I had a boat set up for Ranong. 'The weather will be the thing, Bernard,' I reminded him. We had discussed this before I had left. I wasn't prepared to risk my life and get taken out by one of the violent storms that the tail end of the monsoon creates. He grudgingly acknowledged the point and I hung up with the promise that I'd update him the next day.

'Like a fucking maiden aunt,' I thought as I off-loaded the phone onto one of the pair of bedside tables in the room. Even Bernard had never been this bad before. Once upon a life I wouldn't have spoken to him twice in a month. Whatever was in that damned box on the bottom of the Andaman was really rattling his cage.

The Coro Street Club was jumping when I strolled in. There were perhaps twenty-five people in it, obvious couples and singles; the assembly spanned all ages. Eyes swept over me then came back for more. Shit, this was like a meat market back home. Being reasonably honest, I wasn't the worst-looking banana in the bunch. I had a nose that had been broken long ago but still had all my own teeth. A suntan was rapidly re-establishing itself, and I had a moustache and full head of blond–white hair. Added to those dubious attributes were a pair of blue eyes, a flat gut and enough muscle to make me a nuisance in a scrap. That sort of painted a picture of yours truly. Closer inspection revealed a lot of scars on my body, plus the calluses on the balls of my feet and the knuckles of my thick fingers. A professional, at least, would recognise that I hadn't led a soft life and I was trained in some of the not-so-fine arts.

I came very close to turning on my heel and leaving the club, but instinct made me stay. I thought I might need someone in this place at some time in the future. I pasted half a smile on my face and went to the bar. A couple of guys in shirtsleeves and low-hung ties moved aside to let me belly up.

'New to town?' a walrus-moustached red face asked from behind the bar.

'Just in,' I replied, checking out the barman. He was a jovial-looking character in his fifties, a short barrel of a man with the aforementioned moustache and a fringe of white hair around a tanned dome. He wore a blue polo shirt with a logo that featured a foaming beer tankard and the words: CORO STREET CLUB.

'Just a little housekeeping thing,' he said, pushing a clipboard across the bar and dropping a pen on it. 'If you could just fill in the details. In the meantime, what would you like?' I asked for a pint of Heineken and quickly filled in the blanks. I only lied on occupation and home address, substituting reality with my standard cover. I was a security consultant for Karvonics, a fictitious British alarm and electronics company that existed in all but bricks and mortar. That was close enough to the truth to blur a few lines. The address was somewhere in Surrey, also close enough to smudge the remaining lines. Put it this way, if someone dialled my home phone or my business number, or wrote to my mailing address, they would receive a reply.

The pint was cold and crisp and at thirty-five baht, it was probably the cheapest I'd get anywhere. 'Out from the old country?' one of the pair leaning on the bar asked me.

'Via Hong Kong and Ho Chi Minh,' I replied. I didn't want to get the usual bullshit of, 'You'll notice a huge difference. Must show you around. Christ, you'll have to try the women.' Getting the word around that I was an old hand in these parts would cut a lot of the crap. 'Dan Swann,' I said sticking out my hand. 'Karvonics Security Systems.' The other pair shook with damp, limp hands. Peter Something, trade development. Graham Something, embassy underling. We talked football and beer for a few minutes before two teenage Thai girls entered the club to be signed in by the Somethings. That was my cue to get a refill and wander out towards the patio and the pool.

I pushed out through the swing doors only to be hit by a blast of stifling, thick crud. 'Welcome home,' I muttered as I checked out the surroundings. The patio revealed itself as being quite large. A chest-high green-tiled balustrade separated it from the street below. The pool was a three-quarter-size affair and took up half the space. Loungers, patio chairs and tables scattered amongst the potted palms gave the illusion of a resort setting. Low garden lights were on. It was almost pleasant, but for the lack of clean oxygen. Closer to the bar entrance where I was standing were half a dozen hardwood tables and chairs. Those who had gravitated out from the bar to take in the evening pollution populated several of them.

Four European girls who occupied one of the tables were giving me a very frank assessment.

I gave them a collective smile, turned on my heel and re-entered the air-conditioned comfort of the club. I had no sooner slid into a vacant booth than the patio doors swung open and the four girls trooped in. No, I didn't mind if they joined me.

6

Christ, what a headache! I crawled out of bed and staggered into the bathroom. I didn't recognise the guy who was blinking back at me from the mirror. I sluiced water over my face and fumbled for the magic hangover tablets I'd picked up down at CDS. They were a uniquely Thai concoction and they worked. I decided I would take a suitcase full of them back to the UK with me. If I ever got back there!

I swallowed two of the capsules then turned to the toilet to empty my tortured bladder. There were what looked suspiciously like teeth marks on my right thigh, and a purplish bruise on my belly. It was about then that my memory started to return. I'd been a lucky bad boy.

When I returned to the bedroom I realised there was a shape under the sheets and a tousled crop of red hair on one of the pillows. There were also two used condoms lying on the tiles by my side of the bed. I bent over to pick them up and almost met the bloody tiles headfirst. I carried the rubbers back to the bathroom and flushed them. At least I'd been careful, even if I didn't remember much about what had gone on.

I started back for the bedroom as a series of flashbacks hit me. There had been a lot of laughing and drinking, the four girls and I. A meal somewhere, four thinning down to three, then two in a bar somewhere, then there was me and one other stumbling along a street and falling into a lift. The one had been the redhead. All my befuddled memory could throw back at me were flashes of Red and I lost in a jumble of arms, legs, lips, hips and other bits and pieces.

There was clothing all over the floor, both male and female. A sheer, black G-string was hanging from the wall-mounted lamp above the bed. A black bra of the same material had landed on the side table. I let the shape in the bed be and pulled on a pair of boxers. I found my cigarettes and lighter on the table under the bra and stepped out onto the balcony into the Bangkok morning.

It was early, maybe half five. The traffic was light and the pollution level hadn't climbed past noxious. I realised that this was Sunday. Even Bangkok slowed a little on Sunday morning, but by ten it would be roaring again. I sat on one of the chairs, lit a cigarette and spent the next minute fighting not to cough or vomit. Eventually my system settled down, and the nicotine plus the herbal remedy I had swallowed earlier started to work. After five minutes I was almost feeling human but the sound of retching from the direction of my bathroom told me someone else wasn't. I decided to leave Red to it and eventually the puking stopped. 'Oh God,' a voice said from behind me. I turned and a pale face under a shock of what I knew to be natural red hair shone at me from the slider into the bedroom.

'Good morning isn't appropriate at this time?' I asked.

'No,' she replied thickly. 'Have you got aspirin?'

'Better than that,' I replied, flicking away my cigarette butt. I led her back into the bathroom. There I organised a pair of capsules and a glass of water. Then I remembered her name. Red was in fact Barbara, Barbara from Bristol, an embassy clerk. Unsurprisingly her friends had all called her Babs.

Babs had a wonderful pale body with high, red-tipped breasts, long legs that met at a thick dark red thatch that had been carefully sculpted into the shape of a heart. 'Oh,' she shuddered as she leaned on the vanity and fought to keep the capsules down. Standing the way she was, propped on her straight arms, legs apart, butt pushed back, I had the impulse to press in behind her and see what came up, as it were. I didn't. I was going to be a perfect gentleman, for the moment at least.

'Just keep them down for five minutes and it'll be okay,' I said, leaving her and heading for the coffee plunger. When the brew was made I took two strong black ones back to the bathroom. Babs was still standing at the vanity, her head hanging down, when I landed a coffee in front of her.

'I'm never going to drink again,' she announced. 'Never!' she vowed.

I grinned to myself. How many times had I heard that? I'd never promised me that personally, not since my teens anyway. Alcohol and the conspicuous consumption of it had always been a factor in my lifestyle. I decided that a shower was next on the agenda as the coffee cooled to a drinkable temperature. I dropped my shorts, reached into the cabinet and cranked the control onto full. I'd been in maybe two minutes when the door opened and Babs joined me. I guessed she was feeling a little better. It was soap-and-rinse time with lots of slippery body on body. Nice and sexy, but no sex for the moment. We returned to our coffees and eventually to bed.

Later, much later, when Babs had gone up to her flat on the fifth floor, I made my call to Bernard then went for a walk. I took to my feet as much to catch up on the vibe of the city as to walk off the exertions of the past few hours. I figured if the present rate of sexual expression carried on, I was going to have to get some Viagra. In my more or less sober state, Babs had proven to be some sort of sexual dynamo. I was not a bloody teenager anymore and keeping up had taken some real effort on my part. It had been fun though.

I walked down to Lumphini Park. Being Sunday it was as near to a local holiday as you could get in Thailand, apart from the birthdays of the Royal Family and Chinese New Year. Anyway, the park was full of families and kids. I got the best bits of a barbecued chicken, a cob of steamed corn and a can of Singha and wandered on, letting the atmosphere flow over me. Kids were kicking balls, racing around and yelling. There were a few kites fluttering in the slight breeze. It was a vibrant place. The hawkers and the beggars were about, selling their wares or calling on the generosity of all and sundry. I was always a sucker for kids and cripples, so my pockets were soon emptied of coins.

From the park I headed down Silom to check out Patpong. I wasn't going there for the bars. It was too early for much action but I was just curious to see if anything had changed in the years since I'd last been there. It hadn't, although there was no carnage this time—not that I could see anyway. This was where I'd saved Tuk Tuk's life all those years before. There were still bullet scars on some of the buildings.

'Ah, memories,' I thought as I moved on.

I sat in a little restaurant across from the Ramada and had a delicious early dinner and a couple more beers while the world flowed by outside. I didn't plan on going to the Coro Club that night, nor of bedding Babs or anyone else for that matter. Even if I was able to rediscover my libido, I doubted my body could take it. I was hoping that with the next day being a workday, Babs would beg off and want to do her hair or something.

Funny thing about libido was that it didn't take a hell of a lot of work to rediscover it.

Babs knocked on my door five minutes after I stepped back into the building. I silently promised to kick that dopey-looking security guard in the crotch next time I went out. She had obviously primed him with a few baht to call her when I came in.

Thing was, this time we climbed into bed and made love without wrecking anything much. We went to sleep in each other's arms. It was almost like married life, or how I imagined it to be in an almost perfect world. I'd been there once and there had been perfect moments but they had been few and far between.

The traffic woke us in the morning. We made love again, then Babs got out of bed, dressed hurriedly and leaned down to kiss me goodbye. I sort of expected her to suggest that we do it again that night but she meant goodbye. Her fiancé, a trade development guy, was arriving back in town that very day. 'Jody has her man back from Vietnam so she's not available, but Debbie and Sara are free agents. Their guys are in Japan,' she said, referring to two of the other members of the original quartet. 'They like a little action.' Then she gave me a broad grin that wrinkled her nose and she chuckled. 'You know we tossed a coin Saturday night. They lost and I got you. Aren't you glad?' she challenged.

'Oh yes,' I replied honestly.

'So am I,' she replied, leaning down to kiss me on the lips. '*Ciao,* Dan, it was wild!' With that Barbara from Bristol, alias Babs, was gone in a flash of legs, red hair and a gleaming smile. I started laughing. It was so bloody funny. There was I, Mr Irresistible Stud, and the girls had played me like, well, like I'd played them. Sort of natural justice and in the long run, honour more or less satisfied. I wondered how I could avoid the other two. Apparently fidelity didn't have a big place in their lives. Hey, just like at home, huh? Fidelity had never been my strong suit. That was something, in hindsight, that I had come to regret bitterly on many long, lonely nights. I'd had my chance and I'd blown it. End of story.

7

The only thing worse than a stinking prawn boat is a stinking prawn boat punching its way across a force ten gale that has dragged up a fat ten-foot swell. Okay, the gale and the wave height may be an exaggeration, but it damned well felt like it. Out of sheer self-defence I had been standing on the upwind side of the main deck for the past hour. That meant I was getting a face full of lukewarm salt spray every few seconds, but it also meant I wasn't downside or inside the boat sucking in the odour of rotting fish and diesel fumes, a combination that could turn the hardiest gut inside out.

'You want some food?' The guy asking the question was standing in the doorway that led into the superstructure of the fifty-five-foot-long tub. He was holding out an aluminium plate full of an evil red curry. I could have sworn there were things moving in it.

'Fuck off!' I muttered in English, waving him away.

'You too,' he replied in Thai as he vanished back inside. I had to grin at that. I'd given the crew the standard greeting when I'd come on board. So apart from a couple of *sawatdee khrap*s, I hadn't said a word to anyone in any language. I'd just planted myself out there with my back against the bulkhead and there I'd stayed. I wasn't sure whether it was better to speak their language or plead ignorance and stay with English. I knew speaking Thai could gain me a little respect with this gang of cut-throats. By not speaking it, however, I also knew I might hear something that could ultimately be used to my advantage. Hell, it could even save my life.

Choy and a couple of the crew had had a long conversation as my kit had been off-loaded from The Cabbage's Jeep Cherokee onto the boat. Unfortunately I hadn't been able to put my fake Marlboro pack in Choy's pocket, so I didn't know what the hell had been said. Had he told them,

'When he's shown you where the wreck is, hit him behind the ear and drop him over the side'? Maybe he had said, 'Look after the Englishman well because I want him in one piece when you get back!' I knew it would have been one of those, probably the latter because the bastard wanted to kill me personally. Choy's obsession with my death was as plain as the belly on a laughing buddha. I had no illusions at all that, no matter which way this whole thing went, he and I would have our day of reckoning—Tuk Tuk's word or not.

I'd called Bernard from Ranong and told him he'd have to do without his daily telephone date for as long as I was out chasing his damned lead box, satellite phone or not. I knew once we pushed out beyond the harbour it would be difficult to pick up a bird, even if I had the urge. I also figured I was going to have my hands full. Tough! Strangely enough the old bastard hadn't seemed unduly perturbed at the prospect of not hearing from his favourite agent. Sometimes that arsehole was impossible to figure. What did I mean sometimes? I meant all the time.

Was I scared? Of course I bloody well was. All the fucking secret agents and undercover types in movies come across as having balls of steel. But in the real world, we all sweat bullets and our guts churn. Sometimes I wanted my mummy, but I figured the Walther in the holster in the small of my back was more use in the real world. Sorry mum!

I crossed in front of the cabin to the dry side of the tub. Here, out of the spray and the wind, the smell of dead fish wafted back from the open deck well, set between the raised rear superstructure and the bow. The derricks that controlled the big prawn nets were positioned on each side slightly forward of the three-foot-deep recess in the deck. I'd seen these things working before, swinging their big fine-mesh nets in over the side of the boat and dumping kicking prawns and shrimp by the hundredweight into the well. The take was then quickly sorted for debris and the prawns sent down a chute into ice in the hold below. All very interesting but I didn't think they'd bothered to clean that damn tub since it had first floated. That was why the smell of rotting sea life was so fucking overpowering.

The trawler escort—an unnamed, rusted long-liner about the same size as our tub—was a hundred yards behind and out to one side. Watching it split the waves with its sharp bow as it rose and twisted through the swells before falling and twisting down again didn't do a lot for me, or more precisely, for my gut. I lit a cigarette and shifted my gaze to somewhere over the grey horizon. I was hoping the smoke would hide the rotten fish smell. It worked somewhat, but the smoke and the motion of the boat started to churn my entrails into soup. I tossed the half-finished cigarette butt over the side and then went to the railing. There, I followed the butt with my last meal or two. Fuck, I hated boats!

Eventually we found the lee of an island to hide behind for the night. There were so many reefs, rocks and small islands in the area that to go charging around in the dark was a sure recipe for disaster. The sea behind the island was calm and I finally stopped chucking. I wiped my face with unsalted water from a tap on the bulkhead beside me and risked another cigarette. I had coughed up a storm but I didn't lose it as we cruised closer to our shelter.

Like all good consorts our escort was still following, both behind and a little to our right (starboard as the nautical types call it). The trawler had a crew of eight: three to run the thing and five to run the assortment of weaponry that Tuk Tuk had put on board. I had been impressed by the inventory. There were half a dozen LAW 80 shoulder-fired tank busters guaranteed to take just about anything short of a cruiser to the bottom of the ocean. There were also two Browning .50 calibre heavy machine guns, plus a couple of M79 grenade launchers and the usual assortment of M16s and AK47s. Short of an all out war, we were tooled up to account for ourselves in a damned good skirmish.

The pirate thing in the Andaman and down through the whole region to just about Australia was a reality. However unlike the cut-throats in the Malaccan Straits, there was not a hell of a lot of publicity about the Andaman pirates. The Burmese broadcasted bugger all of anything to the outside world so the pirates existed and prospered, and they were a bloody pack of real villains. Most of their victims were fishermen, but if a nice fat tourist yacht or cruiser happened by, they would have a go at it too. Generally, there were no survivors. The sharks saw to that.

The rattle of the anchor chain broke my musing. There was activity up the pointed end of our tub and shouts from the bridge, followed by the grumble and vibration of an old diesel engine as the boat reversed to set the hook. Two minutes later we were swinging on the cable in near silence. I stood and watched our escort go through the same manoeuvre fifty yards away to starboard.

I noted the other vessels in the big bay. A luxury two-master yacht was anchored to our left and beyond that a string of Moken boats were rafted up closer to the shore. These long, low barge-type boats were home to the sea nomads who were the main occupants of the area. Whole families lived on board the big mother craft, and often they could be seen travelling between the islands with a caravan of dugout canoes strung behind. Once the group arrived in an area they wanted to fish or scavenge in, the larger boat anchors and the owners of the dugouts would go about their business.

The bay in which we had taken shelter had an island mass on three sides of us, and in the gathering gloom I could see sparks of light on the shore—fishing villages or just camps, I guessed. I knew from a briefing long ago, at a time when I had been doing things in these waters, that there were bugger all shore dwellers out there. Almost a thousand islands made up the Mergui Archipelago, the true name of the area. To me back then it was just bloody sea with lumps in it. I hadn't so far seen anything this time round to change my opinion.

I risked going inside the boat. I'd decided, thanks to my rather perverted sense of humour, to name the tub the SS *Odorama*: it was smelly, uncomfortable and sloshed along like a damn bathtub.

The main cabin—a sort of mess and sleeping quarters for the crew—was directly through the door leading to the deck. Mess was probably a good description for it. Hammocks were slung from the ceiling beams. There was a table of sorts that doubled as the engine-room hatch cover, plus there were a few chairs and stools and a built-in bench that was the captain's bed. A crude galley was behind the mess, with an even cruder toilet behind the galley—if a bucket with a couple of rattan screens around it could be considered a toilet.

About two feet behind the toilet, right in the stern, was a second sleeping area. This, I suspected, started life as a storage locker and had subsequently been very roughly converted into a cabin into which four short, hard bunks had been crammed. That was where I was sleeping, along with the three divers Tuk Tuk had brought in. The divers were in the main cabin playing cards when I entered. They glanced at me and grinned. I guessed my face was still glowingly pale. I grinned back to show I had a sense of humour. 'Rotting fish and diesel. I hate the smell,' I said in Thai. The guys immediately laid down their cards and started talking to me ninety to the dozen in their own language. Somewhere along the line I'd decided that speaking Thai and getting alongside these fellows might be a wise move.

It was amazing in any situation what a few words in the native tongue could achieve. Anywhere but Paris that was! Hell, in my opinion fucking Parisians didn't even like each other, let alone their cousins from the provinces. So speaking French in Paris was a joke, especially given that most of the natives could speak English when they chose. No such problem where I was! If you could speak Thai, no matter how badly, you were welcomed with open arms. However, because these guys all worked for Tuk Tuk Song I had no illusions about what to expect from them. They would do as I said only because Choy, on Tuk Tuk's behalf, had told them to. They were terrified of Tuk Tuk and of The Cabbage. They weren't scared of me. Even so, the illusion of camaraderie could be as important as the real thing. That was how most of the intelligence outfits got on together. Mirrors, smoke and big smiley faces up front, sharp knives ready behind the back. I was good at playing Mr Smiley Face.

'Who wants a beer?' I asked and they all chorused very much to the affirmative. I had insisted that we have a good supply of Singha on board. Tuk Tuk had agreed to that readily enough. A big refrigerator the size of a supermarket chest had been squeezed up one end of the mess. As I was boss, if I said drink, they drank. I opened the chest and passed out a string of cans, keeping one for myself.

I let the dive team get back to their game and joined in the banter at appropriate intervals while I stood sipping my beer, looking over the map that had been taped to the bulkhead wall above the refrigerator. I guessed, from the relatively short time we'd been on the move, that we were anchored in Hastings Harbour, right up in the lee of St Luke's Island, or Zadetkale Kyun to give it its Burmese name. A lot of the islands and bays on the map had English names. They were all named after bloody dukes, generals, governors and such. However I guessed the Burmese still called the islands whatever they had been calling them for centuries, and to hell with what a bunch of jumped-up colonial types wrote on their maps. I doubted many Burmese on the mainland even knew this mass of islands existed.

From where I estimated we were I figured that we had maybe half a day's steaming to get to Loughborough Island. We could probably be in position before nightfall the following day. That was if I wanted us to be there. I hadn't yet figured out if we would be better to anchor at the dive site and stay there, or commute. The co-ordinates for the wrecks placed us on the eastern side of the island, with no cover from the westerly winds. At this time of the year it could be calm, it could be shitty and there was no way of knowing which until we got there.

'We are here.' A brown finger tapped the map. I'd been dead right about our anchorage. The speaker was Niran, the captain of this most illustrious vessel. According to Tuk Tuk the boat had once been Niran's but he had lost it gambling to one of Tuk Tuk's syndicates. Now Niran had his chance to earn it back.

Niran was the colour of teak, a small wisp of a man with a straggly beard and long unkempt jet-black hair flecked with silver. He wore what had once been a white singlet, but was now various shades of yellow. He also had on a pair of baggy blue shorts that accentuated his skinny but muscular legs. The legs ended in bare feet that looked as tough as army-issue boots. The toes were hooked, broken and set at odd angles, speaking of years of accidents and abuse mostly on board his boat, I guessed. A European going barefoot on this tub would find it like walking through a fucking minefield of toe-busting, shin-cracking booby traps.

'Beer?' I asked.

'Please,' he replied, taking the can I handed to him. We stood smoking and sipping our beers while we discussed timing and the anchorage for the following night. Without giving too much away, I circled a spot on the large-scale map close to where we would be diving. Niran considered the place I had indicated and pointed out where he thought we should set up our night anchorage. 'Monsoons are finished but there is still too much bad weather to stay out there. We will only be an hour from the dive site. No problem,' he concluded, taking a big swallow of his beer to indicate the can was empty. I opened the refrigerator and distributed another round. For good Buddhists, these boys had a robust thirst for beer. In my book, some rules were just made to be broken.

Food was produced a few minutes later. Curried fish, vegetables and rice was the meal of the moment. I didn't risk any food beyond a bowl of plain steamed rice. After we had eaten, Niran produced a bottle of Mekong and he and I drank a few toasts before I decided to turn in. I left behind the makings of a party. I'd instructed Niran to issue one more round of beer, but I noted that there were a few bottles of the local rocket fuel in a crate in the corner of the mess. I didn't care what the hell they did, short of sinking us.

Back in the shack I checked my emails. Nothing. Then I pulled up the electronic map of the area around Loughborough Island. It told me nothing new. I closed the laptop and pushed it back into its padded pocket inside my holdall and adjusted the bag behind my head. Pillows were in short supply on board the good ship *Odorama*.

I awoke when the others eventually fell noisily into their beds, then again an hour or two later. The makeshift cabin was cramped, hot and bloody smelly with three farting, beer-drinking curry eaters in residence. Despite the fact the door was wide open, the heat and the smell rose up to my top bunk. Maybe having the top bunk was a status thing but, hell, I'd have swapped it for one of the lower ones in an instant. Eventually, however, I found sleep again, or it found me. To many, the famous Thai whisky tastes like shit after bourbon, but it does a job and a half of anaesthetising the brain.

8

We made our second anchorage at a few minutes past 15:00 the next day. This time we were sheltered from the westerlies by a small island tagged onto the northern tip of Lord Loughborough Island. I estimated that our dive site was about another five miles beyond us to the west. I had the GPS in my kit and the co-ordinates all but locked in. I held back on the last couple of important digits—they were my insurance.

I didn't know who Tuk Tuk or Choy had designated as my shadow. On a tub this size, everyone was in everyone's face most of the time. I thought I had Niran on side. The divers, they were okay guys. They were young, none of them over thirty. Apparently they worked for a dive-school chain, a chain owned by, you guessed it, Tuk Tuk Song. Two of them were former Thai navy underwater specialists trained in demolition and salvage. The third was a senior PADI instructor with twelve years under his belt. I had to assume they were all pretty good in the water.

I'd not mentioned the submarine to Tuk Tuk or anyone else up until then. The divers knew we were going after a freighter and treasure, but that was all they knew. I would tell them the rest at our pre-dive briefing the next day. I needed to balance security with practicality. Keeping myself safe was much more of a priority to me than the security of the damned box. I'd probably need help to find the wreck of *Victor*, so I would buddy up with one of the other three divers for the exploratory dive. Once we'd located the sub I'd do the rest myself, leaving the others to mess with the buddha and gather whatever gold Tuk Tuk had instructed them to lift.

The escort boat came alongside and rafted up to us. The Brownings were mounted, one on each of the small bridge wings. The long-barrelled heavy machine guns were covered by tarps, but their shapes remained sharp and intimidating outlines under the canvas. The five pistoleros on the trawler had the look of trained soldiers. Although they were dressed in denim and T-shirts, they may as well have been wearing uniform greens. Each of them carried a holstered Beretta 92 on his belt counterbalanced by a big fucking knife. Sunglasses and baseball caps completed the outfits.

Several of the crew of the other boat came on board, including Tri, their captain.

Tri was a razor-thin, sharp-faced guy of about forty-five. He had the definite air of a former naval man. He was pleasant enough but gave nothing away. As we hovered about the boat, he refused a beer or whisky. Instead he stuck with coffee and, through the open mess door, kept one eye on the boat alongside.

The guards remained on board the trawler, one of them moving between the small bridge wings, binoculars around his neck at all times. There was a second man seated in the tiny glassed-in wheelhouse. No doubt he was on radar watch. Radar wasn't a standard fitting on in-shore fishing boats in these waters. Tuk Tuk had informed me that the Q-boat's radar unit was very sophisticated with a long-range scan. All the better not only to spot pirates and the Burmese navy with, but also to avoid customs vessels!

That night I had a plate of rice with an excellent chicken curry. My stomach didn't roll over on me. I swore off the Mekong but had a couple of beers to wash my food down. After the meal, when Tri and his sailors returned to their own boat, I sat on the foredeck outside and had a smoke. The *Odorama* was pointing into a gentle wind swell. The breeze was fresh and clean. I finished my cigarette, lay down on a pile of netting and closed my eyes.

Having a fucking seagull shit on your upturned face was a hell of a way to wake up. The chortling bird flew out of the rigging above me as I sat up, blinking and cursing. I tore off my T-shirt and wiped the crap off me. It was dawn and the sun was dragging its yawning yellow face over the horizon. I rolled off my net bed, stripped to my briefs and found a hose to sluice myself down. So much for modern amenities, huh?

There was movement on our rafted-up neighbour. The guard on the bridge was changing. I could smell coffee somewhere on our tub, so I followed my nose towards the cupboard that served as a galley. Mug of coffee in hand and suddenly life wasn't looking and feeling quite so bad. The wind had dropped and there was heat in the sun. The sky was cloudless. I think I smiled.

Breakfast was seafood soup and rice. I was following that with my third cup of coffee and a cigarette out on the foredeck when Niran came out to join me. 'The weather will be good. We can go whenever you want,' he said, taking a Marlboro from the pack I held out to him.

'As soon as we finish these,' I replied, holding up my coffee. 'I have a GPS that will get us to within two yards of the wreck.'

Niran nodded. 'I was told that you would have that. Very good,' he said. 'There is a lot of water out there if we don't know exactly where to look.'

'You know what we are looking for?'

'No!' Niran shook his head. 'Tuk Tuk said that I was to take the boat to where you said and do what you said. I didn't ask him any questions. It is not wise to ask Tuk Tuk Song too many questions.' He shook his head and dragged deeply on his smoke. 'I think we are looking for gold,' he added a moment or two later. 'Otherwise why would we have so many guns with us?'

Niran's logic was basic, but quite faultless. Why indeed did we have so many guns? One .50 cal and a couple of AK47s would have done the job against most of the rag tag pirates in these waters. Maybe Tuk Tuk's show of force was for another reason.

Who could tell just how his mind worked?

We weighed anchor at 07:30 and as we started moving west along the Loughborough Passage, I called the dive team together. The first thing I did was get out the Toshiba and show them the two images of the Ruby Buddha. Once they had got over the shock I explained the rest, including the fact that there were two vessels down there, one of which contained something I needed to bring back.

The initial plan was that we would buddy-up and operate in pairs, as was standard procedure, of course. Tan, one of the former navy divers, and I would search out the remains of the sub, while the other pair, Billy and Suwat, would dive into the freighter to seek out the buddha. I passed on the information I had been given and told them that their treasure was in the second hold, and that access was through an open deck hatch. Apparently, and perhaps fortunately for us, the cover had been blown off during the sinking.

God only knows what I'd find at the submarine. The bow would be gone, thanks to the explosion of the bomb and the two or three live and primed torpedoes that had been detonated. However what I was going to be looking for would be in the captain's tiny broom closet of a cabin, which was behind the conning tower, half the submarine's length from its bow section. I only hoped the damned thing had landed on its belly. It would be difficult enough to navigate through it even then, but it sure as hell would be even worse if it had landed upside down or on its butt. Whatever, I guessed we were soon going to find out. The recon divers hadn't figured which way round the sub was lying. They'd seen the wrecked bow section from directly in front. Visibility and light hadn't been good. They'd had no time for further examination before they had had to surface and bug out in the face of an approaching Burmese navy patrol boat.

By 09:30 we were anchoring exactly where the GPS told us to park up. The escort trawler went a quarter of a mile beyond us and dropped its own hook. The sea was a startling shade of blue, but the sky above had turned grey again. The blue of first light was now gone and clouds were building on the western horizon. No matter what the day's weather report told us, we didn't need any electronic help to know that a storm was brewing. Damn global warming, I thought. With the monsoon season over this should have been perfect weather for diving, or anything else for that matter. If it turned sour we'd have to pull back to our sheltered anchorage.

I joined the dive team on the foredeck. Our gear had been brought up from the hold and deposited into piles. Mine was all new, three thousand pounds worth on the company card. US divers four mill suit, double tank rig, compressed-air spear gun, the works. I'd been to Thailand's best dive shop, Divez, and paid their wages for the next fortnight. The other guys had good gear, but it showed signs of much use. My rig drew many admiring comments as I climbed into it. Apart from a tryout in the dive outfitter's immersion tank back in Bangkok, and a swimming pool refresher in London prior to dragging my arse onto the plane, I'd last been in scuba gear a year ago in a lake in Austria. But I hadn't been in the open sea for close to two years, so I had some rapid acclimatising to do.

The spear gun drew further comment from both the divers and our helpers on deck. The other three had powerhead lances in case the sharks got interested. The crude, home-made lances with explosive heads containing a twelve-gauge shotgun cartridge were bad news for sharks when things got up close and personal. I liked spear guns because they allowed me to be a coward and do the business from a distance. I didn't like to be close to anything that had more teeth than my ex-wife.

'Okay. We all know what we're looking for,' I said as I moved to where a section of the railing had been lifted off the side of the boat. Here, a climbing net had been installed to help us navigate the three feet from water level to deck. Three feet didn't seem far, but it was when you were wearing a weight belt and a couple of hefty air tanks.

With a brief, silent prayer I, as the boss of this whole floating circus, led the way. I stepped backwards off the deck and dropped feet first into the water. It was surprisingly warm. There was no need for a wetsuit when you were playing around in the first ten feet of the Andaman, but down at a hundred, it got very cold very quickly.

After a minute of reorganising our bodies, minds and gear, it was time to go exploring. My brief said that the submarine, HMS *Victor*, was on the bottom, some thirty to fifty yards beyond and to the west of the freighter. First step was to find the freighter.

9

Locating the wreck of the former Dutch merchantman was easy. In fact, it would have been damned hard to miss. Once our eyes adjusted to the shifting green water-filtered light, the thing leapt out at us. The remains of the *Ziderzall*, or *San Tao*, or whatever you want to call it, were only forty feet away in a direct line from the whale-like shape of our dive boat's bum. The 4,000-ton wreck appeared as a mass of angles and protrusions against the black of the deep shadow and grey tones of the sand and reef debris.

I kicked and started down, the other three divers fanning out at my shoulders. As we slowly glided down to the wreck, its mass changed from black and grey to a multitude of colours. Our exhaust trails marked our progress as we moved, the silver bubble streams dancing away upwards towards the surface. It was beautiful, very surreal, but the water wasn't crystal clear. The visibility wasn't as great as it would have been in calmer weather because of the haze from sand sediment kicked up by the ongoing storms. Despite the haze we could see relatively clearly to forty or fifty feet, and discern shapes and colours a further twenty yards from that. Beyond that distance it was just grey playing on white light which faded into total murky blackness. I did know from my previous experiences in these waters that in a month or so, by New Year at least, the water would be gin clear with visibility up into the hundreds of feet.

The freighter was sitting spine down on the more or less flat bottom. It was leaning slightly to port and, surprisingly, it seemed to be virtually intact, at least from the direction we were approaching. Over fifty years Mother Nature had worked her magic well on the hulk. Patches of rust-coloured metal showed, but most of the hull and visible superstructure were covered with algae and other marine growths that gave the boat its amazing colours. On the hull proper, the plant and animal life changed and became more drab and sparse. The sun couldn't push its rays all the way down there. On the upper decks, however, there was light aplenty which made visible the corals, anemones, shell dwellers and kelps that clothed the wreck. Everywhere fish of all sizes and colours darted and hovered, eyes on the intruders.

The closer we came, the greater the detail emerged out of the haze. There were shattered and bent derricks. Cables had been thickened by weeds which still anchored them to the deck. The algae-covered shape of a lifeboat hung down the side of the superstructure. A conger eel watched us from a gaping hole where one of the bridge windows would have been. I didn't doubt the rest of the hull would have its usual share of fanged fellows just like him.

A shadow passing between us and the sun caused us all to look up. A huge manta ray was making its majestic way across our artificial heaven. A magnificent sight for any diver, but we had work to do. The sightseeing would come later, if at all.

I kicked again and drifted down to the bridge roof. Here, at only sixty feet, I hung off the remains of a radio antennae and indicated to Billy that this was the place to make his mark. He obliged and came down to join me while the other two hovered above.

Each of us carried a small, deflated fluro marker buoy on a weighted spool attached to our harness. We found our targets and inflated the bags using our regulators, letting the buoys float to the surface. This meant that the next time we dove down it would be much quicker to go from A to B, saving valuable air for the important tasks ahead.

In seconds the bright orange buoy was climbing towards the surface and Billy was looking for a place to tie off the line. I signalled for Tan to follow me and we left the other two to begin their search for Tuk Tuk's sainthood. I checked my compass, watch and depth gauge, and Tan and I pushed on, heading west. We'd already been down ten minutes and were now holding at eighty feet. All was okay so far.

The sea floor beyond the wreck of the freighter rose quite sharply, pushing the shadows back a little as it climbed up into the filtered sunlight. The sand gave way to a mass of broken coral and rock boulders that got rougher and larger the closer we got. The boulders became a reef, created from huge slabs of coral and rock that jutted up from the sea floor like giant teeth. Tan and I held our depth and slowly finned our way over the edge of the reef. I was beginning to get concerned. We should have seen the sub by now. The report said it was only a matter of yards beyond the freighter.

I turned on the torch that I had trailing from my weight belt and sent the beam hunting in the shadows of the reef, looking for debris from the *Victor*, looking for any sign that the sub was where the hell it was supposed to be.

Gauging distance underwater is difficult. A foot becomes a yard becomes a mile. My logical brain told me we had moved less than thirty or forty feet beyond the wreck. I turned, looked back and was reassured to see that the freighter was still visible through the grey haze. Tan's powerhead lance prodded away to the left, attracting my attention. I followed the direction and made out the shape of a big shark moving away from us. I couldn't see it clearly enough to identify it, but the body was thick and barrel-like. My guess was a Tiger, and that wasn't good news. I knew that Tiger sharks were definitely not the nice guys in the fin world, and in some parts they were regarded as worse predators than the dreaded White Pointer. The spear gun in my left hand felt reassuring, but it looked like a big fucking shark and it was a small spear. We carried on heading west.

I was almost ready to concede that we had missed the sub when we saw it, or rather Tan did. He pointed down. We had almost swum right over the bloody thing.

We were holding eighty feet and were still about twenty above it. But it was easy to realise why we'd not seen it earlier because HMS *Victor* didn't look like a submarine from the angle we were at. Tan, like me, had been looking for the shape of the conning tower. The fin was there all right, except that it was lying on its side at an angle that meant we had to be looking down on it from almost directly above, making it impossible to identify it for what it was.

The pair of us hung suspended in the water above the wreck, trying to define its actual shape and position. Yes, the sub was on its side, half-hidden beyond a section of reef. The conning tower wasn't level with the bottom, but rather lay at maybe an angle of thirty degrees. Squinting into the gloom I could see that the bow section wasn't there, as the recon report had stated. The cigar hull, covered in weeds and algae, ended about forty feet in front of the fin. The stern, from the tower back, seemed more or less complete. The rear section lay slightly uphill, propped up by an arm of the reef. The shape of a single bronze screw was clearly visible, now that my eyes were focused to see through the ocean's camouflage.

I indicated to Tan that I was going down to take a closer look and for him to hold his position. He gave me the thumbs up and held his powerhead across his chest, ready to act if jaws came screaming out of the murky shadows at him. I dropped ten feet. I needed to see if the hatch of the conning tower was open, or if there was access through the front section of the hull. There was no way on earth that the hatch could now be re-opened if it had been closed at the time of sinking. After all this time it would be welded shut by rust, and only thermal lances or similar would burn through it. We had a few of those with us but I didn't necessarily want to go that route. I wanted quick in, quick out and away.

I figured if I could get inside the hull and the main control area, I would have no trouble getting into the skipper's cabin. Even in the British navy of that vintage, the old man on the sub would only have had a curtain as a door into his tiny living space. According to Bernard, the 'box' would be in the bottom drawer of the cabin's only desk. It had been too big to fit into the captain's safe.

I was at a hundred feet and beginning to feel the pressure as I came to the top of the leaning conning tower. I propped myself against what had once been the periscope stem, and used the beam of my torch to probe into the deck well formed by the steel spray skirt that surrounded the tower. Through the weeds I could make out the rusted deck plates. The hatch was twisted and jammed half-open. There was no way I could get through it with tanks on my back. Also half-open was the mouth of a Moray that had obviously set up house in the fin. 'Damn!' I muttered. The eel wasn't the problem—not being able to get through the door was.

I turned away and kicked forward, dropping another ten feet so I could see the front section of the hull proper as the cone of light from my torch pushed the shadows back. The forward deck gun was still there, or at least its algae-covered shape was, but just beyond that, the whole front of the submarine looked as if a giant tin-opener had been used to rip it apart. Although covered with crap, I knew that under the weeds and growth there would be razor-sharp tongues of rusted metal that could rip a wetsuit and a diver to shreds.

I moved forward of the remaining hull and hovered there, shining my light back and inside. A tunnel fringed with waving weeds and filled with darting fish faded away into black nothingness beyond the beam of my light. It didn't appear that any of the near hatches had been closed. The force of the explosion could possibly have blown them in. I had no idea if the aircraft attack had been totally out of the blue, no pun intended. Had the sub crew gone to action stations and shut the watertight compartments, as they would have done on a full alert? Either way, the end of *Victor* must have been so damned sudden. One hit on the torpedo section and the whole front of the bloody tin can would have gone. It would have been on the bottom in minutes, seconds even. Maybe no time for anyone to do anything, let alone kiss their arses goodbye.

Above me Tan was flicking his torch on and off. I glanced at my watch. We had been down thirty minutes. While I still had half and hour of air left on my back, it was time to ease my way back to the surface if I wanted to dive again that day. I filled my fluro buoy from my regulator and sent it upwards. When the spool stopped unwinding, I peeled off another yard or two of line, locked the spindle and wound the line around the nearest coral fang to the sub's gaping maw. I now had a road map right to the front door of what was going to become my own personal house of horrors. I didn't want to think too much about what I would find inside, sixty something years on or not.

I slowly started my ascent, letting my bubble trail race away above me. I joined Tan who was hovering at eighty feet and did my calculations. We'd go to fifty and hold that for seven minutes as we swam slowly eastwards. Being rushed off with the bends to the nearest decompression chamber, which was probably down at Patong Beach, didn't figure big in my plans.

When we surfaced ten minutes later, Tan and I were the best part of a hundred yards away from *Odorama*, thanks to the currents near the surface. We didn't have to swim for it, however, because an inflatable from the gunship was heading towards us. When the Zodiac came alongside, Tan and I simply clung to the rope handles on each side of the rubber duck and let ourselves be towed back to the dive boat.

Back on *Odorama,* one look at the faces of the crew told the story. Billy and Suwat were grinning from ear to ear. They'd surfaced quite a while before us, but not before they had been into the second hold. 'It is there,' said Suwat. 'Just like in the picture. It was once in a wooden crate but that has turned to mud. It is so beautiful,' he added, shaking his head in wonder.

'I think we can lift it with air bags.' Billy, the second of the former navy divers, was already planning the salvage operation. 'If we can inflate them outside the hold to take some of the weight, then we can move the buddha into position and blow up another bag to get it through the hatch to the surface.'

'It weighs more than a thousand pounds,' I said as I started to get out of my wetsuit. 'That's a lot of dead weight out of the water.' I'd already done the figures based on what Bernard had given me. 'Three of the smaller bags to move it out of the hold with your help, then add one of the big ones to get it to the surface. The net winches can lift it on board.'

'Let's go and do it,' Suwat was saying. Billy was nodding eagerly. I shook my head.

'Not yet! We have a break and get the equipment organised. Top up the bottles, Tan. Billy, get the air bags and harness organised. Suwat, we need an air hose from the compressor to the freighter's hold. You're linking hoses.' Instructions delivered, I left them to it as I lit a cigarette and went into the mess.

I got a coffee and sat. I was having a problem with priorities. Part of me was screaming, 'Go and get the damned box!' The other side of my brain was calmly whispering to me, 'The buddha. It is good. Return it to the people. What is in the box must surely be bad.' I was damned if that voice didn't sound like Geezer, or an old priest I'd once known who had tried hard to be my conscience at one time. Both of them had liked their grog but each had been, or in Geezer's case was, a wise man. Father Leonard, however, was a dead man of God. He'd been blown up by a car bomb in Armagh.

'Tri says a Myanmar patrol boat is coming,' Niran was calling from the bridge.

'Shit!' I leapt up the steep companionway. Niran pushed a pair of binoculars into my hands and pointed to the east. The gunboat was just a grey smudge on the near horizon. It appeared to be about the size of a MTB. There was a single gun mounted on the bow. It wasn't moving as quickly as it quite obviously could. Rather, it was just cruising. Probably just a routine patrol to see who and what was in its waters.

'Okay.' My mind was working overtime. I grabbed the Motorola hand-held that was our direct link to our escort. I was just hoping Tri would take orders without argument because this was the first time I would try giving him one. He answered almost before I let go of the send button.

'Yes?'

'Get the Zodiac to cut away the two buoys we set, then you sail back to the anchorage and wait for us there,' I said.

'Okay!' he replied. Logic ruled. No argument from Tri. Thank buddha for that. The Zodiac was moving less than thirty seconds later. There were two men in it: one perched in the bow, the other at the outboard. A knife blade flashed twice in the sunlight and they had the buoys in the bottom of the boat within another minute. Our trawler was soon moving back towards the Loughborough Passage with the inflatable in tow. I turned to Niran.

'Cover the dive gear with nets. Pretend to have problems with a winch or something. No weapons in sight! I'll need to hide below.' The patrol boat was definitely heading towards us. We had about five minutes to become a simple prawn boat again. I headed below as Niran started rapidly firing off orders. A European on board a working boat full of Thais was going to arouse suspicion. I needed to be out of sight and pray that *Odorama* wasn't searched. I opened the engine-room hatch and gathered our weaponry from the temporary rack against the rear bulkhead. Then, juggling a pair of AK47s and our single M16 along with a big bag of loaded magazines for both, I went down into the engine room.

Room was a misnomer in this case. The 'engine room' was a dark, narrow stinking hole dominated by an ancient Cummins diesel engine. I knew it was a Cummins because the first time I'd been down there I'd slipped and jammed my right forearm against a very hot manifold cover that bore that name. Light came from a single, dull, greasy light bulb set on the bulkhead beside the steps. It gave just enough of a glow for me to see what I had to.

I lifted a section of dirty deck grating. It was an old smuggler's hidy-hole. The normal bilge hatch was plainly identified by its cut-out handgrips and, when opened, showed oily bilge water slopping about below. This hatch opened into an open-topped aluminium tank installed for moments such as this. I lowered the carbines and the ammunition into the metal trough, then went back up the three steps and pulled down the table hatch. Someone was waiting to scatter some dishes and cards on it the moment it was closed.

I contemplated the metal coffin set in the deck. There really was no point in getting into it and pulling the section of deck down to hide me. If the Burmese searched the boat, they would find the dive gear and know something was up. There was too much sophisticated high-priced kit up there for a simple prawn boat to have on board. That being the case, I didn't want to get into the bilge hidy-hole because the game would be up long before that. I thought of the Walther that was hidden in my bedding. Damn! There was nothing to do but hope and pray. I pulled the section of deck back in place to cover the guns, then sat on the bottom step of the ladder. I flicked the light switch off, letting the stinking blackness claim me.

The stench of diesel and oil was overwhelming. Now, more than ever before, I needed to settle my rebellious gut. The ball was well and truly in Niran's court. If the Burmese were on a social call, no problem. If not, we were totally and absolutely fucked, as the actress said to the bishop!

10

I heard the arrival of the patrol boat. It would have been difficult to miss. There was the sound of powerful diesel engines approaching then fading into an idle rumbling. 'Twin screws,' my brain told me. It was useless information, but the brain did things like that in moments of stress. One such time was when I was returning fire against a bunch of Laotian bandits in tiger country. Outnumbered and outgunned, we were fighting for our lives, but I couldn't help but notice the beautiful display of orchids that grew from the rotting log I was lying behind. Crazy, huh? We won the firefight and I'd never really looked at an orchid since. Such was the way of things.

There was what, to me, sounded like a good-natured conversation shouted between Niran and someone on board the other vessel. Down where I was, I could only guess what the hell was going on. If another vessel had come alongside and hit the tyre bumpers that hung along both sides of the *Odorama,* there would have ben a sudden lurch or thump. I hadn't felt it. So unless they had sent a dinghy over—which would have been totally unnecessary given the size of both vessels—we hadn't been boarded.

Shit, the smell of the diesel was getting to me. My head was thickening and my gut was starting to churn. A few minutes more and I would be hanging my head down into the bilges, chucking my heart out again. I tried to fill my lungs by breathing through my mouth. It didn't make any difference. I tried to think of the plus side of things. For a start, the engine wasn't on. That was a definite bonus for me. Secondly, the sea was calm and thirdly—thirdly the patrol boat had finally engaged its props and was moving away. I could hear Niran wishing them a jovial farewell.

I waited twenty seconds—that was all I could manage—then I went up the steps and pushed the hatch open. I could hear plates and cutlery hitting the deck. I didn't care as I stood there, supporting the damned hatch as I filled my lungs with what passed as fresh air. For the first time the fact the air was dominated by the pong of rotten fish didn't even register. Niran came in through the starboard door.

'It's okay.' He grinned down at me. 'They are just on routine patrol. Once a week they come around here. Said a big storm is coming and to take shelter. They are going to Kawthaung.'

'Okay. Let's make tracks,' I said, feigning a degree of composure I didn't feel as I climbed up onto the mess deck and closed the hatch table. 'How long will the storm go on for?'

'Who knows?' Niran shrugged. 'Maybe two or three days.'

'Just my bleedin' luck,' I muttered to myself. Problem was, once the storm had passed through the seas could stay rough for a couple of days. A big two-day blow might mean four days without diving. I wanted to get the business done and get the hell out of there. I checked on the position of the Burmese patrol boat. The long, low, grey vessel was a quarter of a mile away ahead of us, heading into the Loughborough Passage. I could see our escort trawler almost at the point of the island we had moored behind the previous night. I was praying that Tri had cut away to the anchorage point, letting the Burmese carry on. I thought of the big Brownings on the bridge wings and cursed silently. I hoped like hell he had taken the damn things off their mounts and hidden them. Thing was, if it came to a shoot-out between Tri and his thugs and the Burmese, the chances were the patrol boat would lose. Despite its deck gun, a couple of Tri's rockets would blow it out of the water before it could fire a shot.

There was a rumble from below us and Niran's guys started bringing up our anchor. I went up to the bridge and adjusted the co-ordinates on the GPS. Next time we came calling, we would anchor between the wrecks. My stomach had settled again so I risked lighting a cigarette and sat on one of two stools in the tiny glass-fronted cab. Niran stood at the wheel, his right hand on the throttle. As the anchor was lifted into its holding cleats, he pushed the throttle open and eased the wheel into a slow turn to track the passage of the patrol boat.

Our first dive was over. We had found what we had been looking for. Now it was a matter of collecting it but God knows when we would get back there again. The divers who had first discovered the buddha hadn't been able to return to the wrecks, not that it had been their job to do anything much more than verify identities of the ship and sub. Perhaps they had been after the box but had been thwarted by the arrival of the Burmese. If I had had to put money on it, I would have guessed that at least one of the divers probably had the recovery of the box on his dance card. Who would ever know and who would ever tell? Bernard sure as hell hadn't told me.

Would we be back or would another team have to follow us in to complete the job? There were so many factors at work. How long would it be before some recreational divers found the wrecks? The Burmese hadn't really encouraged tourism in that region so far. However, it seemed that they were warming up to the idea of getting foreign currency into the kitty. Money bought tanks, guns and all those things that military regimes liked to have on hand to maintain their status quo. Already there were some dolphin-watching expeditions out of Kawthaung, and other Thai–Burmese ventures into the archipelago were getting the green light. It was ultimately just a matter of time before someone decided to run a major commercial dive operation in the area. So, in reality, time was one commodity that we were possibly going to run out of if the coming storm really hammered us.

Tri had moored further into the bay than the previous night. The Burmese patrol boat hadn't deviated on its run for Kawthaung, for which I gave a sigh of relief. Several Moken craft with dugouts trailing behind were heading that way as well. A large white cruiser had appeared away to our left, coming around the edge of the island that defined the north side of the passage. The white boat was also making a beeline for Kawthaung or Ranong.

'Dolphin boat,' said Niran. 'They take tourists to see the dolphins. I can take them to see the dolphins,' he added, laughing. I laughed as well. I couldn't imagine any tourists paying to ride on board the *Odorama* under any pretext, dolphins or not.

Niran eased us towards the shore, going past Tri's boat and getting as close into the lee of the razor-backed island as possible. There would be no rafting up the two craft with a big blow on its way. The anchor was dropped and Niran reversed us hard some twenty or so feet to set the hook deep. It didn't matter if he embedded the tines into solid coral because we had divers aplenty to free them when the storm eventually blew itself out. The last thing we needed was to drag our anchor and end up out in the passage.

The sky was darkening by the second and lightning flashed away to the north. The rumble of distant thunder reached us several seconds later. Niran was giving orders and everything that could be latched shut was being tied down. Our dive gear had been taken below. Hatch covers were being secured. I decided it was Singha time and went into the mess. There was the smell of something spicy being cooked. Noy, the designated chef, was working over a giant wok on one of the galley's two gas rings. While we'd been on the move he'd rigged a trolling line and caught a big mackerel. Steaks were now being fried and a second, smaller wok full of spicy noodles and shredded vegetables was waiting to one side.

'The condemned men,' I muttered to myself.

Noy gave me a big grin. 'What you say?'

I realised I'd spoken in English. 'Smells good,' I said in Thai.

'Very good,' he agreed with an even bigger grin. And yes, the meal was very good. Very damned good indeed. We ate and washed the food down with Singha and about the time we'd finished, the storm hit. The rain came down in a curtain. Night had fallen, yet it was only three in the afternoon. The sound of the rain on the deck became a roar. Then the wind came howling down on us like a million demented banshees.

11

Stir crazy! It's more than just an evocative phrase, believe me. After three days stuck in the close confines of SS *Odorama*, with the smell of dead fish and fishy bodies and the sound of the shrieking fucking wind howling above me, I was ready to kill someone, anyone, myself included.

'Tomorrow,' promised Niran. 'Tomorrow we can go. The sea will be calmer.' *Odorama*'s skipper and I were on the bridge. The wind had finally dropped. There was no rain and the white caps both behind us and away to our right were starting to fall away. It was late afternoon and the sun had just managed to burn away the cloud cover. Our gunboat was still in the same position it had been throughout the blow. I could see its crewmembers out on deck, enjoying the fresh air. Some of them, like our guys, had fishing lines down. There would no doubt be something fresh and finned for dinner.

Over the past few days and long nights I had taxed my brain in an effort to maintain whatever sanity I still possessed. I had repeatedly gone over the whole scenario of the box and everything I had to do the moment we hit the water on our next dive. I would retrieve the damned thing and stay long enough to help get the Ruby Buddha on board *Odorama*. Then I would insist we run for Ranong.

I had a built-in radar for things—some called it a bullshit detector—and in the hours of brain-time I'd had over the past few days, I'd come to a few conclusions and raised more questions than answers. I knew Bernard hadn't told me more than he felt I needed to know about this whole deal. That box and its contents were absolute dynamite, political dynamite. That was obvious. But why had our lot been co-opted to get the bloody thing? Why not a submarine full of marine salvage experts and Special Boat Service people? They could mount a hit-and-run, and there would be no way the Burmese navy, such as it was, could detect them or catch them.

So, lying in my bunk listening to the snores, burps and farts of my fellow divers, I concocted my list of answerless questions and questionable conclusions, all of which led back to the former. It was like playing mental rounders.

First amongst my concerns was always the why. Why had we, The Firm, been chosen to pull this damned thing off? Did they want us to attempt it in our usual skin-of-the-fucking-teeth and highly unorthodox fashion, because maybe we weren't meant to succeed? It was a fact that, because of our business and the way it was conducted, we didn't always manage to successfully complete the mission we'd been assigned. A bunch of Special Boat Squadron types, the waterborne SAS and a submarine. That was the obvious option to ensure success.

So if the big boys weren't coming and yes, we were meant to succeed, the next question was why weren't they coming? Was it a matter of detection? The Burmese didn't have technology beyond basic sonar and radar, which were short-range methods at best. The Russian and Western spy satellites zipping around with their sophisticated detection devices knew where most submarines were most of the time. The Russians, the US, our lot and the French were the only main players in this game. But since the great break-up of the Union, the Russians weren't paying that much attention to distant sub-plotting and the like. The French, well, who the hell knew what the bloody French military and naval intelligence outfits were monitoring? But even their satellite access was minimal compared to ours, and especially when compared to that of the US.

The US was the one outfit that could put our lot off sending a submarine on a covert pick-up-and-run operation. With their technology, the Yanks would have the sub's plot on screen from the first turn of their screws. Allies or not, American paranoia ensured that they kept watch on friend, foe and potential foe alike. But if we were trying so hard not to attract their attention by foregoing the obvious means of salvage, it meant that Uncle Sam knew something about this damned box and its contents. Therefore for Sir Bernard and his puppet masters, their desperation to keep this from the Yanks explained the unorthodox, low-key retrieval operation I was fronting. Did they want us to succeed or fail? That was still the twenty-thousand euro question! I would do my damnedest to succeed, even if it was just to piss off Sir Bernard fucking Sinclair, especially if he was relying on my failure.

'Boat,' said Niran, dragging me from my musings. I followed his outstretched arm. Three or four miles away a large white-hulled cruiser was brushing the remaining white caps aside as it slid through the water at a rate of knots. It was either coming from the direction of Ranong or Kawthaung. 'Charter boat. Wealthy tourists. Maybe divers,' Niran added quickly, a look of concern suddenly clouding his wrinkled mahogany face as he turned to me. Images of failure and of him once again losing his beloved boat no doubt caused the turmoil I could see reflected in his eyes. I was feeling more than a little of that turmoil myself. At the mention of divers, my mouth had gone bone dry. I suddenly had a very, very bad feeling. Whoever was on board that boat was in a hurry to get somewhere. The sea was still uncomfortable enough to put off any casual leisure cruises. I grabbed the Motorola and called Tri. He answered after two seconds.

'If that boat anchors anywhere near our dive site, let me know immediately.'

'Okay,' came the reply.

That was it. I'd already learned that Tri didn't waste unnecessary effort as far as dialogue was concerned. I lit a cigarette. The habit was now no longer a struggle to maintain. I'll give up again when this is over, I promised myself silently, knowing full well that any attempt was going to be more than a struggle. I smoked that fag and followed it with another as the white boat went out of sight behind our sheltering island and passed on up the passage.

Travelling at the same clip the intruding boat had been going when it had vanished from view, I figured it would either be passing or pulling up at our dive site within five minutes. I checked my watch and waited. That five minutes dragged on forever. If the boat stopped over the wrecks, what would we do? But I knew exactly what we'd do. We'd send Tri over there to force them off the mooring. We'd become pirates for the day while we hoisted up the buddha and I retrieved the black box.

'They have gone around the western tip of the island. They are a kilometre short of the dive zone,' Tri reported. I waited. I didn't believe in coincidence. It wasn't something that happened in my world, and whatever the white boat's role in this scenario, it was a player, not a spectator. Of that I was certain.

'They are moving on, going around Pila Kyun,' Tri added five minutes later.

'Keep on going, ' I muttered in a prayer to the deities. Was I wrong after all? It had been known to happen, but not often, and not about things like this. Were these guys just tourists or were they after the damned wrecks? I lit another in the endless chain of cigarettes I had been smoking and waited. There was nothing else to do.

'They have stopped in the bay on the north side of the island,' Tri came back at me.

'Will they be able to see the dive site from where they are?'

'No. They are deep in the bay and the hills are high. They may just be a dive party of tourists seeking shelter for the night.'

'Let's pray that's so,' I replied. I put down the Motorola and left Niran to his bridge. Down in the mess I stood in front of the map. It would soon be dark, and that was some sort of blessing. In my book, no one in his or her right mind would dive at night. If the people on the white boat were after our prize, I was figuring they wouldn't start until daylight and then they would have to zero in on the wrecks first. Did they have that sort of technology with them? If they were bad guys, whoever they were, I was betting they had a side-band sonar unit or similar with which to grid search the area, looking for images of the wrecks. The reef formations would help disguise the sub, but once they spotted the freighter, they'd go down looking. If they were Yanks then they would know that, way back in 1945, three of their planes took out a sub and a freighter in one hit, even if they hadn't known the exact location until now. If that was the case, what little birdie had been singing?

Okay. I was paranoid. That was a plain fact, and that was part of what I got paid for. I had to assume the worst. If the Yanks were in the game then they had the technology, including the unseen stuff—spy satellites zipping round above us. If they were plotting our movements, the only hope for us would be if the satellite co-ordinates of our dive position were broad. There was a fair chance they were. There were only so many satellites up there with full-on search and observation capabilities, most of them American and most of them positioned to fly over potential hotspots and enemies. I was prepared to bet that, in the grand scheme of things, Burma and Thailand didn't represent such hotspots to the Pentagon. I went back to the bridge and grabbed the hand-held. 'Tri, call if they move. Will you be able to tell if they put out runabouts?'

'Yes. This radar is very good.'

'Okay. I want us to move back on-site early. We leave at 04:00.'

'We'll be ready,' he said.

'Okay, Niran?' I asked.

Niran nodded. 'Okay!'

I left the bridge and headed down below again. I had the divers get the gear back on deck. I wanted us to be able to get on-site and underwater as soon as possible. Once we were there, possession was everything. If the weather held we could anchor right between the two wrecks. Tri and his trawler would see off anything short of a destroyer, and I doubted if the Yanks—if the guys in the white boat were indeed Americans—had a warship close enough to get to where we were in a week. They could, of course, cut a deal with the Burmese, or the Thais for that matter, and roll up with some serious floating hardware. Time would tell, I guessed. It all depended how badly they wanted the box.

It wasn't a night for sleep and at 04:00 we upped anchors. We didn't even have our navigation lights on. There was a dying full moon heading for the horizon and Tri had his radar. He led and we sat on his tail. A single orange light, low on the water directly in the centre of his stern, was our sole guide. The reason for all the sneaking around in half darkness was simple. I wanted us onto the site before the guys on the white boat knew it. If they had a radar watch, what would the watcher see? A pair of fishing boats heading out into the Andaman, eager to get back to work after days of no fishing and no money? Or would they see a couple of salvors coming their way? Was this white boat operation just a couple of divers with a hired Thai crew, or did it have a full complement of bloody Seals or similar? If it were the latter we would have a real problem on our hands.

'Have they moved?' I asked Tri via the Motorola.

'No. They are still in the bay,' he replied.

So we waited. I wished we could just go full throttle and race to the spot, but *Odorama* had a steady seven knots max and that was that. I fired up cigarette after cigarette and tried to do deals with whatever deity happened to tune into my wavelength. In the end I couldn't stand the bloody suspense. I went down to the well on the foredeck and struggled into my wetsuit. The others soon followed. The chatter was nervous. As we organised ourselves, I went over the plan to raise the buddha. The guys had it figured. The compressor was ready, the air hoses had been coupled. Inside the cargo hold were three small elevator bags, ready for deployment, with a larger one ready to inflate outside the wreck. Once on the surface the net winches could lift the buddha on board *Odorama*. Easy, huh?

The coming few hours would see me go after the box alone and buddy-less, while the other divers concentrated on raising the buddha and appeasing the great god, Tuk Tuk.

'We are close,' Niran called from above. I started back up to the tiny bridge. As I arrived in the doorway to Niran's throne-like room, Tri peeled away to port. He had led us into the city block, no doubt using his radar and charts. Now I had to nail the shop doorway. Standing on the steps I leaned into the wheelhouse, the GPS in my hand. I switched it on and talked Niran into position. When X marked the spot I gave him the nod and, seconds later, the anchor was rattling its way down into the depths. I told Niran to hit the lights. He flicked a series of switches and the whole working area of the boat was bathed in a bright yellow glare. Tri brought the trawler around in a tight circuit. When he was thirty yards off our port side and slightly ahead of us, he also dropped his anchor. I was almost prepared to wager that he had landed it just about right on the bloody sub.

'I don't understand how that works,' Niran said, indicating the GPS I still clutched in my hand.

'Magic,' I replied.

'Yes,' he replied. 'White man's magic. You have good luck down there.'

'I hope so. I really hope so, Niran,' I said as I turned to go. As an afterthought I left the GPS on the sill beside the wheel and grabbed the Motorola. 'Tri, any change of status from the white boat?'

'No. Still anchored down,' came the response.

‘Watch them closely,’ I ordered. Whatever happened above the tide over the next hour or so was out of my hands. Essentially it had passed into the hands of Tri and, to a degree, Niran. I would have more than enough to contend with down below. I went back to the deck and moved forward to where the other divers were going through their final preparations.

Dawn was coming but it was still half an hour away. I wanted to wait for natural light, but a voice in my head was telling me to get into the water and get moving. That damned voice sounded like fucking Bernard. So with every instinct saying no, and that nagging bloody voice saying yes, I gravitated towards where my tanks and harness were sitting. Even in tropical conditions with perfectly clear water and strong sunlight, I knew that light at over a hundred feet down would be pretty gloomy. The water we were about to dive in, freshly stirred and shaken by the storm, would have its visibility cut to a few yards, probably half of what we had experienced on our last dive. Essentially that meant it was going to be pretty black down there, and it sure as hell was going to be pitch black in the sub.

‘I’m going down,’ I announced as I started donning the remainder of my kit. The other divers looked at each other and then, in seconds, all of them were nodding. They were here, the gold buddha was down there. The sooner it was collected the better, and the sooner they would receive the big bonus Tuk Tuk had undoubtedly promised them. Thing was, while the inside of the freighter’s hold would also be black as hell, they had lights and they had each other. I was going into hell alone.

Billy helped me on with my twin pack while Tan dropped a heavily weighted line down into the depths. Once it bottomed, he coiled the excess, tied it off and attached the rope to an orange net float. He tossed the float over the side. We’d lost our buoys so this was the next best thing to guide us down, especially in the dark.

With my spear gun attached by a bungy hanging from my weight belt on my left side, and the strap of my dive torch tied to my right wrist, I went over the side. Light from the *Odorama*’s deck spilled into the water and reflected off the swell which was the colour of tar. There was a steady current pushing away from the mainland. The tide was on the move. I had to work against it while I sorted myself out.

When I was as ready as I was ever going to be, I swam to the float and, with a wave to the others who were standing ready to hit the water, I started down the line. This was one way for me to get down quickly and keep my bearings. Floating free in the blackness would have been totally disorientating. My bubble trail and depth gauge were the only things that told me which way was up. Shit, it was black!

When I touched eighty feet I checked my wrist compass and circled the line, looking for a landmark to lock onto. At the very edge of the beam of my torch, about twenty feet away, I saw a thickly weeded column. It was the radio mast of the freighter. We were bang on target. I continued to turn, hanging from the line until the compass told me due east. If I held the course, despite the tide drift, I would hit the reef head on within thirty yards.

I let go of the weighted line and kicked away. I would hold at eighty. Fish were gliding all around me, little fish, big fish. The torchlight was pulling them in. That wasn't comforting. I didn't want to meet Mr Jaws face to face as he came to the light to check me out. I kicked a little harder and the reef loomed out of the blackness so suddenly that I gasped a couple of breaths and sent a plume of bubbles racing to the surface. Diving in the dark in murky water was never good for the nerves.

Resting on one of the ragged coral teeth, I checked my bearings. Something further on in the jumble of rock and coral glinted in the beam of my light. It was an anchor. Tri's anchor. A chain stretched away above until it merged with the dark. I let go of the coral and swam to the chain. There, ten feet further on, right at the edge of my beam of light, I could see the single bronze screw of the *Victor* raised above a coral slab. Right on target all the way round.

I swam to the screw and paused for a moment. I was going to have to follow the incline and the hull down another thirty feet. Thirty feet doesn't sound like much in the real world, but when you're diving it's a lot and it affects everything you do. I used up a minute's worth of oxygen getting mentally prepared, then started down the weed- and coral-encrusted hull of what had been one of Britain's finest submarines of its day. Now it was just a pile of junk, rotting away on the bottom of a distant ocean. However what was inside the hull was another story. I didn't want to think of how it had ended for the crew and I wasn't looking forward to what I was going to have to do inside their tomb.

I passed the conning tower lying at its drunken angle. Mr Moray wasn't lurking this time. Another few feet and I slid over the gun position. The beam of my torch fought the milky water and the blackness, carving out a cone of visibility that centred on the torn metal where the bow had been. I swam closer and dropped down to hover directly in front of the opening.

This was the part I had been dreading. I knew that if I hesitated too long I would chicken out. Since childhood I had hated confined spaces and the dark. Maybe it was a legacy from my stepfather. His idea of a suitable punishment for misbehaviour—or anything else for that matter—wasn't his belt or a kicking. Instead he would lock me, my brothers and my sister in the coal cellar. The day he did that to my mother was the day I flattened him with a coal shovel and left home. Anyway, the scars that bastard had inflicted on me were still there. They shimmered like the weeds that waved from the gaping hole in front of me. It was like looking in the jaws of a fantasy monster. Enough!

Torch in my right hand, my spear gun in my left, I entered my own personal version of hell. But what a hell it must have been for the men who had died there.

12

The first couple of yards were easy. I glided along the main trunk of the submarine, following the beam of my torch. Because the sub was lying tail up, nose down and at an angle of thirty degrees, the terms up and down were relative. Corroded, rusted pipes lined the bulkheads that were virtually above and below me. Debris, weeds and coral sand filled the corner where deck and bulkhead met. It was like being in a skewed house-of-horror ride at the fair, the sort of thing that had thrilled me as a kid. Right now, I wasn't particularly bloody thrilled.

The first skull gleamed at me from its bed of sand. It was just the dome of the crown. The bone was still clean and gleaming yellow, the colour of old ivory. The eye sockets, fortunately, had been buried. For me there was nothing as haunting as the empty sockets of a skull. Mortality. It was all too human a concept. I wondered whether the big octopus that jetted away from me, moving deeper into the submarine's hull, had a concept more complex than escape. The damned ink it shot out behind it for protection didn't help visibility, but I swam through it and carried on. I hoped I wouldn't run into a predator that really did want a scrap. There was bugger all room to turn and run, let alone fight the denizens of the deep.

I passed through an open hatch. The heavy oval door was buckled back against the bulkhead. One of the hinges was gone and the thick metal lip that would have once surrounded the hatch opening had been torn half-off and blown inwards. Whether it had been open or shut when the torpedoes and bomb had gone off, I doubted it would have mattered. The force of the blast must have been horrendous. Now there were electrical cables hanging suspended in the water. I could see indentations of pipes and tubes in the walls. There were mesh panels covered in algae and debris. These tiny corners were where the sailors would have slept.

I didn't look closely. I didn't want to see what I knew full well would be there, lying jumbled where deck and bulkhead met.

I guessed I had travelled maybe three-quarters of the length of the fore hull when I sensed movement above me. I stabbed the beam of my light upwards, my heart doing double time. What I saw almost caused me to smile. Because of the angle the sub's hull was lying at, with its tail up, my exhaust bubbles looked like little beads of mercury as they merrily made their way along the bulkhead above me, heading for the highest point they could reach. In this case, that was where the lip of a hatch surround met a bulkhead. Here they formed a big shimmering pool. It might have been beautiful in another place and time.

I slowly kicked on again, gliding through the second open hatchway, the beam from my torch probing the pitch darkness ahead of me. I used the butt of the spear gun to push myself off the bulkheads and the pieces of unidentifiable equipment that crowded in on me in places. Mostly, however, there was enough room to move freely—something for which I was extremely grateful. My claustrophobia was just a scream away.

I came to a third hatch. This one was also open. No wonder *Victor* had gone down like a stone. She'd filled with water in an instant. As far as I could tell, this hatch wasn't buckled. It appeared to be resting back in its cleats. It had probably been wide open at the time the sub had been hit; indicating the air attack really had come out of the blue. I pushed through the elongated weed-fringed opening and carried on. Thank God for the light. If I lost that, I'd lose everything, including my sanity.

Then I was in the control room, the heart of this ghostly submarine. There I caught a glimpse of another movement in my light. A huge Moray eel gave me its ghastly grin as it backed away from me, undulating and twisting upwards as it went, moving away to my right and vanishing into what would be one of the lower compartments of the conning tower. I was convinced that this was the same beastie I'd met on my previous dive.

'Shit,' I thought. My pulse was racing. I checked my watch and my tank-pressure dial. I was close to twenty minutes under with forty percent of my air already gone. In my moments of near panic—of which there had been one or three—I had upped the ante. I had to slow my breathing and regain my composure. It seemed as if I had been underwater for hours, but that was just fear playing on my ragged nerves.

I moved on again. There was another grinning skull looking up at me, resting against the base of what had probably been a sonar or radio console. This skull had gaping eye sockets, and one of them was home to a small orange crab that waved its defiant claws in my direction. I didn't dwell on the tiny beast's macabre home. Shit happens, and a whole bunch of it had happened here.

There was still a curtain covering the doorway to the captain's cabin. Remnants of canvas, or whatever the curtain had been made of, were covered by a thick coat of algae. It hung halfway across the tunnel of the sub's core, moving lazily in the water current as if caught in a breeze. It was an eerie sight in a place that didn't need any more nerve-racking props. I reached out to pull the damn curtain away and it disintegrated in a cloud of pale green particles that made the water even murkier. 'Clever, Danny,' I chided myself.

I moved through the cloud of crap and pushed the torch into the cabin. This really was tiny, even smaller than I had anticipated. It was the size of a small walk-in wardrobe. Light from my torch bounced back at me from the remaining fragments of what had been a mirror set on one wall high up to my left. The bunk was down on my right. It was just a rectangle of naked springs covered in brown rust and green weeds. A large starfish sat on the centre of what had been the captain's bed. A small metal table was fixed against one bulkhead. Jumbled in the corner where table and bulkhead met at right angles was a smorgasbord of knick-knacks in a bed of slime. I could make out a mug and a hairbrush. There was also a photo frame, probably metal, its contents long gone. The safe was attached to the floor under the table. Just perfect for smashing one's feet against when one sat down.

I turned the other way and examined the opposite bulkhead. This one contained a wardrobe recess. The curtain for this was gone, but one forlorn weathered coat made of what I took to be oilskin, still hung there at a drunken angle. Beside the wardrobe was a chest of drawers, covered in algae and weeds like everything else in there. I had been told the drawers were metal. Two of the three drawers had fallen most of the way out. The third drawer, the bottom one, was still closed. I let the spear gun fall away on its bungy and removed the short jemmy I carried in the pouch on my chest. It took me just a second to lever the remains of the two hanging drawers away from the bureau. The metal was so thin it just crumpled like tin foil.

I presumed the remaining drawer had a lock, but it was invisible under the crud that had grown across its front. I put the jemmy where I figured the top edge was and pushed. The end of the bar went in effortlessly. I pushed down and felt something give. The drawer wouldn't slide out, but I hadn't expected it to, not after all these years. Instead, the whole front panel simply detached itself and fell away. I aimed the torch closer to look inside. There it was, untouched by time, algae or anything else.

The lead outer casing still gleamed with a dull, deep-grey sheen, even after all this time.

I reached in and withdrew the box. Even with the weightlessness of the ocean it felt heavy, twenty-three pounds heavy to be exact. I had developed a plan of how I would handle it when I found it. I wanted to be able to swim, and if I had to, fight off whatever I came across as I made my way topside. Like my leather holdall, the wire mesh pouch I wore across my chest had been made to carry my prize. I dropped the jemmy and used both hands to fit the box into the pouch. The torch, still attached to my wrist, sent its beam flashing and bouncing around the cabin like a crazy light show as I worked the box inside the holdall.

Knowing the weight of the box had been a bonus right down the line. I had on two dive belts. Just as soon as I had the box stowed, I dropped the smaller belt and my weight equalised. I knew my balance would be altered slightly, causing me to me be a little chest heavy, but that would be manageable.

It was well and truly time to go. I turned and pushed myself out of the cabin and back into the control room. Relief was welling up inside me, but I had to contain it. There was still much to do. I had to navigate the tunnel of horrors and get topside. I settled my breathing and started back the way I had come. Knowing the way back was clear, I didn't hang about. I wanted out of there as quickly as I could. I went across the control room in two kicks and back into the core tunnel. As I passed through the first of the three open hatches I saw it, or rather them.

Trickling along the surface above me was a silver bead necklace: bubbles climbing towards *Victor*'s stern. Except they weren't my bubbles.

I gasped and damned near blew the regulator out of my mouth. There was someone else in here with me.

I jammed my torch and the butt of my spear gun against a tangle of pipes to stop my downward movement, and flicked off the light, my heart thudding louder than a bass drum. There was now no light. None at all! I really was in total darkness. I hung there, fighting my terror. I was cold; the suit's insulating properties 110 feet underwater were being countered by the ice in my veins. The relentless pressure of the water was tightening my chest and giving me a headache.

Where was the other diver? *Who* was the other diver? It wouldn't be Tan or any of the others. They had their own hands full. That meant it was someone else, someone from the white cruiser, in all probability. Had he, she, it or they come right into the hull? Were they waiting for me further down? Or had they just checked the way inside was open and pulled back to wait outside? Had they seen my torch beam? Had they ...?

Then I got it. The bubbles were my own. They'd pooled against the second lip of the watertight compartments. I noted, and in fact almost smiled, at the shimmering puddle of mercury silver formed by my exhaust trail as I'd gone through the hatch opening. Obviously the lip had been fractured in the blast that had sent *Victor* to the bottom and the bubbles were trickling through, moving up to the highest point they could reach. Relief washed over me and my heart rate dropped by about a hundred percent. I was spooking myself. 'Idiot,' I thought. At this rate I was going to be out of oxygen before I got out of the fucking sub. I groped for my torch and was about to flick it on when something stopped me.

There was a very faint flash of yellow in the blackness below. It was moving. I wasn't alone after all. My first instincts had been right. The owner of the light was coming up the gut of the submarine to meet me. I could make out the lip of the second hatch against the brightening circle of light. The diver was just beyond the hatch. Bubbles caught in the beam of light were still trickling up towards me. Maybe his exhaust trail had combined with mine to cause the pool caught by the lip of the hatch to overflow and send the bubbles my way. Whatever the cause, I'd had a warning, and it was up to me to make the most of it.

Was there only one diver or were there more coming? If I stayed, I had some cover where I was. I could probably backtrack and try to get out through the conning tower, but what if I couldn't? I'd be down on air and cornered if there was a fight brewing. At least I knew I could get out the way I was going, so I decided to stay where I was.

Maybe it was one of the others?

The pipes I was wedged against had been pushed away from the buckled bulkhead to my right. I tried to make myself as small as possible and put as much of me behind their protection as I could. That wasn't easy considering I was in a two-tank dive rig. I thought I made less of a target standing, so I hooked my right fin under a pipe to keep me upright. The light from the other diver continued to grow brighter.

I had the spear gun in my left hand. I had no illusions that whoever was coming towards me would be armed and out to kill me if they found me. I knew that recreational divers did not dive in the dark, especially with a fucking gunboat sitting above the dive site. Thing was, did they know I was there? Had they seen me enter? Had they seen my light inside? I doubted the latter because I knew light didn't penetrate blackness like this easily. Their light beam would have hidden the distant glow of my own at first. So, having decided on plan B, I hung there in the dark and waited to try and identify the diver coming my way.

The intensity of the light beam was growing by the second. The other diver was moving quickly. Whether he would see me before he got to my lair or blunder right up to me was in the lap of the gods. I raised the spear gun and pointed it towards the circle of light. This little unit was a very effective weapon at close range. Made from aluminium, with a steel cylinder of highly compressed air to power it, the gun worked exactly the same as a conventional air gun, except the pellet had been replaced by a two-foot spear. The short spear was simply pushed into the gun's muzzle until it locked into position. All it took was a squeeze of the trigger to drive the spear away. Its velocity over ten yards was equivalent to that of a bullet from a .22 rifle. A spear was already locked in position and I had five more in the clips fixed to the air cylinder under the gun's barrel.

The diver was getting close. Was he friend or foe? Whichever, he would see me in seconds. I needed to anticipate he was a bad guy. I aligned the spear gun, pointing the wicked double-barbed shaft straight at the light beam. I had to assume the guy coming at me was holding the torch more or less in front of his face. I thumbed on my own torch as I pushed it around my shield of pipes. The two torch beams met and the inside of the sub hull lit up.

I saw a faceplate, wide eyes then the long rubber-powered spear gun that was aiming at me. I knew our guys only had hand-held powerhead lances. 'Foe!' my brain shrieked. I fired, aiming directly at the mask of the other diver. The razor tip of my stainless steel spear hit the faceplate square on. Time stood still before the short spear punched through the glass.

It might have been a reflex action but the guy's spear gun fired and I felt a thump in my chest. I gasped my regulator out of my mouth in shock. I'd been hit, but there was no pain, which was normal when a body went into shock. I pushed a gloved hand across my chest and turned my torch to see my fate. I would have laughed, but I was in enough danger of drowning as it was.

The head of the other diver's spear had embedded itself into the damned box on my chest. I stuffed the regulator back into my mouth and took a deep breath. I turned my torch back down the tunnel. The diver was no longer moving and the water around him had darkened. His body had drifted down to rest where the deck and bulkhead met. The torch hung from his gloved left hand, its beam illuminating a nest of human bones protruding from a carpet of debris. The long rubber-powered spear gun had fallen to join the bones.

I didn't have time to examine the guy who had tried to kill me. I could see by the shape of his body he was either a bulky guy or a totally out of shape woman. I attempted to pull the four-foot spear out of the box strapped to my chest. It wouldn't move. I grabbed the shaft with my free hand and rotated it against the trapped spear head. As with most conventional underwater spears, the head was detachable. I unscrewed the shaft and let it drop away. I didn't have time to worry about the head embedded in the box. All I wanted was to get out of there.

I loaded another spear into my gun and started down the hull again. I passed over the body of the dead diver without looking down. I had no fear of further attack from him. Having a shaft of steel driven through your head from front to back was inclined to take the fight out of anyone. I was breathing hard again, too deeply, too quickly! Claustrophobia had me well and truly in its grip. I almost didn't care if there were a second diver waiting outside in ambush. I just had to get the fuck out! In fact, it was probably my panic that saved my life as I burst out of the sub's hull like a cork out of a bottle.

As I emerged my torch was pointing straight ahead of me and I immediately saw the second guy through the milky water. He was sitting in the saddle of the underwater scooter that rested on the coral sand right in front of me, no more than ten feet away. The scooter was parked at an angle, its single headlight carving a hole in the darkness away to my right. The guy was wearing twin tanks on his back and the damned things didn't slow him one bit. He came out of the scooter's saddle and launched himself in my direction, grabbing for the dive knife sheathed on his right thigh as he came.

I didn't hesitate. I pointed the spear gun and fired. The shaft caught my attacker in the chest. Its force reversed his motion, sending him back the way he had come. He hit the scooter that was starting to drift off the bottom and slowly tumbled over it. He ended up kneeling on the coral, side on to me. His head was tilted down as he regarded the foot of metal that stuck out of his chest. A foot sticking out of his chest told me that there was a foot of the same unyielding steel inside him. The man was still alive, but a thin stream of blood was escaping from the spear's entry point. I kept him in my torch beam as I debated whether or not to finish him off or just get the hell out of there.

The scooter, freed of the weight of the pilot, was now five or six feet above us, its light stabbing away into the murk as it went into a slow spiral, heading towards the surface. I had my torch on the other diver. Should I finish him or not? Killing someone in cold blood when they are disabled was about as cold-blooded as it got, despite the fact that he would have taken me out given any chance at all.

The debate was short-lived, and the decision taken out of my hands by a most unlikely temporary ally, if you can consider a fucking great shark an ally. I didn't know if it was the same Tiger that Tan and I had seen on our first dive, but it was a big mother. It came out of the blackness and through the feeble cone of light my torch was throwing on the scene. It was moving like a damned freight train as it carved its way across my light beam, gathered up the stricken diver in its gaping jaws and vanished into the darkness in a matter of seconds. I was left looking at a faint black ribbon trail of blood hanging in the water. Maybe it was the blood that had tempted the shark in. Or maybe he had been initally drawn in by the light from the scooter, then the scent of blood had taken over. They say sharks can pick up one part of blood in millions of parts of water. Whatever the reason, both shark and diver were gone in a matter of seconds, leaving me puffing on my respirator like a smoker deprived of weed for too long.

God, I had to get my arse out of there before Jaws or one of his mates came back for dessert. I wasn't cut, so there was no blood trail leading to me. I had to relax as much as I could and quieten my breathing. I did some hurried figures with my watch and gauges.

Three-quarters of an hour had passed since I'd hit the water. I had blown two thirds of my air, most in the last ten minutes, I guessed. I had enough to decompress safely and get me topside but nothing in reserve. I started east, angling up, torch on my bubble trail, making sure I stayed below it. I resisted the temptation to search the darkness around me for any more sharks. I'd be spinning like a top and burning up my air supply like crazy if I started doing that. I'd survived everything so far. I now had to do this last bit right or it all went down the gurgler.

Away to my left and a long way above me, the underwater scooter was accelerating upwards, still turning in a lazy spiral. I guessed it was for safety reasons that they had been balanced in such a way so as to head for the surface if they lost their rider. Away to my right through the hazy water I could make out the anchor chain of Tri's boat. The sun was up and the water was getting lighter above me. I headed for the anchor line. If I had to I'd hang there to decompress, then surface and swim across to *Odorama*.

At fifty feet I stopped and hung from the anchor chain for an agonising five minutes. Nothing came steamrollering out of the dark at me. At twenty feet there was light above. The underwater scooter was bobbing on the surface further away to my left as the current carried it off. Some lucky fisherman was going to score big time, maybe.

The light was brightening by the second. I forced myself to hang from Tri's anchor line for another five nervous minutes, relieved that the sun was starting to drive away some of my demons. I turned off the torch and risked a long look down and around, turning slowly as I hung there. The hull of the boat above me gave me some reassurance. I could hear the grumble of an engine turning over although the screws weren't moving.

I turned my attention down beyond my fins again. No monsters were coming up at me out of the shadows below. I wasted a couple of pounds of air by breathing a huge sigh of relief. The water was clearer up here and the light was tinting it a beautiful shade of turquoise. Now I could plainly make out the hull of the *Odorama* off to my right, a solid black whale shape outlined against the beautiful daylight. I was going to make it.

I had enough air in my tanks to swim the whole way underwater so I released the anchor chain, zeroing in on the prawn boat as I slowly began finning my way towards it. As I moved I gradually eased my way up towards the surface. I had gone maybe twenty feet from the anchor chain when all hell broke loose above me.

13

Underwater the sound of an explosion can travel a long way. This one did. It was a bloody big bang and it came from behind me. I turned. The trawler's twin screws were churning the water into foam. The anchor chain from the gunboat was falling away towards the ocean floor. Someone had smashed a quick-release shackle. Tri was on the move in a big hurry, it seemed. The water all around the black hull was filled with twinkling golden sparks that spiralled slowly down towards the reef below. There was a slapping, banging, drumming sound that cut across the sound of the trawler's engine.

For a moment I didn't get it, then I realised that the golden sparks were the spent shell cases from Tri's heavy artillery. The noise was that of the heavy machine guns at work, transmitted down through the boat's hull. While the big Brownings were doing their thing, brass was being sprayed out of the guns and over the side where it tumbled into the depths. The slow dance of the spent shell casings was almost beautiful. Beautiful! Jesus, I thought, my oxygen must be on the way out. There was a fucking battle under way up above and I was being poetic.

I was about as decompressed as I was going to get, so I started for the *Odorama* at full kick. I didn't want Niran bailing out and leaving me in the water. To have made it this far then to drown, die of exposure or get eaten by sharks as I drifted around the bloody ocean was not on my agenda.

I surfaced twenty feet from the side of the boat. Yes, there was daylight, plenty of it now. More than enough for me to see the faces and waving arms at the side of the boat ahead of me. The divers were back on board. I could hear the slow thud of the *Odorama*'s diesel engine. With my head above water, and even with my dive hood on, the rattle of fire from machine guns was clear. I turned. Tri's gunboat was racing towards a white shape that I could just pick out as I rode the crest of the swell. The target was the white cruiser. Off to the left of Tri's boat, something was sending a plume of black smoke up into the sky.

Then I was at the side of the *Odorama*. I hit the climbing net and was hauled unceremoniously on board the prawn boat by grabbing hands. Niran had us on the move as he ran up his anchor cable. The old winch was in overdrive. He was figuring on picking the hook up on the run. That was a dangerous technique because the damn thing could smack into the hull if it went wrong, or if it snagged on the bottom of our bloody freighter it could pull our bow down, or simply bust up and send wire cable whipping around the deck.

Whatever, it didn't happen. The anchor rattled into its retaining bracket as I pulled off my mask and hood. Then I saw it. The buddha was there, in the deck well, still in the sling that had lifted it from the water. No one but me was looking at it, all other eyes were on the two boats. I dropped my tanks and weight belt and pulled off my fins so I could get to my feet to join the other guys at the rail. The buddha could wait.

The white boat was moving quickly, attempting to run for the passage back to the mainland. Tri was heading to intercept it. The source of the black smoke was what appeared to be the gutted hull of a small runabout, wallowing in the water a hundred yards away.

'What the hell happened?' I asked no one in particular.

'A speedboat came around the headland. They had guns and grenades. They fired at Tri's boat. A grenade landed on deck but I don't think it killed anyone. Tri fired back.' The speaker was Noy. His eyes were wide and focused on nothing but the racing boats. 'Then the white boat came and they have been shooting.'

There were riflemen on the deck of the white boat. Their bullet strikes were all around the trawler that was rapidly closing in. Its speed no doubt surprised them. Tri's boat was capable of thirty knots which made it probably as fast as a big luxury cruiser. But he had the angle on the other vessel and he had the armament. The .50 Brownings were raking the white vessel from end to end, heavy continuous thumping underpinning the sharper sound of the smaller weapons. There was no doubt the white boat was taking a real pounding. If it hadn't been for that it might have made it past the gunboat and away. Then one of Tri's lot fired a tank buster.

The range was about a hundred yards. The rocket was launched from the bow of the trawler and it was right on target. The five- or six-pound package of high explosives slammed into the superstructure of the white boat and a fireball erupted. The ball rolled and twisted within itself as orange flames and black smoke wove themselves together. I saw a flaming figure fall from the boat and then the fireball was gone, leaving in its place a core of flames and twisted, smoking metal and fibreglass.

The bridge of the white boat was gone, but it carried on. Either there was another control panel below deck, or the helm and throttles were jammed because it didn't deviate from its course or speed. Tri's gunboat was closer now and a second rocket went out. This hit the stern of the white boat and a second fireball erupted. They were nasty missiles which burned as well as exploded. Figures were jumping over the side of the stricken boat, but Tri's killers weren't about to show mercy. The heavy machine guns continued to rake the ship while Tri's riflemen shot at the men in the water.

I might have stopped it if I could have. But then again, maybe not. Those two under the sea had been prepared to kill me to get what they were after. Sometimes it paid to just do what you had to in this business. The guys in the white boat had seriously underestimated what they were up against. They had figured on an easy hit against an old prawn boat, and not vectored our escort into their equation. Maybe that caused a change of whatever plan they had. I doubted we were ever going to find out what their original plan had been.

I guessed the two guys I'd taken out underwater had launched their scooter in the bay and homed in on our two boats to get themselves into the zone. Trying to spot two heads bobbing along in the swell would have been damned near impossible for Tri's watchmen. The divers also wouldn't have shown up on radar. Once they'd been close, the scooter jockeys would have gone under, buzzing along at five or six knots and with a powerful headlight, they wouldn't have taken long to spot the sub. I guessed the idea had been to grab the box and get away while their buddies took our boats out up above. Nice plan but they'd screwed it up big time.

The white boat had wallowed to a standstill. Black smoke plumed into the sky and orange and white flames licked out from the holes in the ruined hull. The pretty white cruiser was going to the bottom, as was everyone on it. The shooting had stopped. Tri had slowed to a crawl and was starting to circle the stricken vessel.

I carefully undid the straps which were holding the pouch to my chest and lowered it to the deck. I had a plain lead-covered box, contents unknown with a damned spear head embedded in it, and Tuk Tuk had a wonderful slime-covered gold and jewelled buddha. I squatted in front of the statue. The buddha was a little over four feet tall. It hadn't been made in the paunchy Chinese happy style, or in the aesthetically thin Cambodian one, but rather it fell somewhere in the middle. Even covered with weeds, algae and dripping slimy salt water, it was more than impressive.

A massive explosion dragged my eyes and those of everyone else back to the battling boats. The white vessel was totally gone in a final enormous ball of black smoke. It rolled into the clear blue sky and formed the familiar shape of a noxious nuclear mushroom. But this wasn't an atomic bomb—the fuel tanks had blown up and diesel smoke formed a towering monument to the death of the boat and its crew. The trawler was stationary for the moment. There hadn't been a shot fired for at least a minute or so.

'Ranong?' called Niran from the bridge. I nodded and bent to retrieve the black box. As I did so, one of the tines on the embedded spear head jagged deep into my left thumb. I cursed, grabbed my dive knife from my calf sheath and levered the barbed arrow out of the box. I angrily tossed the offending piece of razor-sharp metal over the side and jammed my injured thumb in my mouth while I examined the damage to the box. The edges of the hole in the grey–black lead shone silver for a moment, and then the hole filled with a milky fluid that bubbled in the wound of the metal and began to spill out of it. I sat back on my heels, startled.

'Fuck!' I muttered. What the hell was that fluid? The liquid foamed as it flooded out of the hole in the box. But it wasn't really liquid, or was it? It was like a grainy paste. Whatever it was in the box it was getting out, and that wasn't good. The flow was intensifying with every passing second. I wasn't panicking but, shit, I wasn't far off. Not knowing what the damned stuff was sent ice rattling down my spine. What the hell was

I to do? Logic said to throw the damned thing over the side.

It was then that a series of heavy swells hit us side on as Niran brought us round, setting a course to take us back through the passage. I stood. I'd had enough of sticking my head underwater for one day. The heavy green seas boomed in through the scuppers and half-filled the well deck before draining away, swirling back the way they had come. We took maybe five big hits before we were turned and the swell was behind us. My eyes went back to the box at my feet. Whatever had been leaking out of it had gone. The edges of the gash in the metal gleamed around a clean black hole. My first instinct was to seal that damned hole before I got very much older. But seal it with what?

I pondered the question for maybe ten seconds before the answer came and I was yelling instructions at Noy, who was standing on the deck down by the door leading to the superstructure. Our chef-cum-deck hand vanished to organise things. My thumb was bleeding. I needed a damned patch on myself. I wondered if whatever had leaked out of the box had contaminated the spear head and, in turn, done the same to yours truly.

The solution to plugging the hole in the lead was simple: more lead. The crew of the *Odorama*, like any fishing boat anywhere in the world, had a plentiful supply of lead on board. The crew used it to make sinkers, net weights and the like. It took Noy ten minutes to rustle up some scraps of metal and melt them in a heavy cast-iron pot over a gas burner. While I waited for the lead to turn to liquid, I gingerly carried my prize to the cabin door. When the lead was molten I poured the gleaming semi-liquid silver into the wound in the box. The gash was filled in seconds and set in a minute. Whatever had been getting out of my personal Pandora's Box was once again sealed inside. But what was it that had seeped out?

I picked up the box and took it and myself down the deck to my makeshift accommodation. There I would hose myself down, dry off, dress and sit on this damned precious thing of Bernard's with my Walther in my hand. Not quite maybe, but having gone to so much trouble to find it and having killed so many people to keep it, I wasn't about to let it out of my sight.

When I was dressed I felt a little more human. The cold had leeched itself out of my bones. I found a Band-Aid for my thumb, helped myself to a coffee with a huge belt of Mekong in it, lit a cigarette and went out on the foredeck again. The black box with its flare of fresh, dulling silver on one side was in the base of my holdall at my side. My gun was in the small of my back under my shirt. If Tuk Tuk had given instructions for someone to whack me before we returned to the mainland, it was going to happen soon.

Tan and Billy were cleaning the buddha while Suwat hosed off the dive gear. 'You guys keep my kit. I won't be needing it again,' I said. They all chorused their thanks. It was a bonus score for them. I'd just given away a couple of hundred thousand baht's worth of the very latest dive gear. Suwat went aft at a run to collect my wetsuit. The boys would either hock it off or rent it to big European clients as a sideline to their regular operation.

Tri was coming up astern of us. The smoke from the burning runabout and the cruiser had dissipated. I guessed he had hung around long enough to ensure there were no survivors. I'd decided from day one that he was a ruthlessly cold fish. I'd decided right. The missing boat and its crew might never be found. The sharks, the tide, the very remoteness of the area would all conspire for that result. If both the hull of the runabout and the cruiser went down, there was little chance their fate would ever be known. Of course, the damned satellite that I just knew was up there above us might have captured it all. I wondered if the Yanks would send a crew to retrieve whatever was left. I had the sudden thought that maybe Tri was the one Tuk Tuk might have entrusted to take me out. I shifted my bag to my left hand and waited.

Tri's boat was alongside. I could see the damage the grenade had caused. It was mainly superficial flash burns and some shrapnel damage. One of the goons had his left arm in a sling. The big Brownings were back under canvas. If the gunboat captain had ever looked smug, it was now. He waved for me to come to the side of the *Odorama*. I did so, slowly, watchful. A crewman reached across the gap between us and handed me a small object. It was a leather wallet. The trawler moved on ahead of us in a grumble of diesel power. I felt a surge of relief. Tri wasn't out to hit me. I now felt that that particular honour would go to Choy, my original pick. It always amazed me the twists and turns that paranoia could cause in one's thought patterns at times.

I watched as Tri set a course to the south, his job done. I guessed that he would off-load his weaponry somewhere down the coast before heading back into Ranong, if indeed he returned there at all. I sat down on the edge of the deck well and examined the wallet. It was sodden as, of course, was expected. I opened it. The New York driver's licence showed a face and a name: Carl Leathem, forty-two years old. There was a Queens address. I didn't recognise the face. I found a photo ID with a State Department seal, but no specific outfit identified. CIA definitely. That was the way they did it. Nice generic IDs with a numerical code that rang the right bells when processed. Just like the one I carried. There was no money in the wallet. I guessed Tri's cut-throats had liberated any cash. I used the bottom of my T-shirt to wipe my prints off the wallet's contents before reinserting them. Then I did an erasing trick on the wallet before I tossed it over the side. I wasn't going to be delivering it to the US Embassy in Bangkok.

I went into the mess with my bag and the mysterious box in tow. I had a Singha and followed it with another good belt of Mekong. I didn't know if I was supposed to feel elated or dejected. I'd recovered the fucking box, but maybe a dozen people had died because of it. I had another drink and then another but I didn't want to get drunk in case any of Choy's playmates had a go at me.

It was only a few minutes after midday and I was bone tired and my damned thumb throbbed. Why was a simple little jag causing me so much pain? Whatever, I was going to get some rest. It was going to take us the rest of the day to get back to Ranong at full clatter, and then I had Choy to deal with. Joy!

I lay on my bunk with the holdall behind my head, gun beside me and went to sleep.

14

I awoke about half an hour from the dock feeling like shit. I washed my face and got ready for Choy and whatever the future held. I pulled on my lightweight leather jacket. I was still chilled, whether from the cold of the dive or because black spiders of paranoia had slipped out of my subconscious to bite me. It happened that way sometimes. I put my few clothes into my bag to cover the black box.

The bag had a steel mesh between layers of leather, all attached to the steel-cored handle and shoulder strap. It had been given to me by Sir Bernard specifically to carry the mysterious box. There was no way this piece of luggage was going to fall apart under the weight of its special cargo.

I had one plan in mind for when we landed. I put the trick Marlboro pack in one jacket pocket, and a full genuine packet in the other. Then I climbed up to the *Odorama*'s bridge.

'What happened today?' Niran asked, his thin face shiny with fear.

'You saw nothing. Nothing happened. You took this crazy Englishman to dive but the weather turned bad. When it cleared he asked you to bring him back here. That is all. You didn't see Tri, you saw nothing, Niran,' I said softly.

'Nothing,' he repeated, nodding his head. 'I see nothing.' I resisted the impulse to smile. 'I see nothing' had been the catch phrase from *Hogan's Heroes*, a television show of my youth. Memories of the show and its characters could still produce a smile, even when life was as low-down dirty and dangerous as it was right at that moment. I went down below to spread the word amongst the rest of the guys. They had all seen nothing. In the mess I got a medicinal beer and stepped out on deck. The light was fading, but a quarter of a mile away I could see Choy and another man standing beside a big black Cherokee parked on the nearest dock. I went up to the bridge, borrowed Niran's glasses and focused on the reception committee on the dock.

Choy usually drove himself. I wondered if he had brought along a driver for another reason. The other guy looked more like a driver than a goon. He was typically slight, maybe in his early thirties, dressed in the standard uniform of jeans, a pair of trainers and a short nylon jacket over a T-shirt. Choy was in his own uniform of a dark silk suit and a black shirt open at the neck to show a gold rope big enough to moor the *Queen Mary*. The ensemble was completed with a pair of black crocodile-skin slip-ons and a pair of platinum-framed snake eyes. The mirrored lenses of the sunglasses completely hid his eyes. He was a very intimidating, very damaged gorilla in expensive clothes. That's my man, Choy Lee, I mused. I gave Niran back his glasses and went down to the mess and the remains of my beer. We were only a matter of fifty feet out by now.

The Cherokee had been parked right there on the dock ready to receive the cargo. The buddha was in the deck well. It had been covered in canvas and was just an anonymous shape now. There was a sling attached to the bundle ready to swing it up onto the dock. It would take some manpower to get it into the back of Choy's Jeep. I hoped he had heavy-duty springs fitted. I was sure he did. Gorilla, yes; idiot, no.

The moment *Odorama*'s tyre buffers hit the wharf I stepped ashore. Choy nodded to me. I couldn't see his eyes through the black lenses of his glasses, but I knew his gaze was focused on the canvas package sitting on the prawn boat. The back of the Cherokee was already open. I moved to the Jeep and put my holdall onto the rear passenger seat. As I did that, I removed the fake pack of Marlboros from my jacket pocket and slid it under the seat in front. I then moved away from the open door and went to lean on the side of the vehicle. I wanted to watch the floor show as the buddha was off-loaded. This was now Choy's game. Or so I would have him think.

Once Tuk Tuk's ticket to paradise was safely on the dock, Choy waved for bodies to help lift the buddha into the back of the wagon. It took six of them to do it, including Choy himself. The Jeep settled heavily on its springs which was my cue to go and bid farewell to Niran and his crew. Would Choy do what I anticipated he would? Harbours were noisy places when you wanted to make a special phone call.

'Gotcha,' I whispered as The Cabbage climbed into the passenger seat of the Cherokee and pulled the door shut against the din of the port. He glued his mobile phone to his ear as I shook Niran's hand and turned away, adjusting the stems of my glasses as I did so.

'We have it,' Choy was saying in Cantonese. His head turned my way as I hid behind a smoke screen and shook hands with the divers.

'So, you will be here by midnight?' Tuk Tuk asked.

'Yes. By midnight or shortly afterwards.' Choy paused. 'What about Daniel? He has his box. It would be easy to get rid of him in the jungle. Then you can take the box and trade it with the British or the Americans. Tri called me. He said it was the Americans who attacked them out on the water.'

'Kill Daniel,' Tuk Tuk replied. 'It pains me, but kill him quickly, Choy.'

My blood ran colder than ice when I heard those words. Without a qualm, Tuk Tuk had consigned me to a shallow grave in the fucking jungle. I kept my face expressionless as I walked back up to the Jeep. Choy closed his mobile phone and dropped it into his jacket pocket. He started to open his door but hesitated as I went to the rear door.

'We go,' he mumbled as I opened the door and got in behind him. No doubt he had planned to manoeuvre me into the front seat and get in behind me. I had checked him in this most deadly game of chess we were about to play.

'Yeah, let's go,' I replied as I settled into the seat behind him. The driver climbed in and cranked the big engine into life. The Jeep felt as heavy as my fucking heart as it moved off. I leaned back against the seat and made a play of closing my eyes. The tint of my Ray Bans hid the fact that my eyes were still half-open. No way was I not going to watch The Cabbage. I doubted he would attempt to kill me in the car, at least not on the move anyway. He was obsessively vehicle proud, so he probably wouldn't want the mess. At some point he would suggest we stop. A call of nature, maybe, on some isolated piece of road in the park as we cut across the peninsula. Then it would happen.

We were heading up the coast on Highway 4. I knew we'd cross over the hill at Kapoh to Chumphon and then run on up to Phetchaburi, again on 4, repeating the run I had done days before. Midnight, huh? It was close to a 250-mile drive to Phetchaburi and it was now 17:00. Choy had plenty of time to do what he wanted to. If I let him! I had already slipped the Walther out of its holster. The automatic was cocked and locked, safety off as it rested under my right thigh. My hand rested casually on the seat beside it.

We passed through Kra Buri without incident, and then started up into the national park. This was where I guessed it would happen. Five minutes up into the jungle I was proven right. There was quite a bit of traffic about, so I guessed it wouldn't take place on the side of the main road. As I saw the secondary road come up ahead on our left, Choy confirmed it would be then and there. 'I have to piss,' he said, indicating for the driver to pull us off the tarmac onto the dirt side road. The man did as he was told. Whether or not he knew what was to come I couldn't tell. He drove us fifty yards along the dirt road and pulled up where the trees started to crowd in. There was no traffic on this rutted track—no doubt a big factor in Choy's calculations. As we slowed I slipped my fingers around the Walther's butt, my finger sliding along the trigger guard.

It was very surreal the way it was happening. I'd never figured Choy for stupid, not ever. Okay, he didn't know I'd been eavesdropping on his conversation with Tuk Tuk, but he must have known that I wasn't a bloody moron and that I didn't trust him. Maybe it was his extreme arrogance. Maybe his hatred for me just overrode his logic. Whatever, it was all over in seconds.

The Jeep rocked on its springs as we stopped. Choy started to open his door with his left hand and as he began to get out, he turned towards me, his right hand rising above the seat back. He clutched the massive Desert Eagle and was still aligning the gun when I started shooting. The butt of my own gun was now resting on my right thigh. He never even saw it before he died. I put five shots through the back of the seat into Choy's chest and left side. That was the thing about those fancy post-production custom seats he'd had installed in the Cherokee. With all that breathable mesh and shit there wasn't a lot between the front and the back. Certainly not enough to stop a nine-millimetre slug, let alone five of them, going through the same big ragged hole.

Choy looked surprised in the second or two it took for him to realise he was dead. His hand cannon fell to the ground outside the car, while he slumped back against the front of the doorframe and the dashboard, his legs outside the wagon. He didn't make a sound. I turned my attention to the driver, raising the Walther to massage his left ear. The guy was frozen in his seat, head turned towards Choy, his eyes bulging. No doubt his ears were also ringing, just as mine were.

'You don't have to die,' I said softly. 'If you have a gun or a knife, open your window and throw them out. He fumbled and produced a small automatic. He opened the window and dropped it out. A switchblade followed a few seconds later. 'Pass me the keys,' I instructed. He did. 'Fasten your seat belt,' I ordered and he scrambled to obey. 'If I hear you release it I will kill you,' I added, probably quite unnecessarily. I got out of the Jeep. The guy had seen first hand how easy it was to die in my little world.

I searched for a pulse in Choy's neck. There was none. The Cabbage had gone to meet his ancestors. However, even in death I had plans for him. The easiest option would have been to simply shoot him in the back of the head, but I needed that big ugly head of his more or less in one piece. I completed opening Choy's door for him, then I turned his body, lifting his legs back into the passenger compartment. I strapped his body back into his seat, picked up his gun and tossed it away into the jungle. I didn't want the fucking thing. I went around the Jeep and did the same with the driver's hardware. Then I had a piss.

As I stood there with my dick in my hand, I felt let down. Not just by Tuk Tuk—I'd sort of expected that—but I'd been forced to kill Choy too damned quickly, too damned easily. I would have liked for him to have seen his death coming. He had brought it on himself with his total obsession to kill me, and I would have liked a few minutes with him to point out the error of his ways. Instead it had all been over in a second and a half. I finished urinating and zipped up.

I moved to the front of the Cherokee and stood appraising the situation. Choy's head drooped on his chest and I could see blood glistening on his shirt. He needed more work. I opened the passenger door again and rearranged his jacket to cover the blood. I wiped the trickle off the corner of his mouth with my thumb, and closed his blank stare. I needed to keep his head back in a more lifelike position. If I'd had superglue with me, I would have glued the back of his shaved head to the headrest. I didn't have any of that magic solution, but I did find an alternative in the elaborate first-aid kit that lived under the driver's seat.

The roll of tape was flesh-coloured. I put a band around Choy's neck under his chin and fixed it to the headrest behind his head. When I arranged his shirt collar, the tape vanished under both it and the thick folds of skin on his neck. The head still leaned forward slightly, but it gave the impression of someone dozing, not of a corpse. I found his sunglasses in his breast pocket and put them on him. That would do. As an afterthought I removed his wallet from inside his jacket. It was thick with both dollars and baht. I took the cash and put the wallet back. It wasn't simple thievery. Until I got back to my stash in the safe at the embassy annex, I figured I might need a lot more cold hard cash than I had on me. I got back in the vehicle and handed the driver the keys. 'Do as I say and you live. Otherwise you know what happens. To Phetchaburi. Okay?'

'Okay,' he replied. I noticed that the crotch of his jeans was stained dark. The acrid smell of urine mingled with that of gunpowder and blood. I had the guy turn up the air-con.

15

Tuk Tuk would come out to the Jeep. I knew that. Normally he would sit and wait for the world to come to him, escorted by Choy. Not this time, however. Not when Choy was coming to deliver his sainthood to him. This was mountain and Mohammed time. The buddha was definitely the mountain and it was truly immovable.

I made the driver pull off the highway just south of Phetchaburi. We found a place with more shadows than light. It seemed the guy thought he was going to die. When I explained what was going to happen next, the relief on his face was plain to see. We waited there for half an hour. I wanted Tuk Tuk to become anxious. He and Choy had an ETA of about 24:00. I was going to arrive at 00:15 precisely. That meant I had twenty minutes to show time.

I removed the mobile phone from my jacket, powered it up and called Bernard. On the third ring, he answered. I pressed the scramble button.

'I have the box.'

'The box!' The old arsehole sounded stunned. There was something akin to disbelief in his voice. 'Daniel?' he asked.

'Of course it's me. Who else? You sent me to get this damned box. I've got it.'

'Where are you?'

'Just south of Phetchaburi. I may be some time getting to the embassy. I have a couple of errands to run first. I'll call when they are complete.' I was starting to hang up when he stopped me.

'Leave your phone on. It may be necessary for a change of plans,' he said. 'It's important. Well done,' he added as an afterthought. 'Did you have any problems?'

'Yeah. Tell you about that later,' I replied and killed the call. I didn't tell him about the CIA ambush because right at that moment it was history and could wait.

I dropped the mobile back into my pocket, lit a cigarette and leaned back in my seat. 'Smoke if you want to,' I told the driver. He stuttered his thanks, lit up and there we sat, smoking like two old buddies. All we needed was a pint and a packet of crisps to complete the party atmosphere.

Something was nagging me about the call I'd just made. Sir Bernard fucking Sinclair hadn't exactly sounded thrilled that I had collected the most important prize in the world for him, whatever that was. Eventually I pushed the thought away. I had other things to do. It was time. I got out of the rear of the Jeep, tossing my cigarette butt away as I closed the door. I quickly opened the front passenger door before my little driver buddy got any ideas. It was time to get the show on the road.

I pushed Choy's seat as far back on its rails as it would go and tilted the backrest to give the illusion that he was just relaxing. It was a fucking squeeze, but I thanked the gods that the Yanks build big cars for big people. I managed to curl myself up, half on the bottom of the foot well and half jammed between Choy's legs and the passenger door. In the dim light I was invisible, as long as Choy remained the centre of whatever attention was directed at the Jeep. I had the gun in my left hand aimed at my chauffeur's groin. He knew he was dead if he screwed up.

I figured we would have to beat a cursory video scan and the gatehouse man.

I'd been with Choy in happier times when he'd go through the main gate. The gate men never used to leave their cubbyhole. One look at The Cabbage was enough. No one who knew Choy got in his face. That fact, coupled with the angle of the gatehouse window and the distance to the side of the car, meant that, technically, the guard wouldn't see me. As for the cameras, I was praying that no one would be looking at them but focusing instead on the live show. To hell with what the video showed later.

'When you enter the second gate, sound the horn. Three short blasts,' I instructed the driver. 'Drive to the bottom of the steps. You stay in the car when we stop.'

'Okay,' he replied. 'We are coming to the first gate.'

I glanced at my watch. 00:14. Perfect!

The Jeep rocked heavily on its suspension as it turned off the street and approached the outer gate. Obviously the goon in the guardhouse had been given his instructions by Tuk Tuk: to expect and expedite our immediate arrival. The cameras picked up the Cherokee the moment it turned into the approach to the palace. The outer gate was open when we reached it. I was picturing us crossing the moat when the Jeep slowed momentarily but didn't stop. The second gate opened. Choy's beautiful mug had done the trick.

Our tyres crunched on pebbles and my driver honked the horn three times as he brought us to a halt. My next trick was to get out of the car as fast as I could. It would be a case of opening the door and kicking myself out backwards onto the driveway. 'Tell me when Tuk Tuk is out of the house,' I whispered to the driver, who sat frozen in his seat. 'Turn off the engine and the headlights and give me the keys.'

He did as I said and sat there stone-faced, the lights from the garden and the palace reflecting white off his face.

'He's coming with the woman.'

'Anyone else?' I was counting on Tuk Tuk being alone. I didn't really want to kill him in front of Sakura.

'No one!'

'Don't move,' I whispered as I reached behind my right shoulder for the door release. I popped it and twisted myself around Choy's left leg, pushing my heels against the transmission hump to give me leverage. I leaned into the door and kicked off. My shoulders hit the shingle and I rolled completely over, landing on my knees beyond the Cherokee's wide door. My gun was locked in a two-handed grip. Tuk Tuk was ten feet away coming directly towards me, Sakura on his right side holding his right forearm while one of his ebony sticks supported him on his left.

Tuk Tuk stopped. Sakura, probably not realising what the hell was happening, stepped beyond him. I came to my feet quickly. I doubted there were any guards in the compound or snipers on the roof, but I didn't want to take a chance. I covered the ground between Tuk Tuk and myself in three paces.

'Daniel, what is ...?' Sakura gasped as I brushed past her.

'Tuk Tuk will tell you,' I said as I kicked the old man's stick away and jammed the muzzle of my automatic under his chin. 'Tell her you stupid, greedy old man,' I said in Cantonese. Tuk Tuk's double whammy of surprise caused him to sag at the knees. I caught him by his left lapel and held him up. 'Yes,' I said, reverting to English. 'All along, Tuk Tuk, I had a microphone hidden. You and that stupid fuck, Choy, just couldn't let it go could you!'

'Choy!' Sakura was standing at the open Jeep door, hand to her beautiful mouth. Tuk Tuk knew then that Choy was no more. His eyes went out of focus for a moment, then they hardened again. He was too slow. I knew all about the knife that he carried in the spring sheath in his right sleeve. As the mechanism delivered the blade into his hand, I caught his wrist and twisted. The blade made an almost musical sound as it hit the stones. 'Daniel, what is happening? Please!' Sakura was coming back towards us, a white angel in the light. I looked beyond her. The driver of the Cherokee sat frozen like the corpse beside him.

'Tuk Tuk gave the order for Choy to kill me. I killed him first. Now I will kill Tuk Tuk,' I replied. I turned back to the object of my rage. 'I came here to offer you something more valuable than gold or my pitiful fucking death, but you just couldn't let it go.' I switched to Cantonese because it was appropriate, perhaps, for my next choice of words. 'Like the scorpion, Tuk Tuk, you sting because you can't not sting. It is your nature and nothing can change that but my own sting.' I pushed the muzzle of the gun deeper into his throat.

'Please don't, Daniel!' Sakura had come to us. She, too, was speaking Cantonese. Both of her hands were on my left forearm. 'Please no, Daniel.'

Tuk Tuk remained silent. He was now looking as he had when I had told him the truth behind Arune's death. Tuk Tuk Song was an old man. Yes, a vicious old man to be sure. He didn't beg or make any excuses. We were far beyond that. But now his eyes had lost their steel. He was sagging against my grip. I let him sink slowly to the pebbles. I could have dropped him. Instead, I lowered him almost gently to the ground. However the muzzle of my gun stayed at his temple. I didn't trust him an inch.

'He's dying, Daniel.' Sakura was speaking softly. She had reverted back to English. Her eyes were huge, either from desperation or fear. 'Prostate cancer. It has spread. He has perhaps a year, no more.'

'He ordered my death,' I replied. 'I saved his life twice, once from his own son, and he rewards me by ordering my death. How can you have any compassion for this man?'

'Because he is my husband,' she said softly. 'We have been married for ten years, Daniel.' I was speechless. I had never heard a whisper, never even suspected they were married. I looked into those beautiful big eyes and could see no lies there.

'Who knew?' I asked.

'No one but Choy.' It was Tuk Tuk who spoke. 'It was to protect Sakura. She had been my mistress for five years before my second wife, Arune's mother, died. When we married we kept it secret.'

'I love him, Daniel. I beg you not to kill him.' Despite the use of the word, Sakura wasn't begging—she was asking a friend for a favour.

'While he lives, I can never come back here,' I replied. 'This old scorpion only knows one way. I gave him the opportunity for eternal redemption, or as close to it as he could ever come, and he rejected it.'

'Daniel. Yes, I made yet one more mistake, but with Choy's death it is over,' Tuk Tuk said, his voice that of a tired, sad old man. 'Yes, you offered and I failed. I let myself be swayed by my blood and my oldest friend. On the life of the woman I love, I promise you that you have my word it is over.'

'My life, Daniel,' Sakura said, a desperate edge to her voice. 'My life. You have no idea how much this man loves me. He would never risk my love or my life.'

'That much?' I said, staring down at Tuk Tuk in something approaching amazement.

'Yes, Daniel. That much! It is over,' Tuk Tuk said staring up at me, his eyes wet not through fear but through something else. Looking down at this old sick man sitting on the stones at my feet, I almost believed his words. 'I am too old and sick to fight any more. I want my last days to be with the woman I love,' he added.

Sakura sank to her knees on the pebbles beside her husband, her arms around his neck, her eyes reaching out to me. 'Daniel, if you kill him, please kill me as well,' she said simply. And there it was. I stood staring down at the pair of them. Later I would wonder how it could be. This thug of a man and the most gentle and beautiful woman I had ever met. Husband and wife? This was the marriage of the scorpion and the butterfly. If I killed him I killed her, and that was something I could never do.

I removed the gun from Tuk Tuk's temple and stood, letting it weigh my hand and drag my arm down to my side. 'I am taking the buddha back to where it belongs,' I said. 'No matter what, you don't deserve to die with its glory added to your name.' I walked over to the Jeep and opened the driver's door, waving the man out. 'Other side. Get Choy out.' I leaned against the truck's bonnet while the driver went around to do as I had said. Sakura and Tuk Tuk stayed where they were, side by side on the white pebbles, she kneeling and he sitting.

A door opened in the inner wall—the change of guard perhaps. The man was dressed in a blue uniform and wearing a sidearm. He paused and stood looking towards the tableaux we had created in the courtyard. 'Tell him everything is as it should be,' I instructed Tuk Tuk.

'Go about your duty,' Tuk Tuk ordered. 'Do not sound the alarm.' Without a word the guard moved on and passed through another door.

Choy lay on his back on the white pebbles. The driver stood beside him, staring down, possibly wondering just how small the scourge of the underworld looked in death. I went to where Tuk Tuk's ebony walking stick lay. The snake-head grip was made of tooled silver and gold with ruby eyes. I examined it and gave the handle a twist. The ebony shaft pulled away to reveal a long double blade that was razor sharp. I closed it and handed it to the old man. He took it.

'Sakura, I want you to ride with me to the outer gate,' I said as I holstered my gun and reached down to draw her to her feet. She came upright so gracefully, weighing nothing at all, or so it seemed. I stood there holding her hand and looking down at Tuk Tuk Song. 'On the life of the woman you love, Tuk Tuk,' I said softly. 'Because if I have to come back, I will kill Sakura in front of your eyes.'

'My promise, Daniel. It is over!'

'Goodbye once again, old friend,' I said.

'Goodbye, Daniel. I am sorry for my weakness. For our friendship's sake I wish I had been stronger,' Tuk Tuk replied as he slowly regained his feet with the aid of his stick.

I helped Sakura into the passenger seat. It was dry and there was no blood or anything else on it. Choy had kept things together even in death. As I shut the door I glanced down at the corpse lying on the white shingle. Tuk Tuk would die lonely without The Cabbage. I didn't have any words for Choy. I walked around the truck and climbed into the driver's seat. I found the keys in my jacket pocket and started the Cherokee, flicking on the lights as I drove around the circular driveway. I headed back to the inside gate.

The gate opened immediately and I drove us across the bridge. Looking back I could see Tuk Tuk standing, watching. He raised his free hand in a gesture of farewell, whether to me or to his lost chance at sainthood, I would never know. The second gate opened. I drove most of the way through but halted when the rear of the Jeep was still on the bridge.

'Would you kill me if you had to come back, Daniel?'

'Kill you or take you off him,' I replied.

'Take me off him?' Sakura whispered, almost smiling.

'Taking you off him and letting him die alone would be the worst punishment of all,' I said. Sakura sat with her head turned, her eyes seeing right into me. It was a long pause.

'You wonder how I could love a man like that. I know,' she said sadly. 'Sometimes, especially in the early days, I wondered too. But there is another man in there, Daniel.' The thought of that other man made her blink and a sad smile touched her lips. 'A man who will grieve that he has lost you as a friend. A man who will cry his heart out at Choy's funeral. I discovered that other man and married him and yes, he is dying, Daniel.'

'Human beings, we never understand each other,' I said, reaching across to open her door.

'Oh, sometimes we do,' Sakura replied softly, 'only too well.' She turned her face to mine, held my chin with powerful slim fingers and kissed me. It was a kiss like none I had ever experienced. It went on and on, then her fingers softened to stroke my cheek and she was gone from the seat, leaving me like a guppy out of water, gasping for breath.

'Daniel, go well, and when you hear that Tuk Tuk Song is dead, please call me.' With that the Jeep's door closed and Sakura was gone. I gathered some composure, and in the rear view mirror I saw the figure in white walking back across the bridge. She turned momentarily to wave, then the inner gate opened and she stepped through. I dropped the Jeep into gear and drove into the night.

It was a long drive down to Pha To. The irony was that it was only fifty or sixty miles southeast of where I had been in Ranong. If we hadn't gone through Choy's little charade, I'd have been there hours ago.

As I turned back down Highway 4 heading south, I wondered at everything that had just happened. I'd killed Choy. I'd let Tuk Tuk live, maybe only because of Sakura. And what of Sakura? That kiss, my God! And then there had been so much promise in her words of 'Call me when ...'. Christ, I was acting like a schoolboy with a crush.

As I struggled to stay awake, I still couldn't figure it all out. And shit, that fucking black box. It was sitting in my bag on the back seat, almost forgotten because of everything else that was going on. I had to deliver the buddha then get my arse and the box back to the embassy in Bangkok. But there was another factor at work here: What about the Americans? They had lost a big team out there in the Andaman. They would be pissed off and looking very hard for the box and whoever had it. If they found both, their revenge would be swift and bloody.

A few miles south of Prachuap Khiri Khan, I was snapped awake by a hell of a bang. In front of me a big tractor–trailer unit was weaving violently across the road. A tyre on the trailer had blown and the automatic brakes had locked on. Great chunks of rubber were airborne. Then another tyre went and the whole damned thing began to jackknife.

I had two choices: try and brake and risk running into the trailer and getting creamed by the traffic coming from behind, or put my foot on the pedal and try and get around. Instinct put lead in my right foot. I went wide across the lane, cutting in front of a braking sedan. I flew past the swinging cab of the tractor unit, my right wheels running down the centre strip. Thank God I was piloting a four-wheel drive as the right wheels ran on shingle and dirt, the left on the road surface. I passed just as the tractor and trailer began to roll. Switching my eyes between the road ahead and the rear view mirrors, I could see the whole unit skidding after me in a slow cartwheel that sent sparks flying. It was like a special-effects crash in a fucking movie, except people were about to die for real. Vehicles behind it were piling up nose to tail. Then the trailer was bouncing free of the driving unit and over into the northbound lanes. The chaos was complete when petrol fires started.

I didn't stop. This was going to take hours to sort out and I didn't have the time, even if I had the inclination, to get knee-deep in burned flesh and smouldering wreckage. I kept my foot to the floor to get some distance between the crash site and me. Cars in front of me were slowing. Some stopped when they realised that hell was erupting behind them. I kept my foot down and threaded my way through, eventually getting beyond them and back into the highway flow of traffic.

As the adrenaline started to wear off I began to lose it and slowed. I needed to sleep. I needed to think. I needed to talk to someone. Geezer! I juggled the phone, noting the power warning light blinking. I thumbed in Geezer's number. I hadn't spoken to him since I had left Patong. I needed to tell him that I'd pulled it off and I needed his advice. I was starting to get a bad feeling. Maybe it was just fatigue and, hell, I'd just offed a guy face to face and, in part, caused a whole bunch more to cash their cheques. I was also fucking scared that the whole of the CIA was going to be looking for me with extreme prejudice.

There was no reply from Geezer. I tried Sami's mobile with the last juice in my battery, but all I got was his voice mail. Maybe he was still in the air on his way home. I didn't leave a message. The phone died about then. Bernard was going to have to wait until I could recharge it. I didn't have a car unit but there was a mains charger in my bag. Later!

A downpour started and, even on full, the windscreen wipers were struggling to cope. I couldn't see the road ahead. I was about done and on the verge of falling asleep at the wheel. I pulled off the highway and found a place to park up. My sanctuary, for the time being, was off a secondary road that headed into a plantation. I had rubber trees on both sides and the highway was three or four miles back. I guessed I was a few miles north of Tha Sae which, in turn, was some twelve miles or so north of Chumphon.

With the vehicle doors locked tight and just the driver's window cracked open for air, I dropped the front seat as far back as it would go and played dead, the Walther lying on the floor under the edge of the seat. The drumming of the rain on the Cherokee sent me tumbling into a deep sleep in seconds.

16

Dawn came early for me thanks to a full bladder and the policeman in the rain cape, hard hat and dark glasses who was tapping on my window. My heart went from a dreamy sleep to near panic, and my adrenaline valve fully opened in a fraction of a second. As I sat up I slid my right hand under the driver's seat. The Walther was positioned for a quick snatch and shoot.

Anyone who wore sunglasses in the rain, cop or otherwise, was definitely a potential problem. It was a matter of attitude. This could mean big trouble. I turned the ignition key and pressed the button on the door to open the side window. My hand went down to the gun as I half turned to face the cop.

'You okay?' he asked in passable English.

'Okay,' I replied, sticking to English. 'Just tired. It's a long drive from Bangkok to Phuket,' I said, trying to see the man's eyes through his glasses. Was he interested in the big canvas bundle in the back? I now had the gun in my hand, holding it close to the door. I wondered if he had a partner with him in the patrol unit. I couldn't see the car as his rain cape was blocking my view. If there were two cops and it came to a shoot-out, I would be in trouble.

'It's good you sleep,' the cop said nodding, suddenly smiling. 'That way you don't have accident. Have a good trip,' he added, turning away. There was no car and I almost laughed as I realised what had happened. My heart rate dropped dramatically and I pushed the gun back under my seat.

The cop got onto a little Honda step-through that was parked a few feet away and waved. So did the young schoolgirl wearing a white blouse and blue skirt with a clear plastic poncho over the top. She was perched on the back of the bike. The girl continued to wave as the Honda pulled away. I did likewise purely out of relief.

I guessed the cop was a country dweller, probably on his way to work at Chumphon after dropping his daughter off at school. He'd only stopped because I was parked on his road. I'd come very close to shooting an innocent guy. I breathed a deep sigh of relief. The rain had stopped. It was going to be a beautiful day and I hadn't killed anyone yet.

By the time I arrived at Chumphon it was hot and the sky was a cloudless blue. I filled up the tank and grabbed coffee and a sweet roll before carrying on to the turn-off for the west coast, just south of Thung Tako. The *wat* at Pha To was about twenty miles in, about the halfway point between the coasts. While the temple wasn't one of the giants of the land it was large enough, and quite plain. Maybe in the days when it was at its prime, it had been the Ruby Buddha inside that had dominated and not the surrounding buildings.

When I pulled into the temple grounds it was a few minutes to 10:00. Several saffron-clad figures stood around, as well as a few Thai civilians. A local bus, one or two cars and a few utility vehicles were in the car park. There didn't seem to be any tourist activity. Maybe without the Ruby Buddha there was no interest in yet another *wat* in the middle of nowhere. I couldn't begin to imagine what would happen when they put this baby back on display.

I got out of the Cherokee, locked the door and headed round to the main building towards the living area. Several monks looked startled as I approached them. *Farang*s were obviously thin on the ground there. I double whammied them when I greeted them in fluent and very respectful Thai. I went through the pleasantries before asking for the head monk. They all looked shocked at the suggestion that the top dog be summoned. 'It is most important for this temple and the people of Pha To that I speak with him,' I announced. 'It is very, very important. I have a gift of great value for your temple.'

With looks of confused consternation, the monks gathered to discuss the implications of my words. I knew that 'gift of great value' was a key phrase in any language and eventually, after much discussion and more than a few raised voices, one of the youngsters departed at a most unholy clip. I waited for perhaps ten minutes. During that time orange-clad figures of all ages—from novices to ancient creatures—came by, all looking at the *farang* who could speak their language and who had a 'gift' for the temple. In Bangkok or any of the other main temples I wouldn't have raised an eyebrow. Here, I was a martian!

Three monks approached through an archway. Two elderly guys in saffron supported a third dressed in white. I had heard of this: a monk in mourning rags, death robes on a living person. It was a rare practice; to put aside the saffron robes and don the white was probably the most soul-felt gesture possible. The third man was ancient. He looked to be older than time itself, like a creature who had forgotten to die a hundred years before. Another very old monk came to my shoulder.

'Brother Thana has been in mourning for more than sixty years,' explained my companion of the moment in a whisper. 'When the Japanese took our Ruby Buddha he donned the white robes and has not spoken a word since that time, other than in prayer. You are the first visitor he has seen that is not of our order.'

That was indeed significant. I just hoped the old boy's ticker was going to handle it. I bowed to the old monk and turned to indicate the Jeep in the car park thirty yards away. 'I have something in my car that will gladden your heart,' I said softly. 'We will need many strong backs to remove it.'

One of the speaking elders raised his voice, and in seconds a dozen young, fit novices appeared. They had no doubt been hiding in doorways wondering what this stranger wanted. They followed me to the back of the Jeep. I unlocked it. 'This is very heavy. You will need a good grip and plenty of muscle,' I said as the swarm of saffron-clad figures gathered. I moved to one side. The old boy in white stood ten feet away with his two attendants.

Clutching handfuls of canvas and the strops we had tied around the buddha back on the *Odorama*, the young men eased the precious bundle out of the back of the Jeep. They lowered it onto the flagstones and stood around uncertainly. I pulled my Gerber folding knife from my pocket and stepped forward to cut away the strops. Then I cut the rope that bound the top of the canvas shroud.

'You can take off your mourning rags,' I said to the old man in white as I flicked the canvas back from the top of the statue. There was an immediate gasp and, as one, the entire assembly fell to its knees, all except the old man and those who were supporting him. It was an image frozen for a few seconds, maybe half a minute. Then the old monk shrugged off the hands that gripped him and walked forward, unaided, to stand in front of me.

'Thank you,' he said in clear, unaccented English as he held out a frail hand. 'Thank you!'

'My pleasure,' I replied as I shook his cool, thin hand gently, fearing I might break it. He turned to look at the priceless relic he had mourned for so long. That was my cue to make myself scarce. I moved away to close the back of the truck, resisting an overwhelming impulse to say aloud, 'My work here is done!' The old man turned back towards me. I could see a thousand questions etched on his face. He was searching for words. One of the other old orange-robed monks was coming towards me.

'Please wait,' he called. 'We must talk. We must thank you, we ...'

'God's will!' I said. 'Plus I have another urgent task,' I replied in Thai.

It was only as I started moving that I realised just how pretentious that must have sounded. As I had done on leaving Tuk Tuk's palace, I looked back in the rear view mirror. The old man in white was looking after me, his hand raised just as another had done only hours before. My final image was of the ancient one lowering himself to his knees in front of the Ruby Buddha of Pha To.

Tuk Tuk Song had missed out on his place amongst the saintly legends of Thai culture. Instead, some anonymous *farang* would become the hero of Pha To. 'Oh, how you stuffed it all up, Tuk Tuk,' I muttered, still remembering and almost tasting my kiss from the angel who had saved his life.

17

Delivery done, I headed back east. I could have carried on to the west coast and either run up to Ranong or gone down to Phuket in order to catch a plane to Bangkok. However, post 911 and everything after, I ran a very real risk of not succeeding. Attempting to get on board an aircraft anywhere carrying a lead box, not to mention a gun and a knife, would damn near get me shot. I opted to double back east for the train, but first I wanted something to eat and to charge my damned phone. I was going to need it for Plan B, or C or whatever lay ahead.

I pulled into a roadside eatery. It was typical of the sort found in Thailand. It was a shack to be sure but there was cold beer and the smells coming from it were delicious. The place had electricity. The owner, a smiling Thai woman of indeterminable age, was happy for me to charge my phone. I got the charger from my kit and set it up while my host started cooking up a storm. My plan was to eat first then do whatever came next on a full stomach. I used the computer to check my emails and the news. Hell, I'd been out of touch for what seemed like years.

Three beers later and a feast that included steamed fish, prawns fried with chillies and other delights, I retrieved my phone and charger. I paid the delighted cook at the roadside eatery far too much. Hell, I was out at least five quid in real money. Try getting a half-decent curry for that anywhere in the UK. I hit the road and whilst on the move I tried Sami again. He was still on voice mail and Geezer wasn't home. I was beginning to feel like everyone had abandoned me until a few miles short of the turn-off onto Highway 41—the highway that links the southwest of the isthmus to 4 at Chumphon—the phone went. It was Bernard, of course. I flicked on the scrambler.

'You've been switched off,' he said angrily.

'I've been out of fucking battery,' I snapped back at him. 'I've just had the damn thing charged.'

'All right,' Bernard conceded with absolutely no hint of apology in his crusty old-maid's voice. 'Where are you?'

'I'm forty miles south of Chumphon,' I replied, guessing he would at least have a small-scale map of Thailand on the desk in front of him. 'I'm on my way to Bangkok,' I replied.

'Yes,' he agreed, 'the original plan is best.' He paused for a moment as if a sudden thought had struck him. 'Now you have your phone charged, leave it on, Daniel.' He was almost pleading. 'There are forces at work over there and we must be able to communicate to save the box.' As an afterthought he added, 'And you, of course.'

'Thank you, Bernard. I didn't know you cared,' I said dryly as I hung up and immediately turned the phone off. The only calls I wanted to deal with at that time were those I made myself. Staying alive was going to take all my energy and concentration from that moment on. I was coming into the turn-off onto 41 so I turned right, not left, to go north. Lang Suan was a couple of miles south of the turn-off but it was the closest main station from which to pick up a train.

I parked the Jeep in a quiet side street a hundred yards away from the station. I took my time to wipe down all the surfaces which could have captured my fingerprints. I almost forgot one vital thing as I prepared to abandon the big black beast: my bugged cigarette pack under the passenger seat. I retrieved it and left the keys in the ignition for some lucky Thai wide boy to discover. The Jeep would be in a chop shop in a day or so.

I was lucky that the next train from Trang was running late. It wasn't the express, but it was going the right way. I got a second-class ticket. The train arrived within five minutes. The carriage I chose was half-full, or half-empty, whichever, and the air-con was working. It was a slice of heaven. I parked my bag under my feet and settled in for an enjoyable trip. I enjoyed travelling by train. There were no responsibilities and it wasn't far to fall if the engines failed or the wings came off.

Just as we started to move I looked up. A flustered European arrived on the station platform running flat out and he wasn't carrying a suitcase. A second figure appeared behind him, also European. The pair were both dressed in what I called 'CIA casual': a pair of jeans or khaki casuals, a pair of sports shoes and a T-shirt or polo shirt hanging loose at the waist, all the better to hide weaponry. One of the new arrivals was in a green polo, the other a white T-shirt that was a little grey from spreading sweat stains. The pair didn't hesitate as the train gathered speed. They turned and headed back for the street at a run.

Where had they picked me up? The wharf at Ranong, leaving Tuk Tuk's palace or on the road? And why hadn't they taken me earlier? Maybe they hadn't expected me to head south from Phetchaburi, anticipating instead that I would go straight for Bangkok. Had they planned on taking me en route? If I'd broken their tail by heading south on the highway, and then getting beyond that damned multi-vehicle pile-up before they did, they'd have been livid. Blind luck may have saved me when I'd turned off the highway to sleep the previous night. They'd probably steamed on south for Phuket, no doubt thinking that was my logical destination. Ducking off for Pha To had been another whammy. It was almost funny thinking of the agents of the mighty CIA chasing their tails up and down the highways of the Kingdom trying to find me, or rather find the Cherokee. So how had they eventually done it? Well, it wasn't magic.

The most important things about any sort of surveillance exercise was manpower and time, knowledge of the countryside and, to a degree, knowledge of the subject in the mix. Enough of each and the game was easy. I knew the CIA's manpower on the ground in Thailand was finite, at least in the short term. They'd have been pulling people out of everywhere in Asia right about then and sending them my way.

Then, of course, there was the technological side of the business. A clear cloudless day and a satellite with a big lens could have tagged my arse. Hell, if you could read a newspaper from up there, picking up a distinctive vehicle and even a licence plate was no problem. Sky surveillance aside, the CIA might have even managed to get a tracer beacon onto the Jeep if they'd had a man at the port. It was the American way to keep throwing resources at the problem to get a solution. I guessed they were throwing heaps my way. They obviously wanted the damned box really badly.

No matter how they had done it, the CIA colours were hot on my tail. At the next stop they would have agents on the train. That posed the immediate question: What should I do about that? It was time for a bit of magic. I had to assume they had a photo of me. I knew I was on their files from when we had been bunk buddies out in the bush. The file shot was probably ten years old, unless they'd updated it. Trouble was, the shot would show me almost exactly as I still was, with blond, medium-length hair, same colour moustache, blah, blah. The few extra scars and wrinkles weren't going to change much of the big picture.

I took my holdall with me and headed to the toilet. Inside I locked the door and started to turn Daniel Swann into someone else. I didn't have much in the bag: the damned lead box, my computer, phone charger, toilet kit and a few choice articles of clothing. However I did have the bare essentials for what I needed.

From experience I knew how easy it was to transform oneself into someone else in the short term if prepared. I stripped and replaced my faded blue jeans with the only other pair I had with me, which just happened to be a pair of black Levis. My white T gave way to a black Harley Davidson cut-off. Colour was the name of the game. My choice of headgear was the clincher: a green John Deere baseball cap with a dark ponytail hanging nine inches down the back. I put it on and pushed any stray strands of my own hair up under it. Then I got every blond agent's friend from my toilet kit—mascara. Using the wand, I quickly blackened my sideburns, my moustache and the fringe areas that poked out under the cap. An almost stranger was staring back at me from the mirror. I had one more little disguise element. The soft camera bag was in the side pocket of my holdall. I pulled it out, knocked it into shape, then put my gun, spare double-magazine pouch and holster inside. I stowed the dark Ray Bans and put on my other disguise: a pair of thin gold aviator frames with orange-tinted lenses. I looked like Joe Tourist out for the sun, cheap booze and Thai ladies.

I stuffed everything else into my holdall, including the leather jacket. Now I was a tall, dark guy in close-fitting clothes. No place to hide weapons. The train was starting to slow. We were about to come into Chumphon. Time to bail out. Before I did so I checked the injury on my thumb. The edges of the gash were red and there was a hint of swelling. I found another plaster in my kit and stuck it on. I didn't want to think about the implications of the wound having been infected by whatever was in the damned box.

I left the toilet and moved to the nearest exit. The attendant standing at the door turned to look at me. I could see he was puzzled. Had he seen me in his carriage? He soon gave up on his speculation and shrugged slightly as he turned back to watch the platform slide into view. Possibly all *farang*s looked the same to him. The moment we stopped he opened the door and stepped aside to let me out.

I jumped jauntily down onto the platform and eased my way through the crowd waiting to board the train. I had my bag slung casually over my left shoulder, my camera case over the right. I presented like a seasoned traveller who knew exactly where he was going. I brushed past Mr White. He didn't even turn his head. His gaze was on the train. He had a photograph or something in his right hand and his eyes were darting back and forth, trying to watch half a dozen carriage doors at once. A good trick if you could do it. Mr Green was further down the platform, and there was a Mr Blue hovering by the exit. I went past Mr Blue and again, he didn't turn his head. This American bum traveller wasn't who he was looking for. If he'd spoken to me for any reason I would have given him a fair hint of Texas by way of return, thanks to months in the late Casey's company. No one spoke to me and I carried on.

In the street outside the station I saw Mr Beige. He was a big black guy in a beige shirt, leaning against the side of a blue Toyota four-door. A silver Toyota was parked immediately beside it. Mr Beige wasn't interested in me either. I crossed the street and walked away. The train was on the move. I looked back. Mr Blue came out of the station entrance and stopped to talk to his compatriot. White and Green, it seemed, had caught the train. Blue and Beige would take the vehicles and head up to the next stop. I needed to be on the move.

A tour bus was parked a hundred feet ahead of me. I could see camera-carrying folks wearing little tour badges converging on it from several directions. The driver and a female tour guide were sitting at a pavement stall drinking soft drinks and eating snacks. I walked up to them and greeted them in Thai. Pleasantries quickly over, it was down to business as I reached for my wallet. Their eyes followed my movement. 'Are you going to Bangkok?'

'Yes,' replied the guide.

'Can I buy a seat?' I asked in English. 'I seem to be too late for the train.' I pulled a thick wad of US dollars from my pocket, most of them supplied by Choy. I peeled off a couple of fifty-dollar bills and handed one to each of them. Fifty dollars at the current exchange rate represented a week's wages for them. They accepted the money with broad smiles.

'We have a seat for you at the back. We leave in five minutes,' the guide said, obviously delighted with her sudden bonus. She opened her bag to put the money away, or so I thought, but after rummaging in it for a moment she handed me a circular decal sticker. The background colour on the sticker matched her green uniform. 'If you put this on your shirt that will be good,' she explained. I peeled off the backing and stuck the decal over my heart. Now I was officially a tourist.

I climbed on board the bus and made my way to the back, smiling at the people already seated as I went. I had just taken my seat alone in the rear section when the two Toyotas drove past, heading for the highway feeder going north. With any luck I would be ahead of them by the time they picked up their disappointed train spotters at whatever stop they would rendezvous at. They would figure I was back on the road and, with no idea how and in what I was travelling, they'd realise they had lost me for the moment. I'd be just another figure in a huge and very mobile crowd. There were hundreds of tour buses plus local transport of all shapes and colours streaming up and down the highway. It was now an impossible task for the CIA ops, or anyone else, to find me. They would regroup and try to tag me in Bangkok, probably as I attempted to get into the British Embassy.

With that thought in mind, I pushed up the aircraft-style armrests on my seat and the next two in the row. With my holdall under my head, I stretched out across my comfortable bed and closed my eyes. After the *Odorama,* this was pure bliss.

18

I awoke as we hit the traffic wall and joined Highway 35 heading into Bangkok. As we drew closer to the river, the traffic got progressively denser and louder. 'Welcome back!' I thought as I sat up. I felt shitty. My mouth and throat were dry and my damned thumb throbbed with a burning intensity. I'd had plenty of cuts in my life, some of them fucking serious, but nothing like this fleabite. Once again I wondered if whatever had leaked from the fucking box had somehow managed to get into my system.

'Imagination,' I chided myself. I was in danger of acting like a big kid on this one. Whatever had escaped from the box had been washed away by the tide. Whatever was still in it was sealed up tight. I had just sliced open my thumb and maybe picked up a slight infection. Face it, the *Odorama* was about as hygienic as a sewer.

I had the coach driver drop me a hundred yards short of the approach to the expressway leading to the Rama IV bridge. I cut down a couple of side alleys and fell back out of instinct, just to reassure myself that I wasn't being followed. I wasn't. I changed direction and flagged down an orange jacket. I had the motorcycle taxi take me down river a mile or two. I was going to get into the city through the back door.

I had figured that the CIA's ground troops would be watching the train and bus stations, the approaches to the British Embassy and, just maybe, they would have the sky train stations closest to the embassy covered as well. I wasn't heading for the embassy. Not yet! I had something else to put in place first. After I had paid off my orange jacket, I grabbed a long-tail river taxi and haggled my fare to Banglamphu. The big six-cylinder car engine in the stern of the boat bellowed as we flew up river. It was always a unique experience screaming up the Chao Phraya River with a cowboy driver wielding a flailing naked propeller. Failing light or not, we hurtled along at a rate of knots. The reflected light from the great hotels that lined the shore turned the river to molten metal, and rafts of water hyacinth riding the current dotted our path. We raced past the Grand Palace and went under the Phra Pin Klao Bridge. Here I gave my man specific directions.

I switched my mobile on and tried Sami again. This time he answered in person. I had to shout over the sound of the boat's roaring engine. 'I'm coming in the back way. Five minutes!'

'Okay,' came the reply. The phone vibrated as I finished the call to Sami. It had to be Bernard. I flicked the thing off. I had the fucking box but there were things to do and speaking to that old queen wasn't one of them at that particular moment in time. I'd never known him to be so damned twitchy or demanding. Where I was going, the forces of evil couldn't reach me. I would be safe at Sami's.

The last time I'd been up that way was when Arune had grabbed me as I came over the border from Laos. My boatman found the canal I was looking for and turned off the main river, heading back into the old city. He produced a big torch and began shining it on the water and buildings that crowded in on us. There were few boats on the narrow, ancient waterway. The buildings—old warehouses and sweatshops—crowded in on us. This canal redefined pollution. The stench was something else. It was one spot that definitely wasn't on the tourist agenda. But I was no tourist.

It took five minutes and a bit of backtracking before we found what I'd been looking for. There were no signs and no street numbers as such. I was relying on a daylight memory from years before, translating it into black, white and shades of night. I generously paid the boatman and took my life in my hands, climbing a slimy wooden ladder up onto a high landing. This was the rear entrance to Sami's place.

The metal door was ancient. It didn't look as if it had been opened in half a century. I knew better. I pulled off my cap with its fringe of fake hair and ponytail and thumped on the steel sheath. I didn't want to be mistaken for someone else when it opened. Five seconds after my knuckles beat out their paradiddle, the door opened noiselessly on oiled hinges. The man who met me was carrying an Uzi. The muzzle of the submachine-gun was pointing loosely in my direction. The face above the gun, however, was split into a wide grin. 'Daniel, welcome back. Come in.'

'Greetings, Sami,' I replied, stepping past the man who had been one of my most trusted companions back in the days when I did things in the bush and over the borders. Sami Somsak still did those things, but these days he was an industry in himself. Sami locked the door with a mechanism that pushed six huge bolts into the metal recesses positioned around the heavy metal doorframe. Basically it was the sort of door that you'd expect to find in a bank vault. When he was done, we embraced. We both had our genuine smiley faces on.

It had been a year and a half since Sami Somsak had been to the UK and we'd caught up. Anyone looking at my friend would see a slight, good-looking Thai male of about thirty, a man who always had a smile on his face. In actual fact Sami was almost sixty. He feigned bad English when it suited him to acknowledge anything other than Thai. In reality, his English was perfect and virtually accentless. He also spoke at least half a dozen other languages.

Sami Somsak was a paradox, just like the country that had raised him. There was some Chinese in his racial mix, amongst other things. Once, over a whisky session with me doing all the drinking, I had coined the term The Onion Man for him. Far from being offended, he had just smiled back at me over his mineral water. Sami was made up of layers, each one more complex than the next. I'd maybe penetrated two or three layers in the years I'd known him. However I had always sensed that there were many more hidden beneath those I thought I knew about.

'Come, old friend,' Sami said. 'I still keep a bottle of vintage Jack Daniels just for you.' I fell in step and let him lead me through a labyrinth of corridors off which dozens of doorways opened. Some doors were ajar. In the rooms beyond I could see vats, burners and people wearing chemical masks. 'Business is good?' I asked.

'Yes, Daniel, business is good. And you?'

'I'm busy, but the business is not of my making.'

'You still working for those arseholes?'

'The same, Sami. The very same.'

'That is a pity, Daniel. Join me and let me make you rich. I'd hoped that was why you'd come. It's time you did, and as the Yanks say, "get a life, boy".' Sami's southern drawl sounded genuine. I had to chuckle. We climbed several short flights of stairs and emerged onto a wide mezzanine that looked like the lounge bar of a luxury hotel. The only thing that jibed with that impression was a bank of television monitors showing street and canal scenes. There were conventional video cameras at work as well as infrared scanners. Very sophisticated! A young and very attractive Thai woman sat at a control panel watching the monitors. One of Sami's unspoken edicts was that all the women he chose to surround himself with, be it at work or for pleasure, had to be attractive, if not stunningly beautiful. I admired that in a man.

'We saw you coming. Or at least we saw the boat. Only those who know us come that way,' Sami said, nodding at the bank of monitors as he pulled his communications earpiece out of his left ear and dropped it into his shirt pocket. He put the Uzi on a side table and moved to the elaborate bar. 'Ice?'

'Please,' I responded, lowering my holdall and camera case to the polished wooden floor. Sami had a thing for wood. He loved it, not in a tree-hugger way. He liked it cut, polished, waxed and pampered. While not a Buddhist in any pure sense of the word, he had always espoused the living qualities of wood.

'It lives on after it is cut,' he'd explained to me one night as we'd huddled beneath our ponchos somewhere over the Burmese border, waiting for a meet with some revolutionary faction or other. 'Wood never dies, not even when you burn it. You burn it and you just release its energy and soul to the sky. And then it returns to the earth and grows again.'

At the time, the theory had seemed intriguing, and it had kept my mind off the fucking miserable night we were spending, at least for a second or two. But I'd never forgotten it. Deep thinker was our Sami. I finished admiring the woodwork as he drifted back with the drinks. 'How is Tuk Tuk?'

'Dying,' I replied.

'And Choy?'

'Dead!'

'You?'

'Yes. It was one or the other and I preferred it wasn't me.' I gave

Sami a hard grin as I accepted the cut-glass tumbler of amber liquid he handed me. For himself he had chosen mineral water with ice. It was his usual tipple. My friend Sami was not a drinker.

'Sit and tell me about it,' he said, indicating a nest of thick leather couches.

We sat and I told him everything because if there was one person in that land or any other that I could trust with my life it was Sami Somsak. I had saved his life half a dozen times in the past and he mine an equal number of times. Ours was a brotherhood based on genuine trust. A trust that was uncontaminated by politics, money, lust, envy or anything else. It just was.

It was midnight when we called the party quits. Thanks to Sami's input I had a plan for the next stage of 'operation black box'. Sami had his operator patch me through to Don Don at his embassy apartment. After apologising to him for the lateness of the hour, I asked him to do something for me. He didn't question it. I gave him the number Sami had written down for me and hung up. I then debated whether or not to call Bernard but rejected the notion almost as soon as it arrived. As I'd decided earlier in the day, 'tomorrow is time enough'. Above the mezzanine were the living quarters, or should I say the luxury apartments that Sami called home—one of his many homes at least.

When I was ensconced in a suite that would have done justice to any of the great Bangkok hotels, my host asked me if I wanted company. I refused the offer. I had a feeling that that night I would be dreaming of an angel's kiss.

19

The next morning as I lay in my wide, soft bed, I called Bernard. He was not amused, as always, and as before I cut him off at the pass and went on the attack. It was the best defence. I told him about the CIA team hunting for me down south.

'So how did they know about the submarine and the fucking black box? How did they track me, Bernard?' I wanted to know.

'I don't know, Daniel. We don't have a leak this end, I promise you that,' he was saying in his most reassuring tone. 'We have kept it close, very close.'

'Whitehall is like a damned sieve when it comes to security, Bernard. You know that. Someone, somewhere tipped the bloody Yanks off and now I'm playing fox to a bunch of trigger-happy hounds. What is in the fucking box?'

'I can't tell you that because I don't know,' he replied primly.

'I'm tempted to open it, Bernard,' I responded, playing devil's advocate just for the hell of it. The reaction I got caused me to pull the mobile phone away from my ear.

'Don't, Daniel! For God's sake, don't open it. If you do you're signing your own death warrant. Believe me on this. Please believe me.' Bernard's words tumbled over themselves.

'I'm joking,' I yelled into the phone. 'Just winding you up.'

Bernard went quiet for what seemed like an eternity. When he started talking again his voice was as cold as I'd ever heard it. 'Don't fool around. This is too damned big. Stay where you are until nightfall, then make your way to the embassy.'

'Why wait?' I replied. 'I've got a plan.'

'For God's sake, you're obviously in a safe house. Stay there until dark. We can arrange a pick-up and escort.' He sounded close to panic. I paused a moment. I didn't want the old sod to blow a fuse.

'Okay, Bernard,' I said in what I figured was a voice of resignation. 'I'll stay here until nightfall but then I'll get to the embassy my way. No escorts.'

'Thank you, Daniel,' came the reply. The sheer relief in his voice was obvious. 'Just stay there until dark and then do it your way,' he said. I smiled. Frank Sinatra Swann at Her Majesty's service.

'I'll call you from the embassy,' I said and closed the mobile. I had no intention of waiting for nightfall. I was getting to the embassy that morning but no way was I going to tell Bernard. The old prick was going through menopause or something. Stop! Go! Go! Stop! Did he want the fucking box safe in the embassy or not? I went into the luxurious bathroom to shower. My thumb was throbbing again. The cut was inflamed and red but there was no pus and the bleeding had long stopped. I anointed the gash with bug killer and stuck a fresh plaster on. If it didn't let up I'd get a shot of antibiotics when I hit the embassy.

Back in the bedroom I dressed. So why wasn't I going to wait until dark? Why didn't I organise an escort of military types from Don Don? Of course, they couldn't carry loaded weapons outside the embassy grounds. Why didn't we hire an armoured car to deliver me to the damned embassy? Simple reason was that calling the embassy and arranging for an escort just wasn't the safest way of doing things. In fact, it was probably the most unsafe because it came with a whole bunch of problems. The circus would get too big, too confusing and too prone to detection and failure, simply because it would attract too much of the wrong attention. If the professionals were watching the embassy and waiting for me to turn up, they would read what was going down and act accordingly. Therefore I had to do the unexpected, and sometimes doing the obvious was the most unexpected thing of all. So we were going to do it just the way Sami and I had planned.

Sami and I met on the mezzanine for a breakfast of coffee and croissants. Stage one of our plan was locked in place and it was dead simple, as all good plans should be. I was going to ride into the embassy on a motorbike. Of course, I wasn't going to necessarily look like me.

We had just finished our meal when a pair of young women appeared on the stairs below us, responding to a signal I hadn't picked up on. One of them carried a metal make-up case, the other a small suitcase. It was time to transform the Swann into an ugly duckling or similar. Mr Black Ponytail wasn't coming back this trip. I knew that Thailand abounded with motorcycle taxis, both licensed and unlicensed, so it seemed like the best idea. Orange-vested official taxi riders did big business with mainly Thai clients, and with traffic snarls around Bangkok a fact of life, bikes were a great way to get around.

Okay, at over six feet tall and being pale-faced at that I was going to stand out—or was I? Instead of the typical 125cc bike, I was going to be riding a 750 Suzuki with a low slung seat to reduce my height. It was all a matter of scale. Small Thai, small bike. Big guy, big bike. Unless we sat side by side, the differential wouldn't be obvious at a glance. But there was more. Jeans and T-shirt were okay, but my tan got worked on, as did my moustache. With a helmet on and my dark Ray Bans, plus an orange vest and a passenger on the back, I was going to look the part—at least at a glance.

I was going to head along Ploenchit into Wireless and cruise for the embassy vehicle entrance. Don Don would have the gate open the moment I made the turn into Wireless. Easy, providing the coast was clear. So was it? That was what the midnight call to Don Don had been about. I glanced at my watch. It was 09:00. Time for him to check in and he was on time. Sami's switchboard girl spoke into her headset and a moment later the light on the phone that was sitting on the table in front of me flashed.

Don Don got straight to the point, and he sounded puzzled. 'We've had vehicles cruising Wireless Road overnight, a couple of black SUVs and at least three sedans. There have been a dozen pedestrians we identified as having been in the area since late afternoon yesterday. I ran tapes from earlier in the day and they moved in about 18:00.' The embassy security chief paused. I figured he was fast-forwarding whatever was on his monitor.

'They mixed and matched as singles and in pairs, but definitely the same faces,' he continued. 'Hell, we have footage of one of them speaking into his sleeve, then getting into one of the SUVs. That was at 08:40 this morning. By 08.45 they were all gone.'

'All of them?' I asked.

'Street's virtually empty,' Don Don replied. 'Hardly any pedestrians, not a lot of traffic and no spooks we can see. It's bloody quiet.'

'Thanks,' I said. 'Any change, call me on my mobile. I'll be there within the hour. Just make sure they open the damn gates.'

'Bet on it,' Don Don replied and we hung up.

'What caused them to pull out?' Sami muttered. 'There has to be a reason.'

'We'll figure it out later,' I replied. 'Let's do it.'

'I've got someone doing a little recon,' said Sami, holding up his hand as another call came in. He spoke to the caller for only a matter of seconds.

'I think we're good to go now,' Sami said. 'I'll explain along the way. Can you still remember how to ride a big bike?' He smiled.

Before selling off parts of its compound, the British Embassy used to front onto Ploenchit, virtually under the line of the sky train. The station entrance nearest to the embassy touched down only a matter of yards from the intersection.

We had to figure that anyone left behind would be stationed there to intercept me coming by train. The reason for the last call was that one of Sami's people had just come off the sky train and taken the logical route to the embassy. She saw no one suspicious at the station, crossed at the intersection and walked up Wireless Road past the embassy entrances. Still she saw no one of concern. Then she crossed and came back down the Swiss Embassy side. Nothing! The reason for our recon wasn't that we didn't trust Don Don's evaluation, but rather that Sami didn't know him. He did, however, know his people and I knew Sami.

My passenger was Mary, one of the girls who had made me up. She was dressed in a smart dark business suit with a crisp white blouse. The skirt was very short and showed a mile of beautiful leg that ended in elegantly high-heeled strappy shoes. She looked stunning. 'Perfect to draw attention away from the driver,' said Sami as he helped Mary into the Thai-girl-with-skirt-riding-side-saddle pose and arranged her legs to maximum advantage. My beautiful passenger giggled. The leather holdall was wedged firmly between my lower back and Mary's hip and held on with a bungy cord. 'Go well,' Sami said as he signalled for the roller door to be raised. 'I'll tell your man to expect you in about fifteen minutes.'

'I'll call you when we get there!'

'I'll hear if you don't,' came the reply. 'Call tomorrow night. I'm heading out of town. No mobile where I'm going,' Sami added, slapping my helmet. 'Go!'

Riding side-saddle or not, Mary was the perfect pillion passenger. I was a more than competent motorcycle rider but having an expert passenger was a real plus. When I'd been based in Bangkok I'd owned a big Kawasaki and that had been my standard means of getting about. I was enjoying the ride but apprehensive as to what we'd find on Wireless Road, despite the all clear. It was all looking too damn easy!

From Sami's place in Banglamphu I headed across to Bamrung Muang Road which becomes Rama I and then Ploenchit as it crosses the city. It was virtually a straight run of maybe five miles. Despite heavy traffic we were passing the Siam Centre ten minutes after leaving Sami's. The big bike mightn't have been the most nimble machine around, but it rode well. I didn't even come close to dropping it or Mary.

My heart did a bit of a flip as I made the turn at the lights into Wireless Road.

This is it! I thought. But there wasn't any 'it'! The designated gate was open as promised. Two armed marines were standing just inside, as was Don Don. I rode into the compound and the gates closed. It was something of an anticlimax. Don Don, ever the gentleman, helped Mary down under the hungry eyes of the squaddies. I lifted the bike onto its stand and got off.

In the top of the holdall we'd put a pair of tracksuit trousers. I opened the bag and gave them to Mary. She pulled them on under her skirt in seconds and the leg show was over. I passed her my helmet. She smiled and kissed me on the cheek before putting on the hard hat and straddling the big Suzuki.

'Good rider, Dan,' she said as the rather startled marines realised what was happening and opened the gate. Mary fired the bike, rolled it off its stand and roared back out onto Wireless Road. I laughed at Don Don's expression.

'Sami's people are versatile,' I said. 'Now,' I hefted the leather bag and shouldered it, 'let's get me and this somewhere safe!'

The room Don Don had set aside for me was the back office immediately behind his. It wasn't a normal office but rather a completely sealed space about thirty feet by twenty with a high ceiling. It had been designed as a safe room before such things were commonplace. 'Sealed unit,' Don Don said needlessly as he led me inside. The door was a heavy mother with a submarine-type lip around it and thick rubber gaskets. 'Separate air, scrubbers, the works. Installed way back.' I didn't acknowledge that I knew about the room from my previous life. The furnishings inside were spartan to the extreme. The joint obviously didn't get a lot of use. There was a small desk on one side, a folding cot and a couple of chairs around a card table that sat in the centre of the room. There was a toilet in a screened alcove, a sagging couch and a couple of bookcases stacked with ancient volumes of *Reader's Digest*.

The kitchen alcove set a few feet along the wall from the toilet recess showed a little promise. That was until I noted that the door on the small refrigerator was held open by a strategically placed roll of newspaper. 'Damn, no cold beer,' I thought. There was also a sink with a mirror above it, plus a couple of cupboards and, perhaps a little incongruously, there was a fire-hose reel on the wall beside the door. Whoever had set this place up had thought of everything except comfort. Basically my new home for the moment was the equivalent of an air-raid shelter. I guessed that, apart from when Don Don brought his Miss Friday back for a good old-fashioned bonking, this forgotten, musty bloody hole was sealed up tight to grow dust mites and mould.

'Papers, food and a few beers coming,' my host said. 'By the way, the fridge doesn't work,' he added as he headed out the door. 'Back in a jiffy.' I hadn't heard that expression in years. I deposited the holdall on the floor beside the table and stripped off the orange taxi vest, removing the Walther from the shoulder holster under my T-shirt. I put it on the table as I fished out my mobile phone. There was no signal, which wasn't surprising given I was so deep inside the building.

I returned to the outer office and Don Don directed me to a scrambled land line. He intercepted Janice returning to the office with supplies and took them into the safe room while I made the call.

Bernard sounded almost stunned to hear from me. Whether he was joyed, overjoyed or ecstatic I had no idea. Thing was, I had done my job as I had understood it, apart from sitting on that damned box until the experts got there. 'They'll be several hours away,' Bernard told me when he'd gained some sort of composure. The conversation was short and there wasn't a single congratulatory word. I went back into my cave, shutting the door behind me. I felt a childish hurt. Teacher hadn't praised me for being a clever bugger.

There was a newspaper, a six-pack of cold Singha and food, such as it was. The embassy sandwiches and sausage rolls tasted as if they had been made a month before in the UK and sent out surface mail. I settled myself at the table. It tilted alarmingly, one leg measurably shorter than the others. I went and got a couple of copies of *Reader's Digest* from the nearest bookcase to balance things up. I proceeded to drink three beers and eat everything in sight. Regulations aside, I lit a cigarette while I scanned the paper. The safe room wasn't fitted with a smoke alarm although there were sprinklers set in the high ceiling.

A huge full-colour photograph of the Ruby Buddha dominated the front page of the *Thai Post*. The article on page two told of a mysterious European who had appeared with the buddha, and how he had vanished immediately afterwards. 'Spooky,' I muttered to myself. The way the reporter had phrased things, it sounded as if the mysterious me had been some sort of supernatural entity. Whatever, the monks at Pha To had their buddha back. Maybe that would put me in line for some luck of the good kind. Although my thumb still throbbed, the swelling and redness had gone down. It appeared I would live so I took that as a sign of good things to come. I leaned back in my chair and sat staring at the image of the buddha. My thoughts turned to Tuk Tuk and how close he had come to sainthood and immortality. Where would things have ended up if I hadn't saved his life all those years before?

20

I woke up lying across the table surrounded by pages of newspapers and the debris of my meal. I felt like gritty shit. I glanced at my watch. It was almost 16:00. I'd been out of it for most of the day. I used the toilet and caught sight of myself in the mirror as I washed up. The make-up Mary and her friend had applied at Sami's was streaked; I looked like a pantomime disaster, a sort of brown and white minstrel. A shower would have to wait. Instead I made do with scrubbing all my visible bits in the washbasin. At least there was plenty of hot water. I was now seriously hungry. I drank one of my remaining beers. It was warm but it was wet.

I did some housekeeping, tossing the rubbish and tidying the newspaper. I hadn't read a lot of it, so I cracked open the last beer and started a serious read. The sort of read only seriously bored people can do. There was a smallish piece on page four about suspected pirate activity off the coast beyond Ranong. Local fishermen had recovered several bodies and body parts from the sea. One particularly grisly find had been made when a large Tiger shark caught in a net was opened up. Inside had been a partially digested human head. 'Nice!' I muttered.

About then I hoped Don Don would come bouncing in the door with more beer, more food and the expert crew who were coming to take charge of my lead casket. Then I heard the door open and a voice beyond it. That was when I knew that no matter what good deeds I had performed over the last few days, my karma was going to be all bad.

'Is that the international man of mystery?'

What the hell was she doing here? Somehow my heart had made it into the back of my throat, jamming my voice box so I couldn't scream. 'Fuck,' I thought. Dracula had arrived in the crypt. I averted my eyes so I wouldn't go blind and fumbled to make the sign of the cross. It was a childish thing on my part. Sort of self-defence for idiots or something.

'Bugger off, Sylvia!' I finally managed to croak out.

'Oh, poor little Danny boy. Haven't you got anyone to play with, all alone in this big cold box?' That was the thing about ex-wives: they could get under your skin without even trying. It was second nature to them. Sylvia Swann, née Dixon, had been my only attempt at matrimonial bliss. Sylvia was a scientist employed by the Ministry of Defence. She was a specialist in things bacterial and chemical which was why, right at that moment, I was extremely grateful that I hadn't succumbed to my childish impulses and opened that damned box. I was also glad that it would shortly be gone from my life, just like Sylvia. She'd entered my life like a thunderbolt and vanished in a tempest.

Sylvia and I met at a mutual friend's wedding and discovered we basically shared the same employer. We dated, and in an indecently short time, discovered we made spectacular sex. We married, had more spectacular sex and then the wheels fell off. It had been an incredibly short-lived attempt at creating eternal wedded bliss for a couple of reasons. Part of the problem was Sylvia's inability to understand the nature of what I did, because she didn't bloody well know and I couldn't tell her. All she knew was that I, like her, 'worked for the Government' and I seemed to be always away doing 'it', whatever 'it' was. We probably could have survived that, but the other major factor was my inability to keep my hands and other body parts off other women. Result: a series of dirty big fights followed by a quick dirty little divorce.

'Hello, darling former wife,' I said finally. I looked up just as Sylvia's lips brushed my cheek.

'And you, sweetie,' she replied. 'Nice décor,' she added, wrinkling her nose as she looked around the room. 'Early trash with just a hint of imperial Victoriana, wouldn't you say?'

'You're the fucking expert,' I said and immediately regretted the opening I'd just delivered to her the moment it left my lips. She pounced like a damned mongoose going for a cobra.

'No, dearly departed, you're the fucking expert if you remember rightly,' she said almost sweetly. 'Anyway, enough of the foreplay. I'm here to examine that little black box you're guarding.' Sylvia turned away, eyes seeking out the object of her interest. As she moved her long, silver–blonde locks shimmered in the fluorescent light. Tall, almost five feet eleven, slim as a fashion model and with a face that could melt a thousand hearts when she so chose, my dear ex was stunning. Fresh from God knows how many hours in a presumably military aircraft, she looked as if she had stepped out of a beauty parlour. She turned and waved two people into the room. I could see a bunch more hovering in the office behind them.

Garston Headley was first into the secure room. Garston always looked like a rumpled garden gnome. He was basically a cross between Bill Oddie and Worzel Gummidge in both the looks and grooming stakes. Garston had been born that way. I remembered at our wedding that he, as a close friend of Sylvia's, had been an usher in the chapel. Even when issued with a cleaned and pressed tux straight from the hire shop, he had managed to reduce it to a rumpled, crumpled and stained mess in five minutes flat. With wild hair, a beard that could—and probably did—hide a battalion of paras, and his silly little John Lennon glasses, he looked like the proverbial mad scientist he in fact was.

'Good afternoon, Daniel,' Garston said formally as he advanced. He put down the large, white hard-shelled box he was carrying with a bright orange biohazard symbol on it and gave me his usual dead-fish handshake. We shook as Sylvia ushered the second figure in my direction.

'Helen, this is Daniel Swann. Never be alone with him if you value your virginity, or what's left of it.' Helen was a blusher and on her, a blush looked good, very good. She was petite, with big dark eyes and dark brown hair cut in a cute pageboy style. Apart from her glowing cheeks, the rest of her complexion was pure cream. I would have said Welsh without hearing her speak.

'Pleased to meet you,' she said in a voice that echoed the sounds of the vales. Her hand was cool and smooth but it twitched in mine like a small, frightened rodent. I released it after an indecently long time and watched it flee back to its owner's side.

'And you,' I replied, trying not to let Sylvia's smirk get to me.

'I presume what we are seeking is in that cute little handbag of yours?' Sylvia pointed to the holdall her X-ray vision had located on the floor by the desk. 'Right as always,' I replied with absolutely no inflection in my voice. Sylvia flashed me a glance to see if I was winding her up.

Satisfied I wasn't, she gave the order for her people to mask and glove up. They were as slick as surgeons at that. The masks weren't standard surgical ones but rather industrial-strength masks with filters fitted. When they were done, Sylvia nodded to Garston and The Gnome went to do her bidding. He picked up the bag and carefully placed it on the table.

'You?' Sylvia queried, tapping the front page of the newspaper she had gathered off the table. There was the photo of the Ruby Buddha and the headline MYSTERY MAN RETURNS RUBY BUDDHA TO PHA TO.

'I confess,' I replied almost smugly.

'How very noble of you, Dan,' Sylvia purred through her mask. 'Now go away and let us get down to work, darling ex.' Garston had lifted the box from the pack and was carefully manoeuvring it onto the desk. The bright slash of fresh lead against the dull aged colour of the rest of the box caused him to pause. The Gnome looked up and beamed a silent question at me from behind the thick lenses of his glasses.

'Spear head went in,' I said. 'When I removed it some damned stuff leaked out and I gashed my thumb.'

'Shit!' Sylvia snapped and Garston's hands came off the box in double-quick time.

'I resealed it with lead,' I added as both scientists turned towards me.

'What about the material that leaked out?' Sylvia wanted to know.

'We had a heavy sea running. Waves washed over it. Whatever it was it's in the fucking Andaman,' I replied.

'Thank God,' Sylvia muttered, a look of relief momentarily flashing across her eyes. Then it was gone, replaced by one of concern. 'Did you get any of that stuff on you or in the cut?'

'I don't know,' I replied. Suddenly I was scared. The look in my former wife's eyes was bad enough, but Garston's was worse. He was close to panic. 'What the fuck was it?'

'Bad,' Sylvia said.

'What fucking bad?' I snapped. Ice had reformed down my spine and my thumb was burning. The mind is a powerful thing. 'What?' I repeated almost shouting now. Sylvia shook her head. She wasn't saying nuthin'.

I felt a rage building, driven by a hundred percent pure fear. Was I infected and if so, with what? I wanted to grab my beautiful ex-wife by the throat and shake her. I took a step towards her and she moved back.

She was shaking her head, silver hair shimmering, one gloved hand held high, palm flat towards me. She was scared, and not just of me. In the stormy debris of our dying marriage I had never once hit her. Now wasn't a good time to start. I took a deep breath and stepped back, fists clenched at my sides. 'Dan, let's find out if you're infected,' Sylvia was saying.

'Test?' Garston asked. She nodded and The Gnome bent to open a briefcase. He produced a small instrument case from which he removed a syringe. He fiddled with the damned thing for a moment, then handed it to Sylvia. She took the hypodermic from her assistant and came towards me.

'I need a blood sample.'

'Damn,' I muttered. I hated needles but the thought of being infected by some damned biological weapon or whatever was worse. I sank into a chair and rested my left arm on a side table. Sylvia made me do the fist thing and I barely felt the needle go in. When she had done her blood-letting she passed the syringe back to Garston. Without a word he went off with it in search of some piece of equipment or other that was still in the outer office. Sylvia reached for my right hand and carefully peeled the plaster off my thumb. She examined the gash closely, nodding to herself.

'How long since you removed the spear head and cut yourself?' she wanted to know. I did the calculations and came up with forty-eight hours, give or take. I told her and a look of relief crossed her face. 'Okay. If you'd been infected you'd have been dead twenty-four hours ago. This is just a low-grade infection, muck on the spear.'

'Thank Christ,' I muttered, feeling the ice along my backbone turn to water.

'Thank Christ,' I repeated. 'What the hell is that stuff?'

'I can't tell you.'

'Come on, Syl!' I implored. She shook her head and turned as Garston came back into the room. He was also shaking his head.

'All clear,' he said.

'Okay, Danny.' Sylvia moved to one side and rummaged in one of her team's cases. She returned a moment later carrying a fresh plaster and a vial of pills. She peeled the plaster and smoothed it in place before she tipped half a dozen capsules from the vial into the palm of her hand and transferred them to mine. 'Two daily with water and that should take care of any residue infection.'

'Thank you, doctor,' I said, pocketing the capsules.

'My pleasure, darling ex,' Sylvia replied. 'We will now run a few tests before we box up your package and get it home in one piece. We might catch up later. In the meantime, Daniel, go and do whatever it is you do and let us get on with it.' She turned to re-evaluate what lay on the desk in front of her. Garston was unpacking what looked like a mini vacuum cleaner, some sort of chemical sniffer, I assumed.

'So you're not planning on opening the thing?' I asked.

'Absolutely not!' Sylvia said, shaking her head which made her sensational hair shimmer. 'We are here to check the exterior for microscopic leaks, contain the whole thing and go home. Now you go!'

'Going,' I replied. I was truly relieved that I was no longer a candidate for the black plague or whatever the hell was in the box, but I wanted to see more of Sylvia. Strange that!

I started to replace the clothes Garston had removed from the holdall but Sylvia held up her hand to stop me. 'We need to run the sniffer over those,' she said. 'When we've done we'll put them in the outer office.' I didn't argue.

I gathered up the Walther and my holster rig and headed for the door. 'See you for a drink afterwards,' I said to the Welsh girl as I passed her. She was crouching on the floor, a case of serious-looking implements open in front of her.

'Not bloody likely,' snapped Sylvia over her shoulder as she answered for the youngster, who immediately turned into a burning beacon. 'Go!'

'Gone,' I replied as I went out the door.

Seated or standing in Don Don's office were half a dozen men, all of them in civilian clothes. The clothes did little to hide their military air. The weapons that several of them held sort of gave the game away. The owners of the hardware had the watchful eyes of true professionals. The big boys were here. No one said a word. There was another technical type squatting over an equipment case, obviously preparing something for Garston and Sylvia to play with.

Hey, hey, the gangs all here, I thought. 'Have a nice day folks,' I said to the room at large as I made my way through the happy throng and stepped out into the corridor where Don Don was waiting along with more men with guns. I couldn't help thinking that me and my little

Walther had done a damned good job of getting us and our package to this point, especially if this was what the damned powers that be figured they needed to protect it. I stopped to slip on my holster rig and hide my gun under my jacket. Walking the streets of Bangkok holding a pistol was not a good look and would probably get me killed.

'Same apartment,' Don Don said as he handed me the key to number eleven. I fell in step as he started walking me towards the stairs. 'Good job, Daniel. Must be something important in that box.'

'Or very dangerous,' I said. 'Sylvia will leave my bag in your office when she has finished checking it.'

'No problem. We've got a couple of staff staying in the apartments. I'll have one drop it in to you when they finish for the day.'

I thanked Don Don and started up the stairs, leaving him standing in the corridor. I was guessing that neither of us would ever know what was in the box. Not unless something went very, very wrong, of course. I didn't really want to give power to the thought, so I pushed it away. 'Get behind me, Satan,' I muttered as I emerged into the evening air. The smog level was up and the air was blue.

I could have used one of the staff entrances but I didn't. Instead I went out through the main gate. In the street I turned down Wireless Road. I wasn't really worried about the CIA colours being back on watch. That part of the game was over now. Why they had vanished when they did would probably remain a mystery. Okay, my playmates and I had caused them serious casualties out in the Andaman and left them with bloodied egg on their faces, but the prize was gone. The dead were just casualties of a black war. God only knows if they would try for the box and its contents when the heavy mob went to take it back to the UK, or wherever.

I kept my eyes open but there was no sign of anyone following. I detoured into the CDS to get some supplies. I figured I'd get to the apartment, shower and have food and a beer or two. I might check out the Coro Club tonight, I thought, check in with Sami tomorrow and in a day or two, perhaps head back down to Phuket to spend a few days with Geezer and make a return engagement with the delicious Nan. It sounded like a workable plan. Funny thing about plans, though, was that there was always someone who would do their best to stuff them up.

21

'Get down here fast!' The voice was Don Don's. He didn't say anything else and hung up in my ear. I rolled over and glared at the digital clock on the beside table. The time was 04:40. Not a good time for me or for many other people. I nudged Babs awake.

'Whash?' she wanted to know. Oh yeah. Babs. Well, it went like this. After I'd had my shower the previous evening I did go down to the Coro Club and, as luck would have it, I ran straight into her. Her man was out of town again. We didn't stay in the club. It was down to a restaurant she knew along the street and then back to number eleven for an exhausting romp. As I'd discovered the time before, she was damned near tireless. No wonder her guy spent so much time out of the country recuperating.

'Gotta go,' I told her. 'Let yourself out. Make sure the door is locked, okay?'

'Okay,' she mumbled as she buried her face back in the pillow.

I quickly showered, dressed and hit the street. I didn't bother flagging down a *tuk tuk*. I was at the embassy in ten minutes and I barely needed to flash my ID. A white-faced Don Don was waiting for me in the foyer.

'What's up?'

'There was a chemical release.'

'Shit!'

'Apparently the box was compromised. Someone bumped the table and it hit the floor. The lead seal broke. Doctor Dixon came to the door, ordered a total lock down and shut herself and the other two inside. The room is completely sealed,' he reported. 'Haven't even got communications, but the technicians are working at getting a phone in to them.'

'Oh boy!' That was all I could think of to say. I should have warned them about the table leg but hadn't thought about it. That part was done but now, what use was I going to be down here? We arrived at the basement corridor to find hawk-eyed armed guards standing around.

In Don Don's office, however, there was a hive of activity. Desks had been pushed against the wall and an inflatable plastic hazard shield had been erected over and around the door to the bomb shelter. Two figures in chemical suits were working a large drill in the makeshift airlock, attempting to breech the wall to the right of the door. Technicians hovered around. There were oxygen and gas bottles, a web of hoses and all sorts of other paraphernalia.

'Carter, Major, 22 SAS.' The grim-faced man who stepped forward was middle-aged and of average build, dressed in denims and a leather jacket. I recalled him from earlier. We exchanged firm grips. 'Out of our depth here,' the major said, nodding at the plastic airlock over the inner door. 'We were told to protect the box, its contents and Doctor Dixon's team, and take everything back to the UK. Apparently we now have a biological substance on the loose.'

'I don't know what I can add, Major,' I replied.

'Dave,' he replied.

'Dave,' I amended. 'I'm Dan. I just acquired the box on orders. I have no idea what the hell is in it.' For a moment my mind played the Dave-and-Dan game but I forced myself to let that one go. Having a trilogy of Don Don, Dan Dan and Dave Dave was pushing everything to the limit.

'We gathered from the doctor that the box fell and a quantity of the contents escaped. She called Code Red. Needless to say we have gone for total containment as option one. We have no idea whether or not they are contaminated, or alive or dead on the other side of the wall. Apparently the telephone that was in there up until a few weeks ago was appropriated for another office.' Carter gave a wry smile. 'All about timing!'

'Yeah,' I agreed. The thought that Sylvia, Garston and Helen, the little Welsh flower, might be dead hit me like a truck. I thought maybe they would be sick, but dead! Did Sylvia have an antidote for whatever it was that was in that fucking box? 'So what can I do?' I asked Carter.

'Make any relevant suggestions as they come to you,' replied the SAS officer. 'God knows we need all the help we can get!' Shoulder to shoulder the pair of us moved to stand beside the airlock. Heavy, clear plastic sheeting had been used to create the tent around the door. The two technical types working inside had a whole bunch of apparatus with them and I could see a telephone handpiece. The connecting wire came out of the airlock wall through a thick plastering of duct tape. The stuff had been used to join all the plastic sheets and seal the openings.

'Duct tape was the hero on the day,' I muttered. Carter snorted in agreement. The guys working the drill had removed the large diameter core cutter from the hole in the wall and one was using a screwdriver to extract a disk of metal sheathing from the cutter blade.

'Good or bad, they built that room to withstand a neutron bomb,' the SAS officer said as the cutter went back into the cavity and started grinding away again. While one of the pair inside the tent worked the drill, the other was preparing a bell-shaped cone of thick plastic. He cut the tip off at the pointed end, passed the phone cord through and connected the handpiece, leaving it in the cone. Once again the duct tape was in play. The man working the drill stopped and pulled it clear to remove another disk which wasn't metal but appeared to be insulation of some sort.

The man with the large drill removed the cutter head and put the drill to one side. He picked up a radically different device. 'Tube drill,' Carter said, answering my silent question. 'Same dimension as the cutter head. Battery powered. Just push it straight on through. Designed for just this sort of situation.'

The man with the tube drill finished attaching the cutting head and carefully positioned the drill in the plastic cone along with the telephone while the second technician held the cone. A glue gun was used to liberally coat the flange around the cone's open end with a sealant before the cone was carefully positioned over the hole. The flange was pushed flat against the wall and, while it was still supported by one of the technicians, the other did his duct-tape trick, using big slabs of tape to completely surround the flange edge. In less than a minute the cone was well and truly fixed into position.

The rubberised plastic of the cone was flexible and, after a little juggling, the tube drill was in position and grinding away on the last section of wall. I drew a deep breath. Would Sylvia and the others still be alive? And if alive, would they be infected with whatever the hell it was that was in that damn box? There was a faint clatter and one of the technicians at the hole turned and gave Carter the thumbs up. The drill had gone through. The phone handpiece followed. Carter turned and reached for the duplicate handset that one of his unsmiling juniors handed to him. He motioned me to stand beside him and turned the handset so I could hear better.

'Doctor Dixon?'

'I'm here,' came the reply. I felt my heart flip.

'Are you infected?'

'I don't think so. We realised what was happening and I think we acted quickly enough to neutralise the release.'

'What's the next stage?'

'We have to stay isolated for twenty-four hours. Call in the Chemical Response Unit. Organise food, please, and can I speak to Daniel?'

'Roger that. Chem Response is already airborne. Here's Mr Swann!'

Carter handed me the headset and went to where Don Don was hovering.

'Hi, Sylvia.'

'Hello, darling ex,' she replied, sounding tired and strained. 'That darned flimsy table collapsed and dumped the box on the floor. It landed on a corner and the lead patch you put on it broke free. Some of the contents got out.'

'What the hell is it, Sylvia?' There was a long pause. I could picture her debating whether or not to answer. I had no doubts that she and her team had been sworn to secrecy and threatened with all sorts of dire consequences. I decided to help her out. 'Sylvia, this is no fucking time for bloody Whitehall politics. Whatever is in that room is obviously deadly in the extreme. If you don't make it, what happens then?'

Despite the crude telephone setup, I heard her catch her breath. I knew she was a brave lady but no one wants to die, especially to some damned bacteria or biological nerve gas. That was generally a really shitty way to go and, in most cases, extremely painful and slow enough to give you plenty of time to enjoy the agony.

'What the fuck is it?'

'It's an anthrax variant,' she said at last. Anthrax! A shiver went up my spine. Of all the dirty tricks in the dirty-trick book, that was potentially one of the worst. I'd gained more than a passing respect for it back in spy school.

'That's not so bad,' I said, trying to remember all I could about the damned stuff. 'You'll have had your shots against it.'

'Yes,' she replied and then she hesitated long enough for me to think she'd stopped bloody breathing. 'But this isn't an ordinary strain, Dan. It's a hybrid. The vaccine won't work on it.'

'Shit,' I muttered, looking for a clutching straw to send her way. 'After fifty years sitting at the bottom of the ocean surely it's dead by now?'

'No, Dan. This is as hot as hell,' Sylvia replied. 'But I think we've managed to neutralise it.' It was then I knew exactly what they had done in there to kill the bug.

'Water, right?' I said. I remembered how she had reacted when I'd told her about the release on the boat and the heavy swells that hit us, washing the bug away.

'Very good, Detective Dan. Good old H_2O! Water kills it dead. When the box hit the floor and we saw the spores being released we got the fire hose going fast—set it on fine spray and drenched the whole place. Then we filled the hazard case with water and put the box inside.'

'Hope you closed the lid and locked it!' I muttered.

Sylvia gave one of her throaty chuckles at that. 'You can bet on that,' she said. 'Now we just have to wait and see if we're dead or not. Can you organise some dry blankets? It's cold in here and bloody damp.'

'Definitely,' I responded. 'And, Syl?'

'What?'

'I'm glad you made it.'

'So am I, Dan. So am I.' I handed the phone to one of Sylvia's technical bods who was hovering, waiting to speak to the boss, then I went to find Carter.

The SAS man was in the corridor with Don Don and the usual suspects. A trolley laden with plates of sandwiches and large urns of coffee and tea had appeared. How the supplies were going to be passed through into the inner sanctum I had no idea. I grabbed a coffee and a sandwich and joined them. One of Sylvia's crew was in the corridor pulling on a chemical suit, and a couple of Carter's men were unrolling a fire hose from a reel further down the corridor. A third SAS man was using the point of a wicked-looking stiletto to perforate a length of plastic tubing.

Now I had an idea of how they were going to get in and out of the bomb shelter without bringing any bugs out with them.

Don Don, Carter and I stood at the office door with our drinks while one of Sylvia's team rigged the strip of plastic tubing across the inside of the airlock tent.

The thin diameter fire hose was a little thicker than a normal garden hose, and with the help of more of the ubiquitous duct tape, the nozzle had been fitted to the open end of the plastic pipe. The other end had been blocked off. The airlock was being turned into a decontamination chamber.

The system worked, and within minutes the prisoners in the secure room were being fed and watered. Blankets were being fetched. Now all Sylvia and her team had to do was sit and wait for twenty-four hours to see if they lived or died. I needed a cigarette and headed for the wide-open spaces up above. I was surprised to find Carter sitting on bench out in the dawn sun. He was smoking and that, too, surprised me. He waved me over and I accepted the cigarette and light he offered.

'Stress smoker,' he said by way of apology or something.

'Goes with the job,' I replied.

'Tell me,' he said after we had been sitting in silence for a couple of minutes, 'were you ever in the squadron?'

'Never even in the army,' I replied, shaking my head. 'I had a different upbringing, but I did spend some time down in Herefordshire with your mob.' In fact, I once thought of trying out for 22 SAS but I didn't like the idea of jumping out of a perfectly good aeroplane. I also wasn't big on marching for mile after boring gut-busting mile, lugging an overloaded Bergen containing three times my body weight in ammunition and kit. All of which was par for the course with the boys from 22 squadron.

'Should have joined,' the SAS officer said. 'You'd have enjoyed it. Comradeship, good friends, lot of laughs at times. I would imagine what you are involved in is a pretty lonely existence.'

'How much do you know about what I'm involved in?'

'I've read the file,' came the reply. 'You're good, one of the very best, but one day that luck will run out. It does to us all, but at least in the squadron we've got people watching our backs. In your line of business there's no one there when you whistle.'

Carter stood and ground out his cigarette. I had nothing to say because he was absolutely right. He clapped a hand on my shoulder, turned and went back to the bowels of the embassy while I sat and pondered my bleak existence.

22

'Bernard, why was the British Government giving the fucking Japanese something like this when we were at war with them?'

Bernard was silent. The time for the truth, or some of it, had come and it was totally against the nature of Sir Bernard Randolph Sinclair to dabble in the truth. Eventually he answered, but it wasn't the answer I wanted to hear.

'We'll discuss this when you return,' came the prim reply when he eventually found his voice. 'Let us just say that there was a very good reason, and it is not up to you or I to presume at this point in time. You have accomplished what you were sent to do. Render what assistance you can to the people on the ground. Goodbye.'

The phone went dead in my ear. I flicked it off and dropped it into my jacket pocket. The implications of what Bernard had not said were absolutely fucking off the wall. Our side had developed some sort of super anthrax strain during the war, and in the latter months, as the fighting in Europe was drawing to its inevitable conclusion, our lot had been in the process of handing the Japs a very potent weapon. It had been just dumb bad luck that the fucking sub had been bombed. Had the super bacteria been promised to the Japs to provide them with their one last shot at the Americans?

A cold finger ran down my spine. Maybe this was supposed to have been the great out-of-the-lab experiment, like the fucking 'A' bomb the Yanks dropped. They didn't have to drop it when they did. History has shown that clearly. The war was all but over. They simply wanted to see just how their new toy worked on living human flesh, and not just on shop dummies, cadavers, cattle and sheep. Maybe the Japs had been planning to use the bacteria to commit mass *hara-kiri*? Maybe this? Maybe fucking that?

I'd made the call to Bernard from one of the outside offices on the second floor. I turned, my mind churning over the ramifications of what I'd just learned as I went back down to the basement to check on Sylvia and the others. It was now 14:09. They were getting close to the twelve-hour mark. If something was going to show, it had to show soon.

There was no sign that any of the prisoners in the vault had been infected, but they still had to sit out the full incubation period. While we waited for the all clear, I took advantage of Sylvia's state of mind. Her relief at not being infected had put her in a near-euphoric mood. She agreed to give me a full briefing on the bug. I wanted to be fully armed with all the facts on the nasty little beast when I went head to head with Sir Bernard.

'Bacillus anthracis in its normal form is nasty, but it's not the great hazard most people think. Not with today's vaccines, especially if you're prepared,' Sylvia was saying. 'You've got three ways of catching it: through the skin, as in cuts and abrasions, inhaling it or ingesting it through the gut. Inhalation is regarded as the most dangerous method of contamination, with the highest probability of death running at about ninety-five percent.'

'Shit, that high?'

'That high,' she repeated. 'Air burst, aerosol sprays, crop dusters, those types of delivery systems are the most logical and easiest for both terrorist strikes and the military for that matter.' I had visions of Ranch Hand, the Agent Orange spray campaign carried out in Vietnam, but instead of those chemicals, these aircraft were spraying anthrax. It wasn't a settling image.

'The thing about this particular variation is that it can lie dormant in a vacuum, apparently for some time. Normal anthrax can live in the soil for years but, seemingly, this one is a sleeper. It simply shuts itself down and wakes only when exposed to oxygen,' Sylvia continued. 'There are four phials of the spore in the box. We must assume that the head of the spear gun broke one. Whether or not the salt water cleaned it out completely we can't know, but it seems likely that the hot lead might have fractured at least one more of them.'

'I hope it did in the whole lot,' I exclaimed. 'We don't need this crap.'

'I agree but we have it, Daniel, and I have to help deal with it.'

The quality of the phone connection and thickness of her mask couldn't hide the resolve in her voice. 'What makes this hybrid so much more dangerous is its size. The spores are much smaller than the normal strain, which means that they disperse in the air that much more easily and over a wider area. Plus, they devour oxygen molecules as nutrition and multiply faster than rabbits.'

'Very nasty!' I replied. I really did need to know as much as I could about this bloody bacteria before I met up with Bernard back in London. I had the feeling that the old queen was jammed up and when he decided to take a shit, it was going to be in my direction. Knowledge was power and I needed that in spades. But more than anything else, I needed to know what Sylvia had on the history of this bug, what was behind it and why, at the end of the day, it was so special that a whole bunch of people had died to get it. I decided to fish a bit further.

'How much do you know about what I'm involved in?'

'Darling, if you remember that's one of the things that screwed us. I don't know what you're doing or why or where. I was just told that you would be waiting for us with a sealed package containing the hybrid anthrax, which you didn't even know you had.'

'Okay.' I lapsed into silence for a moment. 'I'm one of the good guys, Sylvia,' I said, detecting a snort of disbelief at the other end of the line. I chose to ignore it. 'My job was to fetch and carry that damn stuff and make sure no one stopped me.'

'Did they try?'

'Oh yes, they tried,' I replied.

'Did people die?'

'A lot.'

'I knew that I wouldn't like what you did, Dan. That's one of the reasons I couldn't stay the course.'

'The thought of me killing people?'

'No idiot. The thought of you being killed! It wasn't the screwing around, Dan. Believe me, I would have cured you of that if we'd had a normal relationship.'

'Yeah,' I muttered. 'Change the subject. What do you know about the history of this bloody stuff? The who, why, where and how the hell it ended up here.'

Before Sylvia could answer, Don Don appeared in the doorway and with him was a whole set of new faces—tired faces belonging to people who had just flown a very long way.

'Chem Response have arrived,' I told Sylvia. 'I imagine things will get a little hectic. Can we continue this later?'

'I don't see why not, Dan. If you've got 007 to kill, you've obviously got security clearance to the moon and back.' She wasn't laughing and she wasn't joking. There was more than an edge of bitterness in her voice, along with fatigue.

'Later,' I said, handing the telephone handpiece to the newcomer standing at Don Don's shoulder. He nodded his thanks and got straight down to business. It was time for me to exit stage left. My presence most certainly was no longer required at Ground Zero. Don Don fell in step with me.

'You staying around for a while?' he asked.

'Thought I'd stay a couple of days and then head back to Phuket for a while. I've got some leave coming up,' I replied, trying to focus on something, anything other than my ex-wife.

'The apartment's yours as long as you need it. Maybe we can catch a drink or a meal later?' Don Don gave me a sheepish grin. 'Janice would probably come with us if we do the meal thing. We're sort of involved,' he admitted.

I feigned surprise and wondered if Babs was as on for dinner as she was for sex. I also wondered if Don Don and Janice knew Babs's old man. It was a sure thing they did, given the small expat community centred around the embassy. Maybe asking her would be too much of a risk. I decided I would do it solo. Anyway, I told Don Don okay to a meal, and we arranged to meet at the apartments at seven.

I watched the activity in the security office for a moment or two as the new team got ready to enter the inner sanctum. Carter and his men had been relegated back to the role of hired gunslingers. I waved him farewell and got a casual salute in return. I would head back to the apartment, have a shower and catch up on a few winks. I wondered if Babs had woken up and made it to work. If not, I could rule out sleep.

23

I called Sami as I walked back to Soi Chitlom but only got his voice mail. He was still out of range. I'd try again later. I doubled back a few times but no one was following me. I entered the foyer of the apartment block without stopping. The same bored security guard as before was at the podium. I still wanted to kick the bastard's arse. I strangled that impulse and took the lift up to my floor.

The door to number eleven was ajar and the lights were on. Babs was either still in the place, or she had gone and left it open or, third alternative, someone else was in there. I slipped the Walther into my right hand and eased the door open with my left. I went in fast and low, moving left as I did so in case someone was waiting behind the door. They weren't, and Babs was still there.

My beautiful playmate was lying naked in the middle of the floor. The tiles under and around her had caught her body's supply of blood and created a huge dark puddle. 'Oh, Christ!' I physically stumbled. 'Oh, God!' I was calling on all the deities from my Catholic upbringing, but none could help Babs and I doubted they could help me anymore either.

Babs's head sat upright on its severed stump on the glass-topped coffee table. The beautiful green eyes were wide and blank and there was blood on her lips and trickling down her chin. Someone had repositioned the table so it sat right where the ceiling light could best illuminate the macabre centrepiece.

I can't remember how long I was locked there off balance but I forced myself to do what I had to. There was the taste of sour bile in my throat and sinuses, but the charge of pure adrenaline followed closely behind. I hit each room in the apartment in sequence, fast and eager to stitch whoever I found full of holes, knowing in my gut that the killer was long gone. But I had to check, had to hope, because I knew the implications of the ghastly tableaux in the lounge were going to spin me right out when I stopped moving and shock set in.

When my circuit of the apartment brought me back to the lounge I closed the door, locked it and went back to squat in front of the coffee table.

Babs's face was the colour of blue-tinged chalk. Her eyes were impossibly wide open. Her lips were pulled back to show her teeth in a ghastly death grin. Whoever had killed her had positioned a Bangkok telephone book behind the head to keep it from falling over. I stood and turned to look at the body.

The wound that severed the head had been clean. A razor-sharp blade, heavy enough and used with practised skill, had sliced through muscle and vertebrae with equal ease. Bone gleamed white amidst the deep red of the severed neck muscles. The blood pooled like black oil on the white tiles. There was so much blood.

I looked beyond the body. There was a blood spray up the wall beside the door leading into the main bedroom. The door was open. The killer had perhaps been pressed against that wall when Babs had walked into the lounge. He had grabbed her from behind and done the business, pivoting her as he grabbed her and slashed her throat, one hand tangled in her hair, the other pulling his blade right to left through her neck, front to back. He must have been left-handed. Killing stroke made, he had then simply pushed the body away from him and left it to bleed on the floor while he arranged the head in its macabre display.

I got to my feet and went to the bathroom, this time to check on other things. The tiled floor panel which hid the safe seemed undisturbed. In the main bedroom nothing that I could see had been touched. My bag sat in the bottom of the wardrobe where I had left it. The computer was still in its padded side pocket. This most certainly hadn't been a robbery. I looked around the room. Babs's clothes were draped over the back of the chair by the bed, just as she had left them.

'Who and why?' I muttered. 'Why?' I slid the wardrobe door closed and went back into the lounge. I sank into one of the two-seaters and just sat. I didn't look at the head on the table—I would see that forever. I'd turned my mind inwards and was trying to find the invisible and decipher the unknown. Why Babs? It wasn't the CIA way to extract cheap revenge using an innocent. They could play the roughest game in town, but not like this.

I retrieved my phone and tried Sami again. I left an urgent message on his answering machine. I was going to need his help to clean up this mess. Then I was going to have to find whoever did it and exact total and absolute revenge, not only for Babs's sake but also for my own.

Revenge was a noble concept, or in this case, a noble emotion. I remembered people telling me it was a negative emotion, a waste of energy, bad karma, blah, blah. It might have been so in the world they lived in, but in my world of shadows and demons there was nothing sweeter.

Avoiding looking at Babs I got up off the couch and went into the kitchen. If ever I needed a drink it was now. I opened the fridge door and reached for a beer, wishing I had something stronger.

Geezer's head sat on the top shelf of the refrigerator, propped up by a container of margarine and a small block of cheese. Strange how little details like that etched themselves into my mind when my brain hit overload. The eyes, thankfully, were closed and his mouth was shut. There was a smear of dried blood at the corner of his lips. Apart from that, the old bugger could have been asleep but for the fact his tanned face was now purple and green. The late Raymond 'Geezer' Terrant had been dead for some time. He had been subjected to hell before the moment of his release to the next world. I let the refrigerator door swing shut and staggered into the bathroom. I puked up everything that was in my tortured gut. I sluiced water over my face. It didn't help. My brain spun between denial and rage and my heart was thumping hard enough to burst out of my chest. 'Fuck,' I whispered. 'Why? Who?'

The sound of distant police sirens snapped me out of my funk. Were these guys coming for me? Given time I could get Sami to provide a clean-up crew and make it all go away. I didn't have time if those sirens were for me. I could find myself caught up in Thai sticky paper for the next ten years. I went into the bathroom and opened the safe, grabbing my passports and cash. I retrieved the holdall from the wardrobe and dumped everything I owned into it. Then I headed for the door.

'Sorry.' I whispered a collective apology to Babs and Geezer as I went out into the corridor. If she and I hadn't got it together she'd still be alive, beautiful and vibrant, screwing her beautiful arse all the way to a comfortable old age. If I hadn't been to Geezer's, he might still be alive. The fucking world was one big 'if' at that moment in time.

The sirens were louder. Had the motherfucker who had done this been watching for my return to the apartment and anonymously called the cops the moment I had appeared? I guessed he had. Tuk Tuk? That thought crossed my mind as I hit the emergency stairs and went straight to the basement. I didn't think so. A shudder ran down my spin as I crossed the car park. What if he or they had got to Sami as well?

I stepped out into the street through the car park as the first police car pulled up at the main entrance forty feet further down the street. Another car followed close behind. I turned left and headed for the nearest entrance of CDS at a steady walk. Once inside I went through the department store and emerged out on Ploenchit. There were more sirens cutting through the city din. They were going to try and head me off at the pass. Fortunately I had a head start, pun not at all intended. I was on home soil at the embassy before the first car came into view on Wireless Road. I was safe for the moment. I needed Don Don and fast.

Don Don was in an office on the first floor of the main administration block. He would be there for the duration while the party continued downstairs in his own corner of the world. He was completely stunned when I told him about Babs and Geezer.

He didn't need any convincing that I was clean. As far as Babs was concerned, anyway, he and I could prove where I had been virtually every second of the last few hours since I had left her in my bed. Even the fucking keystone cops would figure out that I had a big bad enemy out there who was fucking my friends as he tried to fuck my mind.

As it turned out, Don Don had police contacts high up in the scheme of things.

He made a call and five minutes later the guy at the other end came back to him. Yes, there had been a tip-off that a girl had been killed at the apartment. Yes, it had been anonymous. Yes, they had already found the other head in the refrigerator. Yes, they were about to put out a warrant for Daniel Swann. Yes, they would hold that for the moment, and yes, they would send the detective in charge to the embassy.

When Don Don hung up he opened a desk drawer and produced a bottle of reasonable whisky, not that it would have mattered. I'd have drunk anything at that moment. He poured two glasses and mine contained a quarter of the contents of the bottle. The detective would come and take a statement. If he were convinced I was innocent, I walked. If not, I stayed where I was. I sure as hell wasn't hitting the street until I had absolution. Sitting in a Thai prison on indefinite remand was not an option in my book. Diplomatic immunity was a last resort, but I would use it as a trump card only if I had to. I tried Sami again, and again there was no response. I was getting scared for him and I knew I needed to speak to him more than anything else in the fucking world right then. What the hell had happened to him?

It was 20:40 when the detective in charge of the case arrived in response to Don Don's call. Inspector Tipayakesorn was a dapper little guy in an expensive suit. A suit that I would hazard probably cost a normal Bangkok detective three months' salary. This guy was either on the take or he was very, very high up in the food chain. Don Don had made the introductions and vouched for my presence at the time of Babs's murder. Tipayakesorn didn't need to interview any of the hundred witnesses Don Don said he could produce. 'I have your word, Mr Wisehart, that is sufficient,' the inspector said in accented but precise English. 'You may call me Kit,' Tipayakesorn said focusing on me. 'Kit Carson,' he added with a chuckle.

'Are you a cowboy?' I asked in Thai.

'In my youth, perhaps,' he replied with a smile. 'If you will excuse us, Donald, we will talk in Thai as Mr Swann is obviously fluent. The tape I will make may be transcribed by someone who does not speak good English and we want to be precise.'

Don Don agreed. Kit removed a small Sony dictaphone from his briefcase, set it upon the table between us and began the interview. Don Don, who had admitted to having only a basic knowledge of Thai, sat to one side and tried to follow our discussion as I gave Kit my cover details and explained exactly what had happened when I had entered the apartment. I omitted details relating to the gun, of course, and didn't tell him about Sami Somsak. Bringing him into the picture would cloud the waters. I did recommend that the security guard at the apartments be given a real working over. My bet was the prick would have let the killer into the building. 'Who do you think would bear you ill will enough to do these terrible things?' Kit asked for the recorder.

'I have made a lot of enemies,' I replied. 'Trade is more and more cut-throat every day.' Yeah, I was aware of another bad and very unintentional pun. Kit didn't seem to pick up on it. 'Maybe I have stepped on one set of toes too many,' I continued.

'Gangster enemies?' Kit wanted to know.

'I have had bad dealings with one gangster in particular,' I said. I figured that if I pointed a finger it might as well be at Tuk Tuk as anyone else. Given his record, having him as an enemy would possibly help prove that I was a seriously wronged innocent.

'Who is that?' Kit wanted to know.

'Tuk Tuk Song,' I replied.

The name produced an immediate reaction in the inspector. Kit sat back in his seat with a look of consternation on his face. 'Tuk Tuk Song is a very bad enemy to have,' he said at last. 'Very bad!'

'Yes,' I agreed. 'But perhaps it was not him. It may have been this woman's fiancé, but I think not. My old friend lived in Patong Beach. His death is linked to me and to causing me much pain and regret. It is the same with the girl, I think.' Kit was nodding. I could almost see the thought processes taking place behind his eyes. It didn't take Sherlock Holmes to fit the pieces together. They, whoever they were, had their reasons for wanting to rattle and roll me to hell and back. Kit didn't know that for a fact, but he was no fool. What he did know was that whatever business I was really in, my knowledge and perhaps relationship with Tuk Tuk put a whole different slant on things. He knew I wasn't a civilian and this hadn't been a nice little social killing spree.

'I think we can rule out a jealous boyfriend,' Kit said at last. 'Whoever did this thing wanted you to pay a very, very high price. As you said, someone is out to hurt you very badly. Perhaps it is Tuk Tuk Song. If so, I would advise you to leave Thailand immediately. There will be no charges for you to answer.' Kit stood and scooped his recorder off the desk and then, almost as an afterthought, he paused and held the Sony towards me. 'If you will give me the details of your late friend, we will have people look for the rest of him.'

That was it. Kit and I shook hands and Don Don escorted him out, leaving me alone with the whisky bottle. I poured another solid belt and tried Sami again. Still nothing! Don Don was back. He tipped more whisky into his own glass and sank into his seat. 'What are you going to do?' he was asking. I shrugged and finished my drink in one long swallow. I had to find out what the hell was happening to Sami. I was getting a really bad feeling about him. Sami Somsak could look after himself. That had been proven many times before, but this was a new game. Who the fuck was the mystery player? Something was niggling way back in my brain but it stayed just out of reach.

Don Don asked if I wanted another place to stay, a legitimate safe house perhaps? I rejected that. I looked at my watch. It was 22:34. I knew what I was going to do. I was going to go to Sami's and find out what the hell was happening. Then I stood up and the effects of the whisky hit me. I'd emptied my gut of food and the alcohol had gone straight to my head. I staggered a little and almost fell. Don Don, bless his little cotton socks, steadied me. 'I think you'd better get some sleep,' he suggested and for once I couldn't summon an argument. 'Couch next door, toilet at the end of the hall. I'll organise a blanket or two.' I didn't argue. A few minutes later I spiralled into the blackness of a deep and thankfully dreamless sleep.

I awoke long before dawn and felt like total crap. I used the toilet and splashed water on my face to try and make myself feel better. It didn't. There was instant coffee in a kitchen alcove. I made a strong one and loaded sugar into it. The lights in this part of the building were mostly off. I felt totally alone. I took my brew and my cigarettes, cracked a balcony door and went out into the muggy pre-dawn. There was a patio table containing an overflowing ashtray. I pulled up a chair. It was time to try and put everything in focus. I was tempted to phone and speak to the security types at the US Embassy. Should I apologise to the CIA operative in charge for being sort of responsible for killing off a dozen of his people and for slamming a big helping of egg on their collective face with my decoy plan? I could just imagine his reaction.

'Not them,' I said aloud. Killing Babs and Geezer in that way wasn't their style, nor was it Tuk Tuk's. I instinctively knew it hadn't been him. 'Who?' There were maybe a dozen arms and drug lords and the like in northern Thailand, Cambodia and Laos who would gladly pour petrol on me and set me alight if they had the chance, but that was business. This was a hell of a lot more personal.

I knew there was only one choice. I had to make some calls. Sami still wasn't answering his phone. I needed a phone book for the next one on my list so I went indoors. The battery light of my mobile was on, so I killed it and used the desk phone. It was a local call. I was going to speak to the guys in the white hats before I did anything else.

'I could say you've got a hell of a cheek,' Karl Isbaider said as he stirred the last of six lumps of sugar into his coffee. Then he gave me a hard grin. 'But then you always did.'

'Yeah,' I agreed and took a sip of my own brew. Karl was CIA, the number two or three man in Thailand. He hadn't told me which and I hadn't asked.

It was now 08:30 and Karl and I were having breakfast indoors at the former Hilton in Nai Lert Park. It had been changed to a Swissôtel. Whatever, the food looked delicious but I wasn't eating. Karl and I shared an alcove as far from the rest of the diners as it was possible to get.

'Categorically, Danny, we have not been playing any games with you.' Karl reached for one of my cigarettes. I did the same and lit them both. He was trying to give up smoking he'd told me. It wasn't working. Through a cloud of blue haze he continued. 'We didn't have any team out in the Andaman, let alone lose one. We didn't tail you and we didn't stake out the British Embassy. It wasn't a CIA operation, Dan. End of story.'

'Karl, I saw an ID from one of the dead guys in the water. It was State Department issue.'

'Remember the name?'

I wound back the photographic cells in my brain. 'Carl with a C, Leathem. New York driver's licence, Queens address, early forties, six foot one, weighing over 200 pounds, I guess, silver hair, number-two haircut, moustache, chubby face. State Department standard ID number ZD 437627002,' I recited.

'Damn, I wish I could do that damned memory trick,' the CIA man muttered as he reached for his mobile phone. 'Doesn't ring any bells.' He pressed a directory number. 'Isbaider,' he said. 'Run this ID number for me. ZD 437627002, name of Leathem. I'll hold.'

I poured another coffee and pushed the plate bearing my virtually untouched breakfast to one side. I wasn't hungry. Gallons of blood, severed heads and a missing friend could do that to you. I hadn't known who from the Sheriff's office was still in town, but it had been a lucky break that Karl had been on watch when I'd called. Karl had been a field operative like me way back when. We'd worked together occasionally in those days. Now I was calling on our past to try and figure out the present.

While Karl hung on the end of his phone I tried to stay in focus. Not knowing what the hell was happening with Sami was eating me. As soon as we finished, I would head down to Banglamphu to find out for myself. After a minute or so the CIA agent nodded, grunted and grunted some more before thanking whoever was on the other end of the line and flicking his phone off. 'No State ID has ever been issued with that number. We only have one Leathem on our books and he's an accountant at Langley.' Karl took a final puff of his almost extinct cigarette and ground it out on his saucer. 'Look, Dan, one pro to another and on my mother's grave, we didn't go out chasing whatever it was you were after out there. It was some other outfit. Also, old buddy, we would have got you,' he added.

'But the colours, Karl! Mr Green, Mr Blue, Mr Beige. They had all the hallmarks of you lot,' I said.

'We're not so big on the colour thing these days, Dan, we've become a bit more subtle than that. Believe me when I say you've been suckered on this one. Someone wanted you to think CIA, but we were not involved.' Karl looked absolutely convincing in his denial. Then he paused for a long time, giving me a calculated stare. 'However, old buddy, if you tell me what it was that you found out there we might get very involved.' I believed him. I stubbed out my own cigarette and fought back the impulse to light another or scream with frustration. Karl could see it plainly. He just shook his head.

'Fake IDs are a dime a bushel. The people in this mystery outfit might have been equipped with them to throw everyone off the scent if the shit went down wrong, which obviously it did.' Karl stood. 'I've got a meeting down the street in fifteen so I've got to roll. But believe me when I say it wasn't us. If it had been, I think the only get-together you and I would be having about now would be over a gun. We're forgiving but not that forgiving, especially if you'd taken out a big chunk of our assets. If you figure it out, call me. I think we need to get close on this if some other player in our ballpark is impersonating us. I'll put the word out through our people and see what we dredge up.'

Karl and I shook hands and I watched him leave the restaurant. I was none the wiser.

If it wasn't the CIA or Tuk Tuk, then who the hell was it and where the fuck was Sami? The only good thing for the moment was the fact it wasn't the CIA on my tail. I paid the bill and headed back to the embassy. I needed to speak to Carter if he was still there. The SAS intelligence network was good, damned good. They might have a hint who the third player might be. Once I'd spoken to him I was going to go down into the Old Town to find my old friend, The Onion Man.

24

The retrieval team was due to fly out on a military flight at 22:00. I didn't see Sylvia or the little Welsh beauty in the basement. Carter's people didn't have any intelligence on new local players beyond what we already knew, so it was up to Karl's crew. I was caught in a hellish limbo. My mobile was charging so I found a scrambled land line and called home.

I told Bernard what had gone down in the last few hours. He seemed surprised, but it was hard to tell. No, he didn't have anything else to add. When I hung up I was left with the impression that there was a hell of a lot that he could have added. I didn't dwell on it. I had things to do, including finding a fucking head-hunting killer. In hindsight, maybe I should have realised it then, but I was still rocking from everything that had taken place in the last few hours.

So there I was. My prime mission had been accomplished, but now I was obligated to find the bastards who had killed Geezer and poor innocent Babs. Lone Ranger be damned. I needed to get them before they got me. It was plain that they would come after me in their own time. These guys were pros who knew only too well that when the spring was wound to breaking point, it was so easy to make a fatal mistake.

I was about to get myself organised to head down to Sami's place and find out where he was when Don Don appeared in the doorway. 'Urgent call for you,' he said, indicating the phone I'd just used. It started to chime. Was it Sir Bloody Bernard?

'Daniel, it's Sami.'

'Thank Christ,' I said. 'Did you know ...?'

'Just listen,' he said urgently in a hoarse whisper. 'It's not the CIA, it's Dimitri Chekhov. They hit my warehouse two hours after you left. Killed everyone, then torched the place. They were looking for you and the box so it has to be Bernard. You're bugged, either your phone or your computer.'

'Chekhov!' I said, stunned.

'Yeah. Explanations later,' Sami whispered before I could dwell on the name or the man behind all this. He was obviously in a tight spot. 'Be down at Banglamphu after dark. Chekhov's got the place under surveillance. He's waiting for you or me to show. Disguise. It's a circus. Go stand by the old man with the drinks cart. Use your phone, fake a call to me but only when you're in position. Watch your back. We need one of his people alive real bad. Later, Dan!' With that the line went dead.

'Bad?' Don Don had reappeared in the doorway.

'Sami, my friend. His place was hit. A lot of dead!' I said scrubbing my fingers over my stubble. I felt like shit in every sense of the term.

'I didn't think,' said Don Don, vanishing back into the outer office. He returned with a newspaper and held it out with both hands. There it was on the front page. WAREHOUSE FIRE IN BANGLAMPHU KILLS TWELVE screamed the headline. There was a photograph of a gutted blackened building.

'Oh Christ!' I muttered. Seeing pictures always drove the point home, and now I had to face another fact. A man I had killed, or thought I had killed years ago, was alive and hunting me. I took the paper from Don Don and laid it on the desk. There was a photograph of a gutted, blackened building. Firemen were carrying out a body bag. For a second the image of beautiful Mary astride the Suzuki came to me. She would have gone back to Sami's after dropping me off and ridden straight into the ambush. She and a whole bunch of innocents had died because of me and that damned box.

'Bernard,' I spat. That was why the fake CIA men had vanished from outside the embassy minutes after I had spoken to him. He thought he'd convinced me to do the run at night. He'd passed the information on to Chekhov and Chekhov had pulled his troops off the embassy and moved on Sami's in the afternoon.

'More bad news,' Don Don said softly. 'Kit just phoned. The Patong police went to the address you gave them. They found two bodies, a woman and the remains of your friend, Geezer.' Don Don suddenly looked like a man of fifty on a bad, bad day. I think he was one breath away from changing his career path. I probably would have too if I'd been in his position. I, however, didn't have a choice in what I did. Not at that moment in time anyway.

'The woman had been subjected to some terrible abuse.' The embassy security man paused. 'After she was tortured she'd had her head cut off and then some sick bastard sat it in your friend's crotch. He'd been tied to a chair and probably, according to Kit's people, made to watch what they did to her before he got it.'

Poor bloody Geezer. His death had nothing to do with the fucking box. It was purely personal. It was all about me—me and Dimitri Chekhov. I reached for the phone. I needed to speak to the sheriff. The conversation with Karl was short. When I hung up I told Don Don what I needed and he headed out the door.

It was 15:00. I had time to get ready for what would come next and time to think about Bernard and what I was going to do to him when we finally met face to face. Was I surprised that Sir Bernard Sinclair might be a traitor? No! I hadn't had time to analyse it all, but it made sense. Bernard was the ringmaster in all of it. He'd created the dance routine and I was just a fucking dancer. Coincidence only went so far and the clincher, as far as I was concerned, was the old queen's insistence that I keep that damn mobile phone powered up. With that he had been more than obsessive.

I glanced at the mobile sitting on the side table by a wall socket. The green light told me it was fully charged. If it had a tracer in it that was only active when it was powered, that would explain a lot. It would explain how he'd been able to pinpoint Geezer's place. Geezer had been my friend, not a player, and not known to Bernard. As for Sami's, that was obvious—I'd used the phone there. Down south I'd run out of battery and they had lost me. 'Dumb shit!' I reprimanded myself. But on reflection I wasn't really to blame for not suspecting the mobile. Hey, I knew Bernard was as queer as a two-bob watch but I hadn't known he was a traitor, and I hadn't known I was being targeted and trailed by anyone until I had boarded the train down at Lang Suan what now seemed like years ago. As for Chekhov, the mad Russian was a whole different story.

Dimitri Chekhov had been an ex-KGB colonel. After the break-up of the Soviet Union he had turned his attention to getting rich. The euphemistically named Russian Mafia were, for the most part, former military and they were absolute cut-throats. The original Sicilian mafioso couldn't hold a candle to this new breed when it came to pure viciousness. My lot had been alerted to the Russian mob's presence in our area of operation in about 1996. Operating out of northern Cambodia, Chekhov had become a huge pain in the collective arse of our American allies and us. As a result, he'd been sanctioned and I had been given the task of taking him out on the orders of Sir Bernard Sinclair.

My team and I set up an ambush outside Chekhov's fortified compound in the bush, up by the border just beyond Anlong Veng. Chekhov made regular visits to the town and we simply waited for him to emerge. As his Range Rover started to ford the stream that ran past the compound, I made multiple 300-yard hits with a .50 calibre Barrett, using a mixture of explosives and armour-piercing rounds. The Rover bogged in the stream and turned into a flaming colander. We didn't see anyone escape. We hadn't been in a position to go and investigate up close but we'd chalked up a positive and, to my knowledge, Chekhov hadn't appeared on any intelligence since that day. But he had!

I should have made the connection, but how do you make a connection to a dead man? It was the heads, the damned heads. That was what had been bugging my subconscious. That had been Chekhov's party trick. He had been known as a head-hunter. Legend had it that when he had been seconded to the Spetsnaz and stationed in Afghanistan, on a wall in his unit's camp he had lined up the severed heads of the more than a dozen rebels he had personally killed. Headless bodies had a habit of turning up wherever the maniac was stationed, from Asia to Europe.

I remembered the torso of Ivan Scranner, an undercover operative working in East Berlin. Just prior to the Wall coming down he'd come across the border for a meet. I'd been detailed to provide him with close cover. Point was, when I went to his hotel to do just that he was already dead. I'd found Scranner's naked and tortured remains in the ornate bath of his suite. His head wasn't there. As far as I knew it had never been found. We thought Chekhov had probably taken it back east with him.

We knew it was Chekhov because the hotel's security cameras showed him enter and leave Scranner's room. He entered carrying what looked like a bowling bag and left an hour and a half later with the same bag appearing a good deal heavier going out than when he'd taken it in. As he'd walked towards the camera turret in the foyer by the lift, he had looked up at the camera and saluted. He'd had a broad smile on his wide face the whole time.

I'd never forgotten that smile. It was the broad beam of a jovial grandfather. Picture a bulky bear of a man, a sort of grey-suited Santa with a broad-brimmed hat and a thick, yellow walrus moustache. That was the Dimitri Chekhov I saw on the security video. Thing was, the eyes hadn't been smiling. They had been as cold as fucking ice. They had taunted the camera. He had made no attempt to disguise himself, such was the arrogance of the man.

The next and only other time I laid eyes on him was years later. I was staring through the cross hairs of the twenty-power sniper scope on the Barrett as he sat in the passenger seat of his Range Rover. I'd lost sight of him as I had started pounding the vehicle to bits. Bye bye, Dimitri, I'd thought at the time. Not so, it seemed.

The only way, all these years later, that Chekhov would have know who had pulled the trigger that day was if someone had told him. At the kill zone there had been Sami, Sami's number-one man, Jo, and yours truly. The only other people in the know were Bernard, who had ordered the hit after consulting with CIA brass, and the late Neville Trevaine, my Bangkok controller. My money was on Bernard. But why had Chekhov waited so long to come after me? Unless, of course, Bernard had decided to withhold that little gem until the black box had been discovered. Box or not, I suspected that revenge on me, the triggerman, would be more of a motivator for Chekhov than anything else.

'The chemical team are packing to go. The good doctor was asking where you were. She's outside.' Don Don broke through my meditation. He laid the articles I'd requested on the back of one of the office's guest chairs.

'Thanks for those,' I replied as I stood. I unplugged my mobile phone and ensured the power was off before slipping it into my pocket. This was going to be the key to undoing Sir Bernard. I wasn't sure how yet, but I was going to find a way to use it to turn the tables on the traitorous old prick.

25

Ex-wives and ex-husbands occupy a strange space somewhere between familiarity and distance, attraction and revulsion. Memories of love, smells, taste and touch are things that are never forgotten. Everything is poured into a big blender along with equal parts of anger, hurt and the numbing pain of failure. Then the switch is flicked on to stir it all up. It's a heady mix and it's damned hard to take on an empty stomach.

Sylvia knew that something had changed. Her antennae had always been sharply tuned. Maybe if it hadn't been we might have made it. Who knows? There was no banter this time. She had come to say goodbye. They were flying out that evening. It was 16:20. I'd be at Sami's at 18:00 and Sylvia would be flying out of my life again shortly after that.

'I was going to suggest a late, late lunch or dinner,' she said when I joined her. 'Now I don't think it would be a box of laughs, even if they let us out of here.' Much as I wanted to, I knew she was absolutely right. As before she could still read me like a bloody book.

'Got a really bad thing going down,' I said, attempting a wry grin. 'I'd really like that, but let's take a rain check on dinner until I'm back in the UK.'

'Maybe,' she said, standing and coming around the desk. She leaned down and pecked me on the forehead. 'Maybe not. My boyfriend is the jealous type.'

Boyfriend! I hadn't known. But then, what was there to know? We'd been divorced for five years and only seen each other three or four times during that period. We didn't do birthday cards, Christmas cards or have weekly chat sessions like some exs.

'Lucky guy,' I said.

Sylvia's eyes searched my face, then she smiled. 'I do believe you mean that.'

'I do. Given the chance to do things over, we wouldn't be where we are,' I said, suddenly feeling like a cliché. 'Truth!'

'Well, well. Regrets, huh?'

'Oh yes—about us, about a lot of things actually,' I replied as the images of Babs and Geezer sprung to mind. 'Oh yes!' I needed coffee and I needed food but going outside the embassy compound with Sylvia was totally out of the question. 'Cafeteria,' I said, taking her arm and steering her in that direction.

'Been there, done that,' she replied dryly. 'So upmarket, darling.'

'Yeah,' I agreed as we descended the stairs arm in arm. It reminded me of the day we posed for our wedding photos. I stopped that line of thought immediately. 'Have you tried their scones?' I added as we entered the cafeteria.

'Not likely,' my ex replied as I eased her in front of me at the servery. We quit the banter while we got our coffees and a brace of sandwiches. The place was just about deserted but I led her to an alcove table. We seated ourselves, organised our refreshments and I got straight down to brass tacks. Time was the one thing we didn't have.

'Syl, I need to know the history of the damned strain of anthrax. Why it is so bloody unique? Apart from its size and all that stuff. But even more importantly I need to know how it got here and from where.'

Sylvia spooned two big shovels of sugar into her coffee and started stirring. She stirred slowly, her face thoughtful and young. She looked like a teenager, not a thirty-six-year-old doctor of microbiology. After some time she stopped playing with her spoon and her eyes met mine. 'This is top secret, Dan. I've just had another briefing and it's cut-your-heart-out time if this goes any further.' She paused, her eyes searching mine like beautiful, twin blue–grey lasers. She took a sip of her coffee and grimaced. I tried my brew to keep her company. It wasn't great but it was the only game in town, as the Yanks say, and I needed caffeine.

'Basically,' Sylvia continued, 'this version resembles the normal base bacillus anthracis strain about as much as a biplane resembles a damned stealth bomber. Somehow those researchers fifty plus years ago managed to create something totally and scarily unique. Something no one else, to our knowledge, has even got close to. All of us researchers know about it. It's our very own industry legend, if you like. We all know the details of the brew but not how to make it, and that's why everyone wants it. It's potentially the damned neutron bomb of bacterial warfare.' As she was speaking Sylvia was taking the wrap off her sandwich. I glanced down at mine. I had to eat even if I didn't want to.

'Why not just make up a fresh batch to the original recipe?' I suggested as my ex took a tentative nibble on her tomato and cheese creation and hesitated before repeating the process.

'That's the point and here's your history lesson,' Sylvia mumbled around a mouthful of food. 'The original formula and the remaining samples of that particular strain, along with the team who created it, were destroyed when the laboratory burned down. A US tanker plane loaded with fuel crash-landed on takeoff. Direct hit on the lab at Orford. Killed just about everyone. Couldn't have done better if they'd planned it,' she added, picking up her coffee cup.

'Anyway, the brew was so top secret and had evolved so quickly that nothing was replicated elsewhere. Not only that, there was a lot of politics involved apparently. Very few people even knew of its existence.' Sylvia swallowed another mouthful of coffee and shuddered.

'As Murphy would have it, along with the flames from several tons of aviation gas, guess what?' Sylvia pushed the remains of her sandwich to one side.

'What?'

'It rained for a week. The rain helped to eventually put the fire out, and it killed whatever remained of the strain. That, of course, is how we knew how to neutralise it. The only material to survive was that which you miraculously produced in your little lead box. I honestly don't know where you got it, Danny, but there it was, just waiting for oxygen to bring it back to life.' Sylvia paused and again contemplated her coffee for a moment before pushing the cup towards the plate containing her discarded sandwich. Then those laser eyes met mine again. 'So where did you get it, Dan?'

'Let's just say it's been lying around out in the Andaman since the war,' I replied. 'It was obviously already on its way to these parts when the lab went up. Good timing, bad timing or just plain fate, huh?'

'Yeah, fate. It's a pity you found it,' she said sadly.

'Better *I* found it than the others who were after it,' I replied. 'Much better, believe me.'

'I hope so for all our sakes because there's something else we've just discovered.' Sylvia was now leaning forward, whispering. 'There is absolutely no antidote that we know of for this one. Water kills it, extreme heat kills it, but we haven't got anything to immunise us against it. So you can guess what I'll be involved with for the foreseeable future.'

'Oh boy,' I muttered. She gave me a faint smile and stood.

'I'm going to catch up with the others and get organised for our flight. You take care, and yes, call me when you get back. I was joking about the boyfriend.' She leaned across the table. This time the kiss brushed my lips, then she was walking away. My heart was thumping in my chest. I sat and watched her walk out of my life again. She moved with her long back straight, but there was a sway to her hips and her hair gleamed. She was beautiful. At the door she turned, waved and was gone.

Karl's call came when I was back upstairs dressing for my next role in the bloody game we were playing. He was surprised that I'd already identified the killer as Dimitri Chekhov. The CIA had apparently been running an open file on him since he'd re-emerged in Thailand. Karl was also surprised I didn't know Chekhov had survived the attempt on his life. 'We informed British Intelligence as soon as we knew,' he told me. I felt the hairs on my neck prick. Bernard had intentionally decided not to pass that little morsel on to me.

Karl told me that his mob knew Chekhov had appeared in Switzerland a year after the attempt on his life, and had undergone extensive plastic surgery for horrific burns. When he quit Switzerland two years later, the CIA lost track of him for half a decade. They eventually picked him up on their radar a year or so ago and re-opened the file. They were now digging. Having the Russian mob in the form of Dimitri Chekhov impersonating CIA didn't sit at all well with Karl's lot.

'We're going all out to track the s.o.b down, Danny. When we do it will, I suspect, be a case of extreme prejudice when we make contact. Does that fit with your picture of things?' He was excited or agitated or both.

'Absolutely,' I replied. 'What about the Thais?'

'I believe there are moves afoot to obtain their co-operation with this.' The CIA man paused. 'You might consider talking to your friend, Tuk Tuk. Apparently Chekhov and his playmates are beginning to make inroads into his operations. Tuk Tuk's network may know where we can find Mr fucking Chekhov. We're harvesting all the intel we can find. I'll get back to you when we've got it. I've got some file photos, including one we managed to obtain in Switzerland. Not a pretty sight. I've printed them and a messenger will be there in twenty.'

'Thanks. I owe you.'

'Yes you do, buddy,' he replied before he let a big pause spread its wings. 'Just tell me, what was so bloody important out there in the damned Andaman?'

'Another time, maybe,' I replied. '*Ciao*!' I hung up. I didn't want to tell Karl about Bernard's role in all of this yet. That could wait until we got Chekhov.

As I started applying the make-up that was going to complete my disguise, delayed shock started to work on my subconscious. Bernard and Chekhov! What an unholy alliance! It was obvious I'd been set up to fail from day one.

Every move I made had been monitored by Bernard and passed on to Chekhov. Thank God I didn't always do things by the good book of Bernard. What I couldn't figure out was why hadn't Chekhov already picked up the black box and just whacked me cold before I even found out he was alive? He obviously had the resources he needed to do that with no problem at all.

As I worked on darkening my skin I worried the why to bits. Maybe Bernard hadn't told Chekhov the full story. Maybe he had wanted to stage an attempt at recovering the box to cover his skinny arse in front of his superiors. Could the plan have been to let me recover the box, then take it off me and blame it on pirates? That made some degree of sense. That way Bernard went into his retirement with honour and Chekhov got the bugs for the market. If that was his intent, of course. When did Bernard tell Chekhov I'd been the one to hit him? The old bastard sure as hell wouldn't have let Chekhov know he had ordered the hit. Of course, the other factor might have been that Chekhov had the goods on Bernard and Bernard was hoping like hell Chekhov and I cancelled each other out, leaving him free and clear.

So what was the likely history between Bernard and Chekhov? Maybe back in the days of the cold war Chekhov had been running Bernard, or Bernard running him. The former made sense, given Bernard's background and sexual preferences. Had Chekhov even suspected it was Bernard who had sanctioned the original hit on him, or had he figured it was CIA? Bernard, the clever, foxy old queen, had probably pointed Chekhov in that direction. Of course, perhaps Bernard had been so intent on sterilising his potentially very embarrassing past, that the hit he had called on Chekhov had nothing to do with The Firm at all. Maybe he had simply orchestrated the whole thing and sent me on my mission to whack Chekhov and clear that particular slate. Now, years later, he was pointing Chekhov back at me. Nice boss, huh?

'Bugger!' I muttered. My inattention to the job in hand caused me to poke my eye with a make-up brush. I wished Mary were here doing it for me. But Mary wouldn't be doing anything any more. My gut twisted and I tasted bile at the back of my throat. I forced it down and focused on finishing the make-up job. While I waited for it to set I picked up the phone and called Tuk Tuk. The conversation was short, stilted and very much to the point. Yes, he knew Chekhov, yes, he knew several of his possible locations and yes, he would have his people pinpoint the Russian. When they found him I would be informed. End of conversation. Don Don came in holding a large yellow envelope. 'Special delivery,' he said, passing it across. 'You look very,' he paused searching for words, 'different.'

In the envelope there were three shots, each eight by ten. One black and white showed Chekhov as a young man in full dress uniform. Another was a street shot in an unidentified city. It showed a bear of a man in a black overcoat wearing a broad-brimmed black hat. A white scarf was pulled up high but it didn't hide the shiny white and red of the mass of scar tissue on the side of his face. The left ear, the one nearest the camera, appeared not to exist. The third photograph was taken in hospital. It was from a plastic surgeon's file, no doubt. Chekhov was in a white gown. His entire head was exposed. There was no hair, just what must have been transplanted skin in patches. The eyes were red-rimmed pits. The nose had obviously been reconstructed. It was like it had been formed of melting red and orange Play-Doh. The cheeks were patched with multi-coloured skin and ribbons of deep scar tissue. The lips were puffed, oversized and looked frayed and wet. The left ear was gone. There was just a tiny flap of skin. Most of the right ear was intact but for the ear lobe. That was gone.

'Holy shit,' muttered Don Don. 'Freddy fucking Kruger.'

'Just as terrifying,' I replied. 'Pizza face,' I pushed the photos back into the envelope, shoved it into my holdall and stowed it under the desk in my commandeered office to await my return. I hoped. Don Don pulled a set of car keys from his pocket as I followed him out the door. He was going to drop me down in the Old Town and I was going to go hunting.

26

The entire warehouse was gone. All that remained were blackened beams and crumbling stone work. Tendrils of smoke and steam curled into the night sky. Two fire appliances were still on the scene along with maybe a dozen men combing the debris under the white glare of three or four banks of construction lights. The lights turned the bleak scene into one of desolate, sharp contrasts. A pair of police cars and a large, dark-blue, windowless panel truck filled the street nearest the site.

I faded into the background and started watching everything. I located the old man and his drinks cart at the far end of the short street. I would make my way towards him once I had the scene and the people set in my conscious mind. I needed to observe what passed for normal in this place and time before I started looking for the abnormal.

Sami said Chekhov had people here. I had to spot them before they could identify me. This was a game of chess, with death instead of checkmate for the loser. If Chekhov had just one of his men there as bait, there would be others waiting to take down whoever came sniffing around. I thought, in the first instance at least, that I had a better chance of identifying Chekhov's people than they had of spotting me.

I'd made a bit of effort with my change of image and didn't look anything like the me of a few hours before. I wore a white shirt outside my belt and dark slacks with black shoes. My hair was black, shiny and slicked back behind my ears. I had a thick matching moustache and a pair of large dark-framed glasses. The glass inside the frames looked plain, like normal reading lenses. My tan had been seriously augmented by something out of a bottle. I looked at first glance like an Indian businessman, of which there were plenty in Bangkok. My disguise was completed by a leather briefcase, which contained a stack of newspaper for weight and effect.

No matter what I looked like, I didn't resemble the man Chekhov was no doubt looking to turn into chunky pet food. I wore the Walther under my shirt and the knife taped to my calf. I'd debated wearing my boots but they were a giveaway to anyone who knew me, and I had a feeling that thanks to Bernard fucking Sinclair, Chekhov knew me, right down to my choice of aftershave.

Not as pleasant as my aftershave was the smell of the burned out and doused building, one of the nastiest stenches I'd ever encountered. It was acrid and sickly, clinging to everything, my clothes included. I knew it would sit at the back of my throat and in my nostrils for days afterwards. I also knew that adding water just seemed to make the smell worse. Add a few fried body parts and it went to a new level of nastiness. The paper said twelve had died there, but that had probably been speculation. As I watched, the firemen carried a body bag out of the debris and headed for the black wagon. Beyond the men carrying the grisly burden, another group had stopped digging in the rubble. They were staring down at something they had uncovered. Another body, no doubt!

I moved as close as I could. There were people all around. Some were ghouls on the prowl, others were pickpockets working the tourists who had been drawn by the activity. Local traders hawked food, drink and cigarettes to the spectators. Even though so many hours had passed, the show still wasn't over. A shout from one of the firemen brought a policeman across to where they stood. A photographer followed. Shortly afterwards there was the flash of a camera and, a few minutes later, another black-bagged shape was carried out to the waiting meat wagon.

'That makes fifteen,' an old Thai woman muttered to no one in particular. The old lady was squatting on the footpath a few feet away from me. She was fanning a charcoal brazier as she grilled chicken. Trade was good. Two or three people were hovering, waiting for their snack to cook. Over the acrid stench of the fire, the chicken smelt like heaven. I was tempted, then my eyes went back to the body that was being loaded into the back of the unmarked van thirty yards away. My appetite vanished as quickly as it had appeared.

One more time I scanned the people walking past and those standing watching, waiting for something, or nothing, the way people do when death is around them. Several times I saw faces that caused me to do a double take, but each time I let things ride. Anonymous people in a street were just that until proven otherwise. I needed more. I needed to see someone talk into their sleeve or make eye contact with me and lose it. I needed to see a carelessly exposed gun or a pair of guys trying to pretend they didn't know each other. I needed something, anything. The only thing I could be certain of was that Chekhov had people here.

I moved up the street towards where an old man was doing a fair trade in drinks. It was then that I saw Chekhov's sacrificial lamb, and I'd seen him before. Coincidentally the guy was standing under a streetlight. He was not only wearing colours; he was coloured to boot. It was Mr Beige in his hideous beige shirt. It was combined with a pale straw Panama, red trousers and yellow shoes. The sap had been dressed by Coco the Clown. Subtlety was obviously not one of Chekhov's strong points.

I eased back through the thin curtain of people behind me and moved across the creeping, honking traffic line, angling in Mr Beige's direction. The drinks cart was some thirty yards further up the street. I was perhaps ten or twelve feet away from Beige when a second guy joined him. This one was European. He wore jeans and a tight blue Nike T-shirt. He had the imposing shape of a steroid-swigging body builder and wore a short crop of silver spikes. There was a big gold earring in his left ear. As I drifted closer, I tagged him as Mr Muscles for obvious reasons. 'This is a fucking waste of time,' the new arrival was saying to Beige as I moved past. The language was English, but the accent was Eastern European.

'Orders!' replied Beige. 'You don't want to piss the man off now, do you? Get your white arse away from me. I'm the bait, you fucker.' Muscles looked as if he wanted to argue a little but he grunted and moved back past me without a glance. I kept moving. I was guessing from the accent that the black guy was Jamaican. I didn't pause to talk to him about cricket or Bob Marley. I was past him in two strides and moving on away from the fire. I didn't look back.

I crossed the street again fifty feet further up from Chekhov's sacrificial lamb and moved on to the drinks hawker. The handcart was positioned at the entrance to a narrow alley that ran back towards the canal behind Sami's place. I fished coins out of my pocket. The stall owner was sitting on a stool cooling himself with a small hand-held battery fan.

He grinned at me, took the money and passed me a cold can of Singha. I thanked him and moved back to stand by the alley entrance. I propped my briefcase at my feet and stood sipping my beer, wondering where Sami was. It was time to switch on my phone and make that call.

Drink in one hand, I got the mobile phone out of my pocket with the other, powered it up and tapped in Sami's number. At the other end the phone rang half a dozen times then cut to Sami's voice mail. I left a message, making it up as I went along, then I pocketed the phone again, leaving it powered up. I finished my beer, my eyes on Mr Beige who was still standing under the streetlight thirty or so yards from where I was. Even with the bustling throng going past him, he stood out like a beacon.

I found more coins and got another beer. The old man smiled at me as I retreated to my former position. The second beer certainly tasted better than the first.

I was only a sip or two into it when my phone vibrated. I fished it out, wondering who it was: Bernard, Sami, Don Don or maybe Karl? With the latter I was right on the money.

'I now know why Chekhov is really pissed at you!'

'Because I shot him up and turned him into fucking pizza!' I replied and it wasn't a question.

'No,' the CIA man came back. 'When you hit him his pregnant wife was in the wagon.'

'What?' I replied, totally stunned at this piece news. 'We never knew he was married.'

'He was,' Karl said. 'Russian girl fifteen years his junior. She'd been a ballet dancer and apparently a good one. She was having some difficulties with her pregnancy. Chekhov was taking her out to a doctor at Anlong Veng when you hit them. He tried to get her out of the wagon but she didn't make it. The water must have saved him.'

'Shit!'

'It happens, Dan, but at least you know that this is personal and that means kill him or he'll kill you. There's no middle ground. Take care. I'll be in touch if anything else comes to hand.' Karl cut the connection, leaving me staring blankly at my mobile.

'Christ,' I muttered, pocketing the phone. That explained a lot. Bad enough I'd toasted Chekhov but killing his wife and unborn child, albeit accidentally, was guaranteed to provoke retribution of the bloodiest kind. Thing was, it was only when Bernard had pointed the finger at me that Chekhov would have even had a clue as to who had tried to tap him. Sir Bernard Sinclair and I were going to have an interesting meeting.

Where was Sami? I asked myself as I focused back on our men in the street.

My two Ruskies were gone. Mr Beige was no longer standing under his light and Muscles had vanished from the doorway he'd commandeered. My heart did a double take. The news from Karl had broken my concentration. 'Fuck!' I muttered, desperately trying to pick Beige and Muscles out from the crowd. Undoubtedly there were others there as well. Guys I hadn't picked up on.

I stepped forward to peer around the canvas screen formed by the awning of the drinks cart, checking out the near distance. I pulled back immediately. The two goons were forty feet away and coming towards me fast, splitting the crowd like a pair of icebreakers working thin pack ice. Muscles had his hand down the front of his trousers, fumbling with his crotch, while Beige was reaching under his shirt. I dropped my beer can and drew the Walther as I stepped back into the angle of the wall behind me. 'Where the fuck are you, Sami?' I whispered. The old guy from the stall was kneeling beside his trolley. He'd seen what was going down. 'Watch your arse, old man,' I said in Thai.

27

'You want another Singha, Daniel?' the old fellow was asking me as he removed an Uzi from the bottom compartment of his stall.

'Sami?' I gasped, glancing down. Sami Somsak was staring up at me. He was an old man, his face drawn and haggard under his make-up. He looked like shit.

'I want one of these guys real bad, Daniel. The black guy preferably.'

'Okay,' I said as I thumbed off the safety on my automatic. The old team was back in business but this was not the time or place for a reunion celebration. The Sami Somsak who crouched at my feet was not in a partying mood. He'd lost a bunch of his people and his town base. As he said, he was hurting but then so was I. Chekhov had hit us both where it hurt. I wondered if the crazy Russian really knew just who he had coming after him. Me, he knew about, but Sami, I didn't know. I'd seen Sami in action before many times and was thankful he and I were on the same side. Dimitri Chekhov had started something, but I was hoping and praying he wouldn't be able to finish it. The Russian's two goons weren't real smart. They stayed bunched shoulder to shoulder as they approached, plowing through the crowd. Sami was below their collective line of sight, hidden by the bulk of his trolley, so all they were focused on was me. My white shirt must have been glowing like a neon sign in the gloom. I moved to my left and back into the cover of the alley.

Clear of the nearest pedestrians, Muscles fumbled a small automatic out from between his legs. Mr Beige was now waving a big chromed something in the breeze.

'Show yourself again,' Sami whispered and I did just that, stepping forward into the light to present my attackers with a nice glowing target. I tucked back fast as Beige tried to line me up. Whether they wanted me dead or as a present for Chekhov I would never know because the game was about to change drastically.

Kneeling, Sami leaned around the end of his cart, the Uzi clamped against his shoulder. He took a moment to acquire his targets, then fired single, aimed shots in rapid succession, shifting the muzzle of the gun from one to the other in the blink of an eye. To have used full auto with a street full of people behind the target would have meant certain death for the innocent, but at a range of ten feet and closing, it was no contest. Three rounds hit Mr Beige in the thighs, then three more copper jackets met in a three inch triangle in the centre of Mr Muscles's beautifully formed chest. Both guys hit the street hard. Muscles didn't move, but Beige was curled up into a ball, screaming in agony.

'Grab him,' Sami called. 'Into the alley.' I jammed the Walther into my belt and leapt past Sami's cart. People were screaming in the street, and everyone was running for cover. I was on the injured man in two strides. I kicked the chromed automatic away from Beige, grabbed him under the armpits and started dragging him backwards towards the alleyway. Sami tossed something down the street towards the police vehicles. After a quick glance in that direction, I realised that the cops were in no hurry to get near us. Other figures were heading our way, however. I had to assume they were more of Chekhov's playmates.

'Tear gas,' Sami said as he came running towards me, the Uzi in one hand.

He bent down, grabbed a handful of trouser cuff with his free hand and helped me move the black guy who was screaming like a proverbial stuck pig. The alley was dank, dark and fucking dirty. I stopped, hit the guy hard on the side of the head with a closed anvil fist and quickly frisked him. I found a small automatic ankle gun. I stuffed it into my trouser pocket.

Beige wasn't moving at all and I was faced with hauling a dead weight. I knew the best way to carry someone who was right out of it was the old-fashioned way, just like I had carried Tuk Tuk to safety all those years before. I squatted to arrange limbs and then slung the injured guy head first over my shoulders, legs hanging in front.

'Go,' I yelled to Sami who was watching the mouth of the alley. He threw another gas grenade then came running back. He pushed past me and set off in the lead.

'Not far,' he called. 'Boat,' he added. 'You okay?'

'Yeah,' I muttered. 'Me carry, you lead.' Sami almost laughed. He increased his pace. Not far seemed to me to be a hundred gruelling yards of wet, slippery, slime-covered crap that sloped down towards the canal. I stumbled and skidded, cannoning off the alley walls at every two or three paces. I was tempted to drop my passenger and use him as a toboggan. I could hear our pursuers behind us. There was a whistle and angry shouts further back. It seemed the police were putting on a performance for the crowd but Chekhov's goons were between them and us. Sami raised the Uzi and fired a short burst into the sky. The sound was deafening, amplified by the man-made canyon we were in. He lobbed another grenade over my head as I ran after him.

The alley finally gave way to a narrow wooden jetty just fifty yards up the canal from the charred timbers of Sami's warehouse. His own jetty had been burned down to the tide mark. As we neared the jetty there was enough light for me to identify the boat tied there as a low open cruiser with a fat pair of big black outboards tacked on the rear end. Sami jumped down into the cockpit and perched himself at the wheel. He started flicking switches. The sound of our pursuers was growing louder. I didn't have time to stand on ceremony. It was five or so feet from dock to deck. Mr Beige made it in half a second flat as I pulled my Gerber and went for the ropes holding us to the dock fore and aft.

The razor blade of my folding knife made short work of the nylon and I landed in the boat just as Sami ground the Mercurys into life. It wasn't a coincidence that the cruiser had been parked pointing back towards the river, her engines primed and ready to go. We were moving in ten seconds. Our pursuers didn't even make the dock before we were out of range. In our wake we left several very upset river folk who were fighting to keep their little craft afloat in our wash.

Due to the failing light, Sami turned on the navigation lights and a spotlight positioned on the bow to show the way ahead. He throttled back and the big motors settled into a muted grumble. We could talk without yelling and there was a lot I wanted to know.

'How the hell did you survive?'

'I was on my way to the Gulf,' Sami replied harshly. 'They missed me when they hit the place. They staged an accident in the street—backed a furniture van loaded with their men into the garage door and got in. People on the street only saw it as a bit of shitty driving. They came in fast with silenced weapons and machetes. No one had a chance. They combed the place from top to bottom, looking for you and the box, and me as a bonus,' he added grimly. 'That's the thing about surveillance, Daniel. Got a feed of the whole thing in living colour on DVD at my other place.'

'Was Chekhov there?'

'Oh yes. Pizza Face was there all right. He personally killed half of my people with his damned machete.'

'I'm so sorry I led him to you,' I said lamely. Sami was shaking his head.

'He was after me anyway. It was just a matter of time before it happened. The person we have to settle with after Chekhov is your Sir Bernard. Switch the phone off before we go much further.' I did as he asked and left it on the boat's dashboard while I went to deal with our guest who was beginning to stir. As I move to the rear of the boat, Sami took his own mobile from his pocket and started to make a call.

I grabbed the very hurt Mr Beige and propped him into a seat in the stern. Both his legs were bent at odd angles. The 9mm slugs rather than the fall from the dock had probably done the damage. I pulled his arms behind his back and used a length of mooring cord to tie them to a handy cleat. I looked at the amount of blood soaking his thighs and pondered whether or not to apply tourniquets. I decided to do just that. Sami wanted him alive, and so did I. Grabbing another piece of rope, I sliced off three or four feet. I tied a quick figure of eight around the top of both his thighs and pulled it as tight as I could before tying it off. When I had done my Florence Nightingale trick I went forward and climbed onto a seat across from Sami.

Sami was an expert with the boat. He swung the wheel effortlessly to dodge past a lumbering barge loaded with coffins coming from upstream. I couldn't help thinking that, although coffins were a common enough cargo as any canal watcher would know, it was strangely appropriate to see them at that time. 'I came back this afternoon to wait for them to show again. I knew they'd come looking to see if I was dead, or if you showed up. Fucking predictable.'

'Russians,' I said, 'predictable and violent. You knew Chekhov was still alive and active.' It wasn't a question.

'I knew,' Sami replied as he worked the wheel. 'The ugly son of a whore. I thought we had an arrangement.' He had the power wound up again and we were racing up river, slicing past everything else on the water as if it were standing still. I didn't ask him why he hadn't bothered to tell me about Chekhov rising from the dead. I knew Sami always had a reason for what he did or didn't do.

Sami picked up my mobile phone from the ledge under the windscreen. 'He's got a tracer of some sort in here, an ELB and probably a relay bug,' said Sami. 'Power on and it's live. Every conversation goes back to Bernard and he has your location thanks to a GPS bird up above.' He transferred the phone to his right hand and from out of nowhere another boat virtually the same as ours came alongside us at speed. Sami reached across and the passenger in the front of the other cruiser took the phone. I recognised the passenger as Jo, Sami's invisible warrior. Jo grinned and waved at me as the big black craft peeled away and headed down river. I wasn't in the least bit surprised at what had just happened.

'We'll use it against Sir Bernard,' Sami said as he started to throttle back. 'Jo's taking it to a lab. We'll know its secrets in an hour or two and Sir Bernard will have no idea it's been compromised.'

'Yeah,' I muttered. Sami took a Marlboro from the pack I was holding out. He seldom smoked. I lit for both of us.

'Don't blame yourself, Daniel. I meant it when I said Chekhov didn't hit me because of you,' Sami said. 'He's making a move on me—the timing was probably coincidental. You are another issue altogether. You're personal,' he said, drawing deeply on his cigarette. 'He got my sister's son and my cousin back there, and a lot of others,' he said, sending the words into the slipstream in a curl of smoke.

'Mary?' I asked. Sami just nodded.

'Chekhov wants you real bad but I want him worse.' Sami's voice was flat as he half-turned to look at me. In the reflected light, the pupils of his eyes looked like holes drilled through solid white marble. The holes went deeper into his soul. 'Oh yes,' he whispered. 'I want him and I'm going to get him!' The promise in his voice was absolute.

Sami had now steered us off the main river and we were moving along a canal. There were the usual groups of tired warehouses broken by houses on stilts and docked long-tail boats. Clumps of water hyacinth floated everywhere along with the usual assortment of rubbish. This certainly wasn't one of the more salubrious waterways in the Kingdom. It was almost totally dark, and the spotlight fixed to the bow carved a bright slash through the night.

Sami turned off the canal we'd been running along and we moved slowly into a waterway that was only a couple of feet wider than the hull of the boat. There were no buildings along the banks of this mini-canal, just jungle. All of this in the middle of a damned city!

The canal ended at a high concrete wall with a large pair of solid steel gates set into it, extending right across our path. Sami tapped a button on the boat's console and the gates slid apart smoothly and silently. We moved on into the glare of powerful lights. There were lights everywhere. It was like daytime in this place. I could make out the lake we were crossing. There was a stone jetty in the foreground, and a large three-storey building behind.

'Home sweet home,' Sami said as he turned the wheel to line us up with the jetty. He touched the control on the console again and the gates to the canal slid shut behind us.

'Your line of work certainly pays,' I said in open admiration or just plain old-fashioned jealousy.

'Oh yes,' Sami replied as he nudged us into the buffers on the pier. 'It does that. We'll talk more about that when we sort out Chekhov and your beloved Sir Bernard.'

I mumbled something approaching agreement and took in the amazing surroundings. There were half a dozen other boats moored at the jetty and anchored in the lake itself. They were all long, low craft with big outboards in their sterns. I had no illusions that these were fast-running drug boats designed to get from A to B very, very quickly indeed.

More lights had come on, exposing what appeared to be a huge compound with gardens and lawns stretching off into the darkness. Half a dozen figures came out of the shadows towards us. These guys were armed with M16s and Ak47s. One held the leashes of a pair of what I took to be attack dogs. I couldn't tell the breed, but they were big, black and had plenty of white fangs. Dogs and I had never got on.

The first pair of guards came out on the jetty to meet us. Sami threw the bow rope to one of them and stepped onto the dock. I followed. Sami jerked a thumb at the man lying in the stern of the cruiser. 'We want him alive. Stem the blood flow and prep him for conversation,' he instructed. 'A little truth juice, I think. Call us when he's ready.'

'Okay,' came the acknowledgement. The men slung their assault rifles and dropped down into the boat as Sami and I moved off. I trailed my host as he led the way up towards the house. It wasn't a house, it was more like a damned palace or a luxury hotel. From my perspective it appeared to be U-shaped with the open ends pointing towards the lake. It was truly magnificent. Its splendour was more than driven home when we entered a wide glass door at the base of the U. Sami and I were in a huge, high foyer. The floor was polished cream marble and there were statues and paintings everywhere. This was like Tuk Tuk's palace for Sakura—elegant and so damned lavish.

We didn't loiter in the foyer. Sami led me up a wide, curved teak staircase. As we climbed the broadly spaced steps, I recognised some of the paintings hanging on both sides of the walls. I knew without asking that they weren't copies.

'Fruits of my ill-gotten gains,' Sami said with a thin smile as I paused to check out what I thought was a Renoir. It was! I finally dragged myself away from the two-foot-by-two-foot daub that was probably worth more than I'd make in a lifetime, given I lived to eighty or ninety. I wasn't bitter. Fucking Renoir was dead and, for the moment, I was still alive.

I carried on after The Onion Man and eventually followed him into what appeared to be his study. It was the size of a basketball court, filled with leather and more dark, beautiful wood. Antique weaponry, a dozen more paintings, ceramics and shelves of leather-bound books all vied for my attention. I didn't give in to them but instead headed for a couch and crashed onto it. Sometimes I was on overload, and the last forty-eight hours had just about blown my circuitry to hell and back.

Seated with a big tumbler of bourbon in my hand and a mineral water in Sami's, we started to debate what to do. We began with the most important question: Did Sami know where to find Chekhov? He did.

'Chekhov's main base is in Ayutthaya,' he said. 'It is on the Pa Sak

River, about 300 metres from where the Pa Sak and Lopburi rivers converge, just above the actual town. Looks like a warehouse complex, but appearances can be deceiving.'

I knew Ayutthaya was about fifty or so miles north of Bangkok. I'd been through it a few times. It was probably as good a place as any to set up house. It was close enough to Bangkok to keep a handle on things and, being small, it was certainly a lot easier to keep tabs on who was in town. 'He'll know we took one of his men alive and he'll be ready for whatever we throw at him,' I suggested. Sami nodded in agreement.

'We'll need a lot of help on this one,' he replied, 'and that is being organised as we speak.' Sami stood. 'Relax here. I have a personal matter to attend to.' He hesitated. 'Daniel, we both have grieving to do, but it will have to wait until we have completed our business with Chekhov. I will be half an hour. Help yourself to whatever you want. Company is on its way and we'll eat later.'

Sami left. I lit a cigarette and let my eyes wander around the incredible room. Hell, this was as much a museum and a library as it was a study. There were thousands of books in the cases that lined the walls and a dozen free-standing sculptures and pieces of pottery. As I took in the eye candy, one object caught my attention. Amidst all of the magnificent artworks on display, the figure that caught my eye was positioned in the corner of the room to the left of Sami's huge desk.

It was the statue of a warrior, caught in the white glow of a single spotlight set in the ceiling. The curve of a sword shimmered silver in the light. Curious, drink in hand, I moved to examine it. The figure was Japanese, a samurai warrior, and it wasn't so much a statue as a suit of armour fitted to a mannequin. The armour had been created from highly polished black metal with gold worked into it in intricate patterns. I then decided that it probably wasn't metal but an elaborate creation of lacquered wood, metal and leather. It was hard to tell. The helmet had a beaked crown that formed a visor. The blank eyes of the mannequin were all but obscured behind narrow vertical slits. There were three swords, as was the samurai tradition. I remembered as much from my karate days. The smaller weapons, the *wakizashi* sword and the *tanto* dagger, were sheathed through a leather and cloth rope at the warrior's waist. The gleaming longsword—the magnificent *katana*—was raised, held high above the warrior's head. In heavily gloved hands he held the leather handle, probably made from the skin of a shark or ray. I knew the stroke the warrior was poised for. It was a blow that would send the razor-sharp blade of the *katana* down in an angled stroke that would cleave a victim from shoulder to hip in one ferocious blow.

Despite myself I shuddered. The forty-one- or forty-two-inch blade of the raised sword looked damned sharp. The light sparked off the cutting edge as if to illustrate this fact. It wasn't a tourist article but the real thing, possibly the best bladed weapon of all time, and crafted for one purpose only: to kill. I moved back out of the arc of the sword. Maybe it was just fatigue but I felt vulnerable, as if the mannequin would spring into life and send the razor edge hissing my way.

It was said that the best blades were made with sometimes a million laminates of soft iron and hard steel, folded and hammered again and again to create the ultimate sword. Sometimes master sword makers could only complete a handful of these works of art in an entire lifetime. It was tradition that when the sword was finished, a criminal, slave or prisoner was brought forward and the sword bloodied with the cleaving stroke to satisfy the gods and illustrate that the blade was perfect. Nice touch!

Now that I was on my feet, I drifted along the walls of Sami's study, browsing the artworks and books. When I reached the windows I stopped and looked down into the gardens. I could see Sami. He was to one side of the lake, by a small altar under a tall spreading tree. Two figures holding carbines flanked the tree, facing outwards. On the altar, long candles burned.

My old friend was kneeling, his back to the house, his head low to the ground. As I watched he rocked back, raising his head then lowering it. I could see that there was a white band around his forehead. He repeated the motion and I faded back from the window. I had no idea of Sami's faith. I guess I had always assumed that he was a Buddhist, but there was no buddha on the altar—just candles.

My extremely complex friend, Sami Somsak, was either grieving for his people or he was praying for the strength to bring down Chekhov. I refilled my glass and somehow found myself back in front of the samurai warrior, hovering just out of range of its sword. I was still there ten minutes later when Sami re-entered the room. He came to my side.

'The ultimate warrior, Daniel, the samurai,' Sami explained. He moved around the desk, retrieving his glass of mineral water as he went. He sat in the leather swivel seat and I drifted to one of the equally plush visitor chairs. Sami sat looking up at the raised sword before his eyes turned back to me. He gave me half a smile. 'You know me just about as well as anyone, Daniel, but there is one thing that few know.' Sami paused for what seemed like a minute but was probably only a few seconds. I had the feeling he was choosing the words he needed to plot a verbal course through a complex explanation. Then he started speaking in little more than a whisper. 'You don't know Tuk Tuk Song and I are related,' he said with a crooked grin. It wasn't a question. Now he had me. I caught my lower jaw before it banged me on the knee.

'How?' I croaked.

'He's my uncle. My mother is his sister.'

'Fuck,' I said, shaking my head. 'How come you never told me?'

'Not important in the scheme of things,' Sami replied simply as he lit a cigarette and held the pack out to me. I took one and accepted his light. 'It wasn't a secret, Daniel, it just wasn't important to what you and I were doing,' he added softly. 'Anyway, after Chekhov hit me I called uncle.'

'I called him as well,' I admitted. Sami nodded.

'He told me. He's got a score to settle with the mad Russian as well. But first a little of my family history. It may help you understand more about your future business partner.' Sami looked at me through a cloud of cigarette smoke, his eyes challenging. He was preparing to reveal yet another layer of himself to me.

'My mother, Shan, Tuk Tuk's sister, was taken by the Japanese as a comfort girl,' he said with no infliction whatsoever in his voice. 'When the war ended she was pregnant. She was going to commit suicide out of shame, but Uncle Tuk Tuk stopped her. He cared for her and protected her from anyone and everyone. She gave birth to a boy. That boy was me.' Sami stopped again but only for a moment before he raised his glass and gave me a wry grin.

'Daniel, you coined the name The Onion Man for me many years ago. It was probably more apt than you even dreamed.' Sami chuckled and his face came alive. He looked young again, the years dropping away. 'I am part Thai, part Chinese and my father was a Japanese officer, a samurai, according to my mother. She was perhaps fortunate when she arrived at her comfort camp!' There was emphasis in the words, a contemptuous sharpness accompanied by a grimace. 'Yes, she was perhaps fortunate,' he repeated more softly, 'that an officer took her for his own exclusive comfort. The war ended before he tired of her and she was left carrying me.' He paused for a moment. 'I despised much of what the Japanese had done to Asia, and what they had stood for in my early years in particular. Then I discovered the code of the samurai.'

Sami tuned his swivel chair and nodded at the mannequin. 'There are some things in their code that are admirable, other things not so. I have perhaps tried to live by those principles that are good,' he said. 'Those swords,' he nodded at the samurai, 'are my pride. They are fourteenth century blades made by one of the great masters, a craftsman named Orazawi. He made only five sets during his lifetime. This is the only one to survive to this day.'

'Expensive,' I said for something to say. Sami laughed aloud.

'Ah, Daniel, you are so wonderfully blunt. Yes, expensive,' he replied. 'I won't tell you how much, but let me just say that there are few automobiles in the world that cost more. However cost is not the issue, perfection is.'

Our conversation on the subject of Sami's heritage and magnificent weaponry ended about then with a knock at the door. One of my host's bevy of beautiful women entered the room at Sami's word. She ushered a guest in with her.

28

Karl Isbaider didn't seem surprised to see me. In fact, the expression on his face suggested that he knew I would be there.

'Well,' I said. 'Party time!'

'Absolutely,' the CIA man said with a tight grin.

'In five minutes we'll go and speak to our guest,' added Sami.

'You got one, Sami? Nice going,' said Karl.

That told me Karl knew exactly what Sami had planned all along, even though I hadn't told him. The CIA agent gave me a knowing wink that said, 'You can't keep any secrets from us, Danny boy.'

'Let's go and play question and answer,' Sami said.

'Thumbscrews and needles?' Karl wanted to know. He didn't look as if the prospect of either or both bothered him in the slightest.

'You barbaric Americans,' said Sami, shaking his head in mock disgust. 'I have found that chemicals are an irresistible force if used by a knowledgeable practitioner. I have one such on my staff.'

Five minutes later we went down to a basement room to hear the life story of our Jamaican-born subject. Would you believe it? Wesley was his Christian name. He had an American passport. And yes, Chekhov was really pissed at me. There was more, much more, and he gave it all up very eagerly. The irresistible force coursing in his veins was doing its job.

'It figures that Chekhov knows you're still alive,' said Karl, directing the comment at Sami before he forked a mouthful of something extremely tasty into his mouth.

'Yeah, but he doesn't know where I am,' Sami replied.

It was midnight and we had finished with the Jamaican mafiosa. He was being dumped, still alive but slightly amnesiac, outside a hospital in Bang Sue as we ate.

'Chekhov doesn't know a lot about me, including the existence of this place,' Sami replied. 'No one knows but my inner circle and now you guys.' He paused with a fork loaded with noodles hovering in front of his mouth. 'Damn. That means I'll have to shift or kill you both,' he added without even the hint of a smile.

'We knew,' said Karl as he picked up a prawn and started peeling it. 'You bought the whole ten acres in 1997, flattened just about everything on it but for the jungle fringe and built this place. Took almost two and a half years. You moved in in July 2000.' The CIA man grinned at Sami from across the table. 'Satellite mainly, Sami.'

'Okay, you guys knew, but that doesn't mean the mad Russian does,' Sami replied. Karl and I made eye contact. Sami saw it and shrugged. 'Okay, maybe he does, but I've got thirty people here with enough hardware to start a serious war. What do you suggest?'

'We go up to Ayutthaya and collect the arsehole's singed scalp with all due prejudice,' Karl replied. 'We've been fucked about for years. It's just that we didn't know Chekhov was the man behind a lot of what's happened until just a few months ago. He laid a lot of the action off through people we didn't know he actually controlled. Now that we do know we can put a whole lot of grief at his feet. He's been officially sanctioned, and that comes right from the top.' The CIA agent slapped the table and grinned. 'Let's go get the fucker!'

'Okay,' I said, 'and there's something else you should know.' I'd made the decision to tell Karl about Sir Bernard. I laid it all out for him and he sat there expressionless until I had finished. Then he gave me that smile of his.

'I wondered when you were going to tell me.'

'You knew?' I stammered.

'That he was a traitorous old queer. We've known about him and Chekhov for years,' the CIA man replied. 'Years!'

'Why the fuck didn't you tell me?'

'Fuck,' Karl snapped back. 'I figured you knew.'

'Oh shit,' I muttered. I was getting so sick of being a secret squirrel, especially as everyone else seemed to know the secrets I didn't. 'Do you know how long ago Bernard told Chekhov I was the man who fried him and killed his wife?' I asked. 'And if he's known for years, why didn't he come after me back in the UK?'

'Dunno,' replied the CIA man. 'Maybe he was just busy. He'd been carving up the local rackets big time and perhaps he didn't need the distraction until he was ready. Maybe he was waiting for you to return to Thailand or maybe Bernie boy just kept him as an ace up his sleeve until this fucking black box shit came along. Ask your boss before you kill him,' he added in a tone that suggested he really meant it! To kill Sir Bernard, that is.

'Whatever,' Karl continued. 'In the last year, Pizza Face started raising his ugly profile. Your arrival and that fucking thing you had out there in the bloody Andaman lit the psycho's fuse for real.'

'I'd be pissed off at the man who turned me into a Freddie Kruger clone and killed my woman,' said Sami, joining in the speculation. 'But as far as hitting Chekhov where it really hurts,' he paused, 'wheels are in motion as we speak. Now I think it's time for some sleep. I think we all need it. Karl, will you be staying?'

'Meeting in the morning,' the big CIA agent said. 'We run on meetings,' he added rather ruefully. I imagine he would have liked to have been able to enjoy Sami's brand of hospitality for the night. 'Keep me in the loop.'

'We most definitely will,' replied Sami as he walked Karl to the door. I had absolutely no idea what Sami had going on, but I appreciated he had included me. I tried to stifle a yawn. It didn't work.

29

There was breakfast for two on a table that could have seated twenty comfortably. I had forsaken my Indian disguise for new underwear, faded new Levis that were exactly my size and a black polo shirt. My outfit was completed by a pair of new Nike trainers which, of course, fitted perfectly. Because my kit was still in the embassy Sami, as always, had come to the rescue.

The breakfast spread was lavish. I went for the mixed grill with a vengeance; after a diet of embassy sandwiches this was pure heaven. Sami, as always, showed more restraint and went the route of fruit and rice porridge. We both did full justice to the excellent coffee. At one point Jo came in. He and I shook hands and did the bear hug thing. Jo Darakam, a former Thai Special Forces captain, and Sami had been inseparable in the years gone by. Given my association with Sami that meant we were often musketeers three, generally on the wrong side of some border or other.

Greetings over, Jo put my mobile phone on the table beside me. Like Sami, his English was devoid of any accent. 'A built-in locator beacon and a bug. Beacon is active whenever the power is on and the bug picks up and rebroadcasts every call,' he explained. 'Very clever because it looks normal, except to an expert.'

'That's why Bernard was paranoid about me keeping it charged,' I replied. 'He wanted me with a permanent bull's-eye on my back for the satellite.'

'Let's get Chekhov and then figure how to use that and circumstances to get Bernard,' said Sami, folding his napkin and dropping it onto the table. 'Daniel, I'd like for you to come with me on a run down the Gulf. It'll be educational,' he concluded with a chuckle. I agreed, wondering what I was in for. Whatever Sami had in mind, it would no doubt help make the day go a little faster.

Forty minutes later Sami and I were on board one of his low, mean-looking cruisers, nudging our way down side canals towards the river. The boat, like most of the ones in Sami's fleet, had a pair of huge Mercury outboards on the back. I guessed he must have done a deal to buy the big black motors in bulk, and I also guessed that black was the official Somsak corporate colour because as well as the motors, the entire boat was also black, including the racing seats we were perched in. I had no doubt that the cruiser was as fast as it looked and felt. I was impressed.

Out on the Chao Phraya, the sound of the big motors got louder and the bow raised a little, but Sami didn't give the boat its head. 'Speed limit. Don't want to attract too much attention,' he said in reply to my silent question. I had to chuckle. Here we were, cruising down one of the most heavily populated rivers in the world in the nautical equivalent of a Formula One racing car, and Sami didn't want to attract attention.

It was a pleasant run. The day was overcast and humid; a typical Bangkok day for my money. On the river, however, the breeze we stirred up as we moved was refreshing. I allowed myself to be a tourist for once. Luxury hotels and temples, barges, long tails, speedboats, freighters and rafts of water hyacinth all slid past as we glided down the brown waters towards the Gulf. As we moved on, our speed gradually increased, then we broke away from the river mouth.

'Now we do it,' Sami said with a broad grin as he slammed the twin throttles forward and adjusted the trim tabs. The water was calm and we started flying effortlessly, blasting past the slow-moving vessels in the harbour. I still had no idea where we were going. All I knew was that we were going there fast. We ran south for just over an hour, with the digital speedometer showing a steady seventy miles per hour. We raced past vessels of all shapes and sizes as if they were standing still.

'That's where we're going,' Sami yelled at me, pointing beyond a fleet of shrimp boats to a matchbox shape that sat on the near horizon. 'I was here when Chekhov hit the warehouse.'

I'd seen the big mineral suction dredges many times, but from the air or the shore. We'd passed two of them working the ocean floor for tin on our way from the river mouth, but they'd been a few miles away from us. Now it appeared we were about to pay one a visit. I didn't try to second-guess Sami. I had learned that was almost impossible, particularly after the happenings of the past week or so. I didn't mean it was the oriental mind at work, rather it was just that The Onion Man was as devious a person as I'd ever met in my so far very eventful life.

At a steady rate of knots, we surged on towards the dredge. It grew with every passing second. We were maybe half a mile away when the sheer size of the thing hit me. This monster in the Gulf of Thailand was enormous. It was basically a huge barge the size of a football field. Most of it was enclosed in a giant tin shed which had the dimensions of an aircraft hangar. A huge triangular-shaped boom hung over what was the bow. Suspended from this was a segmented pipe made from metal and heavy rubber. This pipe was a yard across. Effectively it was the suction tube for a giant vacuum cleaner. The bag was somewhere in the shed and the exhaust was at the rear, pumping waste into the water behind the barge and turning it the colour of shit as it created its very own ecological disaster, choking every living thing in the water around it. Nice!

The noise was incredible as we came alongside. The iron shed acted like a giant drum, amplifying the sound of the working machinery inside. Despite the racket, our arrival had been anticipated. Two guys carrying AKs were standing watching us as Sami nosed us into the buffers that edged a small floating landing attached to the dredge's flank. Because the vessel probably had a top speed of half a knot and was basically a floating island, why not tag a jetty onto it?

Another man appeared. Unlike the other pair who were dressed in denims, the guy who trotted down the gangway towards us was dressed in a dark suit, complete with white shirt and tie. He looked like a slick Thai banker. Whatever his role, he grabbed the line I threw to him and fastened the bow to the pontoon. I took the stern line with me as I stepped up and tied the blunt end of the boat to the dock while Mr Suit greeted Sami. The greeting was definitely one of servant to master, and Sami wasn't the one touching his forelock.

'This is Mr Nuampara, Daniel. He is the assistant manager of this noble establishment,' said Sami without a hint of anything in his voice. Nuampara and I greeted each other in Thai, and the formalities were over in two seconds. I fell in behind Sami and the three of us went up on deck, Nuampara leading the way. I was dying to ask my host what in the hell was going on, but I bit back the urge. I had no doubt that all—or as much of the all that Sami was prepared to divulge—would be revealed in good time. In Sami time.

Sami took his mobile phone from his jacket and turned it off. 'No mobiles to be used here, Daniel, and no smoking. That was why I couldn't call you sooner. We have a very volatile process going on. One rogue discharge of electricity could blow this whole place into orbit. Mr Nuampara, please lead on.'

Nuampara did just that. He took us to a door in the otherwise blank tin wall that towered above us. I wasn't really surprised when he produced a swipe card and ran it down a scanner slot. The door looked as if it was made of plate steel. It hissed to one side and we entered. I'd expected a monstrous cavern filled with roaring machinery, not the silence that enveloped us the moment the door closed behind us. We weren't in any cavern. We were in a long, well-lit corridor. The floor was carpeted. The walls were covered in an off-white vinyl-coated material. There were doors along the length of the corridor, but none of those that I could see were open. I didn't attempt to hide the surprise from my face. Sami had been expecting that. He grinned.

'Nothing is what it seems, Daniel,' he said as he reached for the handle on the door nearest us and opened it. He beckoned me forward and stepped to one side so I could get a clear view of what lay beyond. There was a second inner door, completely glass, that remained closed.

The room beyond was at least a hundred feet long and possibly thirty feet wide. It was filled with tables covered in paraphernalia—drug-processing paraphernalia. Several figures in white coats were moving about or working at stations. They all wore hair covers, paper shoes and filtration masks. I stood shaking my head in wonder, entirely lost for words. 'The perfect cover,' Sami explained. 'Right out in the open for all to see. As you have no doubt guessed this dredge doesn't dredge. We simply pick up a little mud, pump it through and out again to give a little cover. The heavy machinery noises are broadcast from hidden speakers. It's a very big sound system,' he added with a grin. 'Most of the interior of this place is devoted to the product. We have a crew of thirty. Some are seamen and engineers, some are guards, the rest work on this.'

'Jesus,' I whispered, still trying to find words. This guy just kept on flooring me at every turn.

'Come work with me, Daniel,' he said with a smile, 'just as soon as we have sorted out our current problems. Come and make yourself rich. Five years and you can retire anywhere in the world and live any life you want.' Standing there listening to Sami Somsak, it all made sense, incredible sense. Sure, I hated drugs and junkies. Many, if not most, of the people I had ever had that conversation with agreed. But for an amoral person in a world that had few morals, why the hell couldn't I just say screw it and throw my hat in the ring? At that moment it would have been easy, but something in me was fighting back. Was I was growing a conscience?

Halfway along the corridor was a set of carpeted stairs set in a recess in the wall. Sami nodded to Nuampara. The man looked vaguely disappointed, but he carried on along the corridor as Sami and I climbed the stairs. There was a landing that cut back, and then we were in a second corridor. Again, Sami chose a door and led me inside. The room we entered was a huge lounge. The wall opposite to where we had entered was mostly glass. I was aware of a couple of people at the far end. I ignored them and followed my host to the window. We stood and looked down into one of the biggest laboratories I had ever seen. Huge vats and pipes filled the complex. Small figures in familiar white overalls were dotted around the vast room.

'Oh shit,' I muttered.

'Plenty of shit, Daniel. Pure shit,' he repeated. 'We can process virtually all the opium we can get.'

'You own it?' I asked, shaking my head in something like dumb disbelief. 'It's yours?' Sami smiled, but it was a smile that contained something else. 'Not quite all mine. I have a partner.'

'May I ask who?' I said, feeling my heart flip. I had a feeling I knew who Sami had in tow.

'Yes, Daniel, Tuk Tuk,' Sami said simply. 'When he goes I am prepared to take you on as my partner.' My breathing and heart stopped for a second. I replayed the words once, then twice before I could manage to get my tongue to work.

'But what can I contribute?' I asked. 'Christ, Sami, this damned barge alone must be worth millions. I'd be lucky if I could pay for the fucking toilet paper for the bogs for a week.'

'You'd contribute friendship and trust, Daniel, and your rare skills in several other areas,' he replied. 'We all need people at our side we can trust. I trust you implicitly. Otherwise, do you think for a minute I would be showing you this?' He chuckled. 'This is The Onion Man's biggest secret, Daniel.'

He was right, of course. Trust was that rarest commodity, a word that was carelessly bandied about. Unfortunately so few people knew the true meaning of the word, and of those who did, most didn't honour it or the concept it represented. Five letters, big word. 'I trust you with my life, Sami. I have done many times,' I replied, 'and you likewise. Let's just get fucking Chekhov and Sir Bernard Turncoat and then we'll talk. Okay?'

'Okay,' came the reply. Sami smiled. He knew he almost had me. 'Lunch, I believe, is being served,' he added with a sweep of his arm. At the far end of the lounge two figures were standing beside the table they had been laying. One was a man in a chef's uniform. The other was a woman, dressed in a conservative European-style top and skirt. She advanced to meet us, smiled and took Sami's hand as she kissed him on the cheek.

'Hello, big brother,' she said in English. 'You are looking well.'

'And you, Anita,' replied Sami formally before his face broke into a broad grin and he embraced his sister.

I'd met Anita Somsak once years before when she had been in her late teens. She had been quietly beautiful then. Now she was an elegant and definitely very striking woman in her early thirties. There was no wedding band on her finger.

'I remember you well, Daniel,' Anita said as Sami and she broke their embrace. She proffered her hand and I took it. It was cool and strong. Her lips were soft on my cheek.

'And I you, Anita,' I replied. 'You are also involved in the family business?'

'Of course,' she smiled and drew me towards a chair. 'It is a thriving industry and Sami needs help. I manage this facility.'

'Uh-huh,' I said, catching Sami's eye. He shrugged. 'He's been talking to you has he?' I queried. Anita smiled disarmingly back at me.

'Just a little. You really should consider it.' She smoothly changed the subject with a wave of her hand as she indicated the food displayed on the table. It was a superb spread. 'In honour of our guest and old friend,' she added.

'I'm flattered,' I replied. I nodded to the chef who was standing nervously by the door that obviously led into his kitchen. 'A wonderful banquet, ' I said in Thai. 'Fit for a king.'

The man's face split into a huge smile. He thanked me profusely and took that as his cue to vanish back into his lair. Anita took her seat between Sami and I, and played mother. She and I split a bottle of excellent New Zealand Chardonnay, while Sami drank Evian. The conversation was light and touched on everything and nothing. No mention was made of Chekhov or the deaths in the family. As Sami had already made plain, the grieving would follow.

We sat and enjoyed a magnificent lunch in that luxurious apartment in a huge floating shed in the middle of the Gulf of Thailand. It was surreal in anyone's language. From the outside, the roaring mammoth was devouring the ocean floor, supposedly sucking riches from the mud and sand. In reality there we were, dining in elegant silence in another world. What genius to see the potential and set up a drug-processing factory out in the Gulf. Thing was, it really was genius and so simple to operate. No one bothered coming near these rigs. They were there, so huge and ponderous, but no one noticed them. They were like mountains—they just were.

The way it all worked was simplicity itself, as Sami explained. Raw materials would arrive by fishing boats, re-supply vessels, ore boats and speedboats. The finished product left the same way, much of it going directly to passing vessels that had already been cleared for departure by customs at the port of Bangkok. Simple and so very effective. It was pure damned genius and it had all been Sami's idea, as he grudgingly revealed during our meal. Tuk Tuk had recognised it for what it was when Sami put his proposition to his uncle. The pair had split the cost of setting up the operation.

It was mid-afternoon when Sami and I made our departure. I left, having made a promise to call Anita when Sami and I had finished our business. I could see something at work in Sami's eyes when she set that up. There was no doubt a man could do a hell of a lot worse than to have Anita Somsak on his arm. Sami's little smile confirmed that. It was one thing to have a friend as a partner. It was even better to have a friend as a partner and brother-in-law. Problem was, Sami knew my past and present with regards to women. Maybe I was mistaking that look and, in actuality, he was warning me off.

'Anita was married for two years. He was an arsehole. She tossed him out,' Sami yelled at me as we peeled away from the dock and waved farewell to Anita and Mr Nuampara who had come to the dock to see us off.

'No kids?'

'No. He couldn't fire a live one. She needs a man and a swag of babies,' Sami said. 'Interested?' he added with a laugh.

'Sami. I'm not the marrying kind anymore. I wouldn't be good for her.'

'I'm not so sure,' he replied. 'After Chekhov we'll have a lot to talk about, my friend.'

'Yeah,' I said, suddenly feeling apprehensive about my future beyond a soon-to-be-dead Russian mafioso. And what about Tuk Tuk? Would the old devil keep his side of the bargain? At the end of the day I'd saved his life, but for what?

30

Bangkok, 19 July 1996

'Your round,' Casey said, pushing his empty glass across the bar with his right hand, while his left slid up the oiled thigh of the girl in the G-string who was swinging her lithe body around the chrome pole that extended from bar to ceiling.

I hated the fucking bars in Patpong. They were for tourists and tourists only. There were other places I would rather have been, but Casey had this thing about dance bars and he and I were partners, sort of anyway. I finished my JD and nudged my glass to sit it next to his.

We were in an upstairs annex bar where there was a little more action than you found in most street-level ones. Up another level and it got wilder still. These were the private bars where money and familiarity gave entry. Casey was a familiar in every single one of them.

The bartender looked thirteen, which meant she was probably ten or thirty. She was topless, her pert little titties crowned with jutting rosy nipples that perfectly matched the colour of her lipstick. She smiled and began fixing re-fills.

I pushed over a handful of hundred-baht notes and retrieved the drinks. Casey's hand had gravitated to his girl's groin. He was doing the boy–girl check. Number Fourteen squatted at the base of the pole, smiling until Casey was done. He nodded and her much practised smile broadened. When the dance ended, she would be joining us. Casey fished out his wad of notes, peeled off 500 baht for the bar, folded it and slipped it down the front of his new girlfriend's G-string.

'Oh shit,' I thought to myself. The mad Yank was planning a night of debauchery, or at least rampant sex, which meant I wouldn't see him until well after noon the next day. Problem was there were things we needed to do and places we needed to be. We had arrived back from Chiang Mai after doing a little business over in what was still Burma in those days. That evening we had been in the Pussy Bar for three hours, having arrived there straight after dropping our kit at our apartment on Yen Akat Road. The apartments were adjacent units in a block of twelve—a hop, skip and proverbial jump from half the embassies in the city as well as a short *tuk tuk* ride from Patpong, or Phat Phong to be annoyingly correct.

The apartment was a halfway house for guys like Casey and me. It was an anonymous plain-white building hidden behind a high wall. With heavy but discreet security, Lot Thirty-Four was an ideal R&R environment for Black Ops operatives in all but one aspect. Casey couldn't take his girl of the night back to his apartment. That was just about the only no-no and it was strictly enforced. Allowing a clever little Asian assassin into the nest of half the undercover operatives in the region was not a good idea. Casey would have to take Number Fourteen to a hotel, which meant he wouldn't be around when I left for a very important meeting down at Thonburi. I could and would remind him of that before we parted, but I knew from almost eighteen months' experience with the horny Texan just what the result would be. When he came out of the bush he was like a tomcat on heat.

As for me, well, I was heading for a little apartment over in Khlong Toey where a friend was waiting. Mai was an eye doctor at the hospital at Phra Khanong down by the university. We had met six months before when I had arrived back with an eye infection from an excursion into Laos. We'd sort of kept semi-regular company ever since. She would take care of my itch and, I hoped, I hers.

Out in Patpong the night stalls were up in both of the short streets that made up Patpong 1 and 2. Casey had his new friend, now clad in skin-tight jeans and a plunge-neck top, hanging off his arm. He was grinning in anticipation of the delights to come. AIDs wasn't as rampant back then, but I couldn't help thinking he'd better have a rubber or two in his pocket. He wouldn't, I knew that as well. It was bareback or nothing for Casey, the boy from Houston out of Langley. Fucking Texans pissed me off. In their world nothing could go wrong until it did. Then everyone else was to blame. Casey had once shaken both of the Bush presidents by the hand, something he was prone to telling the world when he'd had a drink too many. Hell, I'd shaken hands with royalty and I had never told a soul.

Anyway, we stepped out past the show touts in Patpong 2 who were promising sixty-baht beers and free sex shows. Like hell! We gave the stallholders the brush in their own language and made it out to the crowded footpath on Silom Road, looking to flag down some transport.

The first we knew that the shit was about to hit the fan was when we heard an almighty shriek of rubber on the road, coupled with the howl of big engines and the distinctive staccatoed overlapping boom–whack sound of at least three semi-automatic weapons.

The entire throng of humanity that crowded the footpath and the entrance to Patpong 2 froze, eyes locked on the big black Mercedes that was hurtling down Silom towards us, sending traffic spewing in all directions. Behind the Merc was a silver American tank with a sunlit roof. The roof was open and a guy with an AK47 was standing firing at the Merc, along with another guy who was hanging out the front passenger-side window. The second gunman had an M16. These guys were playing for keeps.

'Fuck,' was all Casey could say as he headed for the pavement, dragging his date down with him. I squatted on my heels and made myself small, praying that the whole circus would scream on by. It didn't. The Mercedes was fifty feet away when it lurched and headed for the footpath, taking out a pipe-railing fence as if it was made of pasta. The car slammed into the throng of huddled, screaming pedestrians and started taking them out along with the flimsy street stalls as it careened towards us. A pipe railing which was hanging off one side of the car acted like a scythe, sending broken people spinning in all directions.

At six foot two and fourteen stone I wasn't a small guy, but I became a giant in about a millisecond as I came to my feet and threw myself backwards. I took out a couple of people on the way and landed flat on my back on a stall full of watches and knick-knacks at about the same time the Mercedes arrived where I had been. The canvas awning of the stall collapsed over me and the whole damned thing I was lying on was shunted further back into the broad alley that was Patpong 2. I scrambled to get free of the tangle of clothing, canvas and bodies I was now engulfed in.

The screaming was all around as I kicked myself out of the mess not a moment too soon. There was a roar of horsepower and more screaming. As I made it up the curb to the pavement outside a bar, the fucking Mercedes was under way again. The driver had his foot down hard on the pedal and to hell with whomever and whatever was in front of him. There was a girl sprawled on her back across the bonnet—a street girl, tiny, half-naked and definitely broken.

The Mercedes shunted its way another ten yards past me before the sheer weight of bodies and debris from the crushed and smashed stalls bogged it down. People were running and crawling in all directions. I vaulted several crouching bodies and rolled into the first doorway I could find. I knew what was going to go down next and it wasn't good. I was in a bar and the fucking jukebox thumped on despite the chaos outside. Madonna, it seemed, was still a virgin. Yeah, right!

I peaked around the doorframe. Back on the street the silver Yank tank had stopped and the man with the AK47 was still shooting at the stalled Mercedes. Either the gunman wasn't a great shot or just didn't care. People desperately trying to get out of the way were going down. Two other shooters were now out of the silver car, Mr M16 being one of them. The other gunman had a Mac 10. Both weapons were firing as the men advancing into Patpong 2. The rounds from their weapons were chewing chunks out of the rear of the Mercedes and anyone and anything that got in the way.

I crouched low in the doorway, pressing hard against the doorframe. I could have gone deeper into the bar but it was filled with frightened people, a mix of locals and tourists. I wanted to see what was going down because staying alive might mean making a split-second decision. A grenade lobbed into a bar would take away a lot of the options—especially if I was hiding down at the back.

A large European woman with a shock of red hair and a pale face was at my side, her eyes wider than any saucers I had seen. 'Oh God, oh God, oh God,' she repeated over and over to herself, her hands latched onto my shoulder. What a grip she had! I looked back at the advancing gunmen, but couldn't see Casey or his girl amongst the living, dead or dying.

The near rear door of the Mercedes opened and a man flung himself out. His timing was bad because the Mac 10 had just opened up again. The guy getting out of the car took a hunched step and spun to the ground. At about the same time, the front passenger door of the Merc opened and a huge man with a round moon face and a big handgun got out and crouched behind the open rear door. The gun—I figured it was a Desert Eagle or similar—started booming and Mr M16 suddenly bit the dust. The guy with the Mac, however, had taken cover behind a stall and was walking, crouched down, towards the Merc. Mr AK was coming in fast from further across the street where he had more cover. The guy with the M16, unfortunately, was still alive. He had crawled behind a stall, dragging the rifle with him.

I cursed that I wasn't tooled up. I'd left my weapons back at the apartment.

Being armed in the Kingdom was frowned upon unless absolutely necessary. This was a necessary moment, but it wasn't my fight. Not unless I made it mine, or these clowns did. That was the thing about being a pro. You weren't supposed to get involved in other people's business, which was a laugh because for the last few years, I'd done nothing else.

The man who'd scrambled out of the back seat of the Mercedes was crawling away from the car, moving in my direction. That was good, or that was bad. If he made it into the bar then it would definitely become my fight. I'd be fighting to keep myself alive when the others came for him. I could see plainly enough by the way the guy was moving that he had taken a hit. His right arm was hanging limply as he moved. The injured man was an older guy, Chinese, I figured. He was dressed in an expensive-looking dark-blue suit that shimmered silver in the street and bar lights. Not a good suit to wear in a firefight.

The old guy had crawled to a place where he could hunch behind the remains of a clothing stall. It wasn't much cover but it was all there was. This had a kind of irony to it. There he was, kneeling in his million-baht suit, surrounded by dozens of cheap T-shirts with fake brand names splashed across them.

The old guy looked up and our eyes met. I could see no fear there. It was a look that simply appraised what he was seeing. He turned his head away and peered back at the advancing gunmen. There was no doubt whatsoever that the guys heading our way were out to kill him. This wasn't a case of grab and run. The old man's goon, the one with the big boomer of a handgun, had been forced around the front of the Merc, cut off from his charge by the advancing duo. Despite what happens in the movies, guys with semi-automatic weapons going up against guys with handguns have a huge advantage and it sure as hell was apparent right then.

I felt the injured man's gaze fall on me again, and our eyes locked. It was then that I recognised the man hunched behind the clothing stall. The smooth, round Chinese–Thai face was suddenly all too familiar. This was Tuk Tuk Song, the boss of Thailand's largest Mafia outfit. Way back then we ran continuous intel on who was doing what to whom and who did or didn't know about it. Tuk Tuk Song was the man doing most of the doing and he knew all about everything in this part of the world. He was 'the man'.

My problem right at that minute in time was that the man looked like he was planning on coming in my bar and bringing his own personal gunfight right along with him. So I was going to be in the game whether I liked it or not. There was another thought percolating in my head: if our side were in Tuk Tuk Song's good books, we could gain some big time favours.

So my choices were that I could either meet Tuk Tuk in the doorway and shoulder him back out to his fate, or I could help him to safety. Logic was screaming for me to take the former option. However, being in credit with Tuk Tuk Song was potentially a major plus. I knew that one day that could give me an edge in the deadly game of snakes and ladders we all played.

The decision had made itself. My hat was in the ring.

The butt of a handgun was showing under Tuk Tuk's left shoulder. Probably because he was right-handed and that particular appendage was out of play, he hadn't drawn the weapon, not yet. Maybe he couldn't shoot left-handed. Either way, if he came in the bar I'd take the gun and use it. Then we, all of us, might have a chance of staying alive.

I pried the red-haired woman's fingers off my shoulder, gave her a smile that was meant to be reassuring or something, and gathered myself for whatever was coming next. I could see that Tuk Tuk was getting ready to move. He'd gathered his feet under himself and was in a clumsy sprinter's crouch. Then he was moving in our direction, but moving far too slowly. The big Desert Eagle was booming away like a damned machine gun as his goon tried to give him cover.

The Thai hood with the M16 raised himself to his knees, rifle at his shoulder. He fired maybe twice before ducking back for cover. Tuk Tuk Song, however, had been hit again, this time in the thigh. He hit the deck in front of me. It was now or never!

I rolled over the doorsill across the pavement and down the curb to where the Mafia boss lay. There was no time for niceties. I simply grabbed Tuk Tuk by the lapels, bunched the material of his jacket under his arms and kicked up and backwards. I got over the first high step then dug my heels in and kicked away again to get across the pavement and over the doorsill. It worked, and I hurled both of us backwards into the bar. The doorway where our silhouettes had been framed just a fraction of a second before was scorched by the whining passage of a swarm of angry, copper-jacketed hornets. Somewhere deep in the bar glass shattered and there was more screaming and squealing. Damn Madonna was still maintaining she was a virgin, and the red-haired woman was frozen, crouched by the door talking to her god.

'Back door,' Tuk Tuk grunted as we lay amidst a tangle of limbs on the floor. The Mafia boss's face was close to mine. I could smell fish and whisky on his breath.

'Yeah,' I replied. If I got him away from the firefight with no more bullet holes in him, he would owe me big time. I rolled to my feet and pulled the revolver from the shoulder holster under his arm. He didn't protest and I didn't have time to compliment him on his choice of weapons. The stainless Smith & Wesson Model 66 was one of my favourites.

I pushed the revolver down the front of my belt where I could get at it quickly if I needed to. A hurried glance out through the door told me the big guy in front of the Mercedes was still trying to keep the man with the AK busy. It was a hard ask! Away to the right and I could see Mr Mac 10 coming our way. 'Time to go,' I said, reaching down to grab Tuk Tuk by the shoulders. I could tell it hurt from the hiss of breath, but the Thai Mafia boss knew as well as I that a little pain was much preferable to death.

I hoisted Tuk Tuk over my shoulders, his legs hanging down in front of me, my left forearm barred across the back of his thighs. He was a solid unit and I was going to be running hard. 'Back door,' I yelled in Thai as I headed deeper into the bar. A terrified little dancer wearing not much more than a grimace and a G-string scrambled from behind the edge of the bar and led the way into the bowels of the club.

The door was open. The couple of thugs who would normally have been stationed there to stop unwarranted entry or exit had vamoosed stage left. My little nymph had decided that, near naked or not, flight was a far better option to staying in the bar. She ran ahead down the dark, stinking alleyway while I followed, trying to maintain my footing. Tuk Tuk weighed a ton. Behind us the firefight continued, gunshots echoing down the concrete canyons of downtown Bangkok.

I was gasping for breath and my legs were just about turning to jelly when we finally emerged from the dank, foul gloom of the alleyway. We were on the edge of a loading dock. There were crates of produce and pallets of tins stacked about. I figured it was the loading bay of a hotel. There was a van backed up to the dock with its rear doors open. I could see long canvas bags stacked inside. I guessed it was linen or something similar. Whatever, I staggered into the back of the van and swung Tuk Tuk off my shoulders, lowering him more or less gently onto a pile of the canvas sacks. 'Stay here,' I said, turning to leave and almost falling over the bar girl who was right behind me.

It was a surreal sight, both sad and funny. The girl was standing there in a tiny red G-string, teetering on her ridiculously high matching red shoes. Her arms were crossed over her tiny breasts, her hair was a mess and her huge eyes leaked mascara everywhere. With her painted lips quivering on the verge of tears, she looked like a ten-year-old child. Possibly she wasn't much older.

'Here,' I said as I slipped off my jacket and draped it across her shoulders. 'You stay here. Sit down!' I pushed her down beside Tuk Tuk and stepped out of the van. There were two or three frightened faces peering at us from the edges of the rolling door leading into the bowels of the hotel. I could still hear gunfire, but there were sirens in the distance. Definitely time to be long gone. I swung the van doors closed and barred them before dropping to the ground.

The keys were in the van's ignition. There were no protests from the driver, wherever he was, or the hotel staff. They'd obviously seen the gun in my belt.

I cranked the Hino into life and nosed out of the service alley into the traffic boiling down the street. Ten minutes later I pulled into a side street and stopped. I went around the back of the van and opened the rear doors.

Tuk Tuk used his mobile phone to call up his own people. Once they arrived and took charge of him, I grabbed a cab and took Rutana, the bar girl, to the hovel she shared with a bunch of other working girls. That accomplished I headed back to Lot Thirty-Four and the televised news of Bangkok's latest gangland battle.

Neither Casey, his date nor fifteen other people survived the battle of Patpong. In addition to the dead there had been more than sixty people, both tourists and locals, injured in the fracas.

So that was how I met Thailand's top mafiosi. We became sort-of friends, a situation that remained the status quo until I was forced to kill Arune and shoot the hell out of Choy, who incidentally had escaped the Patpong shoot-out without a scratch. And, oh yes, he succeeded in taking all three gunmen down before the cops spoilt the party.

31

It was dusk when we moored the black boat. Sami and I went to our respective apartments in the mansion to clean up for dinner. Fresh underwear, a pair of dark slacks, a crisp white shirt and a pair of soft black leather slip-ons had been laid out for me while I was in the shower. How the other half wants me to live, I thought as I dressed for dinner. Sami was working me hard, if not too subtly, and I didn't really mind. Obviously my employment contract with Sir Bernard Turncoat was due to be terminated with utmost prejudice on my part. I left my room and headed for Sami's study.

Sami was sitting at his desk when I entered. A huge plasma television screen, which had until then been hidden, had appeared from behind panelling on one wall. The screen was live and the images it showed were of destruction—total, absolute destruction. I could see a river and alongside it a huge area of burned and blackened real estate.

'Tuk Tuk's men have wiped out Chekhov's base at Ayutthaya,' Sami said as I perched on the edge of his desk. 'I'm sure Chekhov thought his fortress was invincible and that was a big mistake.'

'Looks like it was hit by heavy artillery.'

'Close,' replied Sami. 'Uncle Tuk came in over the top with half a dozen choppers with Napalm canisters and petrol drums. Chekhov hadn't figured that would happen in a city. Uncle had half a dozen boats on the canal with flame-throwers, RPGs and guys in trucks with machine guns. He wants Chekhov almost as badly as we do. However I think Uncle missed him.'

'Why?' I asked, my heart doing a nasty flip in my chest. I wanted this to be over.

'My intelligence tells me Chekhov went north just before the attack. Uncle waited too long,' Sami said with resignation and a trace of something else in his voice. 'Maybe a mole amongst Uncle's people, maybe just bad luck,' Sami added and I suddenly realised he wasn't totally disappointed that Chekhov was still alive. I let that thought rest for a moment and focused back on the camera that was panning the scene from a chopper hovering several hundred feet above.

'What the fuck are the authorities going to make of this?' I asked. A full-scale war in one of Bangkok's satellite towns wasn't going to go unnoticed. Sami just chuckled mirthlessly and punched up the sound as a talking head appeared over the scene. '*... in Ayutthaya. The factory was used to make paint, and the explosion from the chemicals reduced the main building and the surrounding warehouses to rubble. Authorities estimate that as many as eighty people may have died and many others were injured. In other news ...*'

Sami flicked off the television and the giant screen vanished behind a pair of ornate wooden panels. 'Industrial accident, just like the one at my place.'

'Familiar pattern,' I suggested.

'Feel like hitting the bush again, like the old days?'

'Oh no!' I muttered. I'm getting too old for this game, I thought.

After another lavish dinner with just us two guests, Sami again asked me if I wanted company. Again I told him I didn't. I thought that for the first time in my life my libido had become stone dead. Everything that had been happening had been about death. Even to me, sex, love, the act, the thoughts, the desires were all a celebration of life. I could only hope that when Chekhov's corpse finally cooled, the fire in my groin will reignite itself. I was too young for celibacy or Viagra.

I bade farewell to Sami, went to my lonely bed and tried to sleep. The whole exercise eventually proved impossible. I just couldn't find that black tunnel and slip away into nothingness, so I switched to plan B. I got up and went into the opulent bathroom, fired up the spa and slipped into the rolling water with a large glass of my favourite spirit to hand. I figured more alcohol and the soothing powers of a hot-water massage might do the trick. It didn't.

When I emerged with my skin wrinkled like a lightly tanned prune, I pulled on a robe and used the suite's coffee machine to make a brew. Mug and cigarette in hand, I went out onto the balcony. The time was a few minutes after 05:30 and dawn was already starting to lighten the sky. The guards were still in place and lights blazed against the grey of the coming day. I noted that half of Sami's boats were gone. No matter what was happening with Chekhov, it was probably business as usual in the drug world. 'Life goes on' was the cliché that came immediately to mind. I supposed it was a reality, but then most clichés started out that way—didn't they?

There was a movement on the top floor balcony two or three rooms away to my left. A young woman wearing a white robe had stepped out of a darkened room. There was the sudden flare of a match. Another smoker in the dawn, I thought. She took a good hit of nicotine and, as she exhaled, she saw me. I raised a hand in silent salute. After a moment she did the same. Here we were, two conspirators waiting for day, each of us locked into our insidious addiction. Was I addicted to nicotine? The answer must have been yes. I'd been addicted since I'd been about seventeen, and even when I'd been off the weed I'd still been an addict just one puff away from damnation. It seemed to be the same with all addictions: drugs, alcohol, food and sex. All the good things in life, some would say. I snorted at the ridiculousness of my philosophical turn and came back to reality.

'Back to the bush,' Sami had said. Were we going hunting or were we going to be the hunted? I dropped the remains of my cigarette into the bin at my feet and waved farewell to the young lady in white as I went back into my room. I figured she was another of Sami's family brought there for safety. A daughter perhaps, a niece, a wife, a concubine? I knew Sami had several wives, legal or not. I had met some on rare occasions. All I knew was that his family set-up was confusing. Whoever the young lady was, it didn't matter, but curiosity was second nature to me.

'Back to the bush,' I repeated as I dressed in yet another set of borrowed clothes. I still hadn't had my kit picked up from the embassy. It didn't matter; the walk-in wardrobe in my suite was filled with clothes, from suits to jeans and even jungle camouflage, all in my size. Was this just another ploy from Sami to get me on board? I was slapped out of my thoughts by the phone. It was he.

'Good morning, Daniel. We have news of Chekhov.'

'Good or bad?'

'A little of each. Come down. We'll breakfast and talk,' he replied.

Breakfast over we relocated to Sami's office. There he did his magic and made the big screen monitor reappear from behind the ornate wall panels. The image he showed me was jungle, with a broad river that snaked down a wide valley. On one of the sharpest bends the snake path formed a peninsula that was narrow at the base but broader towards its head. There was a clearing at the apex of the bend and in the centre of the clearing was a small village. Sami used a hand-held remote to magnify the village and I quickly realised it wasn't a normal Thai hill village. The huts were arranged in precise military rows. There was a perimeter fence and watchtowers.

As Sami brought the image in even closer, I could make out razor wire adorning the fence and machine guns in the watchtowers. I didn't need him to explain who owned this particular real estate.

'Lowland,' said Sami. 'A basin between the mountains. Virtually all swamp and surrounded on three sides by water, so the only clear access is by air or water. He has the water and shore mined, as is the land approach. We know he's got radar and we suspect a bunch of Stingers, so there'll be no sneak helicopter attacks on this camp.'

'Tidy,' was all I could think of to say.

'We have to have him come to us,' Sami said, 'and I think we can arrange that very easily. His desire to get to you will ensure that,' he added.

'Where have you been?' Bernard sounded as pissed off as I'd ever heard him.

'In hiding,' I replied. 'Remember that hit on the Russian, Dimitri Chekhov?'

'Vaguely,' the old bastard muttered.

'He didn't die. He's here in Thailand and he's raising havoc. It was Chekhov's people out in the Andaman,' I said.

'Chekhov,' Bernard mused as if he hadn't heard me. 'Dimitri Chekhov?' The old bastard was playing his senility card.

'Yeah,' I replied. 'He's very much alive and he's taken out friends of mine and he's after me. I'm heading out of Bangkok until Tuk Tuk or the CIA get him,' I said, feigning an urgency I was far from feeling, and all the while marvelling at the old bugger's acting ability. Hell, he was almost as good as I was. I wondered what his GPS would be showing.

I was sitting in one of Sami's boats on the Chao Phraya about mid-way between Bangkok and Ayutthaya. Sami, Jo and I were going upstream to check out the destruction on Chekhov's base personally. The news on the Russian was that he had definitely gone to his northern base. Sami was thinking he'd been tipped off by one of Tuk Tuk's people. 'Trust is hard to come by in our business,' he said. 'That's why I want you by my side.' He wasn't letting up in his efforts to get me to join him.

Because Chekhov was in the north we had no choice but to go there as well, but not yet. Karl, through his people, was busy putting some things in place. In the meantime we three went sightseeing. The call on my mobile was to keep Bernard happy and unsuspicious without putting a big bull's-eye on Sami's palace.

'Call me when you get to where you're going,' Bernard said.

'I will. Wish me luck,' I said, trying to sound at least a little apprehensive.

'I do, Daniel, I certainly do. Call when you get there,' Bernard said in his most fatherly tone. Even given the distance and electronic filters, I could hear the relief in his voice as he cut the contact. I congratulated myself on having masterfully played dumb with him. Sir Bernard Turncoat was convinced that no matter what, his boy, Danny Swann, had no idea he had been set up. In his perfect little scenario he would give Chekhov my location and Chekhov, in turn, would finally get me. Then Bernard's double-play secrets would be safe until he went to his grave.

Officially, of course, the story which would do the rounds would be that he, Sir Bernard Randolph Sinclair, arsehole and bar, had despatched his agent to collect a package. Despite all odds the agent had been successful but unfortunately been killed in a later event. How sad! Bernard would probably get a fucking bar on his knighthood or something. As for failing to get the anthrax for his real bosses or his partners in crime, that would be unfortunate for Chekhov but, on the other hand, Her Majesty's Government would be well pleased. In Bernard's book he would be thinking that, ultimately, Chekhov had a sticky end coming at the hands of Tuk Tuk or the CIA and he could quietly slip into retirement to enjoy whatever millions he no doubt had in his Swiss bank accounts.

'I don't know whether or not he's spoken to his old mate Dimitri today,' I said to Sami as I switched off the phone, 'but it'll be an interesting call when they make contact.'

'I'll believe that,' Sami said as he kicked the big boat into action and sent us racing upstream.

32

Too many cooks and this broth will be turned into blood soup. The thought crossed my mind as we sat in Sami's study for what amounted to a mission briefing. Karl, Jo, Sami and I were there, so was a big, hard-faced s.o.b named Alex. Alex was, Karl informed us, commander of a Special Operations unit. His squad had flown in from the Pakistan–Afghan border just for our little party, all thanks to the CIA paymasters. Karl and Alex had flown in by Jet Ranger just as we three musketeers had arrived back at Sami's compound from our excursion upriver. Coincidental timing? I thought not. Coincidence didn't have a place in the game we were playing. I was beginning to feel like a spare cog.

We were gathered in front of a large-scale glass-framed wall map. The map was of Thailand and the countries that shared its border. Sami illuminated the map panel at the touch of a button. 'We go here!' He tapped the glass, pointing to an unmarked spot on the map in the northeast, close to the border with Laos. The place he indicated wasn't far from Vientiane, the Laotian capital. I'd spent quite a bit of time there once, officially as a tourist recovering from a bout of malaria. The true facts had been a little different, however.

'Chekhov has his base here.' Sami pointed to a red dot on the glass. Then he moved his finger a few inches. 'Here is where we will be.'

'A village?' I said, squinting at the dot he was indicating.

'On a hill,' Sami replied. 'It's the perfect spot. There is only one road in or out.'

'What about the villagers? We don't want them caught in a firefight!' That was the big reality clause for me. I didn't want any more dead and injured innocents on my already overloaded conscience.

'No problem,' Sami said. 'They'll be gone when we get there.'

'They're just going to pack up and go?' Karl muttered, an incredulous expression replacing his habitual poker face.

'You could say I own the place,' Sami said with a shrug. 'It's one of several I have along the border.'

'Does Chekhov suspect that you know where his base is?' I asked.

'Undoubtedly, but that doesn't matter. He'll come after us,' Sami said. 'The urge to kill Daniel is too strong. He won't be able to resist it.'

'Does he realise that this place belongs to you?' Karl was asking.

Sami shrugged. 'I would say probably. We're only twenty clicks apart, but there are a lot of other operators in the area as well. We watch each other from afar,' he added mirthlessly.

'And you're positive he'll come to us?' I asked, worrying that question to death because I just wasn't sure.

'He wants you dead, badly, so he'll come calling,' said Karl. 'The double whammy is that he won't realise that you've got America's finest on your side.' The newcomer almost smiled at that—almost. 'He'll figure you have what, maybe fifteen to twenty men on the hill?' Karl asked and Sami nodded in agreement. 'Okay, and he's probably got about the same?'

'Maybe thirty,' Sami replied.

'That's okay,' Karl came back. 'We'll have a crew of ten Special Forces plus whatever else you've got on site.'

'Six in the village, all fighters,' Sami said, 'and ourselves—say twenty. Is that enough?'

'Oh yes,' replied Karl. 'Agree, Alex?'

'That's enough,' the Special Ops man replied in a tone that ended any argument. I had no idea what Alex and his team were going to bring to the party, but I figured I had no choice but to go along for the ride. It was the only game in town. I knew that when it came to technology and killing equipment, the Yanks would come up trumps.

'Okay, so I confirm with Bernard that I'm in this village here.' I leaned towards the map to look for a name.

'Bang Sai Deng,' Sami supplied for my benefit.

'Bang Sai Deng,' I repeated. 'I speak to him and he alerts Chekhov. Chekhov comes calling and we finish it.'

'Right,' agreed Sami as the others nodded. 'As I said before, there is only one road to it from this point here.' Sami tapped the glass again, indicating a village at a crossroads down the valley from Bang Sai Deng. His hand traced a route back to Chekhov's base away to the west. 'Chekhov has vehicles at the road's end here where the swampland starts. He has to come this way unless he flies in.'

'Okay,' I agreed. 'Bang Sai Deng is where I'm hanging out. I'm waiting for Tuk Tuk or the CIA or anyone to take Chekhov out. I'm ready to flick across the border, just like old times, if there's any attempt on my life, blah, blah,' I finished. We all knew the plot.

'Let's go do it,' said Karl.

33

As we flew in to Bang Sai Deng, I was all eyes. A map and a distant memory were not enough to go on when you were about to put your life on the line. The pilot brought us down almost to within tree-hugging height as we came in on a circuit from the north. We were trying to keep our arrival as low-key as possible. Despite the lack of height there was a lot to see, including a shit load of jungle. We brushed past the shoulders of hills and flashed over little patches of agriculture. A few small villages were dotted around. We could see Vientiane off in the distance and the mighty Mekong showed as a dark ribbon against the green of the jungle just a few hundred yards north of us.

Behind us the borrowed Iroquois kept just as low. Although painted in civilian livery, the old Huey was actually a Thai Air Force machine, one probably used for Black Ops work.

We flew up the northern side of a flat-topped, jungle-covered hill and came over the crest low enough to send dust flying. We were here. The Huey hovered back down below the crest of the plateau as our pilot set up for landing.

Bang Sai Deng hadn't been sited on a hill by accident. The occupants enjoyed the 360-degree panoramic view—a view that was a prerequisite for a village whose cottage industry was processing raw heroin. The top of the hill was about the size of a football field and pear-shaped, the thick end facing southeast. The jungle on the hilltop had been cleared back to where the flat but slightly sloping plateau dropped away towards the valleys below. There were half a dozen large trees left standing, either to provide shade or to make landing anything other than a single chopper really difficult.

The village itself was typical of those anywhere in the north. I could see a dozen bamboo and thatch huts of various sizes on stilts. The only building to break the mould was a long, low corrugated-iron shed situated at the top end of the village on the narrow neck that pointed up into Laos. It was as far from the rest of the village as it was possible to get. A fringe of trees grew around the shed, breaking its outline from the air. I didn't need a degree to figure this was one of Sami's drug labs. It was the place where the raw opium tar was cooked before being sent south for further refinement and cutting.

Beyond the lab the terrain dropped away steeply, and the green carpet of bush rolled back towards the Mekong five or six miles in the distance. The river was effectively the border between Thailand and Laos running down to cut through the heart of Cambodia into Vietnam and then to the South China Sea. I'd seen a lot of that particular piece of water over the years gone by.

There was a welcoming committee of half a dozen hard-looking guys, each bearing a semi-automatic weapon. They were standing motionless in a loose knot by the hut nearest the landing zone. The only things in motion apart from the debris thrown up by Jet Ranger's rotor blast were a few dogs and some scrawny-looking chickens. Upon our arrival, pigs squealed indignantly from half a dozen pens scattered around the plateau. I figured the families had already shipped out otherwise the place would have been swarming with kids.

As soon as we had unloaded our gear with the help of Sami's resident team, the Jet Ranger took off and slid back down the northern side of the hill to be replaced at the landing site by the Huey.

Alex's team was ten, including him as leader. They were a hardened, competent-looking group of young men. As usual they were dressed in the Special Ops mish-mash of casual clothes and combat gear. The common denominator for them all was a pair of dark glasses which each man wore. We were all wearing them but these guys made them look like part of their uniform.

Using my usual method of categorising everyone and everything, I decided Alex's lot were from *The A Team*. Thank god there wasn't an obvious Mr T amongst them, and as for the George Peppard character, there wasn't a cigar in sight. These guys would be using real bullets and there wouldn't be a Hollywood temper tantrum to be seen.

The A Team all had the look of guys who had done a lot of time out in the hard lands. Each of them carried a big pack and wore a sidearm. They didn't talk. They didn't have to because they'd obviously done this many times before. They laid their kit to one side of the chopper and returned to the Huey to haul out several large olive-green, hard-shell holdalls. Within two minutes both helicopters had gone back towards the border. I knew they would skirt the hills and split up, the Huey heading due south to its Bangkok base while the CIA Jet Ranger would head for Udon Thani, fifty or so miles to the southeast where it would remain on standby in case we needed it. That was reassuring to me.

Sami had gone into the village followed by Jo. Each of them wore a holstered pistol and a belt knife and Jo had an M16 over his shoulder. Instead of a carbine, Sami carried a long wrapped bundle of leather and cloth. I had no idea what he had in it. Given the speed of our final preparations, I'd concentrated on what I had needed to do. As personal armament, in addition to the Walther, I carried a Colt Commander, a shortened, telescopic-stocked version of the M16.

While Karl went to consult with The A Team, I walked to the edge of the drop-off where the dirt road started or ended, depending on your point of view. I found a convenient log, checked it for wildlife, then sat and started scanning the countryside with the binoculars I'd borrowed from Sami.

The road, or rather the track, dropped away out of sight immediately below me as it passed into the jungle. It reappeared on the valley floor three or four hundred feet further down. Here it followed the black ribbon of the stream that split the valley floor on its way to join a larger river maybe four miles further down. A hundred yards before the rivers converged there was a village and a crossroads of sorts. A crude log bridge carried another dirt road across the river. This track ran left to right across the foot of the valley. Anyone attempting to reach us by road would need to cross the bridge.

As I sat contemplating the lay of the land and the logistics of the whole deal, I could make out an old green and blue bus rolling away from the bottom village, east in the direction of Vientiane. 'My people taking a holiday,' said Sami as he sank onto the log beside me. 'Nice long approach road,' he said.

'He won't just drive on up here when he comes,' I replied. 'Not

Chekhov.'

'No he won't, Daniel,' Sami said. 'I figure they'll come at night on foot from the bridge and use the bush and the ridge.' He almost chuckled. 'Just like old times, eh?'

'Yeah,' I replied. 'Just hope we do it right this time.'

'We will,' he promised. 'Hopefully by coming in the way we did, any spies he has in the village won't have seen or heard us. There's a lot of aerial traffic up this way. So, with luck, Chekhov won't know we are anywhere up this way until tomorrow when you call Sir Bernard.'

'You got home base covered?' I asked. That had been nagging at me. I was nervous about who in turn was minding the store.

'Oh yes,' he replied. 'Uncle has added significantly to my garrison.' I relaxed a little at that and we sat there in companionable silence and waited, two old friends at ease with each other, each contemplating the hours ahead and his own mortality. At least I was. I had to surmise that Sami was as well, but with Sami Somsak, who could tell?

I glanced at my watch. It was only a few minutes before 15:00. We had time to kill. Right on cue a pig squealed. Sami and I turned. Up at the drug lab two guys had one of the village's many pigs by its hind legs and were wheelbarrow-walking the indignant beast down towards a bamboo and thatch shed that sat alone at the edge of a plateau.

'Dinner,' said Sami simply. 'And breakfast and lunch tomorrow,' he added. 'Shall we get ourselves organised?' I agreed. We stood and strolled over to where Karl and The A Team had gathered in front of the veranda of the largest hut. Karl and Alex were on the deck and a large photographic satellite image of the entire immediate area was attached to the thatch wall.

'Jesus,' I muttered under my breath as I got up close to the photo image. The detail was incredible. It had been taken in the middle of the day because the shadows were short. We were looking directly down on the plateau. I could count the chickens and pigs and virtually name the dogs. There were people in the garden plots and smoke or steam was rising from the lab chimney and cooking fires. The road showed as a vivid brown–yellow slash through the jungle to where it met the black of the stream.

'Delivered half an hour before we were airborne,' Karl told me.

'We know Chekhov won't be able to get detailed current reconnaissance when he identifies this location.' The CIA man gave Sami and I a wolfish grin. 'We can't rule out an intelligence agency from a friendly country requesting up-to-date imagery from our birds. However, should such a request come in the official story is that we have a malfunctioning satellite.' I grinned at that. Karl had effectively shut down any thoughts Sir Bernard might have had about supplying Chekhov with up-to-date images of Bang Sai Deng and its surrounds. 'So here's the plan,' he continued, nodding to Alex who stepped up to bat. I paid attention. I was the bait, but my life might depend on knowing as much as I could about the trap.

The plan the Special Ops man outlined was simple. In the first instance, his team was preparing to put out sound and heat sensors, cameras, decoy devices and Claymore mines at strategic locations on the probable jungle approaches to the plateau. They would install their monitoring equipment in the big hut they'd designated as HQ. They would also check and, where necessary, augment the system of bunkers and trenches Sami had created around the perimeter and under the huts as a defence against drug bandits.

'Given that Chekhov doesn't know where Dan is at this time, we'll set up a basic perimeter defence tonight,' Karl told us when the Special Ops man had finished. 'Tomorrow Alex and his team will load for Russian bear.'

The upshot was that once all of this had been done, the waiting would begin. I confirmed that I would be phoning home in the morning and the party broke up. There was to be a briefing at our evening meal. For Sami, Jo and I that was it for the moment. The A Team dispersed to where their equipment was neatly laid to one side of the landing zone. Several of them proceeded to carry green, hard-shelled cases into their designated HQ, while others began to open the other containers and assemble their high-tech weapons of war. I recognised two long cases amongst the pile of gear.

'Stingers,' I muttered to Sami. 'Nothing but the best!' He nodded his agreement. The ground-to-air shoulder-fired missiles were probably the most sought-after technology of their kind by bad guys worldwide, and we had two of them at about a squillion dollars apiece.

'Just in case Chekhov's got a Hind or two,' Sami replied, referring to the Russian's flying battle tank. Even that would be no match for our missiles. 'Let's sort out our accommodation,' he continued. 'Three of my guys will sleep up in the lab, the others will be on watch, while we three will share a hut.' We detoured to where our packs were stacked and Sami led the way to the hut he had selected.

In the shade it was at least fifteen degrees cooler than out in the sun. I still wasn't used to the humidity. There wasn't a sea breeze or any breeze of any kind to stir things up. Nights could be cool up there but the days stayed hot unless there was a blessed breeze. Sami and I found spaces and angles to sling our hammocks, while Jo elected to use the hut's sleeping platform. 'The old men have gone soft,' he joked.

'But wiser,' Sami replied.

'Absolutely,' I agreed, stripping off my shirt, kicking off my sneakers and trying my hammock for comfort. It would do, I concluded. Jo vanished outside again and Sami went to stand at one of the window openings while I just sprawled out where I was. The perspiration beaded on my skin and the air was like breathing water. Despite that I lit a cigarette and lay looking out at the world from deep in the shadows.

In the bright afternoon sun and the intense heat, chickens continued to scavenge for morsels of food while dogs, smarter or just lazier, merged with the shadows under the huts and trees. It was a peaceful Thai hill village dozing in the sun, but for how much longer?

Several of The A Team troopers bearing what looked like brutally heavy packs passed across my line of vision heading for the jungle below. I stubbed out the remains of my cigarette and closed my eyes.

Dinner was a communal affair held in the lean-to off the cookhouse set just behind the designated HQ. A huge wok was suspended over a large gas burner. It turned out that one of the lab guys had been a chef in another life. In my experience Thai cooks, like many other nationalities in Asia, could produce such a lot from such limited ingredients, and this was another case in point. The rich, spicy pork curry was served with rice and vegetables and washed down with beer. It was an excellent meal. Just about as good as it would get.

The six members of Alex's team not on watch loosened up a bit after the food and beers. They talked in general terms about their experiences in the mountains of Pakistan and Afghanistan. They said it was a tough, dirty war as they hunted down Al-Qaeda. Now the team welcomed the chance to fight a different fight and the change of venue, even if it were just for a week or two. I realised that these guys were young, very young, most in their early twenties. They still had a lot of learning to do in many things, but not when it came to killing.

The A Team members left and Karl produced a briefcase the size of a pilot's document case. He opened it and handed out communication headsets to Sami, Jo and yours truly. The unit was pretty standard comprising an earpiece, stem microphone and a small battery pack with a switch and a dial, all attached to a simple adjustable elasticised headband. 'Essential you keep it with you at all times,' the CIA agent was saying. 'Four channels selected by the dial. Stay on four unless told otherwise. Three-position switch on the battery pack and a pressure button on the microphone stem,' Karl explained. 'First position on the switch is off, the second is stand-by mode which is monitor-only mode, so when any other individual so equipped presses the button on the mike stem, you will hear but can't join in. Three is full live, send and receive, just push the stem button to speak but release it when done.'

We all played with it for a moment, setting the channel and adjusting the headband. 'Stay on stand-by,' Karl instructed. 'If the shit hits the fan you're on four. Control is in there,' he said, indicating the HQ hut in front of us. 'Call anything in to them, anything at all, and because we're a mixed lot of military and civilians we'll talk in plain English, no military speak or codes. That puts everyone on the same page. Some of Alex's people will be on another channel at times,' he added. 'Range is ten clicks line of sight and good for three in the bush.'

Jo was delegated the task of instructing Sami's men how to use the headsets. It was decided in the end that, because Alex's squad spoke no Thai, Sami's two English speakers alone would get the units and share the watch.

When it came time to turn in, I went outside into the cooling night for a last smoke and to empty my bladder. The moon was as bright as an ice-cold searchlight, sending its white light down to bathe the plateau. As I ground out my cigarette, two of The A Team left their hut and walked towards the point where the track crested the plateau. The pair were tooled up with M16 variants complete with all sorts of fancy optics, plus a 40 mm grenade launcher under the barrel. They also had night vision glasses on their foreheads and between them they carried a tripod-mounted device that looked like a cross between a video camera and a large pair of binoculars. I guessed it was an image enhancer of some sort. I hadn't been briefed on the technology the specialists had brought up there with them.

Karl came out of the HQ hut to where I was standing watching The A Team setting up their equipment by the head of the track.

'That's X-ray,' he said. 'Our eyes in the night!'

'I'd love to play with some of their toys,' I said. 'What's that stuff inside?'

'You mean the stuff Alex won't let you, Sami or Jo near?' Karl said with a teasing hint to his voice.

'Yeah, that stuff,' I replied.

'Okay,' Karl hesitated. 'One of the conditions put in place when they agreed to lend it to us was that there was no nosing around the equipment. However, I can give you an overview.' The CIA man paused a moment, either to get his thoughts in order or to engage his mental censor.

'There are high resolution, low-light video cameras in the bush, not infrared which can be detected. There are listening devices, movement detectors, distraction pyrotechnics and remote Claymores, all controlled from in there,' he hooked a thumb over his shoulder. 'The plan is to hear Chekhov's men, see them, distract them and hopefully hit them hard before they get to us. Then we go and hunt down the remnants,' he said.

'Simple as that?' I replied.

Karl laughed. 'Yeah. Simple as that,' he answered, clapping me on the shoulder before heading off towards the drug lab, probably to check that Jo's briefing had been successful. I took the communicator from my shirt pocket and fitted it on. Having all of us wired for sound made great sense. The cynic in me muttered, 'Great, now we can all tune in to hear ourselves die.' I didn't really mean it. In fact I was beginning to feel a bit more confident about the way things were going, particularly when it came to Karl's team-mates. They seemed to know exactly what they were doing. They'd probably done shit like this a dozen times before. I was also relieved that, despite the fact we hadn't broadcast our location yet, they weren't taking any chances with sneak attacks.

I held my communicator to my ear and switched it from stand-by to listen mode in time to catch some of the chatter. 'How's the picture down the valley?' The voice was that of Alex back in the HQ hut. He was obviously checking in with the guys on the imager.

'I could count the hairs on a whore's pussy at five clicks,' came the operator's reply.

'Leave the whores alone until R&R, then you're buying,' Alex replied with a snort. I guessed that somewhere under that stone-faced exterior lurked a sense of humour. I flicked the headset back to stand-by. It was time to sleep and hopefully not dream of headless friends and mad Russians. I stripped to my underwear and crawled under the mosquito net, laying my Walther and communicator beside me. Because I didn't have my old-faithful holdall to use as a pillow, I had to make do with my borrowed pack. Sleep found me very quickly that night.

34

After our breakfast of rice and pork soup, Karl, Sami and I moved to the wide porch of the big house. Karl and I lit up and had coffee while Sami went off towards his iron lab, which I figured wasn't a bad defensive position at all given that iron didn't burn like thatch and was probably capable of stopping a bit more bullet than bamboo. I'd noted the sandbags lining the inner walls when I'd got the grand tour of Chez Somsak the day before.

'Half past nine,' Karl said glancing at his watch. 'Want to start the ball rolling?'

'Might as well,' I replied. The mobile phone was sitting beside my communications unit. I switched it on. There was a strong signal but that didn't surprise me because Sami had chosen this place. Probably the Vientiane mobile phone link was within range and ever-present communications satellites were floating around in the ether.

'I presume there's a GPS bird up there?' I said to Karl.

'Count on it,' he replied as he poured us both another coffee.

Bernard answered immediately, despite the fact it was a late winter's night where he was. I told him I was safely installed in my temporary lair. 'Just a little village up by the border,' I explained. 'Farmers, plantations. Right out of the way. I'll stay here until things quieten down.' For obvious reasons I didn't give him a hint that I wasn't alone. He didn't ask what the village was called. He was getting sloppy or excited. He was no longer playing the game of concerned Mr Need-to-Know-Everything.

'My battery is low, Bernard,' I said. 'There's no power to recharge it here. I'll need to save it so I'm switching it off. Will call you in a day or so.' I flicked off the phone before he could reply. It was hard being civil to the man who was orchestrating my death. Anyway, the deed was done. In a few minutes Chekhov would have the co-ordinates of my new home and he would assume I wasn't alone. Point was, if the spies he probably had in the village below didn't picked up the choppers, especially the one carrying The A Team, we might have a huge advantage. Time sure as hell was going to tell on that one.

'Strategy meeting in two,' Karl was saying into his communicator. I looked around for The A Team as he spoke and couldn't see any of them in view. Then a couple of blinks later six of them were converging on us from all points of the compass, all heavily armed and looking very, very businesslike. No doubt the others were standing watch.

Karl had the chair given that he owned The A Team by association. If I heard something I didn't like, I would speak up, otherwise this was a CIA gig from here on in. Sami and I were just the sacrificial goats, although I hoped that by the end of the day, the sacrificial tag would be dropped, from my perspective at least.

The satellite image was back up on the wall and Karl ran through the situation. 'It's absolutely vital that we don't provide any aerial hints that we are in occupation with some heavy hitters. He now knows we're here but he doesn't know our numbers or the make-up of our crew, even if the choppers are spotted. There will no doubt be a reconnaissance fly over,' Karl added. 'Sami, have four of your men dress as women, men only with weapons in sight as is usual up here,' he gave Sami a tight grin. 'Get them out in the gardens and walking about. Everyone else has to stay out of sight as much as possible.' Sami nodded. He turned to Jo who faded away to pass on the order, while Karl turned the show over to the Special Ops man.

Alex sent his crew off to do whatever it was they did and then proceeded to bring Sami and I up to speed. All the sophisticated gizmos were already positioned at strategic points in the jungle and on the track. They had a two-man ambush in place to take out any vehicles and personnel attempting a frontal raid up the track. The remainder of the team would concentrate on providing perimeter cover in Sami's earthworks. The village guys would be deployed amongst the buildings as a second defence with Jo as their main man. Sami, Karl and I would be the last line of defence along with the two guys working the high-tech gear in the big house. 'We're just preparing the big stuff now,' said the

Special Forces boss. 'Getting ready for a siege,' he added with a hard smile that suggested he didn't mind a bit. Tough cookie!

'The Siege of Bang Sai Deng,' I mused aloud. 'Just like it must have been in Vietnam.'

'Damn right!' Karl replied. 'Only we haven't got the howitzers.'

I didn't do the maths. Karl was one of those guys of indeterminable age, but I guessed he could have been in Nam as a very young man. 'No howitzers, but we've got the next best thing,' replied Alex, nodding towards two of The A Team members as they emerged from one of the huts carrying the unpacked Stingers. Another pair followed, one carrying a tripod, the other a squat multi-barrelled weapon.

'Minigun,' Sami said.

'We call it the mincer,' said Alex. I almost laughed, or applauded.

It figured that when Karl called in the cavalry they would come with the biggest and best hardware, but I hadn't figured on this. 'Nine barrels, .223 calibre, electric-powered, 3,000 rounds a minute on low, 5,000 on maximum. We also brought some tank busters which we will position around the perimeter.' The A Team relay had laid six big fat green tubes on the ground beside the pair assembling the Minigun. 'You've got good earthworks,' Alex told Sami. 'I'll go and assign the ordinance.'

With that, the briefing was over.

'Want to see where we'll be holing up if it all gets bent out of shape?' Sami asked, beckoning us into the big hut. Karl and I followed. The two men sitting at the monitoring equipment in a nest of freshly filled sandbags looked up momentarily, but Sami led us away from their end of the hut and their top-secret gear. He pulled a grass mat aside and exposed a trap door in the centre of the floor. 'Gentlemen, follow me,' he said, opening the trap and dropping through it.

The bunker was huge. Light came through slits spaced regularly along all four walls. The slits were covered with loosely woven mats that allowed the muted light to penetrate into the gloom. 'We dug this and then built the house above,' Sami explained. 'We have a log roof with more than a metre of earth on top. The whole village can fit in here. If the building catches fire, we're okay. We've got air vents and a 360-degree arc of fire. Outside you can't see the firing slots.'

I had to admit I was impressed. I hadn't seen any evidence of the bunker from up above. 'This is also my armoury,' he explained. Along one wall I could see a long bamboo gun rack full of hardware with boxes of ammunition. There were also RPGs stacked further along the wall. Rocket-propelled grenades were common anywhere in the world where there was a scrap going on, mainly because they were cheap, crude, easy to use and bloody effective. I noted that there was also an open crate containing conventional fragmentation grenades. Sami Somsak was set for war.

My eyes were now becoming accustomed to the low light and I could make out neatly rolled and stacked sleeping mats. Along another wall there were stacked cartons of what I presumed was food, along with water containers. There was even a toilet hole in one corner. Short ladders and exposed wooden panels set in the roof suggested that, if needed, the occupants could exit fast. 'Home sweet home,' I said.

'I fucking hope not,' replied Karl, his voice sounding more than a little ragged. 'Let's get back up in the fresh air. I hate fucking earthworks. Saw too many in Nam.' He'd answered my question for me. We climbed up through the trap door and went back up top.

Outside I walked around the big hut and only then did I really notice that it was built on a small rise. Only up-close could I see the woven thatch panels that hid the deep firing slits. Clumps of grass, a tree stump, a water bucket and the remains of an old ox cart served as props to disguise the gun positions. 'Pull a string and it all breaks apart,' said Sami. 'You saw the emergency exits. We can get out quickly if we have to or come up to fire RPGs,' he added.

'Impressive, Mr Somsak,' I said, meaning it.

'You are expecting a war,' Karl said. It was a statement, not a question. 'Always,' replied Sami. 'There are as many bandits up here as there have ever been.' He gave a tight smile. 'You pay the politicians for protection but that's just from the police and the army. There are plenty of other guys who want what you've got.'

'Ain't that the truth,' Karl muttered, fishing a pack of cigarettes out of his shirt pocket. Both Sami and I took one and Karl lit them with a battered old Zippo he'd obviously resurrected from somewhere. His non-smoking campaign, like mine, was obviously over.

'When do you think Chekhov will come?' I asked.

'Tonight!' came the reply, 'and it'll be a shitfest.' Karl coughed and cursed but took a deep drag on his cigarette. He was going to enjoy his smoke even if it killed him. 'In the meantime let's get our fake women out and about and looking busy. Chekhov will have an aircraft over our heads in an hour.'

Ten minutes later there was grumbling, laughter and cheerful but very crude insults as four of Sami's guys made their appearance wearing broad hats and long women's skirts. They picked up hoes and rakes and, implements in hand, they went to the garden plots to make a pretence of working. The other pair strutted about with their AK47s on their shoulders as if they owned the joint. The fact there were no kids about worried me momentarily but I filed it at the back of my mind. We couldn't have everything.

I glanced at my watch. It was now 11:45. I would allow half an hour for Bernard to get back in touch with Chekhov then give him the co-ordinates. Then it would be another hour for Chekhov to organise an aircraft out of Udon Thani, Vientiane, Chiang Mai, Lampang or anywhere else he had people. The satellite image Sami had shown me of the Russian's jungle compound hadn't included any landing strip other than for a chopper, maybe. That didn't mean Chekhov didn't have an airfield elsewhere in the area. Was there one by the boat landing where his vehicles were parked?

I stood looking at the map of the north and did some basic maths. Flight time from Udon Thani was fifteen minutes max and probably less than ten from Vientiane. Chiang Mai was a long shot as it was maybe an hour in a single-engine fixed-wing plane with the hammer down. Bangkok was about an hour and a half to two hours away by small plane, I guessed. Our chopper had done it in two and a half but we hadn't been racing.

My guestimate was out by half an hour. The small Cessna appeared from the direction of Vientiane a few minutes before 14:00. It didn't come across above us. Instead it flew on by between our position and the Mekong. It was possibly a mile away to the north of us. A scenic flight, perhaps? I could imagine that the passenger was taking a lot of photographs with a very big camera. The Cessna carried on out of sight while our fake villagers did their thing.

'A million baht he'll come back,' said Sami jokingly from outside where he was pretending to be an old man resting. Karl and I were sitting in the shadows back in the living area.

'No takers,' I replied.

We were both right. Five minutes later the Cessna came back. This time it was half a mile closer and down country of us. Just a pilot doing a big floppy tourist circuit. It was pretty crude. If I hadn't been expecting it I would have gone onto high alert anyway. Maybe Chekhov's hired help up this way wasn't up to standard? Either that or my paranoia was running on full alert. Of course, when a mad, head-hunting Russian wants you dead, what's not to get paranoid about?

We played out the rest of the day with our people doing their thing around the village while the guys from The A Team did theirs. Some slept, the others sat in their positions, watching and waiting. As always, the waiting was the hardest part.

After our evening meal, Alex, Karl, Jo, Sami and I sat on the veranda of the big hut and discussed the drill for the possible night games to come. Sami would have three men in the lab building along with Jo. The other three village guys would be in a bunker under a hut halfway between the lab and us. There would be two sets of Special Forces troopers in the perimeter bunkers and one pair at the top of the track with the imager and the mincer. Another pair would be further along the face of the plateau close to the lab, with the remaining duo in a bunker on the back side of the hill. Alex and one of the others would man the electronics.

'One on watch in each position,' Alex explained. 'The rest sleep. Two-hour spells. See anything, hear anything, call it in on the open channel. No shooting until ordered or shot at. Direct orders come from me.' The Special Forces leader paused but there was no argument coming. He allowed himself half a smile. 'That's it folks. Let's hope we have a quiet night.'

'What about us?' Sami said meaning himself, Karl and I.

'Stay put and look after each other,' came the reply. 'It's you guys he's pissed at. If it goes down, get your arses in there.' The Special Ops man indicated the temporary HQ. 'Worst case and it's into the bunker.' With that Alex went to speak to his crew who were getting ready to roll out to their perimeter positions.

Now I've been in firefights of various kinds in many countries, but I've never seen so few guys carry so many weapons. Each pair of The A Team could equip a battalion. Each duo had a Minimi—what we Brits called a light squad machine gun with a 200-round box magazine. This was essentially a one-man weapon, which meant the number-two man was free to use his state-of-the-art M16 variant with its grenade launcher and magic optics to seek and destroy at will. On top of that, each trooper carried a sidearm in a thigh holster along with a fighting knife, handle-down, on the harness on his left chest. At each position there were several of the shoulder-fired light anti-tank rockets, the old familiar LAWs, along with conventional grenades. Add to those the mincer, the tank busters and the Stingers and we had the makings of a real war.

The A Team guys vanished into the gloom and Jo moved out with his lot, who all looked to be lacking in weaponry with just a single M16 or AK and a couple of pouches of magazines each. I knew there were RPGs in the lab as well but these guys were still lightly armed compared to Alex's boys. Even Karl admitted he had been impressed by the firepower the team had arrived with. 'When I said prepare for a siege, I wasn't necessarily thinking of Stalingrad revisted,' he said to me with a wry grin as the last of the warriors vanished into the night.

I didn't voice my thoughts aloud, but I was beginning to wonder if Chekhov would come at all. It was too damned predictable. I considered the rather transparent scenario we'd set up. Was the mad Russian mad enough to stick his head in our bear trap? I just didn't know if he was or not. Point was, however, he wanted Sami and I dead and it seemed that his obsession was total. Time would tell, I guessed.

When I did find sleep that night, it was very uneasy. It had been a long day of waiting, and waiting was something I wasn't big on. I had dreams. No, cancel that, they were nightmares. There were a lot of people running around in my night without heads, and bugger, I was one of them.

35

Chekhov didn't show that night and a cool dawn followed one of the longest nights of my life. A mist was rising from the valley below and wet clouds clung to the dense green of the bush. None of the sensors had been triggered and no one had ventured up the track towards us from the village below. 'Where the fuck are you?' I muttered as I stood at the edge of the plateau taking an early morning piss. It was 07:00. I felt gritty, irritable and very, very bloody apprehensive. Where was Chekhov? I'd expected an early morning raid. We all had. Was he coming or was he not?

'Movement to the north! No visual!'

The voice in my ear was Alex's. I'd stuck my head in HQ and he'd been sitting at one of the control screens in his sandbagged nest. I threw away my cigarette butt and went back inside, staying well away from the magic boxes. Karl was standing looking over Alex's shoulder, so I guessed his security clearance wasn't in question. Sami was hovering nearby, a cup of tea in his hand. Even from where I was standing I could see lights blinking on the screen Karl was watching.

'Too regular. Large animal,' said Alex after some time. 'Human contact gives a shorter, sharper pulse. This is big, elephant maybe.'

'There is an elephant training camp about five clicks back towards Vientiane,' Sami called across the room. 'They might be moving through.'

'They might also have some of Chekhov's guys in tow,' Alex replied. 'Trojan fucking horse. We need a visual.' The Special Forces leader didn't need to give the order. One of The A Team in the bunker on the back side of the ridge announced he was on his way. Alex confirmed.

We waited for five minutes, each of us dealing with the nervous suspense in our own way. I lit another smoke. Karl chewed a pen while Alex sat totally motionless, his eyes on the screen. As for Sami, he had found a seat and sat sipping his tea, an AK47 beside him. I'd left the Colt by the door. I went and retrieved it and sat down beside Sami.

'Elephants, three, and their handlers. No bandits,' came the eventual reply.

We all breathed a huge sigh of relief, at least I think it was all of us—it might just have been me. Then we heard it, a distant aircraft breaking the near silence of our misty dawn high up in the countryside.

'Twin engine aircraft approaching from the west,' came the call from another of The A Team.

'Definitely for us?'

'Affirmative. On present course and altitude it will pass directly over us at not more than 200 feet.'

'ETA?'

'One minute.'

'Ready a Stinger. Get a lock and hold. Fire only on my order.'

'Roger that.'

As I sat and listened to the conversation in my headset I felt as useless as tits on a bull, as a rurally orientated colonial friend of mine from years ago was inclined to say in moments like this. I picked up my carbine and went to the window opening to watch the approaching aircraft.

The plane was a small civilian commuter and yes, it was flying directly towards us, straight up the valley. Was it going to drop a fucking bomb, Napalm perhaps, or was it going to strafe us? If Chekhov suspected that I was with Sami and we were tooled up big time, he wouldn't just fly in and risk getting his Russian arse shot right out of the sky. What was he playing at?

The aircraft slowed as it approached. I could hear the noise of the engine drop against the echo it made as it bounced back from the hills all around us. The side door opened and a white cloth trailed in the doorway. A signal of surrender? I doubted it. Maybe Chekhov was calling for a cease-fire?

'Locked,' a voice was saying in my headset.

'Hold.' Alex commanded.

We all watched as the plane cruised over our heads and the white cloth became a ribbon that trailed an object to the ground. It hit the ground, bouncing and rolling, the white ribbon cartwheeling in a pretty looping pattern, reminiscent of ribbon-dancing gymnasts. Then the whole thing hit the side of one of the pigpens and stopped, the ribbon fluttering limply to the ground.

I moved to another window opening and watched the aircraft turn slowly beyond the river and start flying back the way it had come. What was the message in the bottle?

'Make safe!' Alex ordered the man with the Stinger when the aircraft was just a speck on the grey horizon. The trooper acknowledged. I saw Jo leave his cover of the lab and go down the slope towards the object that was lying in the dust. Gingerly he squatted beside it, examining it without touching it. Then he removed the combat knife from the sheath on his hip and used it to slowly prise open the layers of cloth which held the bundle together. When he eventually finished, he stood and turned towards us, his face shining and pale.

'Sami,' he called in a voice that sounded choked and deep in his throat.

'What?' Sami replied getting out of his seat, alarm registering on his face with that single word.

'You must come here,' Jo said as he squatted back down in the dirt, his head turned in the direction in which the aircraft had vanished. Sami started out of the hut and Karl, Alex and I went with him. I knew what it was that had been dropped from the aircraft and shaken Jo. I wanted to grab Sami, to hold him back and tell him I was sorry I had started this whole damned thing. But short of shooting him I couldn't have stopped him if I had tried. I could tell by the way that Sami moved that he knew what he would find, and nothing or no one on this earth was going to stop him reaching the small bundle that lay at Jo's feet.

Her face was a pale oval surrounded by black hair. It was untouched by the dust and dirt it lay on. The fabric that it had been wrapped in had saved it that indignity at least. She had been young, nineteen, and in life she had been beautiful. In death, her blank eyes were wide. They stared up at me accusingly. The lips, which were drawn back to bare her perfect teeth, were coloured with blood. I thought I could hear her screaming at me.

'Oh, Kim,' Sami fell to his knees in the dirt and reached for the head of his child. 'Oh, Kim,' he repeated as he picked it up and cradled it to his cheek. The long, blood-soaked hair hung down Sami's chest. I remembered Kim as a child. Her hair had been her pride and joy, a long gleaming curtain that trailed behind her as she ran beside her father, laughing and chattering. Now the hair hung down in straggly, blood-thickened strands.

Sami got to his feet, helped by Jo. Then, with Jo on his arm, he staggered away from us, walking blindly. Jo steered him towards the nearest hut and kept him on his feet as he stumbled inside. The sounds of Sami's grief started. Karl, Alex and I stayed standing by the stinking pigpen, staring at everything and nothing. Both of the hard-bitten warriors looked shaken by what had just happened. I knew how I must have looked to them. I felt so responsible and so fucking helpless. I wanted—no, I needed—to find Chekhov and batter him into the slime of his own soulless being. I needed to run to Sami and beg his forgiveness and that of Kim. I didn't. I just stood staring at nothing until my eyes hurt. I would have my revenge on Chekhov. That was my silent promise. All I had to do was survive the next few hours.

'Who was she?' Alex wanted to know.

'Kim was one of his daughters,' I replied. 'She was his favourite.' All of Sami's countless children were his favourites, but Kim had been special. I remembered her as an eight or nine year old. A beautiful child, precociously bright and destined for great things. Kim Somsak was a rare combination of beauty and brains. When Sami had visited me in the UK he had told me she was an honour's student at university in Singapore and well on her way to a degree in science. Singapore! That was why Sami hadn't called Kim home for protection. He'd obviously thought she'd be safe there, but Chekhov, in his lust for revenge, had gone after her.

'She wants to discover a cure for cancer,' Sami had told me over dinner one night. 'And I believe she will, Daniel,' he had added, a proud father acknowledging his daughter's dream. Now that dream was over—forever. I was to blame, so was Bernard. If he had appeared in front of me at that very moment in time I think I would have killed him, and it would have been in the slowest, dirtiest, meanest way that I knew how, and I knew plenty of those.

'There is something else,' Alex said, breaking my session of self-hatred. He had seen an object in the folds of Kim's shroud. He knelt and, using his own combat knife, he separated further layers of cloth. Then with a grunt he reached down and picked up a hand-held radio. It was a standard, cheap Motorola clone. Carefully the Special Forces man opened the casing of the radio and looked inside. After a minute he snapped it closed. 'No bombs or poison pins that I can see,' he said as he passed the handset to Karl.

The sounds of Sami's grief were becoming more subdued, which perhaps made things worse. Still, I didn't want to hear his lament for his beautiful daughter. I myself was crying inside for Kim, Babs and the others. I walked blindly away from Karl and Alex, moving towards the drop-off point, groping out a cigarette as I went. The two Americans followed, whether I wanted them to or not. Karl came to my shoulder and handed me the radio.

'We've got to get this maniac, Danny,' he said grimly.

'Oh yes,' I agreed. 'We have to do that.' I lit the cigarette, either to calm myself down or give myself courage. When it was lit I took a deep lungful of smoke and blew it slowly out into the morning sky. I so wanted to kill Chekhov. I wanted to skin him alive, inch by fucking inch. I pressed the send button.

'Chekhov!' I snarled, letting the button go. There was a pause of perhaps five or six seconds.

'Mr Swann ... So nice to talk ... to you ... at long last.' The voice was strange, very strange. 'On our first meeting ... you were very impolite ... Mr Swann ... You shot at me ... from a great range ... and you ... killed my wife and my son ... That was not ... a nice thing ... to do.' I couldn't place the voice as I tried to remember the sound references I'd heard but that had been, at best, very distorted surveillance recordings. On those recordings the voice had been big, a bear of a voice for a bear of a man. But this was different. This voice was high-pitched and stilted, broken by uneven pauses, and there was a light, almost breathless quality to it. Chekhov sounded like an asthmatic fighting for breath. 'We never did ... meet face to ... face. I would ... like to remedy that.' The talk button was released. It was my turn to talk but to say what?

'What do you suggest?' I replied. 'Come on up to my hill top, why don't you?'

I released the button and waited. The man was laughing when he came back on air. The thin wheezing sound was like that of a kiddy cartoon character.

'You have ... Mr Somsak and ... some friends of ... his ... with you ...' It wasn't a question. 'I would prefer ... just you and I ... to meet. That ... would be most ... interesting.' The button at his end was released. I was fighting to suppress my anger, and I was failing, badly.

'Stop fucking around Chekhov. You're down below somewhere, and you have a plan. What do you want to do?' I snarled.

'Yes, Mr Swann ... I have a ... plan ... You start ... walking down ... the road from the hill ... I will start ... from the bottom ... village ... and we will meet in the middle.' Chekhov clicked off the transmit button.

'Fine,' I snapped. 'Your choice of weapon?' I was prepared to give him that to ensure he did his part. I wanted him that badly.

'Knives, Mr Swann ... you might have ... gathered that I like ... knives ... cane knives ... You bring a ... cane knife ... I bring ... a cane knife ... and then ... we see who is the ... man who ... walks away ... You agree?'

'I agree,' I snapped. 'I'll start walking at 10:00. Just me and my knife.'

'I will also start walking ... at 10:00 ... just me ... and my knife,' Chekhov replied with a wheezing chuckle. 'No one else ... Mr Swann ... just ... you and me.'

'Just you and me, Chekhov,' I released the transmit button and stood with the walkie-talkie in my hand. I looked down at it for a moment before lobbing it into the jungle below.

'You going with a cane knife?' Alex asked.

'Yes,' I replied. There was no alternative and I wanted him. I would have gone naked into hell for a chance at Chekhov.

'You can't trust him,' Karl was saying.

'I don't. I want cover, a bullet-proof vest and I'll be carrying a gun as well.'

'Let's get back to the map,' Alex suggested. This was the game he knew best, I would concede that. Right at that moment in time I wasn't thinking as clearly as I might have been. Hate and fear combined were messing up my ability to think logically and rationally. Alex was a trained pro and he wasn't personally involved. Because his emotions weren't in play his perspective was a damned sight clearer than mine.

Karl and I fell in behind the Special Forces man and started back to our HQ. Alex looped us wide around the hut where Sami was still grieving over his lost child. I knew that when those sounds of grief stopped, my old friend would emerge ready for war.

Back inside the command post the satellite map was spread on a table. Alex spent ten seconds looking down at it, then his thick finger tapped a position on the map. 'You stop here where the river comes closest to the track. We'll have four in the bush here in close support.' Alex indicated an arc in the jungle on the opposite side of the track to the river. You get into trouble, hit the water. Looks like its deep enough and there's a bank for cover.'

I glanced at my watch. It was 09:00. There wasn't a lot of time on our side. Alex was calling some of his men in. They arrived in a matter of minutes and grouped around the map. The Special Forces boss laid out the ambush. Then he turned to me. 'Keep your headset on throughout. We need a go word,' he said as he started out to see to his squad.

'Pizza,' I replied, thinking of Chekhov's ruined face. 'I say that and it's all on.'

'Okay,' he agreed, then he was gone. A couple of minutes later and the big boys were off to war. Four of The A Team started for the track off the plateau which had been stripped down for action. They were in pairs. One in each pair carried a modified M16, the other a silenced H&K MP5 in addition to his personal armament. There were canteens, a LAW each and loaded ammunition pouches. Jungle camouflage paint covered any naked flesh. They were gone in a minute.

'Chekhov's probably got people already in position,' I said to Alex.

'We're counting on it,' a voice replied in my earpiece. It wasn't Alex who spoke. I hadn't realised the unit was in full send-and-receive mode. I flicked it back a notch. I didn't want to hear this show take place.

'X-Ray, the guys on the thermal imager are already registering hits. Chekhov maybe didn't count on that,' Karl explained. 'This is the latest technology and far, far better than anything the Soviets had or have. So even if Chekhov has imagers, which I doubt, they're shit compared to this puppy. X-Ray will direct our recon teams in on them. If all of Chekhov's guys are above ground without thermal shielding or not hidden in folds in the terrain, we've got them cold. We just need time to get onto them.'

'Great,' I said with feeling. That was good news. I thanked God for Uncle Sam's technocrats.

'The rest of the squad will stay here and hold the hill,' Karl said. 'I still don't trust Chekhov to do what he says he'll do.'

'Neither do I,' I replied with more than a little conviction in my voice. Chekhov's word wasn't even a consideration in my book. 'Let's set me up so I can do exactly the opposite to what I said,' I added.

'You going to shoot him if you get close enough?'

'You fucking bet on it,' I promised. 'You've seen what this bastard can do with a knife.' It was focused now. A razor sharp, heavy-bladed cane knife could take out bone and muscle with ease. That was obviously what Chekhov had used on all of his victims. I knew without a doubt he'd killed them all simply because, as I'd defined days before, this whole thing was totally personal as far as he was concerned. As it was for me then, for that matter! It couldn't get any more personal.

Then I remembered something that made me chuckle. Karl was looking at me as if I'd tossed my last marble out of the crib. Once again in a moment of stress my mind had wandered, seeking something, anything to take off some of the heat and keep me sane. 'Recall a scene in an Indiana Jones movie,' I asked Karl, 'where this dervish comes at Harrison Ford waving a sword in each hand?'

'Yeah,' replied Karl. 'Old Indy pops him.'

'That's me, buddy. I get close enough, he gets it in the head.' I promised.

'Someone once said never take a knife to a gunfight, and I couldn't have agreed more.'

'I've got an idea,' Karl was saying. 'There's a Kevlar vest in my kit. You get that on, I want a word with Alex.' Karl ran off. He'd come up with a plan! Whatever it was I wasn't about to find out. I retrieved the vest. It was lightweight, of the expensive variety and definitely not standard issue. I stripped off my T-shirt and slipped the armour on, adjusting the Velcro fasteners to get it sitting as comfortably as it was going to get. When I said it was a lightweight, I was talking ten pounds as opposed to twenty. Nevertheless, it would stop a small calibre round or a knife for that matter. I found a cotton shirt in my pack and put that over the top. The loose fit of the shirt would hide the vest and whatever I decided to stuff down the back of my trousers. I figured a Minimi would be just the thing but I'd need to be the size of King Kong to hide that. I settled on the Walther.

Sami suddenly appeared in the doorway. He was minus his grisly burden of half an hour before, but the bloodstains on the side of his face and his shirt bore mute witness to Kim's death. Sami's face was expressionless, except for his eyes. The eyes wore a look that I had never seen in my old friend. It was like looking into the window of a furnace. If I didn't get Chekhov, then Sami was prepared to go into hell after him. We were both of the same mind.

Sami didn't say anything and neither did I. We just embraced and hung together for a long moment before he drew away. 'Later,' he said. 'When this is over! For now we get Chekhov, Daniel. I should go.'

'No,' I replied. 'I saw him first,' I said and Sami almost smiled. 'I need a cane knife, a very sharp cane knife.'

'I will organise that.' Sami turned and was gone, leaving me to finish what preparations I still had to make. I needed a shit, badly. My stomach was churning and it had nothing to do with the food. I went to the stinking latrine set as far away from everything on the plateau as it was possible to get. It wasn't a place to linger.

When I emerged I could see Sami talking to one of his men up by the dope kitchen. The guy was sitting in the shade of a tree by the side of the shed using an old-fashioned foot-operated grinding wheel attached to a machete. I joined my friend and we stood and watched.

The method of sharpening might have been old-fashioned but, by the time the man at the wheel had finished, the machete blade was like a damned razor. 'Very sharp,' he said as he handed the cane knife to me with a big grin.

'Just the way I like it,' I replied, taking a practice swing at nothing. The handle wasn't that great as far as the grip was concerned, but the blade whistled through the air like a scythe. Old man Time—or was it the Spectre of Death?—was waving his big curved blade behind my shoulder. If all else failed and I had to take Chekhov on in a hand-to-hand rumble, this damned thing would be a real asset.

Sami and I started walking back to the command hut without talking. As I walked I swung the blade, trying to get some sort of feel for it. Karl was beckoning to us. Sami pulled me up. 'I will say goodbye and good luck now, Daniel. There is something I must do.' Sami grabbed me in a bear hug and said words I didn't understand. I didn't understand Japanese. Then he was moving away rapidly. Confused, I turned and went to where Karl was waiting on the porch of our HQ.

'Okay,' the CIA man was saying as he led us back to the map table. 'Alex has delegated himself as extra cover. He's getting ready now.' I went to Karl's shoulder. He ran a forefinger down the course of the river on the map. 'He's going into the stream and he's going to go past the meet point to about here.' Karl tapped the map. The point he indicated was maybe a hundred yards beyond the place where I would stop and wait for Chekhov.

'Chekhov might try and draw you further down the track towards him,' Karl continued, 'or he might have a team following him in addition to the ones he's already positioned. If Alex is between them and Chekhov, he can cut Chekhov off from his cover or take him out if he puts you down.'

Alex came back into the war room about then. Gone were the battle fatigues. In their place he had on some sort of skin-tight body suit. It was like a wetsuit but made of some light fabric that was a mottled broken pattern of dark greens. There was a small rucksack of the same material on his back. He had a sheathed knife attached to one thigh and a handgun in a tactical holster attached to the other. There were goggles and a snorkel hanging around his neck and he wore a communicator under his hood. I guessed the damned things were waterproof. 'I'm getting into the river fifteen minutes before you hit the track,' he said. 'I'll get into position beyond you. If the shit hits the fan, you get in the water fast. I'll have Claymores positioned to sweep the track and the jungle fringe in my zone. You stay in the river until you get the all clear.'

'Pizza and I'm in the water,' I confirmed.

'Luck,' said the Special Forces man. He turned to Karl. 'Is our friend coming in?' he asked.

'Be here in ten,' Karl confirmed. Alex nodded and was gone.

I was going to ask what they were talking about but didn't. I had enough going on in my mind and I needed another shit. My gut was turning somersaults and kicking the hell out of my heart with every gyration. I went back to the stinking latrine and delivered up virtually nothing. Maybe it was all in my head.

I came back to our hut, lit a cigarette and opened the half-empty bottle of Mekong the previous occupants had left behind. I didn't care what anyone might say. I was about to do the traditional 'Tombstone Shuffle' down Main Street, and nicotine and a belt of something containing a lot of alcohol were probably the only things in the world that were going to settle my nerves and still allow me to function. Damned shame I didn't have a bottle of bourbon in my kit. That had been a major oversight. I settled on a hefty shot of the embalming fluid. It was way better than nothing.

I had the Walther in the small of my back and two spare magazines in my hip pocket. I doubted I would need them. Either Chekhov would be dead by the time I'd emptied magazine one or I would be. End of story.

My watch was telling me it was time to start my walk. Karl accompanied me to the top of the track. The mist was gone now, and the day had cleared, despite the fact storms still hovered grey and heavy on the far horizon. A good day to die, I thought, remembering an old American Indian saying. Karl shook my hand.

'Go get him, Dan,' he said. 'Remember, I'll be talking to you. The guys on the imager will be talking to the scouts on a closed channel. You won't hear them unless they want you to. Anyone above ground and not hidden behind a fold in the ridge is visible to them. They'll already be calling our teams in on Chekhov's guys. There'll be a lot happening. Just remember, you won't be alone. Just don't get distracted.'

'I'll be praying,' I replied with true feeling as I switched my communicator fully on. I looked around for Sami, but he wasn't anywhere to be seen. Anyway, I thought, any more of this farewell shit and I'll start getting dewy-eyed or chicken out.

'Lone figure leaving the village, walking towards us.' The man on the imager was talking to me from four feet away, sans communicator.

'Roger. Let's get this show on the road,' I replied with a hell of a lot more bravado than I felt. I could almost hear the theme from *The Good, the Bad and the Ugly* playing somewhere in my head as I took that first step down towards the OK Corral, or wherever. Clint Eastwood I wasn't.

I wanted another shit but I held on and prayed for the water in my gut to quickly turn to concrete.

36

Five minutes further down the track the bush crowded in. The light there was no longer as clear and bright as it was up above. This was a world of greens and browns. The clay and mud underfoot supplied the earthy tones. Everything else was a shade of green. The colours of the jungle foliage ran through the entire green spectrum, ranging from light, yellow–green tints to some so dark they were almost black. Welcome back, I thought to myself as I moved down through the mottled shadows. This was the world I had lived in for so long, once upon a time. Then it had been both a friend and a foe, but mainly a friend. This time, I hoped, it would treat me the same way.

'I'm in position. The advancing subject is 200 metres away.' Alex had made it to his position undetected.

'We have a big lens on our subject. We are reasonably positive it is Chekhov.' Karl was back in the act. 'Subject is a thick-set man with a badly scarred face. Age indeterminable. He is carrying a machete in his right hand. There is no other visible sign of a weapon.'

'Chekhov was left-handed,' I said, cutting across the commentary. I remembered the Russian's file. I also remembered Babs. I'd calculated at the time that a left-handed man had cut her throat.

'Injuries may have forced him to change hands,' Karl responded.

'Maybe,' I agreed. I was at the second bend in the track. Soon I would be on the river flat and Chekhov, or whoever it was advancing down the road, would be able to see me. I had no doubt that whatever big lenses we had on Chekhov, he would have some of the very same on us. I reached the flat and followed the track as it curved parallel to the stream. Now I could see him. A tiny figure dressed in white was moving in the distant haze. The track, like the stream, had carved its path out of the green of the jungle and the tall grasses. It appeared as a dark ribbon from down there. The white of Chekhov's clothes was in vivid contrast to both the brown–yellow dirt of the road and the dark green of the jungle mass.

'I see him,' I said aloud to myself as much as anyone else. I passed the cane knife from my right to my left hand. The butt of the gun was positioned for a right-handed draw. Not that I would need the Walther for at least 150 paces. Chekhov and I were still some 300 yards apart at this stage of the game.

'X-Ray has two figures following the line of the ridge down from the village. Sami?' It was Karl speaking.

'Yes,' came the reply.

'Fuck!' I thought but then I realised I'd said it aloud.

'In case you miss him, Daniel!' Sami's voice was a whisper.

'Stay high, Sami,' Karl urged. 'Our killing ground is 200 yards above the track.'

'We will,' came the reply. 'Good hunting!'

Damn, damn, damn, I thought as I tried to refocus on what I was doing. I tried to gauge how quickly Chekhov was moving and how far and how fast I had to move to ensure that we met at the point we had designated as our own personal killing field. I quickened my pace slightly. If I reached where X marked the spot first, I would just wait there for him. If he reached it and came on beyond, how was I to get him to back up?

'At the present rate you will arrive sixty seconds ahead of the subject,' Karl said. He had obviously been doing his maths.

'I figured that,' I replied, slowing slightly.

'Any activity at the lower village?' I didn't recognise the voice.

'Negative. The lack of activity suggests that there is a lot going on,' Karl responded.

'I concur,' Alex said in a close-miked whisper. 'Subject has just passed me. I'm setting the Claymores.'

'Gotcha,' Karl confirmed. 'Recon one reports they have bandits on visual and are positioning for the kill.'

'Roger that. Green One over,' Alex replied.

I felt a momentary shiver of relief. Once Alex's team had been vectored onto unfriendly types, they were guaranteed to take them out. Thank God these guys are on our side, I thought as I trudged on, watching Chekhov grow larger with every combined step we took. My heart gave a grateful thump thirty seconds later when the same voice came back on the line.

'Recon One reports bandits terminated,' Karl relayed to the Special Ops boss. 'Recon Two getting into position on bandit nest number two.'

'Roger. Claymores are hot. Let the party begin, gentlemen!' I detected more than a degree of enthusiasm in Alex's voice. Karl came back again. 'Recon Two reports RPGs and a heavy MG in bandit position. Cannot cull silently. Will cover and terminate at first sign of hostilities.'

'Confirmed. Go to red on verbal Pizza or on gunshot, whichever comes first. Green One over.'

'Roger that.'

Listening to all the rogering and stuff, the uninitiated might have thought we had a boy's-own gathering of Hooray Henrys playing scout games. They slipped in and out of civilian speak but who cared? This was serious shit, and having these guys roger my ears off, pardon the expression, was pure bliss. I wasn't totally alone in wonderland and that was fine by me.

Chekhov and I were maybe a hundred yards apart. Now it was fifty paces each until we would be in each other's faces. I squinted through my sunglasses to get a look at his face. It was just a blur. I needed to get closer, but something still wasn't sitting right. The man walking towards me had on a white shirt. The cuffs of the sleeves had been rolled back up to his elbows. His arms were bare. The machete this guy carried was still in his right hand. His left arm was moving normally as it hung at his side. He was moving too freely for a man with a breathing problem caused maybe by burnt, scarred lungs.

'Decoy to HQ. Get X-Ray to scope our man up close. Has he got a left ear and is there hair on his arms?' I wanted to know. I only had seconds to wait.

'Roger that. Both ears intact and there is hair on the arms, dark hair and plenty of it,' came Karl's response, relayed back from the man with the hundred power eyes. I wondered if he were the one who counted pussy hair. I almost laughed aloud.

'It's not Chekhov,' I said. 'Repeat, not Chekhov. He was fair-haired going grey before he was burned and he lost his left ear.'

'Setup,' Karl jumped in.

'I'll confirm with a voice test,' I replied. We were fifty yards apart and I was in the zone. I stopped. 'Mr Chekhov?' I called out. The man approaching me halted in his tracks and looked expectantly at me. The face was red and silver. Whether it was scar tissue or make-up, I had no idea. I was definitely leaning towards the latter.

'Yes, I am Chekhov,' he said in thick English.

'Anton Chekhov,' I asked, playing out a silly dangerous game. 'The very same Chekhov who wrote *The Cherry Orchard*?'

'You what? I wrote nothing. No Cherry Orchard. What do you mean? I am Dimitri Chekhov!' There we had it. No asthmatic wheezing and no broken pauses, just a bluff Russian voice speaking fractured English.

It was about then that the fake Chekhov realised that whatever game he had been playing was well and truly up. He hunched and began running for cover at the side of the track as I started to grab for the Walther.

'RPGs!' The voice was Alex's.

'Fucking Pizza,' I yelled quite needlessly, forgetting my gun as I launched myself towards the river in a long low dive, praying I wasn't going to hit a damned rock or land on a submerged tree. Something scorched the air behind me as I crashed through the fringe of grass and weeds and hit the water with a clumsy belly flop. As I went under, I heard the world explode behind me.

Yes, the comunicators worked in water. I could hear chaos both over the earpiece and through my uncovered ear as I sank, driven by my momentum and the weight of the Kevlar vest. I had no idea how deep the stream was at this point, but I was happy to stay down just as long as I had air in my lungs. Some seriously heavy thuds vibrated through the water and the rattle of automatic weapons and voices penetrated through my headset. My eyes were open. The water was the colour of tea that had been stewed too long. I kept my mouth shut. No way was I sucking in any of that. Out of the corner of my eye I saw the arse end of something with a long tail vanish downstream.

I grabbed a tree root or branch and held on, fighting against my body's desire to float back to the surface. I rolled onto my back as my feet finally got below my head. Looking up through three or four feet of brown water, I could see what appeared to be flames back the way I had come. It was almost peaceful down here.

Eventually I had to surface for air. I came up as slowly as I could, ready to gulp a lungful of precious oxygen and dive down again. There was still gunfire in the jungle across from where I was, but the frenzy of those first few seconds was gone. Black smoke climbed lazily into the air as dried grasses on the bank above me burned. The grenades Chekhov and his cronies had fired at me had been phosphorus or some sort of incendiary. The bastard wanted me fried, fricasseed or barbecued, as well as dead. Payback! What a hell of an involved scenario for something as simple as that! The guy's hatred knew no bounds, it seemed. Problem was that I could understand that. I probably wanted him dead at that moment just as much, or even more, than he wanted me fried to a crisp.

I kicked for the cover of the bank nearest the track and hauled the Walther out of its holster. Somewhere along the line I had dropped the cane knife. From back along the track towards the crossroads there was a heavy thump. It was followed by another of the same in quick succession. Those, I guessed, were a couple of the Claymores Alex had set up.

I was about to haul myself out of the water when there was another sound. A fucking helicopter was thudding its way towards me. I made myself as small as I could and pressed my body into the clay of the bank. A very large and extremely obnoxious-looking spider was making its merry arachnidan way along an exposed tree root. It stopped and surveyed me with a multitude of eyes. I left it where it was, a scant two inches from my face, as the chopper came thumping through the air above me.

'You okay, Danny?' It was Karl's voice.

'Okay but for the chopper,' I replied. 'Ours or theirs?'

'Ours! We're about to mop up down country.'

'Okay. I'm still in the fucking river.'

'Stay there. We're running for the bottom village, back in five.'

I recognised the chopper now. It was the grey Jet Ranger we'd flown up in. The rear left door was off its hinges and I could see a figure hunched in the doorway. There was a whirring sound, rather like that made by a sewing machine, and I huddled more. The next sound was that of a Gatling gun stitching up the world. The chopper moved on its way.

The sound of the mincer came back over the noise of the turbine as the gunner played his deadly tune. A trail of sparkling shell cases fell away behind it, some of them splashing into the water close to me. It was a variation of that fateful morning out in the Andaman.

'Green One to Recon Units. Check in.' Now that the communicator channels were totally open, I lay there against the riverbank and listened as The A Team checked in. They had all survived and it appeared that they had taken out at least half a dozen of Chekhov's people. Alex confirmed that he had taken out the fake Chekhov and another bandit with his Claymores.

'Green One to Decoy. You okay?'

'Okay,' I replied. 'Sami?' I called.

'Okay,' came the whisper. 'X-Ray, we are moving down parallel to the Napalm strike.'

'Roger, Recon One and Two, copy?' The four guys doing the heavy hitting copied. They weren't going to mistake Sami and Jo for bandits.

'We'll move back up the hill in five. Decoy, stay where you are for the moment while we sweep the area.' Alex was the man in charge. I gave an affirmative and hugged the riverbank, listening as he continued to give orders. X-Ray continued to sweep the bush while the recon guys started to double-check the couple of hundred square yards of bush across from where I lay. I wasn't about to get out of the water and have my behind shot off by a friendly. Dead was dead, no matter who pulled the trigger. As H. Norman Schwartzkopf once commented, 'There is no such thing as friendly fire.'

The vicious-looking spider had lost interest in me and carried on about his business. I looked around for another source of entertainment but there was none, apart from a green grass snake that was wound around a tree branch across the river. I thought the damned thing was probably in a state of shock after all that had taken place, including the miniature gale whipped up by the chopper's rotor.

I could still hear the noise of the helicopter echoing back up the valley. The sound of the Minigun underscored the rotor flap. The gun was firing in short rattling bursts along with another automatic weapon I took to be a Minimi. Shit, this was a full out war. I only hoped that Karl and his happy crew kept the collateral damage to a minimum, and that none of Chekhov's men got an RPG into the Jet Ranger. Why was I so fucking worried? I was alive!

'Clear,' came the eventual call.

I scrambled gingerly up the riverbank, glad to quit the water but definitely cautious. Back on dry ground I leaned against the trunk of a tree, gun in hand, and took a look around. There hadn't just been one missile. It looked as if there had been three, maybe four rocket grenades. There was a small smouldering crater in the road more or less where I had been standing but worse was the stench of phosphorus that filled the thick air. Three separate sticky fires burned on and around the track. I had been right in assuming that Chekhov had been trying to fry me, the barrage of phosphorus grenades had taught me that. Nasty damned things.

I'd been lucky, very, very lucky, thanks mainly to Alex's warning. Being burned alive covered with flames that even water couldn't put out was not my idea of a good end, if there were such a thing. Where was Sami and what the hell was he doing? I resisted the impulse to call him.

The sulphurous smoke curled up to the sky from a dozen places in the grass and bushes that fringed the track, where globs of burning phosphorus had landed. I looked back towards the village at the bridge. Two bodies lay sprawled on the track a hundred or so yards away. One of them wore the remains of a white outfit. I couldn't see Alex, but I figured he was around. The chopper was hovering over the village but the firing had stopped. I was too far away to see what exactly was going on.

Alex appeared in the tall grass across from me.

'Not a fair fight, huh?' he said, nodding at the grenade strikes.

'I didn't expect it to be,' I replied. 'Any news? Did they get Chekhov?'

'No word,' the Special Forces officer replied. 'He could have been miles away.'

'No. He wanted to see me burn up close and in person. He's here somewhere,' I said with absolute certainty.

'We'd have spotted him.'

'Chekhov is an ace jungle fighter. He's around here somewhere,' I replied. 'Believe me, Alex, he wants me very dead but he needs to see me doing the dying. It's totally personal with him.'

'Okay, I believe you,' the grim-faced soldier conceded with a nod.

'He's got his tail between his legs about now.' He indicated the Jet Ranger that was heading nose-down along the bisecting road heading away to the west. They were obviously chasing something. 'That's something he didn't expect.'

'Neither did I,' I replied. 'Nice touch!'

'I thought so.' He almost smiled. 'Let's head back.'

'What about Sami?' I asked. Alex shook his head.

'He's a jungle fighter,' the Special Ops man replied. 'You said that, and he's on a mission. If you're right about Chekhov, he'll be hunting him.'

'But what about the imager? X-Ray would have spotted him if he were there.'

'Only if he was in a direct line of sight. If he was in a bunker, down a gut or had on a chill suit he'd be invisible to them.' Alex gave the order to move out.

Two of his team appeared twenty paces further up the track while the second pair came out onto the track twenty behind us. All of the troopers were carrying more weapons than they had gone into the bush with. Two of them had RPGs over their shoulders with their rockets still fitted. Another had an M60 machine gun complete with ammo belt in addition to his own MP5. We started back the way I had come, with Alex and I in the middle of the column. The guys at the rear walked backwards, eyes and weapons covering our retreat. I walked hunched, ready to dive for the river again. Alex just walked. He moved like a big cat in his clinging camouflage wetsuit, or whatever the hell it was.

'Decoy to X-Ray. Any sign of our guys?' I used the communicator to at least give the illusion I was more than just bait.

'Roger that,' came the reply. 'We have images of friendlies working the ridge. No living bandits in sight. X-Ray out!'

'Chopper has taken out an SUV loaded with bandits. No sighting of principal target. Control out!'

'Damn,' I muttered to myself. If Chekhov were still alive—and I had every reason to believe he was—he had seriously underestimated me, or rather he had underestimated the resources that had been given me. He would never make the same mistake again, and there was absolutely no comfort in that for me. I lit a cigarette in defiance of the gut-busting steepness of the now heavily inclined track. The chopper thudded overhead, heading for a landing on the plateau above. I wished I were on it. What the fuck was Sami doing?

37

I was gasping when I reached the top of the track. Alex wasn't even breathing heavily. One of Sami's drug makers was standing beside the imager waiting for me.

'Message from Mr Somsak,' he said in English. 'In there!' He pointed to the hooch that Sami had gone into carrying Kim's head. I jogged to it, my lungs bursting. Got to give up the cigarettes, I thought as I took the half a dozen steps in one clumsy stride.

The hut was empty but for a bundle wrapped in silk sitting on a small table in the centre of the room. Beside it was a note. I grabbed the single sheet of paper. The words were in English, written in Sami's beautiful copperplated hand.

Daniel
I must avenge my family. If I return, so be it. If I do not return, please take care of Kim for me. Until we meet again.
Your friend
The Onion Man

I almost smiled at the way he'd signed off. I carefully folded the note and put it in my shirt pocket. I had to see what the hell was happening with Sami. Was Chekhov in the bush or back at his base? I ran back to the imager. Alex was standing at the operator's shoulder. 'They're halfway down the ridge,' he said as I joined him. 'If your theory about Chekhov wanting to watch you fry is true, he'll have positioned himself on the slope above the kill zone to get a good view. We never saw an image more than 200 yards above the track, normal rifle range. If he's higher and holed up we just wouldn't have seen him.'

'Can I take a look?' I asked. Alex nodded.

'This isn't Radio Shack but it isn't secret either,' he replied with a grin. The trooper working the unit moved to one side to let me settle my forehead against the rubber headpiece. The green infrared world of the heat sensor filled my vision. 'Magnification left hand,' the trooper said, putting my left hand around a grip. 'Forward or back, traverse with your right,' he instructed and I gripped the other handle. Firstly I pulled the magnification back and then moved the lens left to follow the ridge above the river. The ghostly images showed the cooling bodies of the dead as orange and yellow fading to blue. Two bright orange–red blobs part way down the line of the ridge had to be Jo and Sami.

The Special Forces boss had been right: Chekhov had to have been up there somewhere on the high ground as an observer, but far enough away to avoid being part of the fight. That was why Alex's men hadn't swept the high area after being guided to their targets by X-Ray. They were out to take down the combatants, not any spectators, so had stayed within easy rifle and RPG range of the road.

The gunshots sounded as a crisp three-round burst, followed two seconds later by another of the same. 'M16,' Karl said. I could see only the figures of Sami and Jo in the imager. They were close together but I couldn't tell if they were lying or standing. Another burst of three rounds sounded.

'Controlled fire,' the man from The A Team kneeling beside me said softly. 'Trained shooter.'

'Jo,' I said aloud. 'Thai Special Forces.'

'That's him then,' Alex replied. There was a rattle of full automatic fire and then a short burst from another weapon followed by the thump of a grenade. Then there was silence. We froze, waiting. I could still see my two figures, still close together. A few yards away, another figure miraculously appeared out of the green mist.

'Got three images,' I said aloud. 'One came out of nowhere.'

'Underground,' Alex was saying. 'Update. Sami, what's happening?' he called as I watched the three figures merge.

'Got Chekhov,' came the call. It was Sami, his voice totally void of emotion in my earpiece. 'He and two others were in a cave. The other two are dead. Chekhov is alive!'

'Kill him!' I said.

'My way, my time,' came the reply. 'We're going down to the road. Please do not try and stop what will happen.'

'Be careful!' was all I could think of to say. The only response was an almost chuckle from my old friend, then radio silence. I refocused on the imager. No way was the trooper getting it back. I pressed my face into the mask and watched as the three blobs of colour started to pick their way down towards the road. What was Sami planning?

The trio of multi-coloured figures were moving closer and closer to the road. They were a kilometre away from us but travelling directly across our line of vision from left to right. Who was who? There was no way I could decipher that through the imager. Maybe it was five minutes, maybe ten, until they were at the track, only yards from the edge of the jungle. I raised my head long enough to locate the switch on the side of the imager to change the vision from infrared to binocular and was nearly blinded as a bright, full-colour image flooded my vision.

I was just in time to see the gleam raised in the tall grass that fringed the track. It was the gleam of silver, of naked steel. 'There,' I yelled to the others as Sami Somsak emerged from the jungle. In his right hand he carried his magnificent *katana*, while with his left he was pushing a figure ahead of him. Jo was walking behind Dimitri Chekhov, his M16 jammed in the man's back. 'Yes,' I whispered.

I pulled the image in and Chekhov sprang into view, larger than life. He was dressed in sweat-soaked tiger-striped jungle fatigues, but his head was bare. The passage through the jungle and the heat of the day had flushed him, making his scars an angry red and silver colour. His mouth was moving. He was speaking to Sami but the actions weren't those of a man pleading for his life. Watching I could plainly see that the mad Russian was taunting his captor. Sami turned his head slightly at a comment from Jo, but he was shaking his head. They both had their communicators turned off. In fact, Sami was no longer wearing one. He was instead wearing a headband. It was white, with a red pattern through it. The red was Kim's blood. The cloth had been a piece of her shroud.

'They're going to fight,' Karl was saying. I didn't tear my eyes away from the imager, but I knew that he and Alex had binoculars jammed to their faces. They were going to fight. Jo was moving, backing away from the pair, his rifle held at the ready position. He was leaving Sami and

Chekhov standing a few feet apart in the centre of the track. At first I thought the cane knife Jo stooped to pick up was the one I had dropped, then I realised that it was the one dropped by the ersatz Chekhov an hour before. Mine was probably still in the river.

Jo walked back towards the two figures standing motionless in the sun facing each other. Chekhov was still talking. Under the magnification of my imager I could see that Sami stood impassively, his face set, showing no expression at all. Jo halted five or six yards away from the pair and lobbed the cane knife underarm towards Chekhov. The heavy knife raised dust as it spun to a stop beside the Russian's combat boots. Chekhov didn't pick it up immediately. I could see him still talking to Sami, grinning, grimacing. No doubt he was trying to unsettle his opposition. I could imagine the things he was saying, telling Sami what they had done to Kim before they had killed her. He would be saying anything he could to gain an advantage. Sami continued to stand motionless and emotionally unmoved, the long sword held low across his body.

There was spittle coming from the Russian's lips, his face mottled purple and crimson with silver worms through it as he worked himself into a frenzy. Finally Sami had heard enough. The blade of the *katana* swirled in the sunlight and Dimitri Chekhov earned another scar. This one was across his left cheek, where the delicate backhand sweep of the razor-sharp killing sword kissed it.

The Russian reacted as Sami no doubt knew he would. Chekhov clapped his right hand to his cheek and stooped amazingly quickly for a man of his bulk. He had the cane knife in his left hand and immediately went on the attack. Judging by the ferocity of that attack, the Russian was trying to force the long slim blade of the *katana* against the shorter more solid one of the cane knife and break it. Sami didn't oblige by leaving the blade of his sword hanging in the air as a target. He sent the blade of the *katana* swirling as he pirouetted, spinning away, altering the angle of Chekhov's attack. Chekhov stumbled at the sudden change of direction and the blade of the sword made contact again. This time with the Russian's right shoulder.

Chekhov stumbled, this time backwards. He almost fell. Blood spurted from his injured shoulder. He didn't hesitate to catch his breath or examine his wound. The Russian charged again, like a wounded, enraged bear attacking a smaller, lightning-fast wolverine. Sami caught the cane knife on an angled sword blade and deflected it away. Then he swept the *katana* in an arc aimed at Chekhov's head. The Russian went down on one knee but the long silver blade caught him high on his head and sent him into the dust. Sami had used the reverse side of the blade. If it had been the cutting edge, he would have opened Chekhov's head as one opens a hard-boiled egg.

'He's playing with him,' Alex said. The Special Forces man was right. Sami was playing with the Russian. Dazed, Chekhov got back to his feet, the cane knife still clutched in his hand. The Russian's lips were moving again. I could imagine the words: 'Stop dancing. Come and fight.'

Whatever was said, Sami obliged. He came at Chekhov weaving a dazzling vertical figure of eight in the air and sending the Russian stumbling backwards. Then the figure of eight became a horizontal line. 'Jesus Christ,' Karl muttered. 'I've never fucking seen anything ...'

The CIA man never got a chance to finish his statement because Sami stepped through the Russian's defence and hammered the heel of the butt of the *katana* into Chekhov's face. The Russian went down again, blood now pouring from the wound in his forehead. Kneeling in the dirt, Dimitri Chekhov was looking up at his tormentor through a curtain of blood. He was shouting at Sami. Through the imager I could see the droplets of crimson spraying in the air. Sami was standing motionless, the sword once again resting across his body.

I had to give Chekhov credit for guts, if nothing else. He made it back to his feet and came at Sami again. This time Sami parried the cane knife with the blade of the sword. I could see the sparks as the blades kissed, raised and locked high. Chekhov tried to trip Sami, pushing him back, hooking with his left leg. But Sami had been there before. He twisted his body and brought his right knee up into Chekhov's groin. The Russian released his grip and pulled away.

'Christ, Sami, finish it,' I whispered. The time for playing was over. I wanted him to finish it before Chekhov got in a lucky blow or something fucked up the scenario. I didn't want this to be a false ending. I'd seen too many movies where the good guy gives the villain a chance and ends up dead. The Wes Craven corpse always comes back for one last bite of the cherry. Sami must have heard my prayer because he changed tactics.

The *katana* blade caught Chekhov on the left shoulder. It was a lightning-fast blow, delivered with immense power. The razor edge of the *katana*'s blade bit deep through flesh and bone. The blade was withdrawn as quickly as it had been delivered. In my enhanced vision, it was a surreal scene. The long blade of the sword drew back and the Russian's left arm, still wearing its jungle pattern sleeve, slowly detached itself three or four inches below the shoulder. The arm fell into the dirt, the cane knife still clutched in its dead fist.

'Holy shit!' Karl said. 'Fuck!' The flashing blade stilled, held directly in front of Sami Somsak. Chekhov stood, his head down and turned to one side as he contemplated what had just happened. There was a pause of several seconds before the blood started to spurt from the severed shoulder stump. Chekhov raised his head, the blade flashed again and his right arm fell in the dirt at his feet.

Dimitri Chekhov raised his head to the sky and howled. We could hear the sound from where we were. It echoed back off the ridge and fell back on itself. The sound was purely animalistic. At that moment in time, Dimitri Chekhov wasn't a Russian bear, he was a timber wolf or a banshee or both rolled into one. I'd never heard a sound like it in my life. It was despair, hatred, anger and death all combined in one long, keening song.

Sami then adopted the pose. Standing as he was directly in front of the Russian, he was mirroring the pose of the warrior in his study. The mighty *katana* was about to do the very thing that had birthed it as a killing sword. Chekhov knew as well, I was sure of that. He held his pose, head back as the blur of silver impacted on his left collarbone and passed down through his body, exiting above his right hip. The force of the blow was so great that Sami stumbled forward. He didn't fall but retained his balance. He was standing up straight again, his sword once more raised, when Dimitri Chekhov's body separated on a diagonal through his torso. Blood, intestines and other entrails erupted from the two clearly separate body parts as the remains of the Russian madman hit the dirt.

'Yes,' I yelled. 'Yes!'

'Finally,' Karl whispered. Alex was silent. I raised my head. The Special Forces officer caught my eye and nodded, then turned away. It was over. He had other wars to fight. Such was the life of a warrior.

38

Sami, Jo, Karl and I were in the air in the Jet Ranger an hour after Dimitri Chekhov had finally been removed from the face of the earth. We were silent, lost each to our own thoughts. The A Team stayed behind to retrieve their gear and pack, awaiting the arrival of their ride scheduled for the following morning. I was dozing in my seat, my tiredness a reaction to the amount of adrenaline I'd used up and the Thai whisky I'd drunk.

Sami was in the seat next to me. He'd found a beautiful length of gold and green silk that he had tenderly fashioned into a wrap for the head of his daughter. His precious bundle remained on his knees throughout the flight, his hands resting lightly on top of it. His sword was wrapped in its protective covering and leaned against the seat beside him. My old friend's eyes remained closed most of the flight. Tears occasionally escaped his eyelids and slid down his cheeks as his lips moved in silent prayer.

My heart was right out there for Sami. His loss was my fault, at least on the surface. Deep down I knew that there was nothing I could have done. Sami knew it too. What happened would have happened one day, with or without me. Most of the blame I laid squarely at the feet of Sir Bernard Turncoat.

Despite knowing the realities of the situation, I couldn't shake off the guilt. That was the thing about a Catholic upbringing: guilt fitted like a silken shroud. It was almost comfortable, and we all wallowed in it from our birth to our death without absolution. In my book it was the perfect religion. I had lapsed the moment I'd cracked my stepfather's Catholic skull open. But the Catholic had never left the altar boy, even when that boy had spent his life playing God with other people's lives.

As I sat in my seat, my mental movie screen played a multitude of images. Geezer was grinning at me over a beer, then he was just grinning at me, his tan turning green and blue, the whites of his eyes yellow around the dull raisins of his dead pupils. Then there was Babs, beautiful, bountiful, energetic Babs, every man's perfect red-headed sex machine. One moment she was bouncing on my thighs gasping like a ruptured steam engine, the next she was lying silent and limp on the white tiled floor, blood slowly pooling around her, moving slowly as it spread like hot tar.

Next was pretty young Kim, her head covered with a long silk scarf. She was smiling in the air above me, the scarf trailing as I danced barefoot on a bed of flames to the sound of a balalaika. Chekhov was playing the instrument, or rather his fingers were. His torso sat to one side, his head was at his feet and he was smiling at me. 'Fuck!' I jerked awake as we started to descend towards the helipad at the US Embassy. I guessed it was another lesson learnt in Vietnam: always have a helipad at the embassy in case you have to bug out really fast. Whatever, it meant we didn't have to land at the airport and drive back into town. For that, at least, I was grateful.

Sami was still sitting as he had been when sleep had claimed me. He gave me a sad smile. 'You snore,' he said. 'Even above the noise of the helicopter I could hear you.'

'Sorry,' I replied, thinking of nothing else to say. My old friend managed a chuckle.

'A liability in a bush bivouac, Daniel. I would have had to have gagged you,' he said as he stood and followed Karl out of the chopper, the precious bundle held in both hands. Jo, the faithful retainer, carried the sword in its leather and fabric covering.

'Stay with me,' Sami said as we ducked instinctively under the rotor arc. 'We have much to talk about in the days ahead.'

'Yes,' I agreed. There was much to do. We had many people to bury and a final revenge to be plotted. I already had an inkling of what I would do to Sir Bernard Sinclair, but I wanted something else first—a holiday from death. Apologies to Agatha Christie or whomever coined that wonderful title.

The plan that I had conceived on the flight back was another simple one. Once I'd done what I needed to there, I was going to slip back into the UK without alerting Sir Bernard. Then I was going to visit him at home one night, late and unannounced. I imagined that his suicide would come as a great shock to all those who knew him. The funeral would be with full honours, no doubt. However before I induced that most melancholy and final of all states, I wanted some questions answered.

39

I stayed in Bangkok for the funerals of Sami's family members and his people and then I went south. I didn't want to stay in Patong. I wanted a little space so I checked into a very expensive little resort at Kata Noi. I'd spent a week there in a past life. The resort itself sat back on a hill with five separate villas acting as a luxurious escape. These were set low on the side of a steep cliff that dropped down to rocks and white swells that rolled in from the Andaman. A walkway linking the widely spaced villas ran down to the golden sands of a small crescent of beach. It was beautiful but most of all it was quiet. That was what money could buy in Thailand. The tsunami had miraculously spared the villas, thanks to a small island a hundred metres offshore that had acted as a breakwater.

The first night I demolished the best part of a bottle of bourbon out on my patio and woke up flat out on the golden sand of the beach when dawn found me. Killing people up close and personal could fuck your mind at times.

Geezer's head had been reunited with the rest of his body in Patong and he was cremated along with Yin at her home village in the north of the island. Their farewell to this earth had been pure and simple. Geezer had left papers, diaries mainly. They were for me. His money, what little there was of it, and the house had all been left to Yin but as she had no will, these passed to her family. It wasn't compensation for a daughter but then inheritance never is.

Anyway, that particular part of it all was signed, sealed and as neat as it was going to get. I tried to track down my 'date' from before, Nan, but gave up. She'd obviously gone wherever pretty little ladies of the day and night go. It didn't really matter. For the time being, old JD and I were having our own party. I wouldn't say I was feeling sorry for myself. Really I was feeling sorry for the whole fucked up world.

I didn't call Sir Bernard. I kept my mobile permanently switched off in my holdall. I'd bought a cheap pay-as-you-go mobile phone in Bangkok. I got Don Don to call Sir Bernard on my behalf and tell him I had gone into Laos when the trouble had started. Don Don didn't know where.

After a week, Sami started calling. He wanted me to go back to Bangkok and work with him. He also told me that Tuk Tuk was fading fast, and he added that Anita had been asking after me. I didn't mention Sakura or her parting words to me. Then I thought of my beautiful ex-wife and had another drink. Life was complicated.

I met an Australian girl in Patong one afternoon. Her name was Heather and her accent didn't cut glass. She had a fantastic body, and mine managed to respond. We ended up in her room at some little hotel down the south end of the beach. It was a pleasing encounter that lasted until the next afternoon. When I left in the early evening we tentatively planned on getting together again the following day and maybe go island hopping or something. It appeared I was starting to feel human again.

I had to admit I felt like a new man as I drove back to Kata Noi that evening. I parked the car in the resort car park and decided to walk along the beach. It was nearly dark and the air was hot and still. I should have been falling into my bed, exhausted from a night and the best part of a day of relatively rampant sex, but instead I was feeling invigorated. As I walked I savoured the fine details of my plan to exact my revenge on Bernard. I could be in the UK on a false passport in time for Christmas. The timing somehow seemed appropriate. Endings, new beginnings and all that! I would have my chat with him then be back in Thailand for the New Year and some serious talks with Sami.

The way I was feeling I decided I would make departure plans just as soon as I got back to the laptop in my villa. I would brew a coffee, take the computer out on the balcony and work out a schedule. I needed a maximum of only five to ten hours on the ground to do what I had to do in the UK, depending what time the flight got in. Ideally I wanted to touch down early evening. Then I could go to Sir Bernard's flat in Knightsbridge, do what I had to and get out on an early morning flight. If I did it right, no one would know I'd ever been back in the UK.

I used the key card to open the door to my temporary sanctuary and flicked on the lights.

I wasn't really surprised to see the stick figure of Sir Bernard Sinclair sitting on the couch in the lounge with a gun in his hand. The silenced automatic was pointing directly at me. What did surprise me was the blow to the back of the head that sent me slamming face down onto the tiled floor.

I awoke slowly, in pain and coughing up water. How long I had been out I had no idea, but a jug of water in the face told me that my soon-to-be-ex boss was impatient for us to talk. I was sitting in one of the high cane chairs from the breakfast bar. My hands were behind me, bound tightly to one of the slats of the chair back. I could feel pins and needles starting to form in my hands.

Bernard was still sitting on the same couch. My chair was six feet away, directly facing him. To Bernard's right was a familiar figure. I blinked the water out of my eyes and winced from my pounding headache. 'Roddy?' I said at last.

'Yes, Daniel. Good old Roddy. Roddy the arse,' he said quite amiably, a short leather-covered cosh in his hand. Gone was the bumbling idiot he was at the embassy. This Roddy Thomas was a different person. He gave me what almost passed for a genuine smile. 'You've no idea how difficult it is to always play the class clown, Danny boy.' The tone was a gloating one.

'And you, Bernard,' I said, focusing on my boss. 'How difficult was it for you to play the traitor? Kim Philby, Bernard Sinclair! It has a ring to it, doesn't it? Sir Bernard Sinclair,' I corrected. 'The traitor with the title, huh?' Roddy swung the cosh, hitting me in the mouth. It was a glancing blow because I saw it coming and managed to rock my head back out of the way, well almost. My lips kissed leather and I could taste blood.

'No, Roddy,' Bernard held up his hand. 'He's right.'

Roddy lowered his cosh and stood regarding me with something approaching anticipation in his eyes. 'I guess I'm not leaving this room alive, so why not tell me what the hell was going on?' I spat a dribble of blood out of my mouth and closed my eyes for a moment. I wanted them to think I was hurt worse than I was. It wasn't strictly necessary—I wasn't about to break my bonds—but maybe, just maybe there would be a chance for me to get the fuck out of the chair in one piece. Whoever had tied me up—and I figured it had been Roddy—had forced my hands either side of the bamboo slats and used what I guessed to be a cable tie around my wrists and the slat.

'Oh my dear boy, where do I start?' Bernard looked genuinely confused. Roddy went and sat on the couch by the sliding door leading to the balcony. The door was closed but the drapes were open. From that direction there were no witnesses other than the waves rolling in under the light from the rising moon. Either Roddy knew Bernard's story or he was just bored. He tossed the cosh onto the coffee table and sat looking out at the ocean. Perhaps Roddy had been one of Bernard's bum boys in the years gone by, and he and the old prick had shared intimacies of the verbal kind as well as the physical. Who knows? In fact, who the fuck cared?

I tested my bonds while Bernard started talking. The split bamboo slat between my wrists was flexible but, being bamboo, I knew it wasn't going to break. I looked sideways at the companion chair sitting at the breakfast bar. The slats were slotted into the chair base and the top of the U-shaped frame that formed the back. There appeared to be two small nails, top and bottom, holding the slats in position in the grooves. If I applied enough pressure I figured I could bend the nails that were really little more than tacks, hopefully soft copper ones. Then, with the nails bent, I could hopefully bend the slat enough to get the bottom end out of the groove in the seat. If I did manage to get free I would still have my wrists bound, but I would be clear of the chair at least. As far as plans went, that was it for the moment. Get clear of the damn chair.

I pasted an 'interested' expression on my face and tuned into Bernard's tale while I started work on the slat. Bernard's eyes were half-closed as he searched for words. 'It started between the wars, not with Chekhov, with another man. At first it was a sting, a homosexual thing.' Bernard sounded almost proud of his homosexuality and there was certainly defiance in his tone. 'I was vulnerable so I became a mole. Chekhov took over as my handler in the early 1970s.' Bernard turned to Roddy. 'Can you make some tea, dear boy?'

Roddy went to do his bidding, moving between Bernard and I as he went behind the breakfast bar. With Roddy unable to see my back from where he was, I began playing with my bindings, pushing down against the tension of the slat, willing the tacks at the bottom to come free. I knew that while the bamboo wouldn't break it could splinter, and that was what I was relying on. If I could get the fibres at the bottom end of the slat to break down and release the tacks, I could get to the knife in my boot. Once I had that, I could cut the plastic tie. There were a lot of ifs. It would be a contortionist's struggle to reach for the knife in my boot without being seen, but there was another way if I was quick and flexible enough. Without realising, Roddy and Bernard had helped when they had stripped my jacket off before tying me up.

As Bernard droned on I stayed slumped in the seat, pushing my hands down behind me, bending the slat, worrying at it like a dog with a bone. My wrists were killing me and becoming slippery with blood from the chaffed skin, but I could feel something starting to give. Whether the tacks bent or pulled out it didn't matter. My life depended on getting the slat out of the bottom groove. I increased the pressure, all the time trying to hide my efforts should Roddy look my way or Sir Bernard open his eyes.

Roddy hadn't tied my legs. Another mistake and one I was going to make him pay dearly for, God willing! Why the hell was I thinking of God at that moment? Maybe it had something to do with my impending death if things didn't work out. Bernard's eyes were open but they had gone a little out of focus as he recited his memoirs. I doubted he could see what I was doing anyway because the bulk of my body shielded my hands. Roddy was still off to the side in the mini kitchen, playing mother. He didn't even glance my way. I was no threat now. I was a beaten man slumped in a chair awaiting his fate. I pushed down again and the bottom tacks finally gave way.

I reached up so I could get leverage on the centre of the bamboo strip and put the pressure on. Suddenly the bottom of the slat rasped out of the groove. I held my breath but Bernard was busy talking and Roddy was standing waiting for the noisy kettle to boil. I breathed out slowly and eased my wrists down. I was free of the chair. Now there was just the plastic tie to deal with. I started flexing my shoulders slowly. The next bit depended on me pulling a stunt I hadn't done in years.

'The Russian's didn't need to blackmail me, Daniel. I had already turned, as you say, in both ways really. I think I had always been a Communist from my school days.' Bernard's eyes met mine and every muscle in me froze. He shook his head and closed his eyes again as he returned to his past. I glanced to my left. Roddy had poured the tea and was bent over, looking in the refrigerator. I guessed he was probably looking for milk or something to eat while he waited for the tea to brew.

I changed my position slightly, hooked the toe of my left boot above the heel on my right and pushed down. I got my heel most of the way out and worked on the other one. Now both boots were half off. The stunt I was about to perform would be difficult enough without the boots and impossible if they were on.

Roddy slammed the fridge door. He looked towards me, a slice of processed cheese between his teeth, milk carton in his hands. 'Help yourself, Roddy,' I said sarcastically, hoping he wouldn't focus on my unnatural position and guess what I was up to.

'I will,' he replied with a snigger as he turned away to add milk to Sir Bernard's tea. The old boy's eyes were open. He had a look of extreme annoyance on his face and for a moment he resembled a schoolmaster about to tick off two squabbling kids in class. I pasted a mock apologetic smile on my face, playing my own game.

'What made you a dyed-in-the-wool schoolboy Commie?' I asked, getting the old bugger back on track.

'Not surprising really, Daniel. My father was a miner, my mother a seamstress. Father died of black lung when I was three. Mother got cancer and followed a year later. I was orphaned and brought up by nuns, and that, my boy, was hell. I think it put me off both religion and women really.' Bernard snorted. 'My first sexual experience was being sodomised by a drunken priest in the bell tower of St Mary's in Liverpool.'

That second revelation didn't surprise me as much as the first had. I'd always thought Bernard had been born with a silver spoon in his mouth. Apparently not, but I wasn't really that interested in his damned upbringing. I wanted to know about the box of bugs. 'What was the significance of that anthrax strain, Bernard?' I shot at him. 'Why was the British Government handing what was the most potent bloody weapon of the day to the Japs?'

Bernard looked at me in surprise. Perhaps he expected me to sit and listen to his entire life story in an effort to buy more time. I wasn't going to need more time. I was ready to go. I just wanted answers before I took Bernard and Roddy out of the game forever. At that moment Bernard had my undivided attention. 'It wasn't the government, Daniel. It was a faction in both the government and the military. It was a classified mission. Those in the *Victor* had no idea what was happening.'

'What faction? Communists like you?'

'Some were, but basically it was an anti-American lobby. There were a lot of people who didn't regard the United States as our saviours. A lot who resented the fact they hadn't entered the war earlier.' He sighed. 'Anyway, suffice it to say, Daniel, that ever since we lost the damned colonies there have been many patriotic Englishmen who have hated the Americans. Anti-American sentiment was rife during the war. Some of us would have sided with Hitler, Hirohito or Mickey Mouse in order to deal the smug bastards a real blow.'

Bernard's face was alive with a passion I hadn't seen in all our years of playing master and servant. I did some quick calculations. I knew he was eighty or thereabouts. Given that, he would have been in his early twenties at the start of the war. I could visualise his thin intense face, eyes flashing as he spouted whatever doctrine he had subscribed to at that time. I did know he had been in intelligence, a field he had lived and worked in all his life, up to and including that moment. Intense young homosexuals seemed to favour playing spies and spymasters, and the cynical years of playing with other people's lives had turned them into vicious old queens like Bernard.

'Yes, Daniel, there were many of us. It even went as high as the fringe royals. Some of us had political ideals, some had other agendas, but all of us wanted to see the Americans suffer. The bastards are always late to enter any war they don't start, and then they claim the glory.' Bernard's voice was sharp with spite. 'There were those amongst us who would have preferred the Japanese to win the war in the Pacific. We knew about the Manhattan Project in our innermost circles. We knew that Japan wasn't going to win in the end, but what a wonderful chance to test our new weapon and deal those damned Republicans a truly wonderful blow.'

Roddy arrived back with the tea. Bernard carefully laid his automatic on the side table next to the couch and accepted the cup and saucer. He raised the cup and took a sip before nodding. 'Very nice, Roddy. Very nice indeed.' He closed his eyes momentarily in appreciation. That was my cue to move but I needed more, so I sat and waited, my hands behind my back, feet half out of my boots.

Over his cup and saucer, Bernard focused his gaze back on me. His eyes were tired and rheumy, but there was cunning there. 'Yes, Daniel, imagine a suicide bomber flying down the American west coast, spraying the virus everywhere. Or people walking into places like the Pentagon with it or dropping a little present off a tall building into Times Square. So simple and it could have been so effective.' He sipped at his tea while Roddy went back to watching the waves.

'Anyway, Daniel, luck intervened. Damnable bad luck! The available virus was transferred out of the facility to the *Victor* and it set sail under radio silence. Two days later, before we could move our records and duplicate our remaining stocks, some damn fool American pilot crashed into our laboratory. Everything was lost, including the scientists who had developed the nasty little bug. We couldn't recall *Victor* because it was running on radio silence. When the damned thing went down we had no idea where it had sunk. The Yanks had luck on their side. Through delayed contact with our Japanese people we were sure that *Victor* did meet the freighter as planned. However the Japanese hierarchy didn't know the exact location because both *Victor* and *San Tao* had plotted several rendezvous points and ran at constantly bisecting courses.' Bernard paused again to sip his tea, his lips pursed like the prissy old matron he was.

'We didn't know if an established rendezvous point was used or if the boats met whilst on the move,' he said as he carefully placed the cup back in its saucer and set both on the table. He picked up the automatic again and the muzzle found its unerring way back in line with my chest.

'The Americans didn't have an exact location for the bombing and the damn Burmese wouldn't let us anywhere near their waters when we fell out. So we were forced to maintain a watch on the general area for decades before a survey vessel found the wreckage. The rest you know.'

'How the hell did you get away with sending the bloody virus in the first place. There must have been a fucking enquiry.'

'There was no enquiry. This was wartime, remember!' Bernard was talking to me in his schoolmasterly voice again. 'Officially, *Victor* was taking our secret weapon to try it out on the Japanese. This was our Manhattan Project, our chance to see just what would happen against a real enemy. Everyone bought it, of course. Now, because you succeeded in recovering the bug, heroes will be made. There'll probably be knighthood's for the boys. Ironic, isn't it?'

'Okay. So why send me?' I asked. 'Was it so Chekhov could finally have his revenge?' For a moment Sir Bernard Sinclair looked ashamed, then he nodded slowly.

'I'm sorry to say but yes, that was part of the plan. Of course, Dimitri didn't know who had attempted to kill him until I told him.'

'You, of course, told him you'd ordered the original hit?' I said sarcastically.

'Of course not,' came the prim reply. 'It would have made life so much easier if you had killed him then, but that's life, dear boy. So yes, you were set up to fail in your attempt to get the box. Or rather, Chekhov originally planned to let you retrieve it, then have his thugs board you and take it. He, incidentally, wasn't on board the boat. The orders were for his men to take you with them. I believe he had plans for you.' I shuddered and Bernard saw the movement. 'I did regret the implications, Daniel, but he had me at a disadvantage.'

'Yeah,' I replied as dryly as my bleeding mouth would allow.

'Chekhov always was a bloodthirsty one. He wanted you and Tuk Tuk out of the way. That, of course, was why I insisted you use Tuk Tuk which, of course, ended up as a big mistake on my part, or at least as far as Chekhov was concerned. The weather played against him and into your hands, along with that second boat. You never told me about that.' Bernard shook his head and almost tut-tutted me for being a bad boy. 'His boat was moored in the cove. The plan was to let you retrieve the virus and, when you started back to Ranong, they were going to run you down. It came as quite a surprise when they realised that you had an escort. That called for a drastic change of plan. That's why they tried to get the box from you underwater.'

'Why the hell did his men all have CIA identification on them?'

'Chekhov liked to make sure that blame was never laid at his feet unless he wanted it to be. He thought a little smoke screen and unrest between the Americans, the Thais and us would be good for business. He had some difficult associates in his team on board the boat and, apparently, he planned to leave a body or two behind to be found. He was a devious man.'

'And you're not?' I replied laughing, spraying droplets of blood from my cut lips. 'Two of a kind, Bernard,' I said. As I talked, I was getting ready to move. Roddy bothered me. I didn't know if he had a gun. If he did, I would be dead. Firstly I would move sideways out of the chair and roll to get behind the breakfast bar, out of range of Bernard's gun. I imagined he was still a pretty fair shot and that was my first consideration. If Roddy came for me without a gun I could take him.

'The mobile phone,' I said. 'That was pure genius.'

'Oh yes, that was wasn't it,' Bernard replied, a smug look creeping across his face. 'That was my own idea. When did you realise?'

'After Chekhov burned down the drugs factory in the old town. Things happened too fast from that moment on and it all fell into place.'

'And you played me along after that?' Bernard looked truly surprised, then he nodded and smiled. 'Ah, Daniel, I trained you well. It's a pity what has to be will be,' he said sadly. 'Unfortunately with you left alive, I fear I face a rather bleak retirement in one of Her Majesty's institutions. Now that you have finally got rid of Chekhov, it is time we said goodbye.'

'You are going to do it yourself?' I asked in mock surprise. Bernard looked quite startled at the suggestion he would not do it personally.

'Of course I will do it, Daniel. This is not the sort of thing one has others do. That is just not proper,' he added as he raised the gun. I planted both feet on the floor and launched myself sideways. The chair and I parted company about the same time the silenced automatic spat. I heard a shot ricochet as the slug hit the tiled wall behind me. As I rolled, something broke with a glassy clatter. Once behind the breakfast bar, I pushed my arms down as far as I could. Thank God for a relatively small arse and tight jeans. I worked my behind through my bound arms and then went for my feet, pushing my right boot off as I squirmed to get my legs through my arms. The left boot held me up for a precious second or two, then it was off. I pulled the stiletto out of the sheath and held it in a double grip, blade-upwards. I didn't have time to cut the cable tie because

Roddy was coming around the corner of the breakfast bar.

Roddy didn't have a gun but his cosh was raised high. It was a clumsy move on his part because, crouching where I was on the floor, I had him open from his groin to his chin. Maybe I'd overestimated the talents of Bernard's little sleeper. I lunged forward and up under Roddy's downward swing, feeling the cosh hit me more or less harmlessly behind my left shoulder as I drove the knife straight into the V of Roddy's rib cage. I was going for his heart, and I got it.

Roddy staggered back a pace and then stood, staring down at me with wide eyes. The cosh dropped from his fingers as he gripped his chest with both hands, trying to stem the flow of dark blood. His face had become a big white shock-filled blank.

As the late Roddy Thomas sank to his knees and started to draw his final last breaths, I hunched behind the kitchen counter and twisted the bloodied knife so I could sever the cable tie. It was done in seconds. Now where was Bernard? There was no sound in the room but for Roddy's departing moans. As he started to fall forward, I planted both feet into Roddy's chest and propelled him back out into the room. There was the muted thunk of a silencer and Roddy's falling body took a hit.

I risked looking around the edge of the bar. Bernard was still sitting in his seat, the gun in his hand. I pulled my head back as his automatic spat a bullet. The bullet missed me and hit the wall behind and to my right. Roddy, meanwhile, was lying on his back on the tiled floor. The poor sap raised his head to look at Bernard and opened his mouth but no sound came out. His head made a meaty sound on the tiles and Roddy Thomas was no more. The only movement was a growing pool of dark blood under his body, an echo of poor Babs's final moments.

There was silence in the room, but for the sound of water dripping into the basin in the mini kitchen unit behind me. I realised I'd not noticed that the tap needed a new washer until then. I'd have maintenance look at it when this was all over. Once again, a stupid irrelevant thing like a dripping tap had crept into my mind during such a tense moment. Maybe it was stress. Bernard eventually broke the near silence.

'Very impressive, Daniel. Poor old Roddy. He used to be such a lovely boy,' he added sadly. 'You'll have to come out *some* time.'

'Not necessarily, Bernard. You may have to come to me,' I replied as I squatted behind the breakfast bar, keeping the dishwasher between Bernard and I. I reached up to quietly ease open the utensils drawer. My Walther was out of reach in the safe in the bedroom. However there was a set of very sharp steak knives in the kitchen drawer. I lifted them out quietly and laid them on the floor beside me. My stiletto was an excellent throwing knife but I wanted that in my hand when I sliced Sir Bernard's throat from ear to ear.

I had spent a lot of time learning how to throw knives well. Waiting in the bush for a meet with some bandit or other often meant days of doing nothing. Because nothing and I had never been really good companions, I used to practice throwing knives to pass the time, sometimes for hours on end. I got very good at it. In the movies a single thrown knife, when accurately pinpointed, can cause instant death. In real life it never usually works like that. However a thrown knife inflicting a hit of any sort can distract the recipient. It can cause pain and, occasionally, serious injury. What I wanted was to buy a few seconds of valuable time. Time to get to Sir Bernard.

I would throw the heavy steak knives in flights of three. The range from the counter to the couch was, I judged, almost perfect for one rotation of any decent knife. He would be struck and he would be cut. That I could guarantee. Immediately after I had thrown the second set of three, I would follow.

I pushed the drawer closed and moved so my back was against the cupboards and I had the dishwasher and counter in front of me. I waited for Bernard to make his move. I hoped he wouldn't for the moment because there was one last thing I wanted to know. What was my price? To kill him without knowing that would piss me off. Everyone wants to know their worth—don't they?

'Incidentally,' I asked in a very conversational tone as I fitted the first three knives into my right hand and gauged the weight. 'How did you find out I was staying here?' He started chuckling then and I knew he hadn't moved.

'Oh, Daniel. The mobile phone was clever, wasn't it?'

I leaned across to my left and answered, 'Very clever.' I pulled back instantly. There was a cough and a clank as Bernard fired through the breakfast bar and hit the rubbish bin.

'Damn,' the old prick said mildly. 'Actually my cleverest trick was your bag.'

'What?' I replied, stunned.

'The bag,' he repeated. 'You have a bag with an electronic baggage tag on it. I know because our people made it up.'

'I have the bag,' I replied. At that moment it was in the wardrobe in the bedroom.

'The tag is a baggage tag in one sense. It is also a locator beacon,' Bernard said. I got the icy-spine sensation again.

'You see, Daniel, when your laptop is sitting in its little cubbyhole it is configured to discharge a pulse of electrical energy every twelve hours.' Bernard was relishing this. 'That energy travels to our special little chip in the baggage and the tag sends out a big message saying, "Here I am, come and get me." The steel mesh in the bag becomes an aerial and it lights up a GPS system like a hand grenade. That, dear boy, is how we found you. The bag is totally inert except for that few seconds every twelve hours, so nothing registers at airport security and the like. Not my idea but very clever.'

'Very,' I said, impressed. I didn't try and figure out the twelve-hour cycle, but given the computer was in the bag at that moment in time and I'd been there several days, I'd nailed my co-ordinates for him big time.

'Now I think it's time we stopped all this foolishness and finished it.' The old bastard spoke in such a reasonable tone. It was almost as if he were inviting me to tea.

'Just one more thing. After killing me, what are you going to do?' I asked, leaning away to the right and pulling back again. The fridge took a hit.

'Bother,' he grumbled. 'All right,' he sighed, sounding like a spoilt child. 'In answer to your question, Daniel, I am going to go home, announce my retirement and move to the Bahamas.'

'To be near your bank accounts, huh?' I asked, hunching close behind the dishwasher again. This time he didn't shoot. I figured he was probably still sitting on three rounds but I knew the problem with small calibre weapons was that sometimes you needed more than a few to do the job, especially if your target was pumped up and fast moving. The small, relatively low-powered round also meant you really couldn't shoot through things like dishwashers.

'Of course the anthrax, that was pure patriotism from the start. What followed between Chekhov and I eventually became a fiscal arrangement, as did the recovery of the bug and you, of course. That was my retirement fund.'

'Chekhov paid you before delivery?' I said, not able to hide the genuine amazement in my voice.

'Oh yes,' came the smug reply. 'It was the co-ordinates of the wreck and you, dear boy, with Tuk Tuk and your friend, Sami Somsak, as a side dish. Ten million dollars, US, deposited in my bank account. More than enough for me to see out my days in some degree of style and comfort.'

'Little boys and good brandy.'

'Only little boys to look at. No more buggery! To tell you the truth, Daniel, I'm pleased all that sexual nonsense is over. I'm too old and it was rather messy. I'm just looking forward to warm weather for my old bones and yes, good brandy.'

'I can guarantee it'll be warm where you're going,' I said with very real promise in my voice. Part of ten million dollars was the price on my head. I couldn't really complain. In many places in this world I knew there were people who would gladly kill me for free.

'Would you like to stand up and throw that damned knife of yours at me or do something equally dramatic so we can get this over with. It really is getting very tiresome and I've got a plane to catch.'

'Yeah, why not,' I agreed. 'I'm getting bored as well,' I said as I squatted. The first salvo of knives were ready to go, the second I'd placed on top of the dishwasher. My stiletto, although it may seem unhygienic, was between my teeth. I needed a momentary distraction and it came in the form of the good old rubbish bin. It was steel with a spring lid and foot pedal. It already sported a hole in its side, compliments of Bernard's marksmanship. The bin didn't look much like me, but hell, who cared?

I balanced the bin in my left hand like a bowler getting the feel of his ball. When I was ready I threw it low and underarm towards Roddy's body. As the bin spun away, rattling and clattering, I moved into a half-crouch, sliding along the counter top to my left and rising above it.

Bernard hadn't been expecting two things: the decoy run by the rubbish bin to his left, and me coming from a position several feet to his right. Instinct was a governing factor in just about everything we did. Despite his eyes telling him that the rubbish bin wasn't what he was looking for, he couldn't keep the muzzle of his gun from going that way, or from giving poor old Roddy another souvenir bullet.

I threw the first flight of knives overarm and hard. Then I ducked and moved back to my right, picking up the second flight as I came around the end of the counter in a low crouch. I threw the knives as I stepped over Roddy's body and dived at Bernard, my right hand going for the blade clamped between my teeth.

'Fuck!' I swore as I skidded into the old bugger's knees, my stiletto set for a backhanded rip across his skinny throat from left to right. With my free hand I grabbed for his gun.

Bernard's gun was pointing at the floor, hanging from limp fingers. His eyes were wide with shock. One single, solitary steak knife had actually landed in a such a way that it was like watching a movie scene. It was lodged squarely in Sir Bernard Sinclair's gullet, right where a tracheotomy incision would have been made if he'd been in need of one. The fingers of the old bugger's left hand were fluttering in front of his throat. The other knives were scattered all around the couch. One was embedded in a cushion, another in the wall behind his head.

'One out of six ain't bad,' I muttered, taking the automatic from the old sod's right hand. Bernard's other hand was touching the handle of the knife embedded in his throat. I debated either pulling it out or wrenching it around a bit. In the end I reached over and pulled the serrated blade out as I stood up.

'Sir Bernard Sinclair, traitor to Her Majesty,' I said rather pompously as I dropped the steak knife on the floor. 'I now declare you fucking dead.' I raised the silenced automatic to finish him off, but Bernard was waving both hands. His lips were moving. Amateur tracheotomy or not, he was trying to talk. Curiosity got the better of me, so I knelt down beside him and put my head close to his, the muzzle of the silencer resting over where his heart would have been if he'd had one.

'What?'

'Daniel,' he whispered hoarsely, the fingers of his left hand covering his throat. Blood was leaking from between his fingers and his lips were crimson. 'Don't expose me. Not for my sake! For the sake of the country!'

His voice was fading. I had to lean closer. 'There's been enough of that. Don't give the tabloids another field day. Please, Daniel.' He closed his eyes and I figured that was that. But it wasn't. 'Don't, please,' he pleaded, his voice again a bubbling whisper. 'My wallet, account number. Beacon International Bank, Bahamas. Password is Victor. Just don't expose me for Britain's sake, Daniel.'

With that, the old bugger died. He gasped and went through a classic death-rattle sequence, his body going into spasms and falling back in the chair. I gave him a minute, then checked for signs of life. I still didn't trust him to be dead. I'd seen too many horror movies in real life. I checked for a pulse. There was none. It was truly over.

'Damn,' I said aloud. Trust him to play the loyalty card at the end. He always had been a master of manipulation. I went back to the bar and poured a JD. Then I went and sat on the couch beside my former boss and contemplated my suite filled with dead men.

As I started to lower the level of another bottle of bourbon, I stopped drinking long enough to make a phone call. The call was to Sami. He was sending a clean-up crew down. In a day or two Roddy and Sir Bernard would be involved in a fatal and fiery accident in Bangkok. Sir Bernard would be flown home for his lavish farewell. Who knew what Roddy's arrangements would be? Again, who cared? I just hoped he had plenty of insurance so his poor damned wife could have a fucking ball as she toasted his departure.

So what to do while I awaited Sami's boys? The door was locked with a chair jammed under the handle just in case and the sign displaying Do Not Disturb was hanging outside. I was unlikely to be disturbed for a week if I wanted it that way. I had a bottle of Jack Daniels and there was room service to call on. I was in some sort of limbo heaven.

I glanced at my watch. It was after two in the morning. 'How time flies,' I muttered, thinking about my little Australian named Heather. Hopefully she would find another playmate when I didn't show later that morning.

I had the small square of laminated cardboard that I'd taken from the lining of Bernard's wallet. Victor as a password, how typically Bernard! Before I got too pissed to know what I was doing, I used my computer and modem. After ten minutes I had established another bank account, this one in the Caymans. I left some petty cash in Bernard's old account and transferred a little over ten million dollars across into my new one. It was the price of my life, so I didn't feel at all guilty taking it. I picked up my bottle and glass and went out onto the patio.

What did the future hold for me?

I had no idea but there were now options beyond throwing my hat in the ring with my friend, The Onion Man—several options in fact! One was blonde, two had dark hair and the other option was sitting half-empty on the patio table in front of me. I would explore the latter first and get to the others all in good time.